Hope you
enjoy the
read Maria

Cletyh Whmle

Rayne
The King's Burden

Christopher McMillian

ISBN-13: 978-0-9912989-7-6

First Edition

Cover art by Angela McMillian

Copyedited by Sarah DeCapua

For those that have lost their way

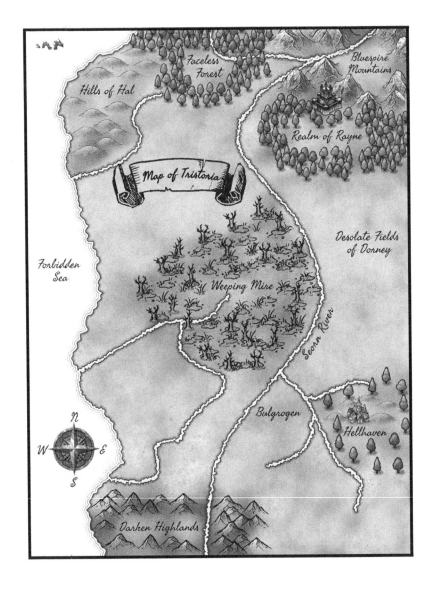

It is said there are five levels of purgatory. There is a pinnacle to these levels and it is called Tristoria. It serves as a vital choke point and a last level of defense to Earth and the heavens. This crucial level is filled with not only hope and destiny, but darkness and evil itching for the opportune moment to feast on the vulnerable and willing. This never-ending scourge of demons and evil trouncing through the levels know that if Tristoria can be breached, Earth is merely a stepping-stone to the heavens.

There are also those who protect the levels, and they are amongst the most fierce and precarious beings in existence: warlocks. Warlocks feed on the very power that threatens their own existence, and their strength is continuously tested and stretched, to the point of ripping them apart. But it is this unceasing, eternal struggle that holds the protective fabric that shields heaven and Earth from destruction. They must ride that perpetual tenuous line of good and evil and never fall. For, if these protectors fail to fulfill their oath, existence as we know it will crumble. We will all be slaves to the most wicked and sinister creatures, birthed in the deepest, darkest pits of hell.

Unknown

CHAPTER 1
The Fevers

*I**t was happening again. Another fever. Great.*
Mrs. Tindal, Alex's fastidious ninth-grade science teacher, was staring down at him through her beige thick-framed glasses, yet again revealing a disappointed frown. He had apparently fallen asleep in fifth period class and was the focus of unwanted attention from around the room.

"Do you need to see the school nurse, Alex?" Mrs. Tindal asked derisively, while glancing down at his drenched shirt collar.

"No–I . . . no definitely not," Alex said clumsily. He knew very little about the fevers but he had found one thing common amongst them: they were sudden and then gone within minutes. By the time he made it to the school nurse, there would be no evidence that he had ever had a fever, besides a damp shirt which could easily be explained away. Sure, a trip to the nurse would give him an excuse to get out of class, but that would only cause more whispers surrounding him — something he did not need more of in his teenage years. The nurse would dismiss him as just another student making up ailments to avoid class.

His cheeks finally settled back to pale and lightly freckled, once the eyes around the room found a more interesting subject to focus on. The distraction was Mrs. Tindal's miniature 3-D model of the Large Hadron Collider — a huge machine in Switzerland designed to smash together subatomic particles. When she suggested the possibility that alternate dimensions could be discovered when these particles collide at close to the speed of light, the choice between paying attention to Alex or Mrs. Tindal was obvious, even to Alex. Considering his current predicament at home, an alternate dimension did not sound all that bad.

Though only ten minutes remained in the period, his eyelids felt like supersized fingers were pulling them down, and the heater by the window pumping warm air was not helping his cause to remain awake. The fevers, as short as they were, drained him, and they were becoming more frequent lately, keeping him in a perpetual state of fatigue. He turned his attention to the window beside him and focused on the groundskeeper. Despite the inclement weather, the snow-white haired man, donning a mud-brown, wide-brimmed hat, trailed up and down the sloped grounds on his dark purple lawn mower in a precise pattern, determined to finish his task.

Alex shook his head a few times as an attempt to stave off the heaviness. He even tried opening his eyes wide and then shutting them quickly, stretching them, but he was no match for the constant drops of rain sliding down the window

2

pane strategically, on a path of least resistance. He sat back up in his chair and rubbed both of his eyes simultaneously with the knuckle of his index fingers.

When he opened his eyes, he was standing in his classroom, only it was empty — no classmates, no teacher, and no desks. There was an enormous gaping hole in the center of the room a few feet from where he was standing as if the earth had opened its mouth and taken a huge bite out of the floor. The air coming from its center was thick and hot, making it difficult to breathe. He wiped the sweat building over his eyes and forehead and stepped closer to the hole, not frightened or apprehensive, but compelled to see what was inside as if it were meant for him somehow. He stepped over cracks in the floor from which puffs of smoke and fingers of fire shot up. He squinted his eyes through the billowing heat and was captivated by the waves of liquid fire far in the depths of the hole. The steep sides were festooned with small holes as far down as he could see and faint, indiscernible whispers echoed from deep within and up to the surface, resonating as if cycling through each of the holes.

The whispers calmed Alex for the moment, until out of nowhere an intense pressure attacked his head, and then an odd pulsing sensation along his extremities. It felt like something very powerful was building inside him and frantically searching for a way out, but there was no exit. He stepped back from the hole and knelt down and gasped for air as the pressure became unbearable to the point of nearly passing out. With his chin to his chest and both his hands grasping his head, he yelled as loud as he could, "Stop! Stop! Stop!"

Seconds later the classroom was back to normal. The soft hum of the lawn mower in the distance filled the silence of the room and he found himself on his knees next to his desk. The pain was gone, but his brief respite from the thought of dying from the intense pain in his head quickly switched to humiliation as he peered breathlessly around the room at the array of furled eyebrows and judging eyes, including an annoyed Mrs. Tindal staring down at him, furious.

Still dazed, Alex desperately searched the room for his best friend, Nick, but he was not in his usual seat. Staring back at him from Nick's desk was a narrow-eyed girl with thick glasses, enraged that he had interrupted the lecture.

Mrs. Tindal's abrasive command, "Sit down, Alex! Now!" quickly sobered him. She smashed a small piece of paper on his desk as he got up from the floor and sat back down in his chair. The bell rang just in time, lessening the potential of long-term encapsulating embarrassment. The paper was a detention slip for Monday.

What the hell was that?, Alex wondered. The experience was new, and disturbing. He slumped down in his seat as the class filed out of the room, with most glancing back at him over their shoulders with grim expressions.

◇ ◇ ◇

Alex felt it was best to just leave for the day to save any speck of dignity he had left. Besides, there was only one remaining period, and it was gym class. He had no immediate plans to become a sports hero; video games and avoiding uncomfortable situations were looking more and more like his future career. The fever followed by an immediate vision were a testament to how things were rapidly changing for him. Sure, the fever had exposed itself during the day before, but the dreams until then had remained veiled at night in dream world and were never that real. This disturbing turn of events could not be good and was another reason for him to leave school early so he could think about what had happened and try and understand it.

Speaking of uncomfortable situations, he thought. He lowered his gaze to his feet and picked up his pace down the corridor. He punished himself for taking this particular route as the two goons approached from the other direction. It was usually empty moments before the bell rang for the next period. The hallway led to the back of the gym, outside to the soccer and baseball fields, and eventually to the parking lot. And since it was raining, the class would change into their gym clothes and make their way to the inside of the gym arena for some lame game of dodgeball or skins vs. shirts basketball.

Alex could already hear the goons' jaws smacking in preparation as they made a beeline toward him. Ever since he could remember, these two, Robby Lauwski and Ted Brody, had made torturing the vulnerable their top priority in school. They were opportunists and had been a pain in his ass ever since the third grade by offering insults followed by shoves and pushes used to incite the victim into a dare to defend themselves. He could turn and walk the other way, meaning he would inevitably run into a teacher and have to return to his last period. Or, he could face the two jerks and laugh at their brains' failed attempt at humor. He decided on the two jerks, hoping it would be over quickly and he could be on his way. He cast a furtive glance toward them before stopping. *Let's see which of their three aphorisms they will choose today.*

"Well, well, if it isn't teeny Sweeny!" Ted spouted.

Yep, right on cue, using his last name once again with the same old rhyme, which didn't work since the one talking was the smaller of the two and was in fact a few inches shorter than Alex.

Alex sighed and said, "Can we get this over with? I have somewhere to be."

"Ooh, so sorry to get in your way," Robby said, blocking the pathway next to Ted and pounding his right fist into his left hand twice, his usual intimidation tactic.

"Yeah, so sorry," Ted mimicked. They looked at one another and linked the one neuron that the two of them shared, then Ted moved aside, allowing a narrow path for Alex to proceed.

"Thanks," Alex said, bracing for the inevitable punch or shove.

He passed cautiously but there was no shove or punch. They were not letting him off that easily.

"Have a nice trip," Ted said.

That's when Alex felt his left ankle give way and ram into his right leg. He fell face-first, coming inches from nailing his head on the linoleum floor. He caught himself with his right shoulder, causing an immediate pain to shoot up his neck.

He was not going to turn around and give them the satisfaction of seeing him angry or hurt. "Tell your dead mom I said 'Hi' for me, will you?" Ted said. "It was fun while she was alive."

Through the loud sound of his heart pounding fiercely in his ears, he could hear the same whispers from earlier, only this time they were not as soothing, and they seemed to be chanting something. Though they were still too faint to understand, they were definitely repetitious, inciting words. Where were they coming from? His conscience? Was this his fight-or-flight response telling him to fight? An overwhelming sense of power pulsed through his veins like a viscous darkness fighting its way to his brain. This experience was definitely different from the classroom; most notably, there was no pain and he didn't feel like he was going to die. Quite the opposite actually. The fluorescent lights flickered wildly above and down the hall. The dual heavy doors ahead of him flew open, inviting wind and rain and a flash of lightning followed by a deafening roar of cracking thunder.

When Alex turned back around, Ted and Robby were sprinting away down the hall. They had not been brave enough until then to bring up his late mom, but ever since his best friend Nick had to transfer schools, they had been way more brazen. He breathed a quick sigh of relief and took off out the doors. The rain felt good on his face as he began his trek home. The odd energy he had felt a moment ago slowly faded, but he couldn't help wondering what would have happened if they had not run.

At home that evening, when Alex removed his shoes he noticed that the sides of his Converses had black smudge marks and the ends of his shoelaces were charred as if a Zippo lighter had burned them — two more things to add to the list of the day's oddities. He let out a deep breath before plunging the back of his head onto his pillow. Riddled with embarrassment from the classroom incident and the wild ride his mind took him on multiple times, he found it difficult to rest that night. He had no control over whatever was happening to him and it was beginning to scare him.

CHAPTER 2
Another Awkward Breakfast

Alex sat on the end of his bed and stared up at the journal on his bookshelf, labeled "fevers". The journal stood out amongst the array of fantasy paperback novels that he had fiercely read and reread over the years, as evidenced by the spines, which were reduced to webs of glue and loose pages. Most recently, the books served as an escape from the constant tension building in his house.

Alex used the journal to jot down pertinent information, then quickly filed it back away on the shelf. He found it best to just forget about the events that had no clear reason or solution to them. In the beginning, he was eager to keep track of the fever riddles, tirelessly attempting to decipher their meaning. Now, he would rather forget about them altogether, but he gave his mom his word that as long as the fevers continued he would keep a journal. And seeing how she died six months ago, there was no bargaining his way out of that promise.

He regretted that promise once again when the humiliating events of the previous day surfaced in his mind. The fever was not unique, but the vision accompanying it and the whispers were something new entirely. He had almost forgotten about his shoes. He glanced down at them on the floor beside his bed in disbelief. He thought perhaps that he had dreamed those black smudges and charred shoelaces last night, but there they were in plain sight. Again, no rational explanation for the events, other than perhaps . . . spontaneous shoelace combustion? Was that a thing?

What Alex needed most was advice from someone he could trust, someone who would not send him off to a psych ward for evaluation. His mom was the first person he had confided in about the fevers, and just like she had always been in his life, she was supportive and encouraging. In fact, her last words to him were, "The fevers are a reminder of how powerful you are." He knew it was just her way of comforting him about his insecurities, a last sentiment, but he desperately wanted there to be more. A deep mystery, a lost diary she had left behind filled with puzzles and riddles leading to something great. No such journal existed. He concluded that it was probably her mind drifting off into the abyss before the sickness killed her.

On his persistent request, his mom had taken him to the doctor several times, mentioning the occasional fever. The doctor eventually did some Blood work and a Chest X-ray and all was normal, so no more tests were done. That was before the visions and whispers and the recent physical signs on his shoes. What would the blood work and images show now, he wondered? No matter anyway, there was no one in his life he trusted enough to confide in about happened in Mrs. Tindal's class yesterday.

Alex had been avoiding telling his dad about the fevers, and as far as he knew his mom never told his dad. Dad had changed, and not for the better. It all began after the divorce a year ago when Dad's new wife Margie inflicted her influence on him and seized control of his mind. Alex knew that if he wanted to be examined again by a physician, he would have to make up something different to tell his dad and regale the doctor in confidence. Patient and doctor confidentiality works with kids too, right? Alex knew better. After his parents separated, his dad and Margie made him go see a head shrink. His dad said he needed to deal with his growing anger toward Margie.

Alex eventually figured out — after many nights of passive-aggressive punishments from his dad — that his private insights into his dad and Margie's marriage with the head shrink were not so private. The only thing he took away from the so-called sessions with the shrink was that his feelings were his fault, and his dad and Margie were only trying to help him. He was told he had to deal with his feelings about his dad's remarriage, plain and simple and had to quit being so selfish. It would have cost his dad much less money to just tell him he had changed and that Alex would have to deal with it in his own way. At least his dad would have been honest, instead of a coward who paid someone else to do his dirty work.

Alex took a deep breath as he rounded the corner to the kitchen for breakfast and performed his usual pep talk to himself about ignoring Margie's insults. He could already hear Margie's overly boisterous mouth complaining about the morning's weather forecast and the detrimental effect it would have on the clump of cobwebs she called hair. He slyly took a seat next to his sister — who was building a structure with pieces of crudely torn waffles — and attempted to avoid notice.

"Nice of you to join us," his dad said sarcastically from behind his open newspaper.

Alex mentally rolled his eyes.

Margie shook her head and sneered at him and returned her attention to her huge stack of syrup drenched waffles and two sides of meat. Margie was a plump, egotistical, no-nonsense woman with much higher than reality expectations for her own two less than average children. Her kids were not quite as nasty as she was yet, but given enough time under her instruction and supervision, along with a little ambition, they would graduate from apprentice to master in no time. They had already inherited a few of her repugnant expressions.

"Sorry," Alex said, doing his best to sound sincere.

"Well, hurry and eat so you can start on the yard," Alex's dad continued. "I tried calling you three times for breakfast. I don't know what's gotten into you lately."

Alex just shook his head and focused on the two waffles he had slid onto his plate.

"I'll tell you what it is," Margie chimed in, through a mouthful of waffles, drooling butter down her thick chin. "He needs discipline."

Alex crammed a forkful of waffles into his mouth before any retaliatory words exited, which would most certainly cause him more grief.

"Just get it done today, no excuses," his dad finished. Alex swallowed deeply and turned toward his dad. "I'll have all the leaves raked and bagged, don't worry."

"I'll believe it when I see it," Margie snarled.

Suddenly, her voice changed to a soft, caring tone when she faced her two children, glued to their handheld video games and ignoring their breakfast. "We have a full day, kids, eat up. We need to get you two new jackets for school. We can't have those sweet little bodies getting too cold, now, can we?"

Alex stifled a laugh.

They continued to ignore her by maintaining their vacant stares toward the small rectangular screens inches from their faces. She tried squeezing their cheeks, but they both dodged her hand as if she were an obstacle in their games. The two boys, ages eight and ten, reminded Alex of two spoiled slugs from the movie *Charlie and the Chocolate Factory* — one of the few seventies-era movies that he and his mom watched together, as eighties was their genre of choice.

"Crazy weather lately. Must be that El Niño at it again," his dad said, as if they were the first words of the morning.

Alex cringed at the drab small talk; this wasn't the dad he once knew.

"Whatever it is, I wish it would make up its mind; I don't know whether to sweat or shiver," Margie said sharply.

Alex begrudgingly held in more comments. He scarfed down the rest of his breakfast and set his plate in the sink.

"You better wash that dish," Margie warned. "Your dad shouldn't have to cook your food and clean up after you."

"Yes, ma'am, I will," Alex said in a bubbly voice. He did not look over his shoulder, but he imagined she was likely smiling at his "disciplined" response. If she only knew what lie beneath. He held in his amusement, remembering how his dad despised cooking and never so much as used the toaster while married to his mom. Margie had somehow persuaded him to learn; most likely by not doing any cooking herself.

"And get your sister's plate, too," Margie demanded. "She can hardly clean up after herself. She makes more of a mess trying to do things."

She's only six, he wanted to shout, but he knew better. His dad did not so much as glance above his open newspaper, safely ignoring the rising tension in the room.

Alex slowly and quietly washed his dish, not daring to take his seat back at the disconcerting atmosphere of the table. After a few agonizing moments of rubbing the same spot on the dish, he grabbed his sister's plate and washed it in record time. He was out the garage door before Margie demanded him to wait and wash the rest of the dishes.

Alex's task of raking the leaves so far was as he expected: solemnly therapeutic. It felt good to be away from the bowels of that insidious house. The leaves could not sneer or scold, nor scoff at him for merely breathing. The cool soothing wind was indifferent, and the swiftly moving dark clouds overhead switched his mood to that of solace, dragging away Margie and her two minions to a place far, far away. The only worry in his mind at that moment was raking back in a stray leaf that had wandered off in the wind.

Though autumn brought the beginning of the school year, it had a few things going for it: cool weather, the fair, Halloween, and then the rest of the holidays were right around the corner to sweeten the deal. It was by far Alex's favorite time of year, and Halloween was once an especially memorable occasion for him and his family. His parents had hosted extravagant parties each year, which usually included intricate costumes from the era from which they grew up: the eighties.

He and his sister were constantly exposed to the eighties pop culture growing up. His parents incessantly played eighties music ranging from Journey, White Snake, Poison, and Guns N' Roses to George Michael and Prince. And not only music but movies, too. Every Friday night was eighties movie night, though occasionally his parents would give in to his request for a current new release.

Not all of his parents' eighties movies were bad, though. One of Alex's favorite movies was *Explorers*, in which a group of friends are contacted in their dreams by an alien race, eventually discovering a way to meet them in outer space. *The Goonies* was another of his favorite movies, in which a group of friends discover an old treasure map in an attic and take off on a dangerous and mysterious journey to find the treasure and ultimately save their neighborhood from being turned into a golf course. He often longed for the

15

companionship and adventure the friends in those movies shared, and when he was bored during summer vacation, he would watch the movies a few times a week.

One Halloween his parents did an entire theme dedicated to the 1984 movie, *The NeverEnding Story*; his parents dressed as the elder eccentric couple near the statued, ominous gate, and Alex was the young adventurer, Atreyu, while his sister was Falcor, the luck dragon. His fondest of the memories were the end of the evenings when the guests had all departed and it was just him and his family. His parents waltzed whimsically in circles around the living room all the while smiling in to one another's eyes; he and his sister playfully pranced around and giggled while attempting to mimic them.

The happy memory funneling through his mind abruptly halted when he suddenly felt warm despite the sporadic cool gusts of wind. An odd feeling of doom washed over him and he couldn't breathe, as if the air had suddenly turned viscous. In front of him, behind a row of tall pines, appeared a pack of snarling creatures the color of charcoal and deep crimson. They were the size of large dogs with huge sharp teeth protruding like Cenozoic saber-toothed tigers and snapping wildly. They remained in place, not moving toward him as if blocked by an invisible fence. He could not move either, frozen in place and unable to speak. Suddenly, a wall of fire hid the beasts from his view and spread quickly toward him. He could feel the intense heat on his face as if he had opened a hot oven door and stuck his head inside. He squeezed his eyes shut and opened them again slowly.

As fast as the vision had appeared, it had gone. His surroundings were back to piles of raked leaves and a coolness enveloping him. Much like the seared shoelaces from his classroom event, he had physical remnants of the vision: the smell of wet dog and smoke filled his nose and there was steam rising off of his shoes and jeans.

A steady rain fell and lightning straddled the sky, followed by roaring thunder in the distance. He had done enough for the day anyway, leaving only a small section of the yard that he could quickly finish the next morning. But as much as he had completed, he knew it would not be good enough for Margie. Inevitably, he would have to endure a degrading comment from her, so before heading inside he weathered the rain and stacked the bagged leaves along the fence in the backyard.

He considered the recent visions and fevers, and wondered how fast this sickness would take to erupt and reveal its grasping tentacles. He noticed that this vision was a little shorter than the last, but what did it mean? Shorter meant closer to something happening, right? Or was it the other way around with illnesses? He wasn't sure. At least the whispers were gone and there was no pain this time. Was this the calm before the storm? Maybe, but snarling huge beasts and fire were hardly calm.

As bad as he wanted all of it to go away so he could return to being a normal teenager, there was something tugging on him. He wanted there to be something wrong with him. There was a darkness swirling around inside that ached to know the suffering and pain that his mom had felt during her sickness. He wondered if it would bring him closer to understanding what was happening to him.

CHAPTER 3
The Ruse

Alex was pleased to see that Margie and her spawn weren't back from shopping, and that his dad was snoring in his chair in the living room after a morning of swinging sticks at the golf course. His little sister had the unenviable task of accompanying Margie's entourage.

He figured he had at least a few hours to immerse himself in an online game with his best friend, Nick. It was their only form of communication since neither of their parents allowed them cell phones; a real embarrassment since most of his classmates had their own, leaving another dent in his barely existent social life.

Being online not only afforded him desperate social interaction with a friend, but it allowed them both to vent about each of their predicaments. Though they were best friends, Alex still couldn't bring himself to tell Nick about the fevers or the visions. If Alex were to tell anyone, it would be Nick. But at the moment they were close to being even in their personal despair and he did not want to tip the scales of pity in his direction.

After jotting down the latest vision in his journal, he logged into the game, crossing his fingers that Nick would be online. Usually, the two of them would spend their questing reminiscing about how things used to be, before divorce had twisted their world. They had grown up across the street from one another for most of their childhood. Nick's parents sold their house after the divorce, and his dad had somehow gained custody of their two children, Nick and his younger brother. Alex didn't want to think about it, nor know the reasons, why Nick didn't live with his mother and Nick never offered an explanation. Whatever it was, his dad now spent most of his time with an occasional girlfriend or out drinking in local pubs, leaving Nick plenty of time to do whatever he wanted. As cool as independence sounds to a teenage boy, caring and reliable parents is an unmentioned desire amongst the club for the children of divorced parents.

With headphones donned, he materialized in the world where he had last logged out — The Pointed Sword tavern. The tavern was a quaint, dark space, lit by candlelight and run by an ornery dwarf constantly spouting, "If you aren't buying, get out of my tavern," followed by a lengthy, boisterous laugh as if he had amused himself.

"Hey, man, what's going on?" Alex said through the microphone on his gaming headset.

"Not much," Nick said solemnly. His mood, much like Alex's, had never fully recovered after his parents' divorce.

"Yeah, same here. Same crap: my dad's still a zombie and his wife is . . . well, you know." Alex had a slew of names that came to mind, but kept them to himself. It wasn't anything that Nick hadn't heard before.

They stepped out from the tavern and into the snow-covered town. They mounted their horses and took off toward the portal where the next part of their quest led them to finish forging a magical ring.

Nick half-laughed, "Yeah, that sucks. How about we trade lives for a few days? I'll deal with your stepmom and you can deal with my little brother. I swear if he comes in here again, I will deck him. He's been a pain in my ass ever since we moved. Probably because my dad's never here, and when he is home, he's drunk as hell."

"That's a deal," Alex said, enthused, and ran through the scenario in his head. If he couldn't have his parents back together, the independence thing sounded much better than a dad letting a strange woman come in and take over. "I wish it were that easy."

It might be good for both of them if there were time restraints. By the time they had learned the detriment of the other's situation, it would be time to switch back. Though Alex figured he wouldn't want to return, except to retrieve his sister from the evil clutches of Margie.

"Hey, man, I don't feel much like doing this quest. How about we take our frustrations out in a battleground? Play some hide and gash with our rogues," Nick suggested.

"Sounds good," Alex said. "Oh, I got detention from Mrs. Tindal."

"You? Alex Sweeny, the acer of tests, got detention?"

"Shut up, I just take the test. It's not like I study all the damn time."

"We all know you're smarter than us humans."

"Whatever."

"Stress, man, you gotta learn to relax. It'll kill you."

"That's why I'm here, playing with you," Alex said emphatically.

"No, we need some out of the house time," Nick said.

"Yeah, that'd be cool, but you know my dad. I barely get to leave and I have to give him and Margie details on where I'll be and who's there. Total bull crap, as if either of them cares."

"Yeah, I know, right," Nick agreed. "My house is the exact opposite. My dad couldn't care two craps about where I am. Okay, I'm ready. Queue us up. It'll give me time to think of something we can do."

"Cool, let's do it," Alex said, excited by the possibility of spending some time with his best friend; even if it was only a digital copy running beside him.

A few games in, and both a little less frustrated having taken it out on a few unfortunate noobs, Alex felt the garage door rumble open.

Alex sighed. "It was fun while it lasted."

"They're back, huh?"

"Yep, unfortunately."

"Hey, I got an idea," Nick said. "See if you can convince them to let you stay over here tonight. My dad's going to be out as usual, I'm sure. And if he isn't, so what.

He'll be so plastered he won't miss me. We can scrape together enough money to get into the fair."

Not only did Nick's dad lose his job not long after the divorce — eventually finding one that paid significantly less — the neighborhood where they had moved was even more run-down than the one Alex lived in. The only benefit was that Nick's house was walking distance to the fairgrounds. Alex knew his dad would not go for him staying over there, remembering his constant criticism of Nick's dad's lifestyle and choices. Alex hid his dad's dislike, which was really Margie's, by mentioning only that his dad did not like the neighborhood. An unsaid fact was that Nick was not welcome over at Alex's house either; any friend of Alex's was naturally Margie's enemy, and would be treated as such.

"I'll see what I can pull off," Alex said unconvincingly. "I'll message you later."

Alex knew he had to come up with an excuse; maybe a new friend at school with a class project that involved a sleepover. He was desperate to get out for a night, not to mention the fair was a welcome nostalgic treat. Also, he had heard rumors the haunted house, known as Doctor Blood, was intense this year.

He hadn't paid attention to the rush of air entering the room as his bedroom door slid open. A few seconds later, he felt a tap on his shoulder. Not surprised by the interruption, he reluctantly turned around, purposely not removing his headset. His dad was staring down at him, wearing his now-permanent irritated frown.

"Did you notice the rain had stopped," his dad asked. It was obviously a rhetorical question because Alex was facing the window with the blinds pulled open.

"Oh," Alex said, craning his neck around the computer monitor toward the window.

"The yard will not rake itself. And, uh, yeah, Margie noticed that it looked like a three-year-old raked it."

Why don't she rake it then; she could use the exercise. Alex held his tongue. "Fine," he said through clenched teeth. He decided it best not to argue the matter, needing to stay on his dad's good side if he wanted his request to be granted. He had not had time to come up with a complete plan, but he winged it anyway. "If I finish the yard, can I stay over at a friend's house tonight?"

"Not Nick's house, I presume?" his dad said warningly.

"No . . . this is a friend from my science class — Mark," Alex said, attempting to sound convincing.

His dad stared at him, but not for long before saying, "We'll see after you finish the yard. And if I approve you're also going to clear it with Margie."

It took everything Alex had to keep his comments firmly inside. His tongue was pressing hard against his front teeth, begging to burst through like a gladiator ready to enter the bloody arena. Passing every request through Margie was his dad's way of involving her and making Alex accept her as his new mom. That would never happen: nothing would impede the memory of his mom, no matter how hard his dad attempted to replace her. Margie's overbearing, emasculating personality handcuffed his dad. But Alex knew a tiny fraction of his dad was still in there; guilt oozed out through Dad's words every time he spoke to Alex.

Alex kept his cool and simply nodded, removing his headset from his head.

It was twilight by the time Alex finished raking the leaves for the second time. Ten black trash bags brimming with crumpled leaves lined the chain-link fence in the backyard. His arms hung heavily by his sides as he lumbered inside the house, deciding he would place the bags by the street in the morning since the trash pickup did not come for another two days.

He switched on his computer and quickly typed out the short message to Nick that he was about to attempt the ruse. He did not expect a response from him until later, but on the screen almost immediately were the words: *good luck.* He would need it, along with a bag full of courage. It was getting more difficult by the day to watch his family disappear into the sludge pit of Margie. With each word she spewed, he could feel his mom drift farther and farther away into the depths. Just a few more years and he was out of there, he told himself often, picturing his mom's beautiful, always buoyant smile. Fortunately for now, he could still faintly hear her voice: *patience, son, patience.*

His dad had his feet reclined in his trusty leather chair, their Jack Russell terrier, Rounder, sitting faithfully by his side. Alex's mom always said that that dog had an unhealthy loyalty to his dad. No matter where the dog's heart lay, at least he had good instincts by snarling at Margie often.

Margie leaned heavily back on the couch where Alex's mom had always sat. Her two kids were nowhere in sight, which made Alex sigh in relief. His sister was playing on the floor next to his dad with a doll she had sadly named Samantha, after their mom. Margie had allowed her to keep the doll, though she was likely working on a plan to rid the stuffed symbol from the house.

Alex took a much-needed deep breath and then stepped into the living room. A simple interaction like the one he was about to perform was once second nature between him and his parents. He looked forward to exchanges with them; always smiles and hugs, jokes and whimsical comments, no matter the subject.

He swallowed the feeling of dread creeping along his insides, threatening his lunch to resurface. He cleared his throat, but no one except his little sister looked up from their activities.

"Dad, I finished the yard. Can I please stay at Mark's house tonight?" Alex focused on his dad, but he knew Margie was listening, likely rubbing her grubby fingers together and waiting on his dad to offer him up on a platter.

"Ask Margie," his dad said, right on cue.

Alex cringed and then straightened his face the best he could manage before turning toward her. He struggled to keep the derision out of his voice and said, "Can I?"

"Can you what?" Margie snapped. She made a wry face, continuing to work the needle in her hand and not removing her eyes from her mindless knitting.

"Stay at my friend Mark's house tonight?" he said, attempting a neutral tone.

She did not care about the details of Mark, who he was or where he lived, parents at home, et cetera. All she cared about was how uncomfortable she could make Alex and for how long.

"Do you think that's a good idea?" Margie said scoffingly. "I mean, considering it took you two attempts at such an easy task as raking the leaves, and you still didn't do it to a standard to which someone would pay for it."

"As you know, I don't get any money for doing it," he said through clenched teeth, his voice not so neutral anymore.

"Nor should you," she said contemptuously. "You live here, don't you? You're fed; you have shelter; you have clothes."

Alex glanced over at his dad; his father's eyes were unwavering from the television. He then looked over at his sister. She had stopped playing with her doll and was now cowering and rubbing her right index finger in a continuous circle into the carpet.

"Not by choice," Alex mumbled.

"Your attitude needs some adjusting," Margie suggested, as if being an objective listener. "A night of reflection may be what you need."

"Dad, come on?" Alex pleaded. "Help me out here."

"If Margie thinks you need to stay home, then it's probably for the best," his dad responded with a rehearsed tone.

"You can't be serious!" Alex said, fuming. "Fine, I guess I'll sit home by myself once again."

"Family time will do you some good," his dad said, keeping his monotone voice.

Alex gazed around the living room, shaking his head. Margie sat with a satisfied expression on her face while still guiding the needle through the material, and his dad sat robotically in his chair. "What family?" Alex muttered to himself before making his way back to his room. He did not say another word; he would not give Margie the satisfaction to see his anger and disappointment over the situation. It would be misinterpreted anyhow. The real disappointment was not about the denial of his request to stay over at Mark's, but his disappointment with his dad.

Alex entered his room prepared to spend the evening on his bed drowning in the sorrows of his miserable life. At least he could still get online with Nick and let off a little more steam. He plopped down on his bed and took a few minutes to gather his thoughts before messaging about his failed attempt.

He glanced over at his computer and noticed a blinking on the screen. It was a message from Nick.

CHAPTER 4
The Long Walk

My dad's in the hospital. He's been in a car accident. I'm going there now, the message from Nick read. The brevity of the message made Alex's stomach churn a little. As much as he did not like his own dad at the moment, he could not help but reflect on what he would do without him. Margie would not take him in, which he was grateful for; he would rather live in a colony of inbred cannibals.

He would be an orphan. And what about his sister? Where would she go? He calmed himself and focused on Nick. He wanted to help him, be there for him as a good friend should be. But how? How bad was the car accident? It could be a simple fender bender, non-life threatening. Or it could be . . . he didn't want to think about it. He needed a distraction until he knew more.

He stretched out on his bed and opened one of his old favorite books, set in the not-too-distant future, where a teenage boy relentlessly searches for a treasure in the vast world known as virtual reality. In this world, there were endless possibilities, where only your imagination set the limitations. Best of all, there was no pain, no death, no disease. Only a desire to seek knowledge and the always popular power — better equipment to progress the story and achievements to keep the player playing the game.

At first he had trouble concentrating on the pages, but as always the pages lured him in and he eventually let himself fall. Just when the young hero was being granted a piece of the first puzzle, he heard his computer let out a beep and a message lit up on the screen. He laid the book on his comforter and clicked on the message.

He could feel his heart pound in his ears as he read the words on the screen from Nick — they yelled at him with an angry sadness as he pictured his friend's face.

My dad died.

The message was stark and raw. He had known Nick a long time and knew his way of communicating; he didn't like the drawn-out drama. A second later, another message popped up on the screen.

I'll be here for a while at Mercy General. There's no one else to identify the body. They only let me use the computer for a minute so don't try and message me back up here. I'll message you when I'm back home.

How did he have the control to write me back, Alex thought? He would have been too traumatized to do anything. But that was Nick. He was always the strong one, the brave one, hiding his emotions until it was the right time in his mind. Good or bad, that was who he was.

When Alex's mom died, he was in shambles, unable to hold a complete thought in his head. He hardly spoke to anyone for a week, although he recalled that he briefly spoke with Nick during those foggy times. His dad was not there for him; Margie made sure of that. Where was Nick's mom? Nick hardly talked to her after the divorce — apparently she had remarried and moved away. But to make Nick identify the body without his mom or any family? Alex had a hard time seeing his mom's face in the casket, but that was after all the cleaning and makeup. He couldn't imagine what Nick's dad must have looked like. He had seen enough reality medical shows to know a little about how things worked in the real-life emergency room. This was too much for someone to take on by themselves, even for Nick.

Alex did not respond immediately, not having a clue what to say. What does one say in these situations? He had never been in this terrible position before with a friend. He supposed he, more than anyone, could at least empathize. Nick would probably believe that Alex understood what he was going through.

He had to be there for Nick, more than a written *Sorry* on a cold computer screen could do. He needed to be there in person and tell him, help him. How would he accomplish such a feat with both his dad and Margie against Nick? They did not like his family, no matter the situation or crisis unfolding.

Still stuck in a surreal, dark pit of helplessness for his friend, he flinched at his dad's booming voice echoing from down the hall and through his cracked door.

"Alex, get in here now!"

Alex mindlessly made his way to the living room where his dad sat fuming in his chair. With the news Nick had just given him, he had a difficult time focusing on anything at the moment. He could hear plates banging together from the kitchen and assumed Margie was in there. The banging stopped when he entered the living room and sighed heavily, "What did I do wrong this time?"

"Margie went outside to take the trash out, which you should have done earlier, and guess what she noticed?"

That she belongs in there? "I give up, what?"

"The trash bags of leaves aren't by the street for pickup."

"Come on, Dad, I was exhausted. Besides, the trash doesn't come until Monday. I was going to put them out tomorrow."

Alex could almost feel Margie's pulsing, impassioned breathing from behind the kitchen threshold, eagerly waiting to enter the ring like a rabid dog.

"You said you were done and I took your word for it; now I found out you lied to me?"

"I didn't lie. I finished. I —"

"Standards son, we have to have standards around here to live by. Margie and I don't believe —"

"Margie, you mean, not you. You were never like this when you and Mom were together. You wouldn't have cared about something so petty."

"That's not true. I have always been me, no matter who I was beside."

Alex shook his head, not believing how much his dad had changed. How dulled and diluted he had become. Alex was mentally weary after seeing his daily deterioration and being the only rational person in their conversations. He could not stand by and watch his dad become someone else entirely. And now his best friend's dad was dead. His brain bulged with excessive, unbridled emotions and he couldn't hold back any longer.

"Not that you care, but Nick's dad died in a car wreck tonight."

For a brief, hovering moment, his dad revealed a glimpse of his former self, a tiny reflection glinted in the dim hallway of his mind from behind the dark, twisted, gnarled foliage Margie had planted. This was her opportunity, her chance to swoop down like a bird of prey.

Margie burst through the door. "He was bound to end up like that, eventually. Trashy lifestyle of his. What did he expect?"

Margie's harsh words snuffed out the iota of hope Alex had seen in his dad. That was too far. Even for Margie.

"What makes you so perfect?" Alex blurted out. "Why do you deserve to live and he doesn't?" Alex could not believe he had just uttered those words.

"Watch your mouth," his dad said robotically.

33

She said nothing, just shook her head as if this was all part of her plan to rile Alex and bait him. And he had tugged on the worm.

"I need to go to Nick's tonight; he'll need someone to talk to," Alex said specifically to his dad, doing his best to shun Margie.

"What about the other friend? Mark, was it? Or was that a lie, too?" Alex's dad said.

"I think he'll understand," Alex said. "And if things weren't bad enough for Nick, he has to identify his dad's body." Let's let it all out, all aboard the sympathy train. It was true, though, and Nick deserved sympathy.

"Where is the rest of the family? Never mind, makes sense," Margie scoffed.

As Alex held back fumes building toward Margie, he watched as his dad seemed to think about Nick's situation. Maybe even picturing Alex's mom after she had died. Alex knew he still had feelings for her no matter their outcome and how things were now. You could only hide so much. If Margie would only shut her huge mouth and let Dad do his own thinking for a moment.

"Fine, go, but Margie still has to approve it," Alex's dad muttered with a wave of his hand.

Margie did not hesitate to respond as if loaded and ready. "I don't agree, Henry. I already told him he needed to stay home tonight and reflect. We can't just change our punishment on a whim. He broke the rules and now he must pay. Can't he just call Nick or something?"

Alex continued to ignore Margie. "Dad, come on, you know he needs me. You remember mom's death, how hard it was on me. I didn't have anyone to talk to." Except the cold, odd therapist. He was expected — no forced — to tell his innermost secrets to that man. He was not ready to talk at the time, much less with a stranger.

Margie huffed loudly, her puffy chins rattling. "That's probably where you got your insolence. Your mother let you spout off anything."

Alex's dad seemed as if he had not heard the comment, but it screamed like a banshee in Alex's head.

Enough was enough. This woman had toyed with his emotions for far too long. They were vibrating around in his head like molecules of water in a microwave, ready to expand, explode, and be free once again. He turned and faced her, staring deep into her empty, dark eyes. As he spoke, a swift shadow moved across the room and then disappeared, and the lamp next to Margie shook as if someone had bumped it. Margie's eyes widened.

"You don't deserve the right to mention her — ever! You wanted her dead, out of your way. It isn't enough for you, is it? Now you have emasculated my dad. What's next? My defenseless little sister? Are you going to enslave her as you do your own little helpless fat minions!? I will not stick around here and watch it happen anymore!"

Margie did not say a word in return. Was it because she was shocked by his words? One would think so, but no. She was beaming behind those evil, narrow eyes. Alex had leaped across the line she had been hoping he would cross.

35

Her weapon was cocked and ready, and she could now reveal it to his father. She would finally have him removed from the house to the boarding school she had threatened many times in the past.

He would not give her the pleasure.

He stormed out of the living room and into his bedroom, ignoring the threats finally emerging from his dad's mouth. He quickly shoved a few items in his backpack and made his way to the garage door. It was open, and he paused before exiting. What would happen once he left? He had never spoken to Margie like that before. What would his dad do to him? Were they really going to send him away to some boarding school?

So what, he thought, letting the embers still hovering around him fuel his next step. He got on his bicycle and sped off down the driveway. He would finally be away from that vile and hideous woman. And it felt fantastic.

Cool wind howled down the dark, desolate street, nipping at Alex's exposed arms and face. The fury that was still steadily pulsing through him created a mental barrier from the elements. He could never have imagined it would go this far. His sturdy dad beguiled by a cold, dull personality. He did not want to believe it. It was not easy letting go of a charismatic and mysterious dad who once shared a passion for video games with him.

In fact, before the divorce, his dad had been constructing an eighties arcade in their spare room, spending countless hours updating plugs and lighting, and even knocking down a small partition to extend the play area. He wanted the experience as real as possible: bright carpeting and neon lights with eighties rock music blaring from overhead, and the subtle sound of spring mechanisms alerting that a credit was available for play, followed by the few seconds of intro music after pressing the Ready Player One button.

The carpet, lights, and speakers looked awesome, but unfortunately his dad had only gotten as far as purchasing two games: *Dragon's Lair* and a tabletop *Ms. Pac-Man* machine. After many hours of his dad's guidance and expertise, Alex mastered the games and they became his favorites. Though Alex had never stepped foot into an arcade, he understood the appeal after hearing his parents' passionate details about them. There was just something about the atmosphere, his dad explained, an aura of excitement fanning around the place. He described the smell of pepperoni pizza, the metallic scent of quarters, and the sounds of buttons being smashed and joysticks jostled in every direction. His parents both described the experience as a euphoric freedom and adventure, exciting Alex to the point of him wanting to travel back to that time and experience it for himself.

An arcade also was where his parents first met, which was probably where most of his parents' passion for arcades arose came from. He heard his parents regale the story often: how his mom, a light brown-haired beauty with a gorgeous smile, lay a pair of quarters on the marquee of the game his dad had been fervently playing. Supposedly, placing quarters there was a way of holding your place in line for the next game, but Alex's dad considered it a challenge. Their math was usually a bit off from one another when they told that part, but they both insisted that they spent over twenty dollars playing each other that day, and neither told of the other one winning or losing, though his dad liked to hint with a smile that he really won.

Sadly, the video games lie dormant and shoved in the corner of a forgotten room and covered by old bedsheets. Though Margie made it abundantly clear no one was allowed in the room, Alex still occasionally snuck in a few games when his dad and Margie were not home. He had been caught a few times and, in the end, decided it was not worth the lectures and punishments. Besides, he was better off not witnessing the remaining tenuous strands of decent memories reduced to ash. Yet another reason to reinforce his decision for walking out when he did.

He didn't know when Nick would have to identify the body, so he picked up his pace. If he kept his current speed of pedaling, he calculated that he would be at the hospital in approximately thirty minutes. Unfortunately, that left plenty of time for his mind to scour the dark depths of fear muddled in his mind because of his solitary, dark surroundings.

Alex tried keeping his thoughts to his purpose by using a tactic his mom had taught him of putting things in order before they happened. It was a focusing technique meant to keep unwanted thoughts from interfering.

First, on arriving at the hospital, he would locate Nick. Next, he would feel out his friend's emotions and see which direction to take the conversation. Mention regret and apologies, or choose a distraction? Nick wouldn't allow much mournful talk, so distraction would probably be the route to take. They'd discuss video games and how miserable school was without Nick in his class. Alex would bring up his latest fiasco with his dad and how he ran away and was now free from Margie. Next, he would —

Suddenly his bike jerked unexpectedly to the right and threatened to throw him over the handlebars. With his stomach pressed hard against the metal bars, he heaved his pedals in reverse. The worn tires skidded along the damp concrete. His eyes widened at the fast-approaching, unavoidable puddle of muddy water. He braced himself as mud and water pelted his face. The front tire wiggled loose from the frame, tossing him onto the wet grass with a thud.

He wiped the mud and water from his face and stared longingly at the bike, nearly submerged in the puddle, then to the front tire leaned snuggly against a tree fifteen feet away.

Walking it is.

Though he was but a few miles from the hospital, the weather made it seem much farther. His temporary mental barrier was now being infiltrated by a mixture of steady wind and rain. He clutched his arms close to his body and began the hike.

A warming cacophony of festive sounds echoed in the distance, accompanied by bright lights beaming high in the sky. He caught a whiff of fried corn dog in the wind and it immediately made his mouth water. He longed to be inside the fair with his friend, Nick, things back to the way they used to be before the divorces. The thought of the two of them enjoying freshly fried corn dogs slathered in mustard while sitting under a dry overhang had temporarily warmed his veins as the cool drops continuously dappled his skin. After disposing of the perfectly cleaned corn dog sticks, they would make their way to the line for the haunted house, known as Doctor Blood, a coil of nerves and anxiety pulsing through them as they eagerly waited their turn in line. He pondered how intense the haunted house was going to be this year.

Each year Doctor Blood seemed as if it were a new experience — probably due to his age and perspective changing — though the house's setup was usually the same. A long, concrete walkway led to the entrance of the ominous pale green gothic-style building. Organizers removed the enormous entrance doors, allowing the entryway to be open, revealing a creepy, crimson-colored light glowing inside, as if it were warming the contents for consumption. Inside the entrance, just visible to the waiting crowd, was a black throne where Doctor Blood, the antagonist of the haunted tale, sat stoically with a bloodied ax draped across his lap. It seemed the screams and echoes of terror surrounding him were charging and prepping him for his hunt.

The most frightening part of the entire experience was not the haunted house itself, but the anticipation: the prequel when Doctor Blood would rise from his throne and tour the waiting patrons in line, all the while keeping his stoic, eerie facial expression. He slowly trailed along the walkway with his bloody ax slung over his right shoulder. Eight minions, four on each side of him, in formation — dressed in red cloaks and their faces painted white and mimicking their master's unwavering stare — accompanied him. Doctor Blood, black cloak covering part of his white-and-red painted face, would randomly point with his gloved finger to a child from behind the roped off area in the grass. Two of the minions would exit the formation and grab the child, sliding the kid over one shoulder and then getting back in formation, dragging the screaming child into the dark haunted lair and never breaking stride.

He had never been chosen and even now wondered if they were preselected beforehand and were part of the show. They had to have had permission from the parents, right? His dad remained persistent that the kids were chosen at random, never to return. Whatever the truth, Alex kept his behavior at the fair in check throughout his younger years on the premise that if he did not, then his dad would offer him up as a sacrifice to Doctor Blood. Alex's mom would intervene and say it was all a ruse, but Alex always had the terrifying thought in the back of his head: what if?

With the fairgrounds well behind him, he was exactly one mile from Nick's house. The two of them had measured it many times over the years and usually they would in unison pedal their bikes faster at this particular point. There were no streetlights, and sitting beyond an open field to the left was an empty restaurant that was supposedly haunted and sat deteriorating. Neither of them had been brave enough, day or night, to venture past the tall weeds to get close to the building. With memories of Doctor Blood still lingering, along with Alex being on foot, he picked up his pace to a slow jog. Though the streetlights ahead were getting closer, the goose bumps running along his neck and back were not going away just yet.

There was a rustling of grass in the empty field beside him. At first he thought it was the wind, but then he noticed the rustling started and halted like an animal stalking its prey in the tall brush. *You have got to be kidding me. This can't be happening. All the times I have traveled along this street. Why tonight?*

He picked up his pace to a fast jog, all the while continuing to hang on to denial and dismissing the sounds as the wind or a small bird. Lightning cracked overhead, almost immediately leaving a loud vibrating rumble of thunder. Having a real fear of lightning, he began to zigzag his pattern as if the lightning were preying on him. A few seconds later, another strike lit the dark field of tall grass beside him and once again vibrated the ground underneath almost immediately. He stopped zigzagging for a second and glanced behind at the field of tall grass with his pace now a run. For a split second, he thought he saw a dark figure poke its head above the waving tall grass; a large dog perhaps, he thought. Whatever it was, it probably was not friendly, and he would not stick around and pet it. He liked his arms and fingers right where they were — attached.

He had already turned back around toward his destination when he heard a low roar followed by a yelp, as if an animal had stepped in a trap. He ran a few more feet and made the standard horror movie mistake of stopping and curiously investigating. He hunched over and placed both of his hands on his knees to catch his breath, then craned his neck to focus on where the sound had come from. He took a few needed deep breaths and then quickly wiped the rain from his eyes, all the while trying not to lose eye contact with the tall brush. After a full minute of quiet and no movement, he considered that he may have imagined all of it.

He caught his breath and restarted his trek toward the hospital. Seconds later he halted in place as if yanked back by his shirt collar in slow motion. He felt three distinct taps on his shoulder from behind him.

CHAPTER 5
An Unexpected Meeting

A lex did not turn around immediately as his instincts had alerted. It was as if time had slowed and allowed him to process his surroundings. A weird calmness blanketed him as he slowly turned and faced the culprit behind the three taps on his shoulder.

A short, gray-haired man, maybe in his late sixties, with furled wiry eyebrows was staring up at him. The man was studying him, slightly moving his neck from side to side as if Alex were on a rotating pedestal and he could see him in his entirety. The man had a pointed goatee matching the color of his hair, only much more groomed than his eyebrows. In his left hand was a black top hat, while in his right what appeared to Alex to be a folded burnished copper umbrella — like no other umbrella he had ever seen before. He wore a dark vest and pants, giving him the appearance of a gentleman dressed from the latter part of the nineteenth century.

The man had not said a word to Alex but continued to stare up at him peevishly. The angst of waiting surged back into Alex's stomach and up his throat. To Alex it seemed like minutes had passed, though it had been only less than half of one. An abundance of questions cascaded through his head: What's the deal with the getup? What do you want with me? And where did you come from? Seconds ago, as far as he could see in every direction, he had been alone. Unless the man had been the one rustling around in the tall grass?

The man finally spoke.

"What is your name, boy?" His voice was raspy and smart and sounded slightly irritated, as if Alex had interrupted his bowl of soup in front of a roaring fire.

"Uh . . . Alex . . ."

"Are you sure? Or do you not know who you are?"

"Yes. . . . I know who I am," Alex said.

"Then you *are* Alex. Your last name, please?" He demanded.

"Sweeny." Alex knew better than to give out personal information to a stranger and so quickly, but he did not have total control of himself; it was as if he were in some display mode.

"Hmmm," the man said skeptically. "You don't look like much." He stepped to Alex's side and tapped his legs with his rigid folded umbrella. Alex took a step back. The entire umbrella appeared to be metallic now that he got a closer look. "Scrawny, slow reflexes, and your mental capacity appears to be even slower; maybe a slight bout of early dementia, it seems, as you could not recall your identity timely."

"Hey, were you the one hiding in the grass a few minutes ago?" Alex queried, as if his voice had just returned.

"Wait, what? Scrawny?"

"I'm asking the questions, boy. And don't be absurd. I would never hide in tall weeds for no reason at all."

"Then if you weren't just there, who was in the —"

"You probably heard the wind. Now, can we get back to where we were?"

Alex's instincts and reflexes were slowly returning, and they were nudging him to take caution with this rude little man. He had never been in a real fistfight; only slight altercations broken up by teachers before they became too heated, or his friend Nick would step in and cool things off. But, all things considered, he felt confident that if he had to, he could at least outrun this guy.

As curious as he was about how this strange, cantankerous man appeared out of nowhere, he remembered he was on a mission to help a friend.

"I need to get going," Alex said. "I have a friend who needs my help."

"Nick, yes, of course. I assure you I have more pressing matters for you to attend," he said, dismissing Alex's plans.

"How do you know . . . wait, what?"

"No matter my first impressions of you, I have a job to do all the same. My temporary employer requests your presence."

The small man had Alex's attention, but only for a moment to explain how he knew Nick. "Employer? And how did you know Nick?"

The man sighed. "I don't have time for this inquiry. I just need you to come with me with no further questions asked."

"Actually, I think you do have time. If you want me to go anywhere with you, which . . . I'm probably not. I don't even know you."

The man appeared to be thinking this over, but only for a moment. "Fine, you have the upper hand for now. But know this: it will not be like that for long."

"You don't bargain well, do you?" Alex said, bemused by the man's boldness.

"I just so happen to be one heck of a negotiator. When it's worth it."

"You're doing a great job. Let's go," Alex said sarcastically.

"See."

"Really?" Alex shook his head. "Seriously, I really need to go. My friend —"

"Yes, yes, needs your help. We'll get to that in a moment. But what if I were to tell you I could bring your dad back to his senses and return him to his former self? Would that be worth something to you?"

"I'm listening," Alex said, furrowing his brows. "But first answer a question for me. Never mind how you know about my dad, but how would you, a stranger, accomplish that? I'm his son and I can barely get him to acknowledge me outside of being punished."

"Details will all come in due time. But isn't it worth it to you if you had a chance at it? To bring him back to the man he once was when married to your mother?"

Alex felt a sadness sweep over him at the mention of his late mom. He had dealt with the feelings until then the best he could, suppressing them just enough to keep his sanity. To have his dad back, joking around, offering advice at every corner in a playful, constructive way, or even just listening, would all be amazing. But that was impossible to re-create without both of his parents: they coalesced into one magnetic personality that yanked even the deepest, darkest rooms into the light.

Alex thought on it for a moment. To have just a sliver of that dad back, he would agree to just about anything, but he could feel the warning signs popping up with loud dings like pinballs hitting bumpers. Do not go anywhere with this strange, little man. How he knows the things he knows is irrelevant. But another part of Alex, the tenacious adventure-seeking part, was curious to see what this was all about. What did he have left, really? He did not even feel comfortable in his own home anymore and no one wanted him there; sure, his little sister, but she was too young to understand what was going on. With his mom gone, and no one left to turn to, he felt there was nothing to lose.

The small man sighed loudly when Alex did not respond. "If you require more information, then so be it. My contract is to bring you safely to my current employer, which happens to be your grandfather, your dad's father. I don't know details as to the reason, and it's not my job to know, so don't ask."

"You know my grandfather? Wait a second. My dad said my grandfather traveled a lot and was basically presumed dead someplace overseas." He sold rare antiques, sometimes in exotic locations. Alex saw him often when he was younger, but then he sort of disappeared.

"So that's what they've told you . . . huh," the small man mumbled while shaking his head.

"What was that?"

"Nothing, I was just thinking out loud," the man said, sighing at the absurdity. "He does travel, but not where and how you think. Anyway, the important fact is he's alive and needs your assistance." He stared at Alex for a moment but Alex didn't seem to be budging from his leery stance. "Okay, I can tell you're still not convinced. What will convince you, then?"

Alex thought on it briefly and said, "Where is he, then? And why send you? Why didn't he come in person to get me?"

"James, your grandfather, sent me because he trusts me and he is getting old. Traveling, especially the distance he would have to travel to reach here, would be way too hard on his body."

"Okay, then, what does he look like?" Alex asked, as if it had just popped into his head.

"Well, to be honest, a little like you, but much older. A little crankier, too, but not by much."

Alex merely frowned, but he knew the man was not wrong. His grandmother used to tell Alex he was a spitting image of his grandfather when he was younger, and he was a bit on the cranky side. "If, and I stress *if,* I say yes, what's the catch?" Alex said. "Why help me? There has to be something in it for you."

For a slight moment, the man lost the irritation in his voice. "Like I said, I work for him and I'll get paid. And once you're there in one piece, safely in front of him, I'll be one step closer to home. We will both be getting back something we lost." He rubbed the top of his head, wincing as if the conversation was physically piercing his mind.

"So, it has something to do with my dad, then?"

The small man nodded a resounding yes.

If this man was telling the truth, it could be the end to his nightmare. He would have his dad back. Too good to be true, he warned himself once again. There had to be a catch; there always was, but the possibility of his dad's return overshadowed his pragmatic side. After all, this man did know his grandfather's name. And seeing his grandfather again would be nice.

"What about my friend Nick? His dad just died and —"

The small man held up his hand and patted the air. "He's a strong young man. He'll be fine, trust me," he said, and then sighed. "But, if you don't believe me, as your dubious expression is suggesting, then I suppose we can take a moment and I'll show you on the way."

Alex knew he would likely regret his next words, but . . . why not, he argued to himself. He had hardly done anything daring in his life, except if you count the time he and Nick had built a bicycle ramp on the sidewalk out of uneven pieces of scrap wood and broken bricks. Not only was his pride injured, his chin received two stitches, and both knees lost a few layers of skin. What's the worst that could happen? He grasped the quarter hanging around his neck and rubbed it with his thumb and index finger. It was the 1976 quarter his mom had placed on the *Dragon's Lair* game marquee the day his parents met. His mom had given it to Alex right before she died.

Alex took in a deep breath and let it out slowly. "Okay," he said.

"Okay?"

"Okay, I'll go, but if it turns out you're lying to me, I'll —"

"I assure you, I am not lying. I take my words and my contracts seriously."

"One last condition," Alex said, sounding as commanding as he could. "Margie has to go. No deal if she remains in the picture."

"How else was I going to get him back?" the man said, as if there were no other way.

Alex began musing how the man would get rid of her, but quickly decided it was not worth his time. The exhilaration of her not being anywhere near him or his sister ever again was enough to not care about the details.

"Let's uh . . . do this," Alex said, with as much cockiness as he could muster. "So, where is my grandfather and how are we getting there? I don't see a vehicle."

"One moment," the small man said, and neatly placed his top hat on his head. Instantly, as if on cue, lightning veined across the sky, illuminating the thick coverage of dark rain clouds. Strangely, Alex noticed, there was no thunder; even far off into the distance there were no low rumbles. Rain began to fall, a drizzle at first, then a steady, soft sprinkle, as if the sky was adjusting its shower knob for the perfect stream. With both hands, the man pointed the closed copper umbrella up in the air. Alex cringed and ducked at the lightning rod that the man was wielding in the air next to him.

Seconds later the umbrella extended a few feet above the man and emanated a loud crunching sound, as if sheets of thick aluminum foil were unfolding. The canopy expanded to three times the width of an average umbrella. Next came a whirring sound. The pole and the curved handle were motionless, but the canopy began spinning like a propeller. The wind it was putting off was a testament to its speed as Alex took a few steps in the opposite direction.

This umbrella appeared mechanical and metallic, not even close to the nylon and fiberglass ones he was used to seeing. Alex craned his neck to peek underneath to see the inner workings of this machine, but to his surprise there were none. It had the guts of a normal umbrella; there were no gears, no motor or knobs as the spinning top had suggested, and it was silent. Maybe it had a sensor or a touch screen like an iPad. Maybe this was a secret Apple or Google product that this man had access to and there was a hologram control panel.

"Ready?" the small man said, motioning for Alex to step underneath the machine next to him.

Before Alex could answer, the pole extended to the concrete at their feet and simultaneously the curved handle transformed into a horizontal platform. Two sets of handles extended on either side of the pole; one halfway up and another slightly lower — a steering mechanism, Alex guessed.

Alex looked on hesitantly, determined not to move from his rigid stance.

"What? Is this thing . . . But how . . . Does this thing hover over the ground or something?"

"It's safe, I assure you. Those handles are yours," he said, pointing toward a pair of metallic handles. "And I suggest you use them."

Alex took a much-needed deep breath and reluctantly inched forward, still not entirely sure that what he was seeing was real. He hesitantly stepped onto the small vibrating platform and reached out to his pair of handles. He was glad the handles had grips, because his shaking hands dripped with sweat in the chilled air.

What the heck are you doing, Alex? This is madness.

"By the way, I'm Nort."

Alex only nodded, as he was too busy holding on for his life as the machine propelled them high into the dark sky.

◇ ◇ ◇

Alex's head was still spinning as he attempted to put some logic to his current situation. He was riding on a mechanical flying umbrella. As asinine as it sounded to him as he considered the words, he could not deny his surroundings.

54

Asleep, awake, or in limbo this was happening to him. He was not sure how fast they were moving at the moment, but his insides were thankful they were not still speeding up like during the initial takeoff. He cautiously lessened his grip and as he did, he noticed that there was, oddly, no wind surrounding them as there should have been. At the very least, his hair should have been blowing madly around.

Alex finally regained enough of his equilibrium to speak, only his parched mouth did not allow for fluidity in his voice.

"What — um . . ." Alex started. He cleared his throat and wet his palate. "What exactly is happening? I mean, when I said I would . . . Look, I had no idea it —"

"It would fly?" Nort said, sighing as if he had been through this before with others.

"No . . . I mean, yeah . . . I mean, move at all. It's an umbrella for crying out loud. Why would anyone in their right mind think it could fly?"

"Of course," Nort said, shaking his head. "Nothing is supposed to do anything other than what its intended purpose is, right? If I thought like you, I would do nothing all day. I would waste away into the nether world letting things be things." He huffed and turned his attention back to his handles.

Alex noticed a gauge above Nort's handles that had not been there a few minutes ago. An altimeter, Alex assumed, seeing the numbers etched on it. He was curious how high they were, but he could not see the needle from his vantage point.

"How about a little gratitude?" Nort said, continuing his rant. "Do you know how many hours and how many trials it took me to complete this masterpiece? How many nauseating trips it took to tame the gyro mechanism for a smooth ride?" Just as Nort finished his words, the vehicle rattled and forced Alex to grip his handles tighter. "Just turbulence. And you see how fast old Bessie recovered; now that's precision craftsmanship."

"Bessie? You named your umbrella Bessie?"

"Do you have a better name?" Nort said testily.

"No, I guess. . . ." Lightning maybe, he thought. Alex was proud of the name he had come up with on the fly, but felt it better not to provoke the testy pilot of the unorthodox umbrella machine.

"This is more than a flying umbrella, boy," Nort said, continuing his boasting. "This is a finely tuned machine. But I wouldn't expect you to understand hard work or to know it when you see it. You kids are all the same. You got it all figured out, no need to see anything but the computer screen. Ignore your surroundings and the world will take care of itself."

"I'm not a kid," Alex contested.

Nort mumbled something indiscernible and then sighed.

Alex regretted his decision to go with Nort; he could get all the lectures he wanted at home. What had he done to this guy for him to be so angry? He had become used to misdirected anger from his dad and direct anger daily from Margie. He figured this was the former seeing as he had never met Nort, although Margie was angry at him from the moment they met.

A few minutes of awkward silence passed in which Alex temporarily changed his attention toward the undercarriage of the canopy. The gears and knobs he had not seen initially were all there and moving fluidly like the inner workings of a clock. Then Alex noticed something even more peculiar about the gears: they were fading in and out as if translucent. He reached up toward them, and as he did, the umbrella shifted and he nearly lost his balance causing him to grab back onto his personal handles. Nort did that on purpose, he suspected from the look on Nort's face: a silent warning not to touch things without his permission.

Alex didn't know what to say even if he had an idea what Nort was so angry about. So, he asked the most obvious and immediate question first; a stipulation for him agreeing to go.

"What about my friend Nick, you said that I could see that he was okay?"

"I did, didn't I," Nort said in a manner suggesting he was hoping Alex would have forgotten. "So be it." He leaned slightly to the right, and the umbrella shot off in that direction and back down toward the ground. A minute or two later, they were hovering above the emergency room entrance, next to a parked ambulance and facing a window.

"Wait, won't they see us?" Alex said in a panic.

"No, not unless they know what to look for," Nort said calmly. "Most wouldn't believe it even if they did see us. They would brush it off as a lack of sleep, or too much coffee or energy drinks, or some other vice your people use for daily life."

Alex scanned the waiting room. Nick was sitting in the corner alone. Don't they have private waiting rooms for the family of the deceased? Alex wondered. He was sure he had seen that somewhere. But even if there were, Nick would decline such a place. He would tough it out with the rest of the waiting crowd, just not so close as to catch unnecessary germs.

"Has he already . . . you know?" Alex stammered.

"Seen his dad?" Nort said. "Yes."

"Then why is he still there?"

"Doesn't want to be alone, I presume. He'll be fine. His mom is flying in tonight."

"And how do you know that?" Alex asked suspiciously.

"I have my ways," Nort said, winking from behind his glasses like a small Santa Claus.

Frustrated, Alex turned his attention back toward his friend. Though Nick was not actively crying, he could see that he had been from his puffy eyes. This brought back his own grieving after his mom had died. It was the hardest thing he had faced so far, and he wondered if there could be anything harder in the world. He could not imagine such a thing existing, and if it did, he wanted nothing to do with it.

"Have you seen enough?" Nort said impatiently. "Can we get back on track, please?"

Alex nodded, though he wanted to sit and talk with his friend. His brief interaction with Nort and his crazy umbrella would be enough to distract Nick until his mom arrived.

Although afterward Nick would insist that he made it all up, and Alex wasn't sure just yet if that would be entirely untrue.

"Now that that's out of the way, back to my mission," Nort said testily.

"And where exactly is my grandfather?" Alex asked, reluctantly turning his attention away from his friend.

"How about a little patience? If you want to impress me, start with that."

What reason would Alex have to impress this man he had just met? None, but he agreed to go, and he was not one for pushing an already tense situation further. It was not as if he could just step off the platform and return home. For now, he would have to trust this Nort.

"Okay, I'll have some patience about your mission. That is, if you'll answer a few surrounding curiosities of mine," Alex said, attempting to negotiate.

Nort huffed and then nodded.

"Why is there no wind?" Alex blurted out before Nort changed his mind. Alex glanced down and realized that they were already so high in the wet sky that the hospital was a mere dot now.

Nort seemed to like this question, for he almost grinned. "Perceptive. Well, it's about time. Even though you have insulted Bessie, she still protects you. You can let go of the handles if you choose. Even if you fall, you will not fall far."

"Huh? Are you insane? I'll die," Alex said. "There's nothing but wet clouds and the hard ground beneath us. And the clouds won't catch me."

"Suit yourself," Nort said, and then yanked on a handle above his head.

They immediately ascended upward at a steadily increasing speed and Alex felt his grip loosening. He could not catch his breath as he braced with white knuckles. A few seconds later, his fingers gave way and he fell.

"Ahhhhh," he yelled, until he realized he was not falling. He shook his head in disbelief. "What the . . ." He felt around at the invisible floor underneath him, which seconds ago he swore was thin air. He did not believe what he was feeling, but there it was, holding him up seemingly in midair. He firmly pressed both of his hands against the structure, making sure not to press too hard. It was pliable and soft like a balloon, but surprisingly sturdy. "What is this?"

"A drop. A raindrop, more precisely," Nort said nonchalantly, as if this were common and not incomprehensible, as it should have been.

"A what?" Alex asked, as if he had heard something absurd.

"A single drop of rainwater," Nort said, losing his patience.

Alex pushed aside the absurdity of Nort's explanation and entertained it humorously. "Then why am I not wet? If it's water and all. And raindrops are tiny," Alex contested.

"We shrank, but only temporarily," Nort said, as if reciting from a book he had read many times over. "You haven't noticed our size? Our reflection in the window next to the ambulance was clear. I take back the perceptive comment I made about you earlier." He shook his head. "We are the size of a drop of water, smaller actually. And as for the other question. Well, that one still baffles me a little if I am to be honest, but I presume it has to do with water molecules and our molecular structure."

Alex began searching around in the drenched, dark sky for a comparison in size. He did not believe this crazy idea of shrinking to the size of a drop of rain, nor did he believe his own eyes at the moment, or his hands. He was sure he was about to wake up; he could feel it tugging on him.

"I'm on a time schedule but, for your peace of mind, I will slow us enough so you can get a better understanding of our size in relation to our surroundings," Nort said.

Nort pressed his right index finger on a button on top of his handle. He then twisted a knob counterclockwise above him. Alex immediately felt the machine decelerate and he could see what he could not before. Drops of water similar to the size of Alex and Nort, shattered into mist as one after the other pummeled the exterior of their vessel. Nort had been avoiding them somehow: expert flying skills, Alex presumed. But did that automatically mean he and Nort were small? They could have been huge raindrops. Alex turned his attention to the clouds surrounding them and how massive they appeared. Then he remembered the hospital. It made sense that they were tiny because no one saw them. As terrifying and mad as his situation had become, somehow he was not drowning in trepidation.

"Okay, I think we're ready," Nort said when Alex had no more questions. "Get back up on the platform. You'll want to hold on for this one."

"For what!?," Alex said, quickly heaving himself up from the balloonlike floor and back onto the platform. He searched the sky around them for what Nort had seen, but there were just heavy, dark rain clouds in all directions. "Is something coming at us?"

Nort said nothing, and then something happened, which made Alex grip the handles tighter than he had yet. A force, significantly greater than the burst takeoff he had experienced moments ago — greater than the one where he lost his grip — propelled them upward at a tremendous speed. He felt his insides being dragged into the soles of his feet. He clenched his eyes shut and held on, waiting desperately for the painful, wickedly fast ascent to slow down.

Suddenly a deafening boom echoed all around them, and they immediately began slowing down. One more second of that terrifying speed and Alex felt sure he would have ripped apart like a poorly sewn doll.

When he finally gained the courage to open his eyes, the sky surrounding them was quite different.

CHAPTER 6
Tristoria

A lex could not believe his eyes. One moment the sky was midnight blue and full of rain and the next a dry, loud burst of fire orange. He immediately felt the heat all around him and deep into his lungs when he inhaled.

"Nort, uh, where exactly did we go?" Alex asked, as he attempted to process this new environment.

Nort continued to focus on his flying, keeping his attention forward, and said, "Not as far as one would think, but not so close one would bump into it in the middle of the night."

This answer not only confused Alex, but annoyed him. He began tapping his fingers repetitively on the handles as the irritation wrapped around his unsteady nerves.

"Can you not do that, please?" Nort said, eyeing Alex's fingers.

Alex didn't stop his finger tapping. He was not doing one more thing this Nort said without some answers.

Nort sighed, "Look, you will not recognize nor understand where we are, but since you apparently don't have patience . . . you're in Tristoria . . . the horrible part of it at the moment. Though horrible is a relative term here."

Nort's answer did not help, as he had suggested it would not. Alex began to wonder if he was even on Earth anymore or in the same dimension. He had read many books and seen tons of movies and cartoons, especially of the eighties genre where kids end up in other worlds, usually fraught with danger and mayhem. The *Dungeons and Dragons* cartoon from 1983 came to mind, though he had not recalled getting on any amusement park ride as the group of kids did in the series. They were, however, close to the fair and Nort had a slight resemblance to the Dungeon Master, along with the master's obscure explanations of things.

"Is there anything else I should know about this place?" Alex asked, removing one of his feet from the platform because it was falling asleep.

"There's much —" Nort started, then turned his attention to the platform where they were standing, "Um, I wouldn't do that if I were you. Things work differently here."

"What?" Alex asked, unsure of what Nort was referring to. He continued to lower his foot to the invisible barrier surrounding them.

"The barrier is no longer there," Nort warned.

Alex suddenly remembered the heat and nearly lost his balance. Nort grabbed him from under his right elbow, and Alex yanked his foot back to the safety of the platform and hugged the handles.

"How was I supposed to know that?" Alex said, gasping. He took a few thankful deep breaths of sweltering heat. "Thanks."

Nort nodded and just as he was turning his attention back to his driving, the umbrella shook once, then again, and then the canopy stopped spinning all together. Alex felt like he was floating in midair as his hands loosened themselves from the handles. The feeling was short-lived. The umbrella's copper canopy flipped inside out, sounding like an aluminum soda can crushed under a giant foot. Next came a burst of heat as they hurled downward as if they had just been launched out of a cannon. Alex struggled but somehow seized his handles. He wasn't sure how far they were up in the sky, but eventually they would run out of open space.

"Nort . . . do . . . something," Alex yelled through clenched teeth. "Nort!"

"What do you think I'm doing over here, sleeping?" Nort said calmly as if sitting and having a casual conversation. To Alex, it seemed like Nort was not doing much but standing still on the platform, waiting for the ride to end. In actuality he was working diligently to get his contraption started up again by meticulously twisting a knob Alex couldn't see on the other side of the handles. Nort explained, as he worked the knob, that it was the backup starter, and that it had to be precisely turned at the correct degree to get it to work again.

Alex did not dare look down, not immediately. He held on tight with eyes clenched closed. He believed that if he kept them closed long enough, he would eventually wake up and he would be safe in his bed under a cluster of warm sheets. The intense wind muffled his hearing and disrupted his ability to sink softly into dreamworld. *This is it,* he thought. He could at least face his doom with his eyes open. He harvested just enough nerve to open one of his eyes, and when he did, he saw a solid layer of ground quickly approaching. Then, he heard it, a revving sound. It was like breathing in a gulp of fresh air after being submerged to the bottom of a deep dark pool. The canopy returned to its proper shape and was spinning overhead again.

Just when Alex was about to sigh in relief, they suddenly jerked violently upward and then horizontally.

"Not again," Alex mumbled to himself. "Nort, what are you doing?"

"Not me this time. Seems a dust devil has captured us. And these are a little trickier than restarting an engine."

"What . . . what do you mean? A dust devil as in, like, a tornado!?"

"Yes," Nort said, annoyed, twisting a different knob that had popped out from the pole above him. He grabbed the pocket watch off the chain connected to his pants and retrieved a key from the back of it. He then placed that key inside the middle of the knob and twisted three times. A loud pop came from above the spinning canopy.

"What was that?" Alex asked nervously.

"The glider. Not something you want to engage in mid-flight accidentally, hence the key. But we have no other choice."

Before this moment, Alex had not been nauseous. Likely because his mind had other things to do, as in process

66

this entire event happening. Nausea overcame him as they twirled around and around in the sky, as if dancing with a giant.

"I'm going to be sick if you don't do something quick, Nort," Alex warned.

"I'm trying," Nort grumbled. "All right, that should do it."

"We're not stopping," Alex sang, filling his cheeks with air and trying his best not to hurl.

"I got it," Nort said confidently. "Okay, brace yourself."

But Alex didn't hear him. It wouldn't have mattered anyway for he was holding on as tightly as he could muster at the moment.

Nort leaned forward, and the umbrella thrust up at an angle and to the right, and then finally downward. There was a slight beading of sweat down Nort's forehead as Bessie finally made it out of the dust devil's vortex. But he still did not have total control because of the continual strong gusts. He attempted to restart the engine, but it only sputtered for a second and was quiet once more.

"Sand and dirt must have gotten past the filters," Nort said. "We have to land to fix this."

"What!? How!?"

"Jump," Nort said.

"What!? Are you crazy?" Alex cried, feeling the speed at which they were falling.

"Now!" Nort demanded, and Alex did not question the command this time.

There was something in Nort's voice, a growl that made Alex leap immediately from the platform without another thought.

When Alex regained consciousness, he sat up slowly, shaking off the pain in his neck. "How long was I out?" he said wearily.

Nort shook his head and rolled his eyes. "We just landed. Dust yourself off and help me with this, please."

Alex dusted his pants and shirt and then made his way to Nort, who was gathering pieces of Bessie that had been strewn about from the crash. The umbrella machine was on its side, but appeared to be mostly intact despite the rough landing.

"Grab that side and lift," Nort said, pointing to the pole of the umbrella.

To Alex's surprise, the umbrella was much heavier than it had first appeared. Nort had been wielding the thing when they first met like an ordinary umbrella.

Alex was apparently missing something here, unless Nort had some super strength, in which case Alex intended to be nicer to him so as not to get pummeled. He started thinking about how glad he was that he had not challenged him further when they had first met.

"Heavier than I thought it would be," Alex said. "How do you lug this thing around? It's got to be even heavier in its smaller form, right?"

"Quite the opposite. It's but part of its functionality. I mean honestly, how can it be the same?" Nort shook his head and began working on the undercarriage of the canopy.

Alex sat on the dry ground and waited for Nort to grumble his way through repairing the flying umbrella. He understood nothing in this place, and Nort was not exactly forthcoming with information. He was starting to think that Nort wasn't who he said he was at all. That he was the bad guy and was luring him to his evil master and not to his grandfather at all. He had put himself completely at this Nort's mercy, as he was completely out of his element and vulnerable.

A scratching sound in the distance interrupted his thoughts. It sounded as if a dog were digging in gravel. He peered around in every direction for the source, but could not pinpoint the location. He was merely curious about the sound and not frightened at first, but then he remembered his ominous surroundings: empty small hills and a dry, hot wind whipping reddish brown dirt in the air, contrasted by the burnt red sky above, leaving a feeling like he was on some alien planet. The noise halted. Alex shuddered and jerked his head nervously around in every direction.

Seconds later the scratching returned, and this time it sounded like it was getting closer.

"Nort, do you hear that?" Alex whispered.

"Hear what?" Nort said, with irritation in his voice.

"That scratching sound."

Nort sighed and then pulled his head from under the umbrella canopy and glanced around quickly. "I don't hear anything. Now, if you don't mind, I would appreciate no more interruptions until this is complete. I'd like to get back before supper."

Alex nodded his head in understanding. He was not the cleverest boy around, but he knew what he had heard. Maybe it wasn't something dangerous, but it was still there. And given the looks of his surroundings, caution seemed like a great attribute to have, no matter what Nort the cantankerous said.

A long, deep growl echoed in the air.

Alex stood up and began backing toward Nort. Nort even craned his head out from under the canopy and peered around curiously. This time his eyes held concern rather than annoyance.

Out of nowhere, a giant, dark beast on all fours landed a few feet in front of Alex. The beast snarled, barring its teeth. It snapped twice, drool dripping onto the dry dirt below. It was taunting, as if it were trying to terrify its victim before killing it, tenderizing the meat. Alex had no weapon or anything in his immediate surroundings for defense. But even if he had, the beast was twice his size, and its teeth were the size of Alex's forearms. All he could do was shield his face and neck and hope the beast was seeking a challenge, and would move on to a more worthy opponent. Before Alex could call for Nort, the beast let out a horrible yelp.

Alex lowered his arm and saw that the beast had a dagger sticking out from his horned head with blood dripping down into its cracked open, burning red eyes. Alex wiped the spray of blood from the top of his head with the back of his hand and backed away from the slain beast.

Nort smoothly walked up to the beast and yanked his dagger out from the skull, then wiped his blade clean with a handkerchief. He then sheathed the weapon back in his belt. Alex had not noticed the blade's handle protruding before then, but apparently it had been there the entire time.

"Thanks for, uh, you know," Alex said in a shaky voice. Nort nodded. "What exactly is that thing?" The encounter was still spinning around in Alex's head and his hands still trembled wildly.

"That was a demon. A tracker demon to be more precise," Nort said, now standing on Bessie's platform. "We need to get out of here, and now. There'll be more along soon."

"But it's not . . ."

Bessie revved to life and Alex smiled nervously, cracking the now dried blood on his chin.

"Are you coming?"

Alex nodded without question and all but leaped onto the platform.

CHAPTER 7
Gnarled Spirits Inn

With feet firmly back on the ground, Alex gulped down a much-needed breath of relief, thankful that his insides and his spinning head would finally get a break. He could not understand how he had kept what remained in his stomach from lurching out, but he had, and Nort made a comment that he was grateful for him doing so.

Alex took in his surroundings and noticed that once again, they were in a much different place than the vast desert where they had crash-landed; there were actual trees and hills here. And the scenery was not the only change: the weather had transformed in the blink of an eye from mid-August in the South to a bitter January morning in the Northeast. Remembering his coat before he dashed out of the house would have been a good idea right about that moment as the soft, white flakes dappled his skin, causing him to shiver. With twilight fast approaching, he desperately hoped that they were close to their destination.

As Bessie began her deconstructing sequence back into a normal-sized umbrella, Nort said, "This is my current place of residence, Hellhaven." He said it in a way that suggested he was not planning on staying and that he would not be returning for nostalgic purposes.

"Where?" Alex asked, peering around at the surrounding trees. He had seen nothing that resembled houses when they were landing, but to be fair he had not really been paying attention to much of anything other than holding onto Bessie's handles and counting the seconds before they were safely back on the ground.

"Just through there," Nort said, pointing to the crumbling brick entrance up ahead near the tree line. Alex squinted his eyes in the direction and sure enough there was a brick sign. Though undergrowth and vines had taken over much of the structure, he could still easily make out the words. Alex shook his head and swore that there was nothing there moments before Nort pointed.

The sign read: *Hellhaven, outlaws and outcasts welcome.* Another sentence, in a different and smaller text read: *or anyone with a thought of their own!*

"It may seem harsh, but once you get to know this place you'll understand," Nort said. "We're not here to judge or oppress. We offer a place of solitude to avoid the norms of the world."

"Whatever that means," Alex mumbled to himself as they walked through another crumbling structure. An archway with sconces on either side flickered brightly against the brick despite their dilapidated appearance. He hurried through with crossed arms, trying to keep warm.

"I know what you're thinking," Nort continued. "We're not criminals. This is a place where one can earn their way home on their own terms."

Alex was leaning the way of criminal activity; the sign actually had the word *outlaw* on it, but if the entrance was any indication of what lay ahead, they were not very good criminals. He did not understand what Nort meant by earning a way home, but he did not care at the moment, for he was too busy staring in awe at the structures on the other side of the brush that they had just entered through. He had even forgotten about the cold and dropped his arms by his sides.

The place was, well, strangely awesome in Alex's eyes as he gawked. The village appeared ancient, medieval-style fused with some awe-inspiring architectural marvels. The houses, mostly made of different shades of gray stones, seemed to lean precariously as if some invisible arm were holding them up, and the chimneys were much the same, hanging in the sky uncertain of which way they wanted to go. But, despite the unorthodox construction, they all seemed in working order, with each billowing fingers of smoke high into the cold sky.

The streets were cobblestone and lined by ten- to fifteen-foot-tall thick trees, spaced out to what Alex guessed was about fifty feet apart. Each tree was beautiful and full and ornately unique, with each possessing a protruding branch brandishing a glowing lantern that stretched out over the street. Alex thought the branches looked suspiciously like a grasping hand reaching out into the night to light the way. The cobblestone street even seemed to slightly glow a faint orange, contrasting the flickering light above.

Despite the twilight hour, the streets appeared to be mostly empty. He thought a village of outcasts would be out and about most hours of the day and night. They were rebels, right? Going against the grain, doing what they wanted when they wanted? Though Nort was cranky and odd, Alex did not think he looked like someone who would be in a rebellious gang of sorts, hanging out on the street corner harassing younger kids. Looking over at Nort's top hat, which reminded him of Abraham Lincoln's, Alex tried to imagine Nort as a short Abraham Lincoln bullying kids on the street corner in front of a 7-Eleven.

He pondered that the streets were likely empty due to the people's fear of the creature he had encountered. If Nort was telling the truth, then he had encountered a real demon, face-to-face. The thought made him cringe and dimmed the wondrous sights surrounding him. Before now Alex had never really given much thought to demons, considering them to be more of a way to describe an evil person and not a tangible beast. This brought back memories of his brief encounters with religion. He had heard of demons possessing a person's body and taking over their minds, but he was not sure if he believed the idea.

There were crazy people in the world, he knew that; all one had to do was to switch on the news once in a while. But something inside him, the part he liked to call his "mom reasoning", told him never to dismiss all aspects of an idea:

there was a genesis to everything spoken. Were these creatures the same ones written about in the religious texts? If so, what did that mean? He did not know, but he felt sure it wasn't good.

They were now standing at an entrance door with a wooden oval sign above their heads that squeaked and swung back and forth from the snow-filled wind. The sign read, *Gnarled Spirits* and had a picture of a mug and a bed surrounding the name, leaving Alex to assume that it was a tavern and an inn.

Nort pulled a small white rag from his front pocket. He then swiped some snow from the nearby window ledge to dampen the cloth. "Wipe your face before we go inside."

"Huh?" Alex said, and then he remembered the demon. He quickly and thoroughly wiped the demon's blood from his face, and then tossed the stained rag in an empty can next to them. "Where are we?"

"This is where you'll be staying for the night," Nort said.

Despite his eagerness to get inside and out of the cold, Alex held at the door when he noticed that Nort said *you'll* and not *we*.

"Wait, what? Alone, by myself?" Alex said. "In a place of outlaws and —"

"You'll be fine," Nort said dismissively. "The innkeeper is a close friend of mine. Besides, it's only for a night. The morning will come fast and then we'll be off to the Bluespire Mountains, where your grandfather will be awaiting our arrival."

"You're joking, right?" Alex said, but Nort was not changing his expression. "After what just happened with that creature? I'm not staying alone."

"Get inside and quit your bellyaching."

Alex did not have time to object a second time before Nort pushed open the heavy wooden door to the inn, introducing a warm, inviting rush of air.

"Keep in mind some of these people are a little on edge," Nort warned from the doorway. "They were driven from their homes from the direction we crash-landed. They aren't as . . . how do I put it . . . optimistic as we are."

"Speak for yourself," Alex whispered loudly and shook off the cold as the door shut behind him. The apprehension in the air was thick and palpable as he swept his eyes across the unfamiliar room. The few patrons spaced out amongst the tables briefly stopped their conversations and turned their attention to Alex and Nort.

"Ale and mead," Nort said, "are most important to folks in times of uncertainty."

Torches lined the walls, dimly lighting the room, and a huge, round, stone fireplace in the middle warmed it. The U-shaped bar sat in the place's rear, and that was where Nort was leading them. The roaring fire looked inviting as Alex passed by it, leaving him a sense of longing to be near it, but he was in a strange land and had to stay with his guide. He followed closely and shyly behind him as if walking into a classroom mid-lecture. It was futile trying to hide as Alex towered over Nort, but he tried to slouch anyway, avoiding eye contact with the patrons who were watching them.

"Wiley, my friend, how are things?" Nort said, greeting a bearded man not much taller than himself, though much broader. He looked like the bartenders Alex had seen in the movies and on TV. He imagined he had an ear to lend for a tale, but also a temper to boot you out if things got out of hand.

Wiley lifted a stained towel from the bar and slung it over his right shoulder. "Hello, Nort. What can I do you for? A pint of your favorite dark?" He had not noticed Alex yet, or if he had he had not realized he was with Nort.

"Nah, not tonight," Nort said. "I need a favor, though. I need a room for the night."

"A lady friend? Well, it's about time you —"

"No, not for me," Nort spouted, and quickly turned toward Alex, who was attempting to shroud himself behind him. "Come around here, boy."

Alex did as Nort said and sheepishly stood at his side.

"Who is this?" Wiley asked. He eyed Alex suspiciously. "A straggler you picked up on the way back home?"

"No," Nort said, as if the question were asinine. "My contract."

"Anything to it?" Wiley said, staring inquisitively at Alex. "Was it tasked to you by the big guy?"

Alex did not particularly enjoy being referred to as a contract, but he remained quiet until he had a handle on what exactly was going on.

"Yes, sir, and it didn't come cheap for him this time. I can tell you that," Nort said proudly. "This kid may just be my

79

ticket out of here." Nort rubbed his head as if a headache were brewing. "So, how about that room?"

My grandfather is 'the big guy'? What does that even mean? Alex queried himself silently.

"You're not going to like my answer, Nort. Sure, normally I would have a few rooms open, but as of late, for obvious reasons, we've had more guests funneling through."

"Wiley, I need this favor. Just for a night. He'll be gone first thing in the morning," Nort assured him. "I'll even pay you double."

"Would if I could, honestly. It's not about the money. I just don't have the space. Unless he wants to sleep on one of the tables here in the tavern."

Nort seemed to consider the idea, but Alex intervened, interrupting his thoughts. "I'm not sleeping on a bar table. What's wrong with your place?"

Wiley, being an experienced bartender, knew when to leave the conversation. He turned his attention to the tap behind him.

Nort sighed. "Because I don't mix work and my personal life. I fulfill the contract, and then I'm done. Finished. I don't bring it home with me."

"I didn't choose this," Alex said angrily, and then realized what he had said. "Okay, I did but . . . I'm a contract, remember, so you can get paid. And you're going to leave me to sleep in a bar, alone? After a demon almost killed me!? My grand —"

Nort cupped his hand over Alex's mouth and loudly whispered, "Keep your voice down!"

Wiley eagerly turned his attention back toward them at the mention of a demon and the word he only half-sputtered out. Nort seemed to change his tune and considered Alex's words.

"You weren't in real danger. Stop your squawking," Nort said. "And don't mention the word *demon* in public, please, or your grandfather. There's enough tension in the air."

"What demon?" Wiley asked.

"Great, see what I mean," Nort said, shaking his head. "Just a tracker demon to the west. Nothing to be concerned about."

"How close to the border?" Wiley pressed, nervously.

"Not near our border; northwest Bulgrogen," Nort said dismissively.

Wiley seemed to accept Nort's answer and breathed a little easier with his next question. "What was it like? I mean, are they as big as they say they are this time, this new breed?"

"Dead, and yes, bigger," Nort said.

Wiley shuddered a little and then turned to Alex. "I don't know who you are, boy, but you got yourself the best blade this side of Tristoria. Anyone will tell you that."

Alex did not know what to say, so he nodded in agreement. The outcast villagers respected Nort for his fighting abilities; it definitely was not because of his bright personality and delightful charm.

"Any word from the realm?" Wiley continued.

"Only whispers, but nothing out of the ordinary. Another pathetic horde of demons trying to cross through, unorganized as usual. Probably slipped through another carelessly left open gate."

"What about the rumors of a demon lord leading an army of those demons? There's word they're not just trying to cut through this time, but trying to occupy."

"Just rumors," Nort said. "But, on the slight chance it happens to be more than a few roaming tracker demons, we'll be fine as usual. Our barriers cannot be breached. Remember, it is us who the realm calls on when a task needs to be completed the right way."

What barriers? Alex wondered, recalling that he had not seen so much as a fence when they entered the village.

"I suppose so," Wiley said with unease. "But it sure would make my family feel better knowing the realm will come help if it is something more."

"You mean you sleep better," Nort said. "And believe me you don't want them here; brainwashed soldiers fighting for a never-ending righteous cause. No beginning and no end. No thanks."

Alex was attempting to put the pieces together. Nort was a mercenary, fighting for himself and his own interest. He seemed as if he would help his fellow villagers, but to heck with the realm and their beliefs. Alex wondered where he and his grandfather fit into it all.

"I guess you're right, Nort," Wiley said. "I hope so, anyway."

Nort shrugged. "How about that ale now?"

"Sure thing." Wiley turned to the keg in the wall behind him and filled the mug with a dark ale.

Nort turned to Alex, who had been intently listening to their back-and-forth. "I guess you must stay at my place," Nort grumbled.

"Thanks?" Alex said, as if it should have been an easy decision from the beginning.

Wiley swiped his towel across the bar by Nort's mug and then leaned in close and whispered, "There's also another rumor." Alex inconspicuously craned his head closer. "People are saying there is a demon witch also involved."

Nort scoffed. "What do they know? This is no organized invasion. Come on, Wiley, we've been through this before. Many times. Invasion or not, nothing will breach our defenses. Even a . . . whatever you just said . . . a demon witch."

Wiley did not seem convinced. "This time seems different," Wiley said. "I've never seen this many people displaced. There's even been talk of sending a small group to consult with the realm to join forces."

Nort shook his head in disappointment. "That goes against all we stand for."

"There may be nothing left to stand for," Wiley argued.

Nort waved a dismissive hand in the air. "Look, the realm will send soldiers and scouts as usual to handle the problem. Sure, there will be an occasional few that slip by, as in the one I killed, but that will be it."

Wiley grabbed another tarnished silver mug and filled it with ale and shoved it in front of Alex. "You'll be needing this before this is over, boy."

Before Alex could say anything, Nort slid the mug back toward Wiley.

"He has not earned his way yet," Nort said.

Okay? Alex thought. He did not want it anyway. He had once tasted a sip from his dad's beer can and remembered how bitter the beverage had tasted. He had spat it out immediately.

Nort downed his ale in a few gulps and then wiped his chin with the back of his hand. "Let's go, I'm starving," Nort told Alex. "I'll be seeing you, Wiley."

"I hope so," Wiley mumbled.

Alex followed Nort, waving back to Wiley as he left. Alex noticed that Wiley held a concerned look for him as he waved a heavy hand back. He wondered if Nort was actually hungry or just did not want to answer any more of Wiley's pressing questions. Was Nort secretly concerned or was he concealing something bigger?

CHAPTER 8
Nort's Horns

Nort's house sat on a hill, just far and high enough from the rest to show his importance in the small town. Behind the back door to the house, merely feet away, was a steep cliff well over a hundred feet deep that led to a vast canopy of trees. Alex shivered at the dizzying height, taking a safe step back, but still leaning over just far enough to take in the view. He felt a chill slip along his arms and neck, wondering what dark creatures lurked in the forest below, recalling the demon he had faced earlier.

Nort did not help Alex's growing fear when they entered the house through the rear door instead of the front, explaining that a surprise was better from an unexpected entrance than an obvious one.

When the comforting smell of something cooking hit his nose, the ominous feeling pulsing through him slid aside. Maybe it was because he had not eaten in many hours, or the exhausting nature of what he had been through so far, but whatever was wafting in the air when they opened the door reminded him of the first time he had eaten his mom's chicken and dumplings. Alex wanted to run toward the source of the mouthwatering aroma and devour it, but then he remembered his manners and Nort's stern demeanor. Nort was not exactly exuding hospitality toward him.

"Are you some sort of leader in your village?" Alex asked, shutting the door behind him and attempting to ignore the rumbling in his stomach.

"Why do you ask?" Nort said, his voice trailing. Somehow he had already moved from the back door of the house to the front foyer.

Alex followed Nort's voice to the front foyer and stopped at the threshold and watched as Nort placed his umbrella in a cylindrical container, which seemed to suck it in at the moment he touched the lid. The container was much too small for the object, but Alex didn't question it; he had seen enough so far to know that things were much different here than they were back home.

"I don't know . . . the bartender, the way he talked to you, and your house on a hill away from the others with much more space than the rest," he said, following Nort into what he presumed was the living room. "And then when we ran in to that lady on the street outside of the tavern, she hung on every word you said."

"*No* is the short answer, but they respect me because the realm respects me. They respect my right to not agree with their agenda and followers. And I don't panic like a mindless rube."

Alex nodded. "Fair enough."

"You must be hungry," Nort said, changing the subject. "I suppose I should feed you. I have stew and bread."

"Yes!" Alex nearly yelled. "I mean, yes, that sounds great. I left the house without much of anything."

"I noticed," Nort grumbled. "I would loan you some of my clothes but seeing as how my head is much closer to the ground than yours it wouldn't make much sense."

"I'll be fine," Alex insisted. "I just need to dry off."

"Suit yourself, but if you change your mind, there's a place in the town that has your, uh, shall we say . . . style?"

Alex realized he probably looked way out of place at the tavern in his jeans and sneakers and his *Goonies* T-shirt. The less attention the better in a place as ambivalent as this one seemed. He may reconsider Nort's offer of clothing in the morning.

He did not know what to expect when entering Nort's home, only that the furniture was probably like the inside of the tavern: medieval style; thick, heavy tables and benches; sconces with torches; and a huge fireplace somewhere. He was partially correct in his assumption. There was similar furniture and a nice-sized fireplace in the living room and many candles letting off a soft light throughout. But there were also other things that were not like those in the tavern: many ornate and intricate mechanical objects and devices scattered on the numerous shelves and walls. It was obvious Nort had a thing for steampunk, but Alex knew Nort would probably have a different name for it.

"Thank you," Alex said, taking the steaming bowl of stew and half loaf of bread from Nort's hand, along with a mug of cool water. Alex then sat on a soft rug in the center of the room, noticing that there was only one chair. He would not dare take the only seat that was obviously Nort's personal chair. He nearly scarfed down the entire bowl of stew in a matter of seconds, but on seeing Nort glare at him like he was a starving dog devouring a steak, he slowed to a respectable partly starving teenage boy. "You're not going to eat?" He wiped his chin with the back of his hand.

"Not hungry," Nort said, tossing him a napkin, and then pulled a pipe with a long handle from an inside pocket of his vest. He stuffed it with some dark stringy stuff and lit it, then opened a small, round window next to his rocking chair. "My pipe is much more satisfying at the moment."

Alex remembered Nort's statement in the tavern about how hungry he had been. So he was hiding something from Wiley, but what? Nort seemed concerned about something that he was not telling Alex.

Beside Nort's chair and angled just right in the corner sat the fireplace — taking up most of the wall — heating the cast-iron pot he had spooned the stew from moments ago. The mantle had beautifully carved writing Alex had never seen before, a language full of symbols and strange letters. He likened it to a cross between Egyptian hieroglyphics and the elvish language from Tolkein's *The Lord of the Rings* books.

After finishing his soup, Alex set his bowl beside him and scooted against a nearby wall and enjoyed the warmth of the fire. He felt good and satiated, but the feeling was shallow. There were many questions he wanted answers to, now that he had time to think, and Nort so far was unwilling to give many details. But he felt he deserved at least some minimal information.

Nort rubbed his head with his empty hand in the same spot Alex had noticed him rubbing earlier. That's when Alex saw them: two white protrusions poking through his gray head of hair. He stared at them, perplexed, and unable to determine exactly what they were. He could not tell if they were part of his hair or skull, or an added piece of an odd style, like jewelry.

"What?" Nort said irritably when he realized Alex was staring at him.

"Sorry, I was just noticing . . ." Nort impatiently waited with wide eyes. "The bumps you keep rubbing on your . . . uh . . . head."

Nort sighed as if he had known the question was imminent. "They are my curse in this place," Nort said, running his hand across the two protrusions.

"Curse?"

"I guess you'll learn the truth eventually about where you are. This isn't my place to tell you, but seeing as you have to spend the night and it's taking longer than I expected. . . ."

Finally, Alex thought. *Now we're getting somewhere.* Alex scooted closer to Nort on the other side of the fireplace and leaned forward, anxiously expecting Nort's words. Even though the snow was now falling harder out of the half-moon windows on either side of the front door, the fire somehow expelled a perfect amount of heat to balance the cracked window next to Nort.

Nort took another puff of his pipe. "I was not always like this, you know."

"How do you mean?" Alex said, with a clueless look on his face.

Nort frowned knowingly. "I mean, I come from somewhere spectacular and somewhere I miss dearly." Nort stared off into the room absently.

"So, what happened?"

"I made a mistake," he sighed. "The details are . . . complicated and suited for a different time. But when it happened, and I came to this place, they also appeared. The horns."

"Horns? You mean those are actual horns on your head? Like a deer or something?"

"Like a demon." The room seemed to darken for a second as if a shadow blinked by them. Alex was searching Nort's eyes for amusement, as if he were about to let out a laugh, but it never came, leaving a lump in Alex's throat.

"Wait, so you're telling me you're a —"

"No!" Nort stopped him. "I'm not a demon. Not yet, anyhow. They're there as a reminder. You can think of them as an hourglass where you can put in more sand or take it out depending on the situation. But, like an hourglass that is always flowing, so is my time. The more advancements I make, the smaller they become, and the opposite if I do not perform honorably."

"Advancements?"

"Learn something new; *mature* is a better word, I suppose."

"Okay . . . so how big were these things to start?"

"Let's just say, my neck hurt for the first few years I was here."

"And what happens if you make enough advancements and they disappear?"

"I go home," Nort said, with a longing stare through Alex.

"If . . ."

Nort sighed. "If I don't . . . mature in time and the hourglass is empty? I go somewhere more unpleasant and begin another arduous trek. But that would take a very long time. As frustrating as it is, I would most likely spend much more time here. But one could see the appeal over time . . ." Nort trailed off.

Alex felt the bumps rise again, this time along his spine as he thought about the place Nort was talking about. Though he had not admitted it to himself yet, he had a bad feeling rising inside. Alex jokingly said with a partial laugh, "Are you saying you'll go to hell?"

Nort took a long puff of his pipe. "Hell is a relative term, but if you have to use it then I would say it is a level closer, yes." He blew out a plume of smoke and said, "And now you know why I'm a little cranky at times. I've been here for a long, long time and I'm tired."

"Wait . . ." The gears in his head were spinning wildly and the bad feeling took shape. "That means we're in —"

"A middle world, yes. The pinnacle, in fact, of the middle levels."

Alex chewed over the thought in his head for a few moments, but it did not register completely. Part of him did not believe it was possible, so he continued with the inquisition, letting denial shroud him until he had more proof to accompany the dread filling inside of him. He turned his attention to a glowing, blue, ornate hourglass on the mantle he had not noticed before then. There were two of them actually, but one was empty.

"Is that the time you have left?" Alex quipped, motioning toward the hourglass with sand still in it.

"Figuratively, yes. Only the king truly knows how much time I have and he keeps that to himself. He is the keeper of time in this place and only he has the power to release us."

Alex had been waiting for Nort's tone to change or a slipup of words, but neither had happened. Nort was very convincing. What if this is not a dream, and this is all real? "What about me?" He heard himself say the words, but they hung in the air like a thick fog. He stood and lost all composure, frantically feeling around on the top of his head. There was no more amusement on his face anywhere. "Wait! Did I die!? Am I dead!?"

Nort smirked as if he were waiting for Alex's response to unfold. "No, you're hardly dead, and you're not here because of something you did or didn't do. I was contracted by your grandfather to retrieve you. You are a guest and can leave whenever you desire."

Alex settled back down to slightly just below terrified. "I can leave? Like, now, if I want?"

"Yes, but you made a commitment, remember? Are you sure you want to break that vow knowing where you are and what I just told you?"

"Yes," he hurriedly said. But then he thought on it. If he was in some middle world, then reneging on his word would not be wise.

Nort was staring at him, as if willing him to answer correctly.

"I guess not," Alex said. "So, if what you are telling me is true, then isn't everyone here dead? My grandfather?"

"No, he's not dead either. You and his situation are . . . let's just say complicated and better explained directly from him."

"Okay," Alex said, realizing Nort was not going to tell him any more about his grandfather. He was at least answering other questions, so Alex pressed on. "But isn't that how you reach this place?"

"Death is such an ugly word," Nort said. "I've never liked the term. For one, death means the end, which it is obviously not. Souls pass through here, a stop if you will, a very long one sometimes, but a stop nonetheless, to determine their next step."

"Are you dead?"

"No," Nort said, rolling his eyes. "Not all souls here are from where you came."

Alex's confusion was beginning to spiral out of control. "Not everyone's dead here? Is anyone dead here? Does everyone have horns as a way of showing their time here? I didn't see anyone else with horns in the tavern or on the streets. And no one looked like ghosts to me."

"Take a breath and sit, please," Nort said, and then heaved a sigh. Alex reluctantly took his seat back on the rug. "Let me give you a very condensed explanation. Souls take forms, just like you right now. The ghost form is only a piece of the soul visiting another place without permission."

"Oh," Alex said, still not grasping the concept.

"Your world is obsessed with ghosts. Those are just souls stepping in and out from their realm. Which, by the way, they aren't supposed to do without strict permission." Alex nodded silently, so Nort continued. "And no, not everyone has horns. They are a personal touch to a select group from a very disappointed . . . No, not all have them."

"But those that are dead — I mean passed over — did something terrible in their other life to get here, right? They are paying for it like you are with the horns? Do they have something else in place of the horns?"

"I never said I was paying for anything," Nort said curtly. "But I guess one as young and inexperienced as yourself could see it that way. Anyway, *terrible* is, well, a horrible word to describe a mistake from a not fully matured soul. And yes, there are many devices one can choose to keep their time."

"I don't understand, about matured and —"

"Your grandfather will have the answers you seek. It will make much more sense once you two speak."

"Wait, but you said I was a guest, not here because —"

"I know, calm down. I'm just messing with you. Look, you only have to worry about what your grandfather tells you tomorrow. These rules about this place aren't necessary until they are, okay." He placed his pipe on the table beside him and got up from his chair. "Now, off to bed. We have a long journey ahead of us tomorrow."

"One more question," Alex pressed. He had countless more but did not push him further. Nort nodded. "Why are things so different here? I mean, physics and . . . well, pretty much everything seems much different from back home."

"The obscurity from where you came from is one's own eyes. Here, things are not obscure. Now, off to bed, please."

Alex nodded reluctantly, even though he could feel the weight of the extraordinary day taking hold as he let out a yawn. But, despite how mentally and physically exhausting his journey had been so far, his mind was no match for the deluge of thoughts as he lay on the makeshift bed that Nort readied for him on the floor by the fireplace. Tristoria, a middle world for souls, was a real place. Whatever his mind had formed about such a place existing, he never could have readied himself for what he had seen so far. Two things were certain in this place: one, demons were definitely real and terrifying as the deep-red burning eyes still stained his own when he closed them, and two, it was never a good thing to be closer to the underworld. Good or bad, Nort's vagueness left gaps for way more information.

If there was one saving grace so far, it was that Alex was a guest in this place and supposedly could leave anytime.

However, Nort's warning against breaking commitments was clear. As badly as he wanted this nightmare over and to wake up back in his miserable and boring life, there was an aching curiosity about him. What was he doing in this place? What was his grandfather here for? Why was Alex brought here?

He jarred his memory and considered his life the past few years. Nothing immediately came to mind that would warrant a visit to this place. He had been fairly decent, not withstanding his demeanor toward Margie and his dad, but that was merely a response to her instigations. After a few frustrating attempts, he realized that he could go on forever on the philosophy of good and bad choices, and what determines judgment. Unfortunately, he would just have to wait until he met with his grandfather to get more answers.

Sleep did not come easily that first night.

CHAPTER 9
Hellhaven

Nort was sitting in his chair and staring out of the cracked window next to him when Alex woke. *Has he been there all night?* Alex wondered, noticing that he was still wearing the same outfit. Alex sat up and stretched his arms high above his head, dropping the warm blanket to the floor. Feeling the cool draft from the window, he shivered and quickly covered back up. The logs were still burning, though not raging like they had been before he had fallen asleep.

"You sleep well?" Nort asked.

"No, not really." Alex rubbed his red eyes. "You?"

"My usual," Nort said, still staring off into the distance.

"What time is it?" Alex asked and yawned.

"Seven thirty," Nort replied, removing his pipe from the small table beside him and sliding it back into an inner pocket of his vest. "Which means we are already off schedule. There is breakfast on the table in the kitchen."

The mention of food distracted him enough to not linger on what Nort was pondering by the window all night.

Alex figured Nort was more worried than he let on in the tavern the night before. Alex draped the blanket over his back and made his way to the kitchen. His brain worked overtime during the night, he supposed, causing the ravenous hunger when he saw the plate of food. He scarfed down the biscuits and eggs, not taking the time for butter and jelly as he normally would have. Once again, the food was pleasing. It reminded him of his mom's cooking, and quite the opposite of what Margie described as cooked food. When Margie cooked — which was rare, thankfully — the food was tasteless and reminded Alex of notebook paper or some other inanimate object not meant for consumption. *The food one prepares represents the cook's personality,* his mom used to tell him as he sat at the barstool in the kitchen and conversed with her as she whimsically worked the food.

A loud knock on the door startled Alex as he finished the last bite of biscuit.

"Who the heck is rapping on my door this early?" Nort grumbled, making his way to the door from the living room.

Alex craned his neck to see through the kitchen opening into the entryway. The wall partially blocked his view, but he could see enough.

"Nort," the male voice said enthusiastically. "Good to see you!"

"Jorn," Nort said suspiciously. "What brings you to my door this early in the morning and is so urgent it could not wait until I made it into town?"

"I didn't want to miss you. I hear you're on your way to the realm to deliver an important package."

Nort sighed. "Why is that any concern of yours?"

"I have a request."

"Another request," Nort huffed. "As I have told you in the past, you can travel to the realm just as I can. I'm not your errand boy for information on how to gain the realm's favor."

"This time it's different."

"Sure it is. How so?" Nort said skeptically.

Jorn stepped aside. A cloaked figure in a violet robe, slightly shorter than Jorn but taller than Nort, stepped forward.

"Karissa," Nort said excitedly. "How are you, my dear?"

Karissa nodded from behind the hood of the cloak that partially covered her face. "I'm fine, Nort, thank you for asking."

Nort turned his attention back to Jorn. "What's your request?"

"I want you to take her with you. She will serve the realm well."

"And how does Karissa feel about serving the realm?" Nort said smugly.

"I'm her dad and I make the choices for her. She'll do what I tell her."

Nort ignored Jorn and looked over at Karissa. "Is this what you want, my dear?"

She nodded a slow *yes* from under the hood.

"I'll take her with me, but this is the last request I want from you, Jorn. I mean it, no more."

"I promise," Jorn said, making a cross symbol over his chest with his right index finger.

Nort shook his head at Jorn's animated gesture.

"She turned fourteen the other day," Jorn added. "She won't be a burden, I promise. She knows how to take care of herself. And she can cook."

Alex lost his balance and toppled over in his chair, sending his mug of orange juice crashing to the floor.

"Is that the boy in there with you? Can I meet him?" Jorn said, pushing Karissa aside and moving closer to the door.

What boy? Alex wondered. *Does he mean me?*

"Who told you . . ." Nort started and shook his head knowingly. "I don't think that would be a good idea. He's still adjusting to his surroundings."

Nort blocked the entrance from Jorn, but moved just slightly to the side to allow Karissa by and then waved her inside.

Karissa never turned around to say goodbye to her father, nor did he offer any sentiment in return.

"If you say so," Jorn said disappointed. "Thanks for —"

Nort shut the door with slightly more strength than was necessary.

Alex immediately got to his feet and grabbed a towel from the sink and hurriedly wiped up the juice he had spilled. He pushed aside his curiosity about how the man knew he was here and absentmindedly ran his hand through his hair and took in a deep breath.

"Alex," Nort said from the entryway as if he knew he had been eavesdropping. "I have someone I would like to introduce to you."

Alex leaped forward and met them at the threshold of the kitchen and the entryway, shoving the dirty towel behind his back with his left hand.

"This is Karissa," Nort said. "She'll be joining us on our trip today."

"Nice to . . . meet . . . you," Alex stammered. He reached out his empty hand for introduction, nearly revealing the towel, but caught himself at the last second.

"You, too," Karissa said shyly. She quickly shook Alex's outstretched hand and then hurriedly returned hers to her side.

"I can take your cloak if you would like, though we're not staying for much longer," Nort told Karissa. "Once your father has made his way out of sight and far enough away to not bother us, we will be on our way."

"I'd like to keep it on, if it's all the same to you," Karissa said. "I'm still a little cold."

"The fire is still burning in the living room," Nort said. "Make yourself at home while I gather a few things for the trip. You two take these few minutes to get acquainted."

They both nodded, then Nort left the room before Alex had time to consider his situation. He stood stiffly a few feet from Karissa, a girl around his age. His experience with girls was, well, really, nonexistent. He had talked to a few in class through a few cross words about classroom material, but none on a personal level. Not that he didn't want to talk with them, but he always acted awkward and the words just did not form easily. Girls were unfamiliar territory and filled with unpredictable unknowns. *Much like the world I've found myself in,* he thought, smiling inwardly at his epiphany.

He had to say something, but he knew he must tread cautiously. There was more awkward silence while he debated with himself on what words to choose. After a few minutes, he finally gained the courage and played off of Nort's offer. Not his best idea, but at least it was something.

"So, uh, I can show you where the fireplace is if you're still cold," Alex offered.

"I'm okay, but thank you." Karissa said with her eyes still glued to her feet.

He felt the rush of blood in his cheeks and immediately began berating himself. What a stupid idea; she knew Nort and had probably been here before and knew exactly how to find the fireplace. He needed out of this situation and fast, but he could not just walk away and leave her standing by herself, especially after Nort had suggested he get acquainted. He could hear Nort shuffling around in the other room as sweat beaded on his forehead. *What could you possibly be doing for this long?* Alex thought, convinced Nort was purposely taking his time.

The awkwardness between him and Karissa had turned palpable. He wanted to say something again, anything really, just to cut the silence. Nort had put him in an awkward situation and he felt obligated for some unknown reason to talk to Karissa. He could talk about the weather. Nah. He could talk about her cloak. Nope. It was best to stay quiet until he had something interesting to say. It would be less embarrassing that way.

He sighed in relief when he saw Nort round the corner.

"Okay, now that the two of you have had time to acquaint yourselves with each other, let's be on our way, shall we," Nort said, wearing a partial smirk.

Alex had been so distracted by the situation that he almost forgot that he was barefoot. "I'll be right back," he told them. He marched to the living room and hurriedly slipped on his socks and shoes. The flush filling every part of the flesh in his face finally subsided, leaving a cool sweat across his brow. He made a quick stop in the kitchen and splashed some water on his face, then his hair, and met them back in the foyer.

"Okay," Alex said, nearly out of breath. "I'm ready."

Nort handed Alex a leather satchel that for its size was surprisingly light, and he slid it on his back without question.

The snow had settled nicely on the grass and rooftops, reflecting brightly in the warm, morning sun. The air was just cool enough to allow the snow to stay in place. Alex trailed behind Nort and Karissa, caught up in the sights all around him now that some light was blanketing the town.

After gawking again at the spectacular houses and buildings now that he could see them in their full glory, he noticed the people of the village, most notably how they dressed: a collage of time. There was a couple holding hands and wearing clothes as if they had just left a drive-in movie and now headed to the malt shop. A woman wearing bell-bottom jeans and a bandanna tied around her head was sitting on a bench with her toddler daughter dressed like a wildflower. And then there was Nort in his late nineteenth-century garb. Alex's smile broadened even further when he saw a man about his dad's age wearing a pair of acid-washed jeans. The jeans were tight-rolled over a pair of Reebok high-top shoes, and he wore a "Save Ferris" T-shirt from the John Hughes 1986 movie *Ferris Bueller's Day Off.*

"What was all that about last night?" Alex asked Nort, picking up his pace to catch up with him and Karissa.

"What do you mean?"

"The atmosphere in the inn was dark and . . . well, nothing like this out here."

"The sun pokes its head out about an hour a day if we're lucky, so when it's out, people temporarily set aside their sorrows."

"Oh," Alex said, thinking how depressing it would be to see the sun for only one hour a day.

"Like I said, there is a realization here instilled in souls. It is a step in a maturing soul to see things, all things."

"Okay," Alex said, more confused.

"Don't worry, the doldrums will be back soon enough," Nort said, as if torturing himself with the inevitable news.

"I wasn't saying I wanted —" Alex started, but stopped because they had just arrived at a storefront. The bay window next to the entrance door revealed many shelves of clothes and shoes with no sort of theme or age. There were also books and trinkets scattered about.

Before Alex could look more closely inside, Nort said, "We have a schedule to keep, so let's get in, get what you need, and get out, okay?"

"Okay," Alex said, still unsure of what he was searching for, but then he peered above the door at the sign: *Wear from Home.* He remembered Nort mentioning a jacket the previous night and figured this was a thrift shop.

He followed Nort and Karissa through the door and stood at the entryway for a few moments and peered around at the enormity of the place he had just entered. He could not have guessed from its outside appearance how huge it was inside.

"Find something warm for the road, Alex," Nort said. "Karissa, if you need something, grab it. We'll meet back in the front in ten minutes."

"How do I pay?" Alex asked, searching his pockets for money. "I don't have but a few dollars." He pulled out a wad of three one-dollar bills from his front pocket.

"It's on me," Nort said. "Just get what you need and hurry."

Alex nodded and looked around. "Okay, but where do I start; this place is huge."

"You'll know, just walk a little. The pattern will reveal itself."

Alex shook his head and sighed and took a few steps forward. In a blink of an eye, a long hallway appeared just as Nort had said it would. There was corridor after corridor leading to section after section. They were each labeled by time period: Late 1800s, early 1900s, 1950s, 1960s, 1970s . . .

Then he came to the decade that he should have been born in: the 1980s. With a broad smile, he entered the short, silent hallway, which was lit by bright green and blue neon lights. Once he stepped down into the section, Journey's "Don't Stop Believing" song blared all around him. More neon lights lined the shelves and walls, and bright colored carpet straight out of an eighties arcade filled the place wall to wall. "This is freaking awesome," he whispered to himself. He shook his head in disbelief when he noticed a Sony Walkman perched on a shelf next to a wide variety of cassette tapes; he remembered borrowing his parents' Walkman often and how hard it was to find one in good working order online. Even though the sound quality was much better on his iPod, he would play *Dragon's Lair* or *Ms. Pac-Man* for hours listening to his parents' extensive tape collection of eighties rock and pop music on the Walkman.

Alex considered asking Nort if he could have it, thinking it would give him some solace in this place, but he didn't know how money worked here and he did not have but a few dollars on him.

Remembering Nort's time restriction, he quickly grabbed a navy-colored Members Only jacket from the rack. But, before leaving, he couldn't help himself from playing one game of *Donkey Kong.* An original 1981 arcade version sat in display mode next to the exit to the section. Alex had a quarter in his jeans pocket and could not resist plunging it into the machine. The familiar sound of a credit being added made him feel at home for just a moment.

He had never played the game, but understood the concept having heard his mom speak of it as one of her go-to games back in the arcade. He did remarkably well on one quarter, considering he had only seen the game played on YouTube, and also the fact he was in a hurry having exceeded Nort's ten-minute window.

He began preparing his apology on his way back through the maze of corridors and made one more brief stop to settle a curiosity he had. He poked his head in the fifties section and back out again, and then to the sixties section and back out again. He couldn't believe how there was no bleeding of songs into the other section and how immersed one was while inside. *Amazing,* he thought, considering there were no thick walls or sound barriers that he could see between the sections; there were only open walkways.

He was still preparing his apology for being late when he arrived back in the store's front. He saw Nort was eyeing a gold pocket watch in a case and approached him slowly.

"What took you so long?" Nort said on seeing Alex's reflection in the glass display.

"I was just . . ." Alex started. "Sorry, I got a little distracted."

Nort turned around and faced him, nearly cringing. "That's it? That's all you could find in all that time?"

"What's wrong with my jacket?" Alex asked defensively.

"Oh, nothing, it just lacks the sophistication of —"

"What? Your proper clothes?"

"Style. But I suppose it's your choice."

"Thank you," Alex said proudly. "It is my choice."

Karissa remained quiet during their bickering as she glanced around in the local section in the very front of the store, appropriately named Tristoria, that had no time stamp on it. Alex had not noticed the section when they first entered, but then again he hadn't seen the hallway either.

What represented Tristoria? Pretty much everything. There were countless hats, from western cowboy hats to fire helmets and every type of vest you could imagine, along with belts and buckles, boots and shoes for all occasions, and even leather sandals. There were even full suits of armor, if that was your fancy. There was also a section labeled Fantasy that reminded Alex of the characters in the plethora of RPGs on his computer.

Karissa bought nothing. She seemed perfectly content just browsing in her plain violet cloak. She did, however, briefly hover over an ornate wooden bow displayed in an intricate cabinet.

"Everyone set?" Nort asked. They both nodded. "Good, let's get to the stables and be on our way."

"Stables? What for?" Alex asked.

"Horses," Nort said. "What else are in stables?"

"Sorry, jeez. I was just wondering how come we aren't using, your . . . um . . . umbrella?" Alex wasn't even sure his stomach could handle another trip in that flying machine, but horses were just as foreign to him as Tristoria, and they would take much longer to get where they were going. And longer meant more chance for danger.

"It's built for two," Nort said. "And seeing how there are three of us now . . . Anyway, this will be fun."

"I don't see how," Alex mumbled while shaking his head.

CHAPTER 10
Riding a Tormented Horse

Thankfully, the horses stood saddled and ready to go when they arrived at the stables. On the walk over, Nort gave Alex brief riding instructions along with a few commands to use. Alex had never been closer to a horse than a computer or television screen and did not have the first clue about the equipment or commands. "Giddy up" was the extent of his lingo. But these horses didn't look like the ones he had ever seen, or he suspected anyone has ever seen where he was from. They were as dark as night and had glistening, blood-red horns that curved menacingly toward the sky. But it was their eyes that caused a sense of foreboding to hover like a thick fog; they glowed white, like a bright full moon on a cloudless night, without pupils. He was intimidated before he had seen the creatures, but their appearance elevated things considerably.

"They are tormented, just as many things here are," Nort said. "They may seem a little irritable at first, but they'll warm up to you in time."

Great, more cranky things. "What are they?" Alex surveyed the horses nervously. "I mean, they aren't . . . you know . . ."

"Demons? Certainly not," Nort said, as if Alex should have known. "They're just horses. Now go on, don't be afraid."

"No horses like I've ever seen," Alex grumbled.

He edged closer to the horse he was expected to ride, doing his best to avoid eye contact with those sinister glowing eyes. After a few seconds of staring from a safe distance, the horse neighed and Alex got a strange feeling the horse was telling him to "get on with it already."

Karissa looked on helplessly, having already mounted her horse brilliantly moments before, while Nort stared at Alex like a patient teacher, offering advice but insisting that this was a lesson Alex had to complete on his own.

"I don't see the point," Alex spouted between nervous breaths.

"This is it, you know," Nort said, ignoring Alex's scoffing. "Your last chance to back out."

"Why are you telling me that?! I'm in the middle of . . ." He took a deep breath and regained his composure. "You told me it wouldn't be a good idea to break a commitment here."

"Yes, but I also have the responsibility to remind you of your free will."

Alex had enough doubt circling around inside that he hardly needed any more, especially from Nort, the one who had convinced him to come here in the first place. If he was trying some sort of reverse psychology in front of a girl, well, it was working he had to admit. Without another word spoken, he made his first attempt to mount the horse, but it was unsuccessful because he underestimated the horse's height. Frustrated, but determined, he tried again; his foot slipped out of the stirrup and he lost his balance and fell to the ground. He got up quickly, not bothering to dust himself off, and faced the side of the horse. Avoiding eye contact with both Nort and Karissa, he placed his right shoe in the stirrup and grabbed ahold of the reins. He grunted and hefted himself up, struggling with all of his might and humility to get his left leg over the horse's wide back. A few seconds later and out of breath, he sat atop the dark beast proud of his new feat.

"Are you done? Can we go now?" Nort said impatiently.

"Yeah, no thanks to you," Alex said.

"I gave you instructions. Karissa had the same instructions her first time."

Alex glanced over toward her, but she had her head lowered, avoiding input to the back-and-forth.

With red cheeks, he grabbed the reins snuggly and leaned forward to the horse's ear and whispered, "Don't let me fall, please." The horse tilted his head down as if nodding to him. Alex shook off the oddness and turned his attention to Nort.

"Ready now?" Nort said.

Alex straightened himself upright and said pridefully, "What are we waiting for?"

Nort shook his head and turned his horse north, and Karissa did the same. Alex needed a second to go over the brief instructions Nort had given him on guiding and instructing the horse. After a few moments of mumbling the words to himself, he pressed his heels into the horse's sides and the horse shot off at great speed.

Alex was nearly flung off from the initial burst, but somehow hung on. Recalling the sudden burst of speed of Nort's umbrella, Alex thought to himself, *It's happening again;* only, this was a different power from Nort's umbrella: the horse moved smoothly and gracefully as if it were traversing a peaceful meadow. Alex caught a blur of Nort and Karissa as he zoomed by them and heard a faint yell from Nort that he could not understand. He tried to look back, but the momentum was too great. He had no clue where they were going. He needed to stop, but how? He quickly rummaged through the information in his head and remembered Nort saying something about a command to slow or stop the animal.

He tried "halt" first and then "stop," but neither so much as fazed the horse from its intense momentum. "Think, Alex, think," he scolded himself, eyeing a ridge up ahead. *Please tell me these horses have the presence of mind to stop and not go over a cliff.* He remembered the horse from the movie *NeverEnding Story*, Artax, and recalled Atreyu guiding him through the swamp of sadness and saying, "Come on, boy." *That's it,* he thought.

He yelled, "Whoa, boy!"

The horse immediately halted, skidding its hooves in the soft dirt. Alex grabbed ahold of the horse's bridle, barely missing being gored by a horn as he toppled over the front of the horse. The horse shook his neck, making Alex release his hand and fall to the ground. His head missed a rock by mere inches. He lay still and stared up at the gray clouds, not wanting to get up just yet.

"You could have used a little common sense and slowed down first," he told the horse. The horse neighed and turned in the other direction as if pouting.

A few seconds later, Alex heard hooves approaching and then Nort was hovering above him wearing a frown. Oddly, Nort's horse was looking at Alex with the same expression.

"I said a nudge, not a bloody bludgeon," Nort lectured.

Ignoring Nort, Alex searched around for Karissa. He could see her a few feet away behind Nort, thankfully looking the other way. Was she ashamed for him? Or was she giving him the courtesy of privacy and dignity until he gathered himself? He hoped for the latter.

"Let's try this again, shall we," Nort said. "My plan was to acclimate you for a half mile, but seeing as you aren't one for easing into things, we'll be on our way."

Alex got up and dusted himself off. He mounted the horse after two attempts, feeling a little better about it this time and keeping a smidgen of pride.

"On my mark," Nort said. He looked to Karissa, and then to Alex.

Nort shot off into the distance like a fast-moving train. Next, Karissa did the same, with her cloak flowing in a perfect line behind her swiftly moving horse. Alex cringed and gripped the reins much tighter this time. He counted to three and then pressed his heels firmly, but much more gently, against the horse's sides. He barreled forward, only this time he braced himself. After a few minutes, he loosened up the reins and enjoyed the rush of wind and speed.

Alex could still feel the adrenaline pumping freely in his veins as his horse slowed to a trot. It was just what he needed to separate the tangled mess of angst rattling around in his head. Karissa was on the other side of Nort a few horse lengths ahead when Alex slowed and heard them conversing back and forth over something about the realm. Alex heard the word *hand* before they stopped and acknowledged him. He pulled the reins of his horse and moved alongside Nort with surprising ease.

"That was great," Alex said. "I think I'm finally getting the hang of this horse riding."

Nort nodded. "Good, because the terrain up ahead is more challenging."

"And no offense," Alex continued, "but it was smoother than Bessie." *An understatement,* he thought.

"She's a machine, and these are graceful, beautiful creatures. There is no comparison."

Nort's response surprised Alex, seeing as how he went on and on about his flying machine's abilities. He must hold a serious soft spot for these creatures.

"Wait a minute," Alex said, just now catching Nort's earlier words. "How challenging? And where exactly are we?" Not that it really mattered because he had no reference points or any idea of the place. It just felt right to ask. He peered around nervously at the barren, rocky terrain where they had slowed their horses. He noticed the wind was picking up and stirring up dust in the distance.

"We are on the outer edges of the desolate fields of Dorney," Nort said. "You'll see the peaks of the Blue-spire Mountains soon."

"Whew, well that didn't take as long as I thought it would," Alex said relieved. "But you mentioned something challenging."

"Indeed, I did," Nort said. "And we're not quite to the realm's land; we have a few hours yet to go."

"Why did we stop, then?"

Nort pointed up ahead.

"I don't see anything."

"Look closer at the ground in front of you."

Alex looked on, horrified at the sea of sharp, jagged rocks jutting out from the dirt like pieces of broken gems glimmering in the light.

"What the heck are those?" Alex asked.

"A common and very poisonous ore, appropriately named daemonium mortem, demon death, for its only usefulness is that it is very lethal to demons. That is if you can mine enough without getting yourself killed first. Many have died mining them. And all for the protection of the realm."

"So, this is like a fence to keep the demons out?" Alex said, ignoring Nort's continued discontent for the realm.

"Precisely," Nort said.

His earlier plea to the horse to not throw him off was well past merely avoiding humiliation; it was now a matter of life and death.

"Is this the only way in?" Alex asked warily.

"No, but the shortest, and least dangerous," Nort said.

"Okay, well, in that case —" Alex said.

"Yes," Nort nodded, "this way. And follow closely and make sure not to sway from the path."

"What path!?" Alex said in a near panic. He had noticed no path.

"Just stay close behind Karissa," Nort said irritably.

After Nort was out of earshot Karissa told Alex, "He's not always like this, you know. You'll be fine if you stay close."

"Not a problem," Alex said, pulling his horse's reins to edge closer to hers. His horse neighed in rebellion as he nudged it so close to Karissa's that her horse slapped its tail in warning. "Sorry," he told all three of them.

"Maybe not that close," Karissa said playfully.

"Oh, okay. Got it," Alex said, feeling the heat rising in his face once again.

An hour later, they were clear of the minefield of poisonous rocks, and mostly unscathed, except for some tense shoulders and neck muscles. Alex rolled up the sleeves of his Members Only jacket and enjoyed the cool breeze on his skin, then took in a much-needed gulp of fresh air.

"I have an extra piece of cloth if you want it," Karissa offered.

"Huh?" Alex said. He had been so focused and tense that he had not realized he had been riding alongside her quietly for at least five minutes. Nort was in front of them a good distance, but still within earshot.

"Your face."

"Wait, what's wrong with my face?" he said in a panic, and immediately began fingering all around on his face. "Did I get hit with a piece of that demon rock?"

He sighed in relief when he felt that his face was still intact and there was no blood on his hands.

"No," she smirked again from under her cloak, keeping her composure. "It's just sweat."

Alex noticed for the first time that she had dimples and pretty teeth. Something that would normally never cross his mind. But there was something mysterious about this girl, and not only the fact that she was wearing a cloak and hiding her face most of the time.

"Oh," he said and instinctively wiped the sweat with the back of his hand. He felt the chill of the wind hitting his drenched neck and he took the piece of cloth from her outstretched hand. "Thank you."

"You're welcome."

He wiped his face and arms, noticing a pleasant but strange floral scent on the cloth.

"You can keep that," she said. "I have more."

"Thanks," he said, placing the cloth in the back pocket of his jeans. "You make it look so easy; where did you learn to ride?"

"My dad," she said with discontent. "He made me."

"Made you? How come?"

119

"We traveled a ton when I was a little younger. I can't tell you how many trips we made to the castle."

"Castle? There's a castle here?"

"Of course there is. We're going there now to meet your grandfather."

"Oh, okay . . . sorry. I'm still getting used to this place. Did he work there or something?"

She scowled. "Not hardly. My dad only wanted one thing from the realm and it wasn't work. He wanted favor, and I was the bartered merchandise."

"Sorry to hear that. That's pretty darn cruel. Yeah, my dad's nowhere that extreme, but I know what it's like to be disappointed in my dad."

"Thankfully, Nort knows my dad and his intentions. My dad has been trying to get Nort to take me to the realm for a long time. I think Nort could see my dad's desperation this time."

"Desperation? How come?"

"My dad's getting close to his time and he thinks I'm his only way to get more of it."

"Isn't he defeating the purpose? Good deeds and intention and all."

"Exactly. I'm just currency to him. Nort has told him I'm special and that I possess a delicacy that needs grooming. My dad took it to mean I was worth more, letting Nort's true intentions slip right past him. No one has ever accused him of being smart."

"What about your mom? Where is she?"

Before Karissa could answer, a gust of wind blew back the hood of her cloak just enough for Alex to glimpse a scar along her face. She quickly covered it back up by whisking her cloak back over her head.

"I need to ask Nort something, excuse me," she said, and quickly galloped up to Nort a few horse lengths ahead.

Was it something I said?, he wondered. He thought he was doing well talking to girls this time around. He felt sure she was just being self-conscious about her scar. And if she wasn't, he was still telling himself that she was.

When they came to the top of a large hill a few minutes later, all his worries halted. The sight in front of him was amazing and breathtaking, sending confusing chills up and down his entire body. He did not know if he should cower in fear or bow in respect.

CHAPTER 11
The Castle

With twilight fast approaching and a thick gray blanket of clouds hanging low in the sky, the massive structure in the distance was even more ominous and beautiful to Alex as it plastered him in place and in a state of awe. Its dark, gothic architecture haunted the mountain that held it securely in place, and the blue-gray rock formations lifted and fortified its position along the vast mountain range. Each of its many towers staggered in height and stood crowned with a keen-edged tip that kissed the clouds. *Menacing and strategically placed,* Alex thought, as he glanced down at a winding path leading from the castle to a small dense forest below: a mountain on three sides and a forest in front.

Near the entrance to the forest, he could make out a faint flickering light that he assumed was a torch stuck in a sconce on a tree or a guard standing perfectly still.

"Yes, it's beautiful in its own way, I guess," Nort said. "Now, this way, and when we reach the forest let me do the talking, please. If it's even necessary."

Neither Karissa nor Alex had objections, so Nort turned his horse and trotted down the valley. Once they made it to the entrance of the forest, there was no one there to converse with; only a sconce wielding the torch Alex had seen. Thankfully, there were many more torches along the path and no one to greet or challenge them, although Alex noticed that Nort tipped his hat a few times. Alex presumed they were being watched, and if the field of deadly rocks was any sign of security, they likely had a weapon pointed in their direction the entire time.

Once they cleared the tree line, they traveled up a narrow pathway to an elevated stone bridge. The bridge hovered at least twenty to thirty feet above a moat and at the other end was an entrance to the castle. Though it was dark, the reflection of the moat glowed emerald green, leaving Alex to shudder at the thought of what creatures lie beneath in the dark depths. There were always creatures in moats, he recalled from his books, usually some huge snakes or crocodiles. But in this place who knew what deadly behemoth lie in hiding, so he was careful to keep to the center of the bridge as he crossed over it.

Ahead, an iron portcullis laced with vines lay open for them. Two large sconces on either side of the gate shot wide, bright flames along the castle walls up to a pair of sinister gargoyle statues. The statues stared down at them warningly as if to say one wrong move and we'll fly down and gouge your eyes out. Alex cringed and considered that they were actually entering Dracula's lair, and that they were about to be dinner guests to a feast featuring them as the main course.

A man's boisterous voice startled Alex from his eerie thoughts. "Welcome all, please come in."

The man wore a nicely tailored, dark navy tunic and bark colored pants. He had a well kempt beard with long, light golden brown hair pulled back behind his ears. He had a welcoming demeanor, unlike the feeling of dread the castle portrayed from the outside. He nodded to two young boys flanked on his sides that appeared a few years younger than Alex, and who also dressed similar to the man. They immediately helped the three of them from their horses and then led the beasts away. Alex suddenly felt way underdressed and somehow even more out of place.

"Jarren," Nort said with a stern nod while straightening his clothes from the ride. "Where's the king? He's usually here when I return."

"Same old Nort. Right to the point," Jarren said. "This is the boy, I presume."

"Of course it is," Nort said. "As agreed."

"Very good," Jarren said, offering an outstretched hand to Alex. "Nice to finally meet you. I am Jarren, the king's hand."

Alex had his hands clasped behind his back, but quickly pulled his right arm around and shook the man's outstretched hand. "Yes , . . you too."

Jarren smiled brightly and then looked over at Karissa. She was staring at the floor with her cloak still donned. He walked over and stood in front of her and said, "And who else have you brought with you?"

"This is Karissa Spurnlock," Nort said.

"Karissa Shade, sir," Karissa chided.

"Are you Jorn's daughter?" Jarren asked.

She didn't respond, so Nort intervened. "Yes, she is but — "

"Nort, I have to object once again," Jarren interjected. "As I have told her father before, she is too young to join the guard, by any means he offers."

"She is not here on her father's behalf," Nort said. "She's with me. She is my company and will leave with me when I go."

Alex noticed Karissa crack a brief smile from under her hood when Nort said she was his company.

"Very well, Nort," Jarren said. "If you two could excuse us for a moment, Alex and I need to speak in the Great Hall."

Nort stared at Jarren suspiciously, but after a moment he nodded to Alex that it was okay. "I'll stay until you have met with your grandfather," Nort assured him.

"Wait, what about our deal?" Alex asked Nort.

"Your grandfather will have the answer you're seeking," Nort said.

"Okay, but where is he?"

"Soon, I promise," Jarren said with a half smile, and cast a curious glance toward Nort. Nort seemed unfazed by his look, not offering elaboration. "But first we must discuss a few small things while your grandfather is being summoned."

Alex nodded and thought, *What choice do Ie have at this point?* He followed Jarren and as they walked to the Great Hall one room over, he hadn't noticed until then that there were two guards standing in the shadows of the entry hall.

They were stoic and wore dark armor, similar to a knight's but lighter somehow; it appeared very agile but still sturdy and strong. There was also a crest on the breastplate that he could not quite make out because of the shadows.

The Great Hall stood up to its name, and not only from its vastness but with the items it held. There was a massive, thick wooden table in the center surrounded by various mammoth-sized paintings and tapestries along the walls. The paintings depicted a variety of scenes of cloaked figures and armored men battling various types of demons. They told a story in what Alex assumed was a timeline of battles. There were colossal wooden barrels jutting from the walls with names of the beverage the barrels held written in script. An elaborate hall for drinks and tales of past battles.

"Have a seat, please," Jarren offered.

Alex sat in the closest high-back arched chair to him and Jarren sat across from him, moving aside a multi-tiered ornate black candelabra from between them.

Jarren clasped his hands together and cast a concerned look across his face as if on cue. He then let out a heavy sigh and said, "I know this . . ." he peered around the room dramatically, "this place can overwhelm and you're probably nervous and scared, among many other feelings scrambling around in there. And if I know Nort, he hasn't told you much." Alex nodded his head. "Well, I trust he told you where you are, just not why? Am I correct?"

Alex nodded again. "Sort of. Only that my grandfather wanted me. But not the reasons."

"First, let me get it out of the way. You have done nothing wrong. None of your life choices has anything to do with why you are here."

Jarren was the second person to iterate that point. Alex let out an audible sigh and relaxed, having the information reaffirmed.

Jarren smiled briefly, but it quickly faded. "Alex, you are here because you have blood running through your veins that comes with great responsibility. A dark one, but nonetheless a responsibility."

Alex hung on the word *dark,* but continued to listen intently.

"What's your middle name?"

"Rayne, why?"

"Your mother's name?"

"Samantha."

"Do you know her maiden name?"

Alex thought on it for a moment, but couldn't recall ever knowing. "No, I don't remember," he said, shaking his head.

"Sweeny, and your father's last name is actually Rayne. Rayne also is the king's last name."

"Are you saying I am related to the king or something?" Alex asked, attempting to process the information and where Jarren was going with it.

"Yes, something like that. But I'm not the one to elaborate on these things. Your grandfather would like to speak with you and discuss these matters. I wanted to inspect you alone, before I bothered him. And now I see that Nort has performed as we instructed him." Jarren stood and held his hands out toward the door behind them, "After you."

Alex got up from his chair and walked to a side door opposite the one they initially came through and entered a candlelit corridor. After a few turns, they came to a set of double doors with two sentries standing guard. On seeing Jarren, the sentries moved aside immediately and pushed open the doors for them.

Alex entered but stopped only a few steps inside once he saw the man standing next to the fireplace. He couldn't believe his eyes, but there he was, only much older and more frail than the last time Alex had seen him.

The huge bedroom was well lit by a massive fireplace with an intricately carved mantle and an array of candles spread throughout the space. The figure standing in front of the fireplace wore a dark robe with the hood resting on his shoulders. His hair was thin and gray, but long, to his shoulders, and he had sunken cheeks, giving his face a skull-like appearance. Though he appeared different from how he remembered, Alex knew this man well.

"Grandpa, is that you?" Alex said hesitantly. "How . . ."

"Long story," he said dismissively, followed by a brief coughing fit. "My boy, come here and let me get a good look at you. It's been too long."

Alex, still stuck in a dreamlike state, did as his grandpa said. *Yes,* Alex thought, *he appears to be my grandpa and his voice is correct, but what the heck is going on?*

"We'll have to fatten you up a bit, I see."

Now that the man was closer to Alex, the firelight revealed a more disturbing feature than his frailness: his eyes had changed from a pleasant copper to a crimson that seemed to glow as burning embers.

"What is all of this?" Alex began. "And why am I here? A bad dream, right? I'll wake up soon?"

"No dream, I'm afraid, but it's not all bad."

"Okay. . . ." Alex said tentatively.

His grandpa looked over at Jarren and nodded to him. Jarren bowed and left the room, closing the heavy, creaking double doors behind him.

"Have a seat and let's talk," Alex's grandpa said, motioning toward the two adjacent chairs facing the fireplace.

Alex sat in one of the high-back chairs and then watched his grandpa wince as he slowly sat down in the chair next to him.

"You've had some unexplained fevers recently? Quick to come on and leave just as suddenly?"

"Yes!" Alex said enthusiastically.

"And with them you experienced visions, either before, during, or after. They felt very real to you."

"Too real," Alex said, remembering the huge beast he had seen while raking leaves. "I had remnants, burnt shoelaces and I could smell smoke and —"

"Yes, yes, it's all part of it."

"So, I'm not crazy, then? Wait, part of what?"

"No, not entirely," he said, and winked. "You are coming of age, my boy."

"Puberty? Fevers and visions weren't part of the class they taught me in school."

His grandpa stifled a laugh.

"This has nothing to do with your endocrine system, my boy. This is your powers revealing themselves in tiny bursts. Those remnants you mentioned were you crossing through."

"Powers? What are you talking about? And crossing through what?" He wanted to ask his grandfather if he was out of his medications, but decided it best not to.

"Never mind the crossing through stuff for now," his grandfather sighed. "You've made things move without touching them, have you not? Maybe a little persuasion over others at a particularly important moment to you?"

Alex thought on it and remembered a few instances, notably the lamp in the living room with Margie. But the persuasion part eluded his thoughts. He nodded, but still not entirely convinced.

"That is your emotions tampering where they should not. They will attempt to control you when you are not aware. They are both an attribute and an adversary."

"Are you saying I can do . . . magic?" Alex winced at the word, hearing how absurd it sounded saying it aloud. But Nort has done a few things that Alex could consider magic, he presumed.

His grandpa smiled, followed by another coughing fit. "Well, in a manner of speaking, yes. But it's not as easy as 'poof there it is, or there it isn't'. There is discipline and incantations and rituals . . . anyway, we're getting ahead of ourselves." He grabbed a small cloth from his robe pocket and wiped his mouth. Alex glimpsed the blood-tinged cloth before he shoved it back inside his pocket. "I have little time and I need you to listen closely. I'll get straight to the point. You're a warlock. So am I. So was my dad and his dad and so on."

"A warlock?" Alex said, furrowing his eyebrows.

"A sorcerer, dark magic user, male witch, we've been called many things."

"Wait, but aren't warlocks evil?"

"Not all, no. Only the ones who allow themselves to be corrupted by the ones from whom they draw their power."

"You mean demons?"

"You catch on quickly. Yes, in short, we summon and use their power. But we remain in control. Total control. Which brings me to why you are here. We, meaning our family, have developed and perfected many incantations over the centuries. We are stingy with our powers and prefer to keep them in the family. And for a very good reason. The Raynes have been guardians of Tristoria for many ages. Alex, you are a Rayne. Your true name is Alexander Henry Rayne. Your mother's maiden name was Sweeny and it was given to you as a protection. Your current middle name, which is Rayne, is your true surname. Your dad is a Rayne, not a Sweeny."

"Guardians? So that would mean you're the . . . king here?"

His grandfather nodded, "Yes."

"Wait, so Dad is a warlock? He never told me anything —" Alex said, as he attempted to piece together the insane puzzle he was being given.

His grandpa lowered his head and sighed. "Our weapon can also be our curse. Warlocks can be easily corrupted, and it takes a strong mind to resist the powerful evil that we call on for our powers. There is a balance, a strict balance, that must be maintained. Your father passed all of his tests but one. The one that says above all that he will put Tristoria first and protect it at any cost. He felt there was too much uncertainty in him and didn't trust his ability to keep this place safe. I tried over the years to give him another trial, but he refused over and over again. He never gained the confidence to succeed me, which means . . ."

"You can't be serious?" Alex contested. "Me?"

His grandfather nodded once again.

"You want me to run this place? A place I never knew existed until a few hours ago?"

"No, I want you to rule," his grandfather said firmly. "Of course, there is a ton to learn but what feat worth it in the end is ever easy? I'll save you the time, the answer is none."

Alex sat back in his chair and absorbed the information, unsure of how to respond to his ailing grandfather. He had homework due by Monday, not to mention after-school detention given by Mrs. Tindal. He didn't have time to rule whatever this place was; Tristoria. Yeah, he wanted to get away from his miserable life, but he wasn't expecting to be ruling a world in return.

"What about Dad? Does he know I'm here?" Alex asked, entertaining the absurdness.

"Things will be handled. Your dad is fine where he is. He knew this day would eventually come. In fact, he was supposed to have had the talk with you on your fourteenth birthday. I don't know why he was waiting. This wouldn't be so overwhelming for you if he had told you."

"I can tell you," Alex said, feeling the anger rise up his throat. His grandpa arched his left eyebrow. "Ever since he married that Margie woman, he hasn't been the same." One more thing to blame her for.

His grandpa shook his head in disappointment. "His weakness continues. No matter. He has made his choice several times over, and now it is your time." He coughed a few times into his cloth and then continued, only this time his voice held a sadness Alex had not heard before. "Alex, I'm dying."

Silence hung in the air as Alex grasped ahold of the words. His grandpa stood and untied his robe, revealing a necrotic, black and dark green wound the length of his entire right side.

"It's poison," his grandpa said. "I've slowed it, but I cannot stop this." The dark poison moved under his skin like a snake slithering through sand.

This is real, he told himself, *crazy but real.* His grandfather was right in front of him and he was dying. He could feel the panic rising in his throat as the reality sunk in deeper.

"You can't die. I mean, you're a warlock, right? Can't you heal yourself or cast some spell. . . ."

Alex's breathing became rapid and then a sharp pain twisted in his side with each inhalation.

"Alex, I need you to focus," his grandfather said calmly. "There will be plenty of time for grieving later. You have a legacy to continue. You are a Rayne, and with that comes a powerful responsibility. You will learn the ways of the warlock and will become a great leader." He wiped his mouth and winced, holding his injured side before retying his robe. "I need to lie down," he said, coughing and wincing at the pain.

Alex assisted his grandfather to the bed and sat beside him gingerly. His grandfather winced again as he slowly lowered his head to the soft pillow and shut his eyes.

"Grandpa," Alex said, with alarm in his voice. "Grandpa!"

His grandfather opened his eyes lazily and said in a tired voice, "Tell Jarren to bring Nort to me, please."

Alex, relieved to see that his grandfather was still there, did as he asked without question. A few minutes later, Nort was standing in the doorway. All along, Nort had actually been referring to his grandfather, the king, when mentioning the realm. No matter how much discontent Nort held for the king's policies, he could see the forlorn expression on Nort's face when he saw the king.

"Nort, my friend. Please come here," Alex's grandpa said weakly.

Alex looked on from the other side of the room as Nort and his grandpa conversed quietly. He couldn't make out

135

much of what they were saying, only a few inflections that sounded like concern in Nort's voice.

Before leaving the room, Nort placed a gentle hand on Alex's shoulder and lowered his head and said, "This changes things a bit."

"Come here, son," his grandpa said before Alex could question Nort's comment.

Alex carefully sat back down on the bed next to his grandpa and grabbed his brittle hand with his own. It was cold and weak, he noticed, so he slightly loosened his grip. "I know I'm a Rayne, but I'm only fourteen. I can't do this . . . this ruling or warlock stuff. Can't my dad have one more chance? Another attempt or something? I can talk with him —"

"He has made his choice. This is *your* time now, *your* destiny. I am sorry for the process in which it has happened, but Tristoria needs a guardian. You are the first line of defense to Earth and in the scheme of things, ultimately, heaven. Tristoria is the true middle world and is a gateway. If the evil spreads and takes over this world, it could mean the end to everything."

No pressure, Alex thought.

The king coughed again, this time spraying blood into his hands. His strength was fading fast. He could not stifle a cough long enough to retrieve a cloth. "There has to be a Rayne on the throne."

"Grandpa, I'm not . . ."

"You must seek Krunk and tell him that the book is missing and that Helenia lives; he'll know what that means.

And I did not open a portal. That's important, okay?" Alex said nothing. "Okay!?" his grandpa reinforced.

Alex nodded with fearful eyes. "Okay."

"Oh, and despite Nort's sometimes churlish demeanor, he is trustworthy."

"Grandpa, I'm not ready," Alex pleaded.

"Beware of the eager."

"Huh, wait, what does that —"

"And one more thing . . ." His eyes darkened, Alex noticed. "Once the dust settles, and after you have found Krunk, only then will you inform the council of my passing. It is up to you now, Alex Rayne. Tristoria is in your hands. Surround yourself with trustworthy companions and you will not fail."

"There's a council? Why haven't I —"

"I see you share your parents' love for the eighties," he said, and used his last bit of strength to stretch a smile across his face. "It was a good decade for music."

Anger, fear, sadness, self-pity: they were all waiting eagerly at the doorway like an angry mob with pitchforks. When he finally released the latch, the door flung open, releasing tears and shouts. "You can't go!" Alex shook him, repeatedly, begging for his return, but he didn't move.

His grandpa — the warlock king of Tristoria, the true middle world — was gone.

CHAPTER 12
The King is Dead

Alex sat with his grandfather's body for a long while, attempting to process what had just happened. It was all surreal. Nothing made sense. He knew his grandfather was eccentric, according to his mom, but a warlock king of a middle world? That was just ridiculous. And even more insane: he was next in line to rule the world.

While he ran through this absurd turn of events, his grandpa's body had disappeared, leaving only his robe. *Great, another kink in my reality,* he thought. *Is Grandpa in heaven? Do warlocks even go there? Is he in some other form?* Alex's head pounded as his reality sank in the murky depths of this world. He sat back in the chair next to the fireplace and attempted to get a mental grasp on anything he could.

Before now he had a solid understanding of death, which was only what he could see. This experience definitely changed things, though he did not quite know to what extent.

Jarren knocked on the door, startling him and dragging him out from his thoughts. "Sir?" Jarren said, peeking his head through the cracked door. "Are you okay? If you need more time, the others will understand."

"No, it's fine," Alex said, wiping his eyes with his knuckles and getting to his feet. He cleared his throat and attempted to sound normal, as if he hadn't just lost his grandfather. "What do we do now?"

"We talk," Jarren said reassuringly, opening the door fully and standing to the side.

"Okay," Alex nodded, and solemnly glanced back in the room one more time at his grandpa's wrinkled empty robe.

Jarren led Alex back into the Great Hall where Nort and Karissa sat next to one another on one end of the massive wooden table. Alex silently took a seat across from them and Jarren took the seat at the head. A spread of meats and fruits and breads filled the table, along with pitchers of water and juices and ale and mead. Intricate candelabras spaced out along the table shed an elegant and serene light, as if the dinner were a way to simmer the moods due to the recent grim event.

Alex's plate sat empty in front of him. He was in no mood to eat. He did, however, eye the pitcher of mead sitting within arm's reach. Though he had never tasted the honey wine, he knew people consumed alcohol for many reasons, including to calm their nerves after a hectic day. And this day was definitely hectic.

Alex stretched out his hand to grab the pitcher's handle, but Nort was quicker, as if he had expected Alex's move.

"After we have had our discussion, then we can consider letting our wits linger in the shadows for a while," Nort said.

"You're not my dad," Alex snapped.

Nort kept his composure, but held a stern glare toward him, keeping the gold liquid safely out of Alex's reach.

"Fine," Alex said, huffing and crossing his arms. "I don't see how any of you can eat. Your king just died. My grandpa is dead. And guess what? I'm clueless about this place and I'm supposed to take my grandfather's place as king. Yeah, right!" He lowered his head and felt himself tremble. "This makes no sense at all."

Alex was supposedly a warlock, but still had no clue what that actually meant. Where are these supposed powers, and how does one tap into them? The one person he fully trusted to help him was now dead. And this council, whoever and wherever they are, could not help him yet either. His frustration was roiling, leaving him teetering on the edge of another outburst.

The silence echoed in the large hall for a few awkward moments as Alex sat brooding.

Finally, Jarren cut the silence by clearing his throat and said, "I can speak for the realm when I say how sorry and truly sad we are about the king's death. He was an honorable king and ruled fairly. Unfortunately, a king is always under threat."

"Isn't it your job to protect him?" Alex said indignantly. He immediately felt remorse for his misdirected anger. He hardly knew these people, and he didn't know who or what was at fault.

Jarren didn't have an immediate answer. "Yes, but . . ." He sighed. "We don't yet have all the evidence, but I promise to you and the entire realm that we will avenge him. As long as I have breath in my lungs, I will not stop the pursuit of justice. And there is no doubt in my mind that you will follow in his shoes and rule just as honorably and —"

"Yeah, yeah, the kingdom and honor and all that stuff," Nort interrupted. "The boy needs direction, not a speech. There will be plenty of time for ceremonies and speeches of greatness later."

Jarren looked over at Nort with stifled anger. "Nort, the realm appreciates your service and we will compensate you as discussed." His eyes narrowed. "You have completed your mission here."

"Are you kicking me out, Jarren?" Nort asked slightly threatening.

"I am simply saying your job is complete," Jarren said with a forced smile. "We can handle it from here." Jarren scooted his chair back and stood. "You may finish your meal before departing. I'm sure you have some mercenary or outlaw business to take care of elsewhere."

"If you think I'm just going to leave this boy to —"

"Nort, don't test my patience," Jarren warned, elevating his voice. The guards by the door turned toward the noise and placed their hands on the hilt of their swords.

Nort remained seated and stared tauntingly back at Jarren.

Ignoring Nort, Jarren turned his attention to Alex and seemed to erase any displeasure from his voice and expression. "Alex, will you please join me in the throne room? There will be much more privacy where we can discuss your part and the future of the realm."

Despite the chaos of the situation and his defusing anger, there was one thing Alex was sure of, and that was he wasn't going anywhere without Nort. He had kept Alex alive so far, and could have killed him on multiple occasions if that had been his mission.

"My grandpa trusted Nort enough to bring me here," Alex said. "I would like him with me, along with Karissa."

"Nort is a mercenary who fights only for himself, Alex," Jarren said. "I have to insist on protecting the sensitive nature of the information. A need-to-know basis, and the only ones who need to know are the ones accompanying you on your mission."

Alex's tone changed to a more assertive one. "I don't care about Nort's motives. He has kept me safe and I'm not going anywhere in this place without him and Karissa. That is, if they agree to go with me." *Please say yes,* he said silently. He felt the heat rising again inside his belly.

Nort nearly revealed a smile, but remained tight-lipped and nodded firmly. Karissa also nodded from under her hood. Alex sighed in relief to himself.

"Very well," Jarren said begrudgingly. "No matter, I'm also sending a few of my best soldiers with you."

"Sure, of course," Alex said as if there were no other way.

Nort huffed while Jarren sat back down in his chair and poured himself a tall mug of mead. He took a long sip and set the mug in front of him. "I know this goes without saying, but knowledge of the king's death must not leave this room. The king's last order was not to alert the council until Alex has returned." He turned to face Alex. "He will become a powerful warlock and the realm will go on as it has for millennia."

"That is, if he passes the tests and he doesn't run away," Nort said.

Nort's words shocked Alex, especially since he had just taken up for him. He knew Nort doubted him, but a little confidence wouldn't hurt.

"He's a Rayne. It's his destiny," Jarren said emphatically.

"Have you forgotten his father? It was also his destiny, and where is he now," Nort said.

Alex's face turned a few shades of red. "I'm not my dad," Alex said between clenched teeth.

Jarren stared at Nort with his brows furrowed. "This is not helpful, Nort. Don't take out your distaste for the realm and the king's rule on Alex."

"The king and I had an understanding," Nort said. "He was a great man, and I considered him a friend. My problem is this place and the suffering that comes with it. This has nothing to do with Alex personally."

"Paying for your mistakes isn't supposed to be a pleasant walk in a meadow. We pay our debts with much more vigor and energy than our mistakes took to make them. That's what we do!" Jarren exclaimed.

"Thanks for the lecture," Nort sighed.

"There must be order in this place or it will crumble," Jarren said. "Even you know that, Nort."

"Good, maybe we should let it crumble," Nort said as if he had taken a bite of a rotten apple.

"You will have heaven and Earth destroyed because of what?" Jarren said. "Your view of how things should be? This is bigger than you, Nort. Bigger than all of us."

"Stop!" Karissa shouted, and then stood up from the table with her cloak still partially masking her face. "Please . . ." she looked down at Nort pleadingly. "This place is all that I know. I am part of it, no matter how I feel about it. And if they destroy it, I will no longer exist. Say you don't mean it." She looked as if she could start crying at any moment. "Do you?"

Alex assumed she meant that the demons or some other enemy would kill her, but her tone and passion said something more.

"No, I do not," Nort admitted, apologetically. He gingerly touched her shoulder for her to sit back down.

She nodded from under her hood and sat down, lowering her gaze to the table.

Jarren used this opportunity to begin his speech on the mission. "We must have a ruler in Tristoria and that means a Rayne on the throne." His tone changed to a more severe one. "What I am about to say does not leave this room. Do we all understand?" He peered around the room, one by one. They all nodded, even Nort, though he rolled his eyes while doing so. "The Book is missing. And I don't have to tell you how dire this makes the situation."

145

Alex raised his hand. "What book?" He remembered his grandpa mentioning something about a book, but the circumstances didn't allow for him to elaborate.

Nort chimed in, "Incantations created by your greedy warlock ancestors. Knowledge kept only to them, for them."

"They keep their powers to themselves, and for good reason," Jarren defended. "That knowledge keeps the demons at bay."

"Until now," Nort interjected. "And don't forget, it also summons them."

Jarren cast a glower toward Nort. "Yes, until now. In the wrong hands, the Book can be very dangerous. But . . . they still have to know how to read it and use it. The king was very strategic. If, and I stress if, one of those creatures from the underworld deciphers the spells they could summon their own kind here, theoretically releasing a flood of powerful demons."

"There was a contingency plan in place, correct, were this to happen?" Nort inquired mockingly.

"Yes, and he's sitting in front of you," Jarren said matter-of-factly.

"No offense, Alex," Nort said, glancing over toward him and then turned his attention back to Jarren, "but you've got to be kidding me. That book, as you so eloquently put it, can end everything. Was there not a spell or a curse or whatever placed on that thing to self-destruct if it were stolen?"

"Certainly not. That book contains ancient, priceless knowledge."

"Worth more than everything being destroyed?"

Nort has a point, Alex thought. *If something is that powerful, there should be a contingency plan if it were to get into the wrong hands.*

"Yes," Jarren said, not wavering. "They will destroy nothing. I have every confidence in our new king that he will return the Book intact."

"Fine," Nort relented. "Obviously we will not agree, so let's just move on to what we know. The king was powerful and smart, correct?"

"Yes," Jarren replied. "Where are you going with this?"

"Then this was no ordinary scout demon that made its way into the king's chamber to kill him and steal the most powerful book in Tristoria."

"Correct."

"Helenia lives."

Jarren didn't respond, but held a look of dark surprise on his face. "How did you come about that information?"

"Like I said, the king and I were friends. He trusted me."

"My grandpa mentioned that name," Alex said, interrupting. "Who is Helenia?"

"What is she is a more appropriate question. And how is it she is alive?" Nort asked darkly.

"That thing is Helenia," Jarren said, pointing to the painting centered on the wall behind him that was much larger than the surrounding ones. In the center of the painting, there was a huge beast the size of a small house, standing upright on hind legs. Its black and dark green skin resembled scales on a dragon. Protruding from its back was a pair of leathery dark wings, and on its massive head was a set of horns the size of a child. A circle of fire surrounded the menacing beast as it screamed in agony to the heavens above. Beyond the fire was a group of cloaked figures with their weapons drawn.

"Yes, and your grandfather and his coven had supposedly killed her," Nort said, disappointed. "That's what the painting represents."

"You're saying that thing killed my grandfather?"

"Apparently," Nort said. "Helenia was . . . is a powerful demon witch from the deepest, darkest parts of hell."

"So, basically the worst thing I can imagine, multiplied times a thousand. And you're saying we have to face this thing? If my grandpa couldn't kill it, I certainly won't be able to."

"You will not be alone," Jarren said.

"I guess that's reassuring. . . ." Alex said doubtfully.

"Your role in this is to survive and become a leader for the kingdom," Jarren said. "In time you will learn to fight."

"I know I'm new here and everything, and I don't quite understand how things work, but how did that huge thing get inside the castle and into the king's chamber unnoticed?" Alex asked, bringing the obvious to light.

"She can take on different forms for short periods of time," Nort explained.

"Oh, great," Alex said. "This keeps getting better."

"Yes, but she still couldn't get past the barrier that the king placed around the castle," Jarren said. "No demon, no matter what form they take, can cross through. In fact, it extends well past the tree line."

"Wait, back up, how do these demons get to Tristoria in the first place?" Alex queried.

"Warlocks summon them," Nort said with discontent.

"And then send them back, or kill them, after they have served their purpose," Jarren added.

"And sometimes a lazy warlock will leave a portal open for too long," Nort contended.

Jarren relented, giving the impression that it was sometimes the case.

"Could my grandfather have summoned her on accident?" Alex asked, but then remembered what his grandfather had told him. "Never mind, I remember him specifically telling me he didn't open a portal."

"That's the thing," Jarren said. "Only the king has permission to open a portal inside the castle. It was his rule, his spell, but like you just said, he didn't open a portal."

No one spoke for a few moments. You could almost hear the gears in their heads cranking away, attempting to figure out how such a thing could occur if every fail-safe had been in place as the king had said.

"The king was obviously dumbfounded by this, too, which is the reason he instructed me to put a team together and seek Krunk," Jarren said. "He will accelerate Alex's training and may also shed some light on this mystery."

"Krunk? Are you mad?" Nort contested. "He couldn't resist the corruption of his own summoning."

"Wait, my grandpa said I was to find him. Who is he?"

"A powerful, yet weak warlock, who sought more and more power by summoning huge demon monsters until he eventually went insane and was unable to resist the demons' persuasion," Nort said. "In fact, he's probably the one behind all of this. No wonder your grandfather left out that piece of information. He knew I would have protested."

"Highly unlikely," Jarren said. "The king kept in touch with Krunk, until a year ago. But he still trusted Krunk with his life."

"Isn't there another warlock that can teach Alex?" Nort said. "A more stable one . . . if such exists."

"Not with Krunk's skill set and knowledge. If a Rayne isn't to teach him, then he's the next best thing. Also, they fought Helenia side by side. If anyone would know how to defeat her, it would be him."

"If he is still alive, how do we trust him?" Nort said. "If I recall, wasn't it he who left the portal open that let Helenia in the first time? And wasn't he responsible for the destruction of an entire race of mountain giants in the southern region, Darken Highlands?"

"I never said he was without fault, but he is the best one for this task."

"How do we know he will even help us?" Nort said.

"I have every confidence because the king had every confidence. Especially once he finds out that she has murdered the king, his friend; he will make it a personal fight to avenge his friend."

Nort leaned back in his chair and sighed, as if giving up the brief fight with Jarren. He then clasped his hands together and said, "Are you positive there is no one else?"

Jarren shook his head with an emphatic no.

"Well, it looks like we don't have a choice," Nort said. "But don't say I didn't warn you all." He cleared his throat, then said with exasperation, "So, when do we leave?"

"First light," Jarren said. "My men have the supplies ready and packed. There will be eight in the party, and that's including Karissa, which I have to contest one more time. This is a dangerous endeavor, and a little girl could get hurt or even end up dead."

Before Nort could put Jarren in his place yet again, a woman's voice echoed from behind them and startled them all.

"Nine will be in this party."

◊ ◊ ◊

"Jayda," Jarren said, not surprised. "How many times have I asked you not to sneak up on me?"

A beautiful woman with a bow strapped to her back and hair the color of warm honey pulled tightly around her head in a braid revealing perfect high cheekbones, leaped down from somewhere above. She had piercing dark green eyes and a soft but confident voice.

"It's what I do, brother. And don't insult this young woman with your false intervention to protect her because she is a little girl," Jayda said defending Karissa.

"Everyone, this is Jayda, my twin sister," Jarren introduced with subtle irritation in his voice.

"Nice to see you, Jayda," Nort said warmly with a slight bow of his head. "When are you going to leave this ridiculous place and join my village where you belong?"

She smiled brightly while Jarren frowned at Nort's words.

"And who is this young lady you were insulting, brother?" Jayda said, turning her attention to Karissa.

"I'm Karissa, ma'am," she said shyly.

"Don't hide, sweetheart," Jayda said, referring to Karissa's cloak. "Hold your head up and be proud of who you are."

Karissa nodded shyly, but still did not remove her hood.

Alex stood, anxiously waiting his turn to meet the beautiful woman.

"You must be Alex," she said, stepping in front of him with an outstretched hand.

"Yes," Alex said as confidently as he could. Her hands were firm yet soft and delicate.

"I'm sorry to hear of your grandfather's passing; he was a great king," Jayda continued. "If you wouldn't mind, I would like to join you on your expedition."

"Please do," Alex said a little too quickly.

She smiled and said, "Thank you. I'm always up for an adventure that includes killing demons."

The very mention of demons made Alex cringe. How was it this woman wanted to seek out demons? But he was glad that she was with them. There was something about her that told him she could hold her own in a fight.

"She has an affinity for it," Jarren said. "An unhealthy one, if you ask me. She claims the title of 'demon hunter'."

"No one asked you, brother. But yes, I am proud of that name," Jayda said, and then turned toward Jarren with furrowed eyebrows. "And why was I not invited to this meeting in the first place?"

"I thought you needed a break from your . . . avocation."

She shook her head in disgust. "I will not rest until they're all dead."

"So," Jarren said, "how much did you eavesdrop?"

"Find Krunk the warlock and return the Book. Kill demons. Sounds cut-and-dried to me. Oh, yeah, and my favorite part: hunt down the infamous supposedly dead demon witch, Helenia."

Alex shuddered at the thought of facing that huge beast from the painting.

"Yes, that is the brunt of it," Jarren confirmed. "Our mission, above all, is to keep Alex safe and return that book."

"When do we leave?" Jayda asked excitedly.

"Dawn," Jarren said.

CHAPTER 13
The Paths of the Dead

Alex sat alone in the courtyard on a wooden bench propped against a dramatic ancient tree. The massive limbs stretched and hugged the sitting area warmly, inviting guests to stay and sit for a while. He stared at the moonlight-dappled cobblestone at his feet and contemplated what he had gotten himself into. The demon, Helenia, was enough to make him want to be back in his warm bed waking up from this nightmare, thankfully soaked in sweat and not blood. He kept telling himself it was still possible to wake up; he was still unsure if it was all real. He knocked on the bench he was sitting on and then the tree behind him. He even opened and closed his eyes multiple times to force himself awake, but to his disappointment he did not.

"Would you like some company," a female voice breathed from behind him.

He jerked his head around toward the voice and nearly fell off of the bench. "Karissa . . . oh . . . hi," he said through an exasperated breath. "You scared the —"

"Sorry," she said in an even softer voice. "May I sit?"

"Yes," he nearly shouted, and then scooted over to the far end of the bench.

"I don't need that much room, but thank you," she said and smiled from behind her hood.

Embarrassed, Alex said nothing. He inched back toward her, leaving plenty of room for one more person to squeeze between them.

"May I ask you why you were knocking on the tree?" Karissa asked. "I wasn't spying on you or anything; I was sitting on the other side of the tree and heard your mumbles."

Alex could feel the warmth around his ears and acted as if he did not understand the question. Patiently, Karissa asked again, but he stopped her mid-sentence. "You saw that?" He lowered his head and sighed. "I . . . was . . . just testing to see if all of this was real."

"I hope it is," she said. "Or it would mean that I'm not real."

"I didn't mean anything by saying —"

"I know," she said lightly. "But I can tell that you probably don't want to be here. Your home is likely much more sane and less chaotic than this place. And less dangerous, too."

"Actually, it's not," Alex said, thinking of the reason he left in the first place, and that was just his home. That was not including the constant conflicts around the world.

"Okay, but I bet you don't have demons trying to kill you."

Alex thought on it a moment. There were many bad people who did horrible things to one another. And those people, he supposed, would probably end up where these demons originated. In fact, he was sure that there were demons roaming there in human form.

"No, not like the ones that are here, but there are a lot of evil people there. My stepmother is a prime example. And the worst part is, my dad doesn't get it."

"I sort of know how you feel. I don't have a stepmother, but my dad's not exactly what you would call a caring parent."

Alex's dad may have been a jerk and not taken up for him as he should have, but at least he was not trying to give him away every chance he got. Karissa had him beat on the worst father, but Alex still was not giving his dad a pass.

"Is he the one that gave you that?" Alex said, pointing to the small scar along her right cheek, but immediately wanting to yank the words back into his mouth. "Sorry, I —"

"It's okay," Karissa said. "It would come up, eventually." She turned toward him. "Don't judge me too harshly, please. And no, my dad did not give it to me."

She then removed her hood, and Alex could not help but stare. But he was not staring at the scar; instead, he was looking at her hazel blue eyes, her thick dark hair lying softly on her shoulders, and her lightly freckled nose. She was beautiful, stunningly so.

"I know I'm not anything to look at like Jayda," she said shying away.

"What? Are you kidding me?" Alex said sincerely.

"It's okay, I saw how you looked at her."

"Wait, what . . . how did I look at her?" Alex said, honestly not realizing that he had gawked at Jayda the first time he had seen her.

"The same way everyone does, in awe."

Alex felt the warmness saturate him once again and quickly changed the subject. "If your dad didn't give it to you, how did you get it?"

"We all get one. Everyone born here, that is."

"Why?"

"A mark of this place, meaning we are not from anywhere else. We are permanent residents and can never leave."

"That's what you meant when you said if this place is destroyed then so will you."

"Yes," she said solemnly. "I am truly in the center for eternity. And even worse, I cannot be rewarded, but I can be punished."

"No one, not even my —?"

"No, not even the king. I'm considered a product of impurity. Basically damaged goods, irredeemable."

"But why? That doesn't make sense or seem fair at all."

"No, but I can't do anything about it. It's the way things are. The way they've always been." Her voice trailed off.

"I'm sorry," Alex said. "If I am king one day," he swallowed the words. "I'll do whatever I can to help you. I promise."

"Noble, but I'm afraid it's impossible. The children of Tristoria must pay for the sins of all who enter. It's stamped in small letters on the king's crest. I think you have enough to worry about anyway." She changed her tone to sound more upbeat. "On a different note, I can see the future to a certain degree. I consider it a curse, though, mainly because it's so frustrating."

"You can see the future? That's cool."

"I can't control it, though, and I only get small glimpses at a time. Nort says I'm blocked by my dad, meaning my emotions have been getting in the way. I don't think it's that simple."

"My grandfather mentioned my emotions getting in the way with my supposed powers, too."

"Because we're young and stupid and can't control anything, according to my dad."

He shook his head and said, "Yeah, I've been told that, too, on occasion."

"Obviously, it's deeper than a teenage hormone problem," Karissa said. "We never lose our emotions as we age; we only learn to deal with them."

"You're way smarter than I am. I haven't even thought about my emotions, much less being in control of them, until my grandfather mentioned it."

"My situation sort of demands me to face certain things. Believe me, it's not by choice for me to think like that."

"Can I ask you something?"

"Sure."

"I don't want to seem selfish, but I am curious if you can see my future?"

"Honestly, you're a broken piece to me and scattered everywhere."

"What?" Alex asked, confused and somewhat disturbed by the reference.

"You know how you wake up from a dream and it was so vivid that you want to hurry back to sleep and finish it, no matter if it was bad or not?" Alex nodded. "And then there are dreams you can see pieces of when you wake, but you're really not sure what you were dreaming about or if it was a dream at all. Well, that's you. I can see fragments but nothing solid."

"Are they bad pieces?" Alex asked anxiously.

"There's not enough there to tell, but I would like to fall back asleep and see if the pieces connect. Sorry, that's all I really have."

"That's okay, thanks anyway," Alex said deflating. "I knew it couldn't be that easy."

"Come on, let me show you something," Karissa said, getting to her feet.

She left her hood down, Alex noticed. "Where are we going?"

"I want to show you how you're destined to be here no matter how much you doubt yourself, or that this place is real."

A few minutes later, they were standing in front of a wrought-iron gate guarded by two stone gargoyles staring off into the distance, as if whatever were inside could handle guarding itself. Behind the gate a bright blue glow emanating throughout the small area.

The gate creaked open, and the glowing's source became clear. The huge gate, once opened, revealed a

160

massive tree trunk bigger around than any he had ever seen; a car could easily fit inside it if there were a hole. It dwarfed the tree in the courtyard. It stood over ten feet tall and had many sword handles of all varieties jutting out from the top of the stump as if it were a knife block for a giant chef.

"Are we supposed to be in here?" Alex asked, peering around nervously.

"You tell me. It's your family's plot."

"Huh?" And then the realization hit him when he got closer. There were blue glowing faces spaced out around the stump, at least twenty of them. And at the very peak was the most recent, he surmised, as it was his grandfather's face.

"Are they in there?"

"No," Karissa said, laughing softly. "This is only the world's memory of them. They leave soon after they take their last breath. There is nothing left but the clothes they were wearing."

"Okay," Alex said, and then he remembered. "Makes sense now seeing how my grandfather disappeared when I turned away for just a second after he died."

"We don't bury them as you do; Nort explained to me that is how you honor your dead. And the stone above them is your memory. It must be strange having to see the body without the accompanying soul and only have a stone to visit."

"Yeah, it is," Alex mourned, remembering his mother. A glowing portrait of her face with lively expressions would have been much more pleasant than a stone with her name on it above her empty shell buried below the earth.

Alex circled the tree and recognized only a few of the faces from old photos his mom had shown him when he was younger. All had the last name Rayne and were wearing a cloak, either hood donned or resting on their necks.

"What are the sword handles for?"

"Those are the kings' personal swords. They're placed there by the successor."

"So I must do that?" he furrowed his brow. "Like King Arthur, only placing it instead of removing it?" He noticed her confusion and realized she was unfamiliar with the reference to King Arthur. "Sorry, all I'm saying is that it doesn't look easy, cramming a sword into a tree stump."

Karissa laughed again at his honest observation. "No, there are premade slits in the top for the next sword. Once you place your grandfather's sword in, another will appear beside it where your sword will eventually be inserted by your successor."

Another reminder of his mortality, and also the thought of having children. A son or daughter to take his place one day. But first that involves having a girlfriend and then a wife. The thought was overwhelming, for he had never even been on a serious date before.

"Our dead are honored every night at midnight, when the moon is allowed to shine through. Its brightness amplifies the trees along the many Paths of the Dead around Tristoria."

"There are more of these places?"

"Yes, every town has its own path. Every family has a tree full of ancestors that will glow for eternity. This is the Tree of Kings that was once the center for this world until it was burned two millennia ago during one of the many wars. The king built his castle around the remaining stump to protect the remnants. It's the oldest tree in Tristoria."

"Wait, so all ancestors are on the trees? Meaning my mother's family that died is somewhere here?"

"No, sorry, only if they passed through Tristoria. I don't understand it fully myself, but I was told each step or world has its rules. And just like other worlds, when we die here we leave and go somewhere else."

"What about you? You said you could never leave?"

"I can still die."

"Where do you go?"

"You know, I really haven't given it much thought. I've spent most of my life trying to figure out where I fit in; that or avoiding my dad. I'm not sure."

"I guess none of us knows exactly where we're going. And I can definitely relate to the fitting in part."

"Now you see that you have a place to fill," she said, smiling. "Your slit will soon appear on the Tree of Kings, and your face will one day be on this tree."

"Hopefully not soon," Alex said with unease. "But what about you? Don't you want to know more about what's next for you?"

"Maybe later. First, we have to get you believing in yourself so we can save this world."

Alex lamented but still could not help but feel for her situation. He looked over at her, but quickly looked away. He had been so distracted by the sight in front of him he only just realized how close they stood beside one another. He pictured his dead ancestors' faces suddenly judging him and smirking at the awkwardness that he was exuding.

"This place is real, Alex, along with the very real danger facing it," Karissa said and then turned toward him. "You need to believe in yourself and trust in your abilities, or we are all doomed to face the evil coming for us." She touched his arm gingerly as if to reinforce her words.

He instantly felt a tingling along his entire body as his head swirled with warning signs of the opposite sex penetrating his weak defenses. He panicked inside. *What do I do? Do I turn toward her or stay staring forward?* He could feel beads of sweat growing along his forehead.

"You need your rest," she said abruptly and turned to leave.

He breathed a heavy sigh of relief and called out clumsily, "You're still going, aren't you?"

"Definitely, I wouldn't miss it. Besides, who's going to give you pieces of worthless information about what may happen to you." And with that she walked out of the gate and disappeared into the night.

Alex stayed a while longer next to the tree and stared up at the faces, waiting for one of them to chide him for being so lame and boring in front of a girl. Did his awkwardness run her off? He sat at the base of the stump for some time, punishing himself over and over, wondering if he should have said something more or done something different.

CHAPTER 14

A Warlock's Attire

Alex could not remember the last time he had fallen asleep so fast and slept so hard. He shook off the odd night of dreamless sleep and lazily sat up in bed and yawned, then heard a knock on his door.

"Just a second," Alex said, edging his legs over the side of the bed. The cold stone floors revved him awake a little faster than he had wanted.

Jarren stood at the door with a neatly folded cloak in his hands. "It's yours until you have your own. Time to look the part." Jarren's eyes seemed to linger on Alex's sleep worn *Goonies* T-shirt. "You are part of this world now." Alex took the robe without question. "When you finish getting dressed, we are all meeting for breakfast in the dining hall before your departure. We have a few last-minute items to discuss."

Jarren turned and left while Alex stood in the doorway, thankful that it had been Jarren at the door and not Karissa, remembering that he was wearing only his boxer briefs and T-shirt. He quickly shut the door and unfolded the dark green, nearly black robe. On the inside collar were the initials J.R. — James Rayne. It felt strange holding his grandfather's robe so soon after his death. But everything so far had been strange. Even the fireplace that was still roaring just as true as it was the night before. He surmised that someone could have come in and placed more wood on the fire while he was sleeping, but he suspected the explanation was more of the weirdness of this place.

He quickly put on his jeans and then stood in front of the mirror. He slipped on the robe over his shirt and jeans. The robe fit well with even a little room to grow if he kept it. He noticed a patch sewn into the front middle of the robe he had not noticed when his grandfather had worn it. The patch was the same crest on the armor the guards wore. A gold triangle formed from three elongated infinity signs, intertwined with a blood red demon tail. A black sword penetrated the symbol from top down. There was writing surrounding the triangle: "Dark straddles the light into eternity as our children remain prisoners for the sins of the world." He ran his fingers across the triangle and it glowed brightly in the firelight as if his fingers were a power source to light it. The symbol entranced him. His eyes remained transfixed on the mysterious symbol as he absentmindedly donned the hood of the robe.

Once the hood covered his head, a rush of energy thrust throughout his body as if he had just absorbed a jolt of electricity from an open light socket. His grandfather's words of him ruling whispered in the air as he stared at himself in the mirror with only his chin lit by the flickering firelight. A darkness pulsed through him that frightened him enough to yank the hood back and turn away from the mirror.

What the heck was that? Was it some sort of residual powers of my grandfather being transferred to me? Does the cloak hold a power of its own? Whatever it was he knew he did not have the knowledge or the discipline to wield it. Yet he yearned for it and could not explain the overwhelming feeling.

He sat on the end of the bed and doubt intervened once again when the questions began flooding his mind. *Will I pass the tests? Or will I be like my dad and fail the final and most important one?* He did not feel that he desired dark power, but he also had not wielded the power of a demon yet. *Can I maintain control of my desires?* He hoped so, but he could not be certain. He had always thought he was more like his mom than his dad, and if there was one person who was strong enough to resist evil, it was his mom.

There was only one way to find out, and that was to embrace his destiny and start the adventure.

◊ ◊ ◊

Alex felt a little odd wearing his grandfather's robe, but no one else seemed to share the sentiment when he entered the dining hall for breakfast. Each of them greeted him warmly, and all had waited for him before they began eating. All except Nort, but Alex did not take it personally. He knew it was likely just another gouge in the eye of a monarchy and Jarren.

"I liked your other attire better," Nort said gruffly.

"Don't worry. I'm still wearing my *Goonies* T-shirt and jeans underneath," Alex said smirking, while Nort shook his head in disapproval.

167

Before Alex could pull the chair beside Nort fully from under the table, Jarren cleared his throat. "A king sits at the head of the table." Jarren had a chair pulled out and ready.

Alex looked back to Nort for direction, but he was already looking the other way. "Okay, fine," he said, deciding not to argue, and made his way over to the chair and sat down; Jarren took the seat next to him on his right side.

Jayda had been sitting across from Nort and Karissa, but Alex made a conscious decision before entering not to stare in her direction. He wanted to prove Karissa wrong about his admiration for Jayda, and in the process went a little extreme and avoided any eye contact with her at all. He could not be rude, though, so he glanced her way and waved an awkward hand toward her. "Hello, Jayda," he managed and then stared down at his plate.

"Once you return and we have notified the council, you will officially be addressed as King Rayne around the realm," Jarren said, thankfully interrupting Alex's thoughts about his latest attempt to not be awkward. "There must be leadership and respect for the crown."

But Alex had no crown and did not remotely feel like a king. He was a name, nothing more. He had done nothing to deserve such a title or respect.

"I'm not king yet," Alex reminded Jarren and those around him.

"Be that as it may, you will be soon enough," Jarren stressed. "This information is not common to the people. This is for the ones in this room only. Your party needs a leader and what better way for you to learn your new responsibilities than to lead them. And most importantly you can avenge your grandfather by following through with his orders."

The thought of avenging his grandfather sounded pretty great, but it was the leading part that was the problem. Everyone in the room he was supposed to lead were all older and more experienced than he was in every way. Even Karissa, his only peer, was way more prepared for this.

Alex sighed. "I'd much rather follow than lead, but if I —"

"That's the spirit," Jarren cheered.

"Can we get this started?" Nort interrupted. "I'd like to reach our destination camp before nightfall."

Jarren had somehow kept the cheer on his face as he glared at Nort. He then turned his attention to the doors behind them and snapped his fingers. Seconds later, three servants filed into the dining room and removed the metal covers from the platters of meats, eggs, and fruit on the table in front of the group and filled their goblets with juices.

"Fill your bellies, for the journey ahead is long and riddled with many dangers and strife," Jarren said.

Alex did not feel much like eating, but he knew he needed his strength, and Jarren was there to remind him by nudging him until he finished what he had placed on his plate. He forced down a few eggs and slices of bacon and finished a glass of apple juice. Wherever the journey took them, he knew it would not be a nice stroll in a meadow, as Jarren so pointed out, and food may not come as easily.

Jarren finished his plate quickly and began his farewell spiel while the others continued to eat. Alex presumed he had

169

planned it this way so Nort hopefully would not interrupt him. "First, I'd like to wish you all a safe journey. The team assembled here would send shivers down any creatures' spines, including my own." Nort sighed loud enough for all to hear and loudly moved around in his chair, but Jarren held a closed-mouth smile, ignoring Nort. "The horses are all assembled and ready, along with your provisions. And if you all were wondering about the group of men at the other end of the table," Jarren motioned for the group of men to stand, "they are a hand-selected group of men, by me of course, to serve as your guards on my — the kingdom's — behalf."

Alex had not noticed the five men in full gunmetal armor until then. They were not there when he had arrived in the hall. *When did they sneak inside? Probably during Jarren's speech,* Alex surmised.

One of the men stepped away from the table and to the side so the group could see him. He had a full, well-groomed beard the color of coal and broad shoulders that spread like a beefy bird. His hands were thick and veins bulged as he held a heavy goblet in the air toward the group and then set it on the table with a loud clank.

"Thank you, Jarren, for the introduction," the broad-shouldered man said with a deep and unfaltering voice. The two men's eyes met and they nodded to one another. "My name is Karmac and these are my loyal companions."

He motioned to the men standing beside him, who all nodded in unison. He introduced them one by one, each sitting back down after his name was called. Their armor possessed the same crest on the chest that his grandfather's robe had embroidered on it. They all appeared disciplined and respected their leader. None of the men smiled, but raised their mugs with a nod. They were not all as well-groomed as Karmac; they had long, stringy, dirty hair, and beards that looked as if it they had never seen a pair of scissors. Alex had a strong feeling it was not apple juice in their mugs.

Karmac continued, "We're tasked to make sure this journey goes smoothly and safely, and above all protect the king by any means necessary. Anything in our way will suffer the full wrath of the king's army and my blade." He smiled toward Alex and tapped the hilt of his sword.

Alex felt an uneasiness and wondered what the man was hiding behind that smile. *Probably nothing,* he reminded himself. He just did not trust anyone in this place yet except for Nort. But there was something else creepy about this Karmac guy other than his lingering stare; it was as if they shared a thought. He just could not put his finger on it yet. Alex glanced over at Nort and saw the smirk on his face and the shaking of his head with eye rolls toward Karmac's gestures.

Putting his own apprehension aside that this group gave him an uneasy, sinister feeling, Alex was glad to have more protection. It was always good to have more than one watching your back, and especially in a place crawling with demons.

"Would you like to say anything to the party, King Rayne?" Jarren asked Alex after Karmac had taken his seat.

Alex swallowed nervously and cleared his throat. He then stood and felt the flush return in his face. "Good luck to us all," he blurted and quickly took his seat. *What else is there to say?* he wondered.

Thankfully, Nort interrupted the silence. "Short and to the point. Good job, Alex," he said with a nod.

"King Rayne, you mean," Jarren said, correcting Nort.

"Precisely, Jarren," Nort said smugly. Nort wiped his face with his napkin and stood. He looked at Alex and said, "I'll be in the courtyard." He then made his way to the door not looking back. Karissa hurriedly shoved her chair back and followed him, not wanting to be in the room without Nort.

"I'll never know what your grandfather saw in him," Jarren mumbled to Alex.

"We should be on our way," Alex said and pushed his chair back, acting as if he had not heard Jarren's comment.

Jayda also stood and gathered her bow from beside her chair.

"Yes, I agree," Jarren said with a smile, but it was a forced smile, Alex noticed. Nort had irritated Jarren; that much was obvious, but there seemed to be something else bothering him. Alex wondered if Jarren's confidence was a shroud hiding a deeper worry about the kingdom falling. It was a huge task to manage a kingdom in the absence of a king, he imagined. And now, Jarren must do so while preparing the next in line to be king, a young boy without a clue about this world or himself. Alex wondered how many kingdoms in history had started out the same way. There was always a Hand, one who knew the day-to-day activity of the kingdom.

That has to be a ton of responsibility, he thought. Maybe he owed Jarren a little more credit than he was affording him.

CHAPTER 15
The Faceless Forest

The party exited through a secret door in the castle's rear not too far from the king's chambers. The door led to a long winding corridor through the mountain lined with torches along the wall that Karmac began lighting as they trudged through heaps of spider webs. Alex cringed at the sounds of rats scurrying their claws along the stone floor and tried not to think about how many were actually running beside their feet.

"One way in, one way out," Nort told Alex. He felt his stomach lighten as the array of dark thoughts washed over him.

"Forget the spiders and rats," Alex said. "What if there are demons waiting for us in the darkness, drooling impatiently, and primed to rip us apart?"

Nort snickered at Alex's paranoia and told him the real reason for the secret passage: it was constructed long ago, a short time after the castle was built, for smuggling. Anything from banned liquors to women and even demons. Anything forbidden by the council eventually got trafficked through this tunnel.

"Yeah, about this council. Who are they and why aren't they counseling me on things?" Alex asked, ignoring the more disturbing fact of sneaking in demons. His grandfather told him warlocks needed demons for their powers, but he was not quite ready to face that disturbing fact just yet.

"There have been many councils over the years," Nort started. "Initially, it was comprised of elected officials around Tristoria, but if you know anything about politics, things revolving around it eventually became corrupt. Just like a monarchy where the king has too much power over the people, a council can become too powerful without checks and balances in place. That very thing happened and King Karl had had enough one afternoon and killed them all in a fit of rage. He wanted absolute rule back how it used to be with no interference. If he wanted something, he didn't want to have to ask a governing body for permission, especially ones that weren't comprised of warlocks. He ruled as a monarchy his entire reign, though his son, after he took Karl's place, reinstated the council once again. But it wasn't like the old council. He agreed with the people that there needed to be multiple voices deciding matters, but they all had to be warlocks. So, the coven of Rayne was born."

"Are they still around?"

"Yes."

"Wait, so why haven't I met them? Shouldn't they be the ones training me?"

"They do not train the king, nor do they interfere with the process. They are under strict orders to assist the sitting king with matters he deems necessary for help. If they were to train you, then they would learn your weaknesses. And you can figure out the rest."

Alex considered this and agreed with the logic. "The king still has most of the power, then?"

"Yes," Nort said with indignation.

The torchlight was too dim, but if Alex could have seen Nort's face he was sure it would reveal disgust. Yes, Nort was an outcast mercenary, but he was only rebelling against a system of absolute power. Though Alex would possibly be that power one day, he could see Nort's point. How unfair it appears from the outside looking in. He wasn't sure he would change such a rule, but he knew at the very least he would be a fair and just king.

Nort continued, swiping a cobweb from his face. "The last time this passageway was likely used was by the late king's father to sneak in and out a lady friend. He had a prearranged marriage waiting for him he had been rebelling against, but he wasn't one for letting others decide his fate. Eventually he gave in and married the woman, but he never closed the passageway, if you know what I mean."

No one had mentioned a prearranged marriage to Alex, and he wondered if such a rule still existed. The story of his parents' meeting didn't sound prearranged, but who knew? They also never told him all of this existed either. Was there a princess somewhere waiting for him?

Alex had a ton of questions for Nort, but before he could ask any more, there came a knock up ahead. He could see Karmac's helmet in the front and realized it was he who was doing the knocking. They had come to a door, and the knock suggested a secret code to someone on the other side. A moment later, a door opened, revealing a guard who greeted them and began shaking Karmac's hand earnestly. The sky was gray and dim. He could see how dismal this place could be in time, remembering Nort's comment about the sun only coming out for an hour each day.

The man showed them to their horses that were all waiting just as Jarren had said, including the provisions hanging on each of the saddles. Alex stared at the dark horse and then down at his robe. Mounting the horse would be a little trickier than before, as if he needed a new challenge at the moment. He watched Karissa's flawless mount once more and immediately leaped on his horse, attempting to adopt her technique. He was not nearly as graceful and nearly toppled over, but he somehow managed it in one attempt. He looked around proudly as he sat perched on his horse, to see if anyone had noticed what he had accomplished, but no one seemed to pay attention as they were all situating themselves on their own horses.

Still admiring his own feat, he heard Nort say, "On your count, Alex." Alex looked at him dubiously. He didn't have a clue to where they were going or even which direction to begin. "West, until we reach the stream." Alex continued to stare blankly. Nort sighed and pointed toward the direction they should go with a stiff hand.

Alex nodded, because he finally understood what Nort wanted him to do. He then leaned forward and whispered to his horse, "Same as last time, for both our sake." The horse looked back at him and seemed to pause for a moment as if considering his words. Alex caught its gaze and felt chills along his neck. He wondered if he would ever get used to the horse's haunting white glowing eyes.

Alex didn't like this new leader role that Jarren had given him. He was much more comfortable as a tourist following the crowd and following orders. "What about the poisonous rocks?" he said hesitantly, looking over his shoulder at Nort.

"Not on this side of the mountain," Nort said. "The steep jagged edges are plenty protection."

Alex peered up at the dizzying height of the mountain and agreed with Nort's assessment.

"One, two . . . three," Alex said and leaned forward and heeled his horse. The horse propelled forward like a bottle rocket. Though Alex remembered the last time very well, there was no way that he could completely prepare for the horse's initial thrust. He tilted his head down at just the right angle, allowing the wind to keep his hood plastered to his head.

A few minutes into the ride, as Alex's mind was drifting off to the unsettling information about his great grandfather having a prearranged marriage, Karissa pulled her horse beside his and looked over at him with a smile from beneath her hood. He glanced back at the others, who now looked like dots in a mirage; he hadn't realized how far he had gotten ahead of the party.

"Race?" She asked, not losing stride and with her eyes driven forward.

"Shouldn't we stay somewhat close to the others?" Alex said, remembering the certain dangers that lie ahead.

"Scared a girl will beat you?"

"No, but, . . ."

She cast a furtive glance over at him. "Last one to the stream loses."

"Well, Pronto, looks like we got a challenge," Alex said with a wry grin.

"You named your horse Pronto?" She said with a smirk.

"What about yours?"

"My what?"

"Your horse's name."

Karissa thought on it for a second and said, "Winner," and then shot off a horse's length in front of him.

Alex grinned and immediately nudged his heels firmly into the horse's sides. Pronto grunted and sprinted forward toward Karissa and her horse. He was edging closer to her when he noticed her grab the reins in her right hand and then lightly began slapping them on either side of the horse's lower neck.

"Now, why hadn't I thought to do that," he mumbled to himself.

She had pulled ahead of him two full horse lengths, so he attempted to mimic her movement once again, only this time he wasn't successful. However, he maintained the two horse lengths behind her, which he thought was decent considering his level of riding skill compared to hers. Still, he lost, and to a girl no less. Nort would probably love to have seen the race, but thankfully Nort was far enough behind not to see it. Though Alex was humble enough to admit her riding skills impressed him, he wouldn't be bringing it up to Nort in casual conversation.

Their horses began drinking from the stream that seemed to be out of place in the middle of nowhere. The terrain was desolate, except for a few sporadic naked trees. While they waited for the others to catch up, Alex felt brave enough to spark a conversation now that they had spoken more than a few words to one another. It wasn't near as difficult as he had made it out to be in his head. Besides, he had heard girls liked flattery, and she had earned it.

"That was impressive," Alex said. "You got any tips that you would like to share with a rookie like me?"

She laughed it off and then realized he wasn't poking fun. "You're serious?"

"Yes, of course I am." He could see the genuine humility in her watery eyes when she realized he wasn't mocking her. Alex surmised that her dad had probably put her down countless times.

They talked for a while before the rest caught up to them. Karissa regaled him on her start to riding, not embellishing one bit. Alex stood next to Pronto and listened enthusiastically as she was relaying the information. In return, he told her a little bit about his world and his school life, and she seemed just as enthused as he did about her stories. It felt odd, but great having a conversation with someone his age. Though they were from very different places, teenage life was pretty much ubiquitous.

The day wore on and the shadows lengthened. They had stopped only once more after the stream and that was to eat a quick lunch. Nort warned that he could feel a storm moving in, and no one seemed to question the weather report. A half hour later, the air cooled a few degrees, and the wind began howling. They all agreed that once they reached the forest entrance, they would find a suitable camp for the night.

The trees were huge and ancient, wielding trunks as wide as a car, and their peaks stretched high enough to poke their heads through the clouds. Their thick, gnarled roots coated the forest floor like tentacles waiting for prey to pull in and devour beneath its thick undergrowth.

Once the party crossed the threshold into the forest, the vast canopy of limbs and leaves immediately encapsulated them, leaving the heavy cover of clouds to a far-off world. Alex shuddered once inside as if a door had slammed behind him and the key lay hidden on the other side of the forest.

They decided it best not to venture too far inside until all had the proper rest to face whatever cursed creatures lurked within. Alex definitely agreed on the decision for he had an unpleasant feeling about the place aching in the pit of his stomach. It left him anxious and cold, leaving his body unable to decipher which to grasp on to and focus.

"There's no need to tie up the horses," Karissa said, as Alex grabbed a rope from his saddlebag. "They feel right at home in this forest."

"And rightfully so," Nort added.

Karissa nodded. "This is where they were first discovered. They were wild and very temperamental. But, over time with much training and care, they learned to trust and became milder, eventually accepting riders."

"Yeah, home sounds pretty good to me too about now," Alex said. He would even settle for a short lecture from Margie and then a long, lonely night in his safe bedroom amongst his books.

"It calms them," Nort said, grabbing his bag from the saddle. "Which is more than I can say for myself about this forest."

They made two camps next to one another: Alex, Nort, Karissa, and Jayda in one and the soldiers in the other. The soldiers had quickly gathered enough wood for both of their camps, but Nort insisted on getting his own materials. To all of their surprise, Nort had his fire assembled and roaring before the other camp even had their rocks spaced out. And being the gentleman he was, he even offered Karmac and his soldiers advice in return for their gesture, but Karmac only grumbled with a wave of his hand. Nort smirked knowingly at Karmac's pride that wasn't unlike his boss Jarren's.

Alex found a suitable spot of grass, far away from any of the giant roots. It worried him they might grab him in the middle of sleep and slowly digest him over many agonizing years. He laid out his sleeping blanket and sat on top of it next to the bright, warm glow of the fire Nort had prepared. The air was crisp and cool with a musty odor. Though there was no wind, the trees still creaked and groaned, like old bones rising from a front porch chair. He scooted as close as he could to the fire without getting burned.

Alex pulled out some jerky from his bag and before he could fully unwrap it, Nort held out his hand to stop him.

"We will have a proper dinner," Nort said. "Jerky will not do at the end of a long day of travel. Karissa, if you wouldn't mind, could you make the preparations for dinner, please? I will be back shortly."

And before Alex could object, Nort had disappeared into the darkness.

"How does he do that?" Alex said, astonished.

Karissa shrugged with a shake of her head. Alex was sure that she knew, but she just wasn't telling his secrets. He admired her for her loyalty.

"So, why do they call this place the Faceless Forest?" Alex asked, while assisting Karissa in setting up the metal frame that would hold the cast-iron pot over the fire.

"These trees are unlike any trees in Tristoria. They don't — or rather — they can't hold the glowing faces of our dead. This entire forest grew from demon blood that spilled in battle."

"The death fields," Jayda said hauntingly. She was sitting on her makeshift bed, bow in hand, rubbing a cloth along the intricate handle. The blonde of her hair glowed softly in the firelight and her captivating green eyes narrowed as she spoke. Alex stared again, and when he caught himself, he nearly knocked over the pot Karissa had just placed on its hook.

"Death fields?" Alex asked, as a knot grew in his throat. "That doesn't help to ease the super creepy vibe of this place."

"This was once farmlands that provided food and life," Jayda said. "That was until demons desecrated it and waged a war. Since then, many battles have taken place on this land and countless numbers have perished. More demons perished than others, but it was not enough. It will never be enough until they're all dead." Her bow was shaking from her intense grip as she spoke. "This is a dreadful place that needs cleansing."

"Some say the demons haunt the trees themselves and possess them for their bidding," Nort said, appearing out of nowhere and startling Alex from behind him.

"What bidding?" Alex asked, peering around nervously for rogue branches. "What can a tree do?" The creaking of branches filled the air as if a gust of wind had blown through; only there was no wind.

"I'm not entirely sure," Karissa said, "but I don't think insulting the forest's intelligence is a good thing."

Alex nodded in agreement and whispered, "Sorry" to the surrounding trees.

"Let's get ready for dinner, shall we?" Nort said, patting Alex on the back. He pulled a ladle from his pack. "Great campfire tale, huh?"

"It's not true, then?" Alex asked, hopefully.

"Oh, it's true all right," Jayda added.

"Yes, which makes it all the better of a tale," Nort said. "But not to worry, someone will be on watch until dawn."

That reassurance did little to ease the growing fear surrounding Alex over the demon-possessed trees.

◊ ◊ ◊

Dinner was settling nicely in their bellies and most of the soldiers were already snoring. All except Karmac, who was taking first watch in the center of the camps and leaned up against a tree. Jayda was writing in some journal, and Karissa was lying on her back staring up at the trees. Alex couldn't tell if her eyes were open or not.

Nort sat on the other side of Alex, out of Karmac's view, and whispered, "Now that we are a safe distance from Karmac, I can give you what is rightfully yours."

Nort handed Alex an elongated wrapped object.

"What is it?" Alex asked, gingerly taking it from Nort's hands.

"Just open it, will you," Nort whispered testily.

Alex unfolded the brown fabric carefully and revealed the shiny object.

"Did you make this?" Alex asked, holding the sword by its hilt. Nort shoved it down out of Karmac's view.

"No," Nort whispered, looking back toward Karmac, who was more interested in his own sword at the moment than their conversation. "That was your grandfather's sword."

"So, why are we hiding it? Wait, isn't this supposed to be in the tree with the others?"

"Yes — wait, how do you know . . . never mind. Yes, but not until the next king has taken the throne. Some in the kingdom, namely Jarren and his followers, don't see things as I do. They would not approve of you touching your grandfather's sword until you have earned your own, forged by a master blacksmith and then sealed by the warlock council. Then and only then can you place your grandfather's sword in its rightful place. I, however, am more practical in my thinking. You are in an unfamiliar and dangerous world, and you need a weapon to protect yourself. And what better weapon to wield than one that has been proven in battle?"

"It's killed demons?" Alex whispered loudly, staring in awe at the sword's blade. "So, my grandfather actually killed demons?"

"Of course he did," Nort said. "Keep your voice down."

Alex nodded and shuddered a little at the thought of demon blood on the sword. "But wait, I must use it eventually and then Karmac will see it."

"He has never seen the king's sword unsheathed. Yes, yes, I know, then why hide it? Some things are better left covered until it's necessary to reveal them. Anyway, the scabbard is from an old sword of my own and if he asks about the sword, refer him to me. I gave it to you from my personal collection and it's none of his business."

Alex slowly removed the blade from the dark scabbard and focused on the carvings and writing along the grip. The crest that appeared on every piece of armor and shield attached to the king was also on the base of the sword's blade. This was the first time he had seen the writing up close and as he looked closer, he noticed that it was like the writing he had seen along Nort's fireplace mantle. The tiny elegant writing wrapped around the crest.

"What's it say?" Alex asked, admiring the script.

" 'Shadows are but temporary, light within is eternal,' " Nort said. "And the words near the pummel, 'If stones are all that you cherish, then your heart will crumble as one'."

"What's it mean?" Alex asked, mildly disappointed. He wasn't sure what he wanted it to say, but maybe something a little more complicated.

"I never asked, and he never told me. But, if I had to guess, it had something to do with his personal battle with darkness."

"As a warlock?"

Nort nodded and said, "Yes, and also as a man. One day you also will have to balance that same burden. That is, if you pass the tests."

"Yeah," Alex said and swallowed, feeling the dread churn in his stomach. He ran his fingers lightly along the blade.

"Careful," Nort said. "The sword is enchanted to have an eternally keen edge. Every king's blade has it once the smith forges it. The council enchants the blades so they are unbreakable and will never dull. And every king, being a warlock, has put their own spin on their blades."

"Spin? What do you mean? The writing?"

"Yes, anything really; as simple as different shaped hilts to enchantments to warn of approaching demons. One of your relatives enchanted his sword to glow when women were interested in him. He wasn't one for the adventure of courting and romance, if you know what I mean."

Alex sort of knew, or at least he thought he did, but shrugged it off, more interested in the sword in front of him than his ancestor's love life.

"What did my grandfather do to his sword?"

"For one, the hilt is his personal touch."

Alex glanced at it, turning it over in his hands. He noticed a deeply engraved shape of a heart on the bottom, but didn't linger on it; he was more interested in the magic it possessed. "What about enchantments?"

"The wielder usually keeps that to himself. Security reasons, but I'm sure you will find out soon enough what secrets the blade holds."

"How am I supposed to do that?"

"By using it, of course. You share the same DNA, which means whatever enchantments your grandfather placed will reveal themselves when they're needed."

"Okay," Alex said. But he didn't want to wait. He needed to know his limitations in a battle to form strategies. Not that he had any experience in battle, but even he knew that all possibilities need to be on the table. He could feel the excitement building at the potential of the sword, though the anxiety of a battle was much greater. "So, what kind of language is this, anyway? I saw the same writing on your fireplace mantle."

"An ancient one not known by many."

Nort wasn't offering more, and Alex did not press him further. He had learned so far that Nort was hardly forthcoming about things he did not want to talk about.

He handed Alex the scabbard, motioning for him to sheathe it. "Morning will come fast, so get some rest. First light we are moving out. It shouldn't take longer than a full day to reach the other side."

"We have to spend an entire day in this place?" Alex said dreadfully.

"If things go well," Nort said, and then sat on the blanket he had laid out.

Alex laid back on his own makeshift bed and clasped his hands behind his head and stared up at the labyrinth of branches that looked more like elongated old men's fingers. The fire crackled and the trees shifted about as if they, too, were having trouble getting comfortable for sleep.

CHAPTER 16
The Woodblood

Alex had just fallen into a deep sleep for the first time of the night when Nort nudged him awake with a light kick on the bottom of his feet. He had woken up multiple times, swearing that he had heard awful guttural howling and dark incomprehensible whispers only to wake up drenched in sweat to the soft sound of crackling logs on the fire. The canopy of dense trees left a sense of permanent twilight. He groggily shook off the restless night, wanting to sink back in his sleeping bag until he realized his surroundings.

He stretched and began mindlessly gathering his things, which did not take long for he had only a pack and a sleeping bag. Nort and Karissa had put together a quick breakfast of eggs and sausage biscuits for the group and they all ate while preparing for the ominous, and apparently dark, journey ahead. Everyone agreed that the shorter time they spent in the forest, the better.

Nort had just gathered Alex's horse for him and hitched it to a nearby tree where Alex began situating his saddlebag.

"I couldn't help but overhear the fear in your dreams last night," Karmac said to Alex, making small talk while gathering the rocks they had placed around the fires and tossing them randomly in the forest as if to hide their tracks.

Alex tightened the seal on the bag he had just situated and stared up at the trees as if lost in thought. "Yeah, they were definitely weird. I kept hearing some deep growl, but every time I woke up there was nothing there."

"You're hearing the Woodblood: the sound of the dead attempting to rise," Karmac explained.

"What? Wait," Alex said, turning toward Karmac. "They told me spirits moved on when they died and left an imprint in a tree." He looked around for Karissa to confirm what she had shown him.

"Yes, that's correct, but I'm not speaking of them," Karmac said, smiling deviously. He paused and then said in a loud whisper, "Demons dwell in these trees, whispering to those able to give rise to them."

Alex pointed a finger to his chest and a bewildered look spread across his face. "But, I'm not a warlock yet. How can I . . ."

"Not fully, but you give off a scent a demon's keen sense can detect."

Alex smelled his armpit, attempting to bring humor into the absurdness. "Huh?"

Karmac kept his serious face and tone. "It's more of a dark energy emanating from you."

"That'll be enough for now," Nort said, interrupting Karmac with a sneer. "I would prefer to leave the teaching of the warlock to someone more qualified in the art."

Karmac nodded, not objecting. Alex had a feeling that Karmac was suppressing something, but if he was, he never let it show more than a forced smile.

"So, Nort, how are we supposed to find this Krunk? We were given vague coordinates," Karmac said, tossing the last of the rocks into a nearby brush. Alex noticed how he quickly changed the conversation after the brief humiliation by Nort.

"I'll know once we're close," Nort said. "His last known location is somewhere near the Hills of Hal, a few miles outside the eastern edge of the forest."

"The shorter we stay in this forsaken place the better," Karmac huffed.

Alex couldn't agree more; the farther he was away from this woodblood the better he would feel. He wasn't sure if Karmac was speaking the truth or not, but he held a dreadful feeling deep inside that there was some validity to it. With this possible new development that he possesses dark energy that can summon demons, it gave rise to the aching itch bothering him: he needed guidance in his new role. He had heard enough about the seductive nature of the darkness and how it could quickly become too powerful and overwhelming. Especially to a young and inexperienced mind.

◇ ◇ ◇

The Faceless Forest is turning into the never-ending, gloomy forest, Alex mused as the day wore on. They were forced to travel at a snail's pace due to the thickness of the underbrush and the occasional huge thorn bushes that sprouted up as if they sensed prey nearby. The perpetual twilight and the sinister vibe that the place exuded didn't help the doldrums that Alex was slumping into. But there was something else bothering him, something immediate, and it lived in the trees above them.

Huge spiderwebs, the size that could capture and incapacitate a small person, were becoming more and more prevalent and thicker the farther they traveled inside the forest. They had yet to spot the spiders that had spun the webs, but Alex thought it was inevitable if they continued on this path.

"I know I'm not the only one seeing these giant webs above us," Alex said with a voice riddled with apprehension. "Is it possible to take another route around these things before we run into the creatures that made them?"

Karmac laughed. "They won't bother us if we don't bother them. Besides, if we take another route it would mean a few more days in this dreadful forest. And I'm sure you don't want that. None of us does."

"Yeah, right," Alex mumbled sarcastically. "I'd rather be alive, though."

Alex noticed in a tree ahead something large encapsulated in web and hanging from a branch. As he got closer, it appeared to be a large rodent or maybe a bird. It would soon be a meal, and it was definitely no small insect like the spiders back home ate.

"I've heard stories of the giant spiders here, but never believed them," Karissa said, riding up to Alex and causing him to flinch as she spoke. "I thought they were just tales to keep people away."

"You mean other than demons being here? Isn't that enough to scare anyone?" Alex asked. "Why would you need to add giant spiders for more deterrence?" He peered around nervously and then raised his voice slightly to reach Karmac who had moved to take the lead. "Can we pick up the pace a little, please?"

Karmac did not respond to his request. Alex didn't repeat himself, but looked around at the others who also seemed on edge. Even Karmac's soldiers were on guard, periodically glancing up at the webs above.

On hearing a rustling in the trees over his head, Alex felt along the saddlebag where his newly gained sword was snuggly shoved inside. He found the hilt and loosened it slightly from the scabbard so it would be easier to remove on short notice. That's when he noticed the soft hum coming from the sword: *one of my grandfather's enchantments,* he considered. *Maybe warning of approaching spiders? It's in my genes, right? Grandpa must have also hated spiders.*

"Alex! Above you!" Karissa shouted.

Before he could respond, he heard the thump of something heavy hitting the forest floor near him. He pulled on the reins of his horse and halted before the creature that now lay twitching in front of him. It looked like a spider all right, a huge one, the size of a large dog with fangs as big as Alex's head. There was one of Jayda's arrows jutting out from between the spider's red burning eyes, along with black ichor dripping that Alex assumed was the creature's blood.

"That's not an ordinary spider!" Alex cried, out of breath and backing his horse away from the thing. He took a few deep breaths and said, "Not just their size, I mean their legs. These things have . . ." Alex counted the legs again, "four huge legs the size of mine."

"Let me guess, demon spiders?" Karissa said revoltingly.

Nort nodded his head. "Yes, and very disturbing. I've only heard rumors of these abominations."

The party surrounded the dead creature. Despite their fear and disgust, they all stared for a moment. The horses also seemed on edge and didn't allow them to linger, jerking their heads away from their riders' commands.

"Well, so much for letting each of us pass our own way peacefully," Karmac said derisively toward Jayda.

Jayda glared at him, her nimble hands and bow ready for another demon should it retaliate for killing a comrade.

"Thank you," Alex said sincerely to Jayda.

"You're welcome," Jayda said with her eyes still glued to the trees above. "I'll take the rear. And I believe we should heed Alex's advice on picking up our pace."

Karmac sighed and then nodded and took the lead once more, but moved the group now at a horse's trot. He also had his sword unsheathed and lying across his lap. The rest of the group followed suit with their weapons at the ready.

No one spoke; only the hooves of the horses hitting the mud echoed through the trees. Alex wanted to close his eyes as if in the Doctor Blood haunted house, following closely behind the group until they were clear of the webs, but he couldn't. *I am their leader,* he thought, *or at least in training to be the leader. I have to at least act like I have courage to guide others out of harm's way, if it comes to that.*

There was a movement above them again that Alex had caught out of the corner of his eye. He gripped his grandfather's sword tightly and could still feel the soft vibration from the humming and a slight warmth, from the friction, he supposed. The vibration was oddly calming, but also alarming at the same time.

Alex looked ahead when he heard a sword hit wood from Karmac's direction. Karmac yanked his sword from the now dead creature without so much as a pause and began moving forward again. Alex cringed and tried not to stare as he passed the huge spider curled on its back. The movements above them had grown substantially and sounded like thousands of legs scaling the trees and webs being spun all around them.

There was no clearing in sight; only thick webbed trees surrounded them now. Alex had his sword drawn and head ducked defensively and began slicing madly at every web near him.

Out of his peripheral vision, a sudden light flamed from the rear of the group. Alex glanced back and saw Jayda holding an arrow with a burning tip aimed forward and above their heads.

"Once we pass under, I will burn their webs," Jayda shouted from the rear.

No one questioned her choice. The party moved as one and Jayda shot her flaming arrow high into the trees. The webs began to burn and high-pitched squeals of pain and anger filled the air above. Jayda's fire arrow rang true and separated the creatures' horde, cutting their numbers in half.

Nort stopped and looked back, and then to the trail in front of them. He then hurriedly dismounted his horse.

"What are you doing, Nort!? We have to keep going!" Alex pleaded.

"We will have to make our stand," Nort commanded. "Or they will pick us off one by one. They're too damn fast and too many in number. Even with the fire."

"Yes," Karmac agreed and signaled his men to a halt with a raised hand.

Alex felt his stomach plummet to his feet at Nort's words. He wanted to plant his heels firmly in the horse's sides and not look back, but he couldn't leave his party. He took a deep breath and reluctantly dismounted his horse and joined the rest. They all armed themselves and on Karmac's command they formed a tight circle: Alex stood between Nort and Karissa and fumbled to draw his sword.

"Now would be a good time for some of that warlock training, Nort," Alex said, hefting his sword out in front of him with a death grip. His eyes searched the dark trees, one to the other from branches to trunk.

"I agree, but I'm not the one to —" Nort began, but stopped short from the sight in front of him. In the distance, the smoke from Jayda's fire was thinning, and through it scores of spiders were speeding toward them in all levels of the trees.

"I really hope you thinned the herd enough for us to get through this," one soldier said in a shaky voice.

"Me too," Jayda said, as if she couldn't care less. "If not, oh well, more demon blood to spill for me."

"I'm glad you're okay with it," Karmac sneered.

"Here we go!" Nort shouted as a wall of spiders began marching toward them and moving as one massive nightmare.

Jayda began firing her bow with insane precision and speed, picking them off one by one. Alex cheered her silently, but his anxiety grew as the horde got closer and seemed unfazed by Jayda's death rockets. He turned his attention in the other direction toward Nort and noticed that he hadn't even armed himself.

"Aren't you going to draw your sword?" Alex asked tensely.

"Stay close," Nort warned, ignoring his question while gently edging Alex behind him with an outstretched arm. Nort pulled out an odd-looking device from his backpack and assembled it with uncanny speed. It appeared to be a . . . gun? It had two barrels like a shotgun, only the barrels were the size of small cannons. Perched on top was a rotating scope with three lenses that Nort adjusted in seconds. It also had a strap hanging to the ground that he wrapped snuggly around his right boot.

"What is that?" Alex asked, as Nort unfolded a handle from the rear of the device. Nort yanked back on the handle and immediately a loud boom vibrated the ground beneath them and then smoke emerged from the huge barrel. In the distance, they could see three spiders immediately shredded to nothing. The spiders behind the now decimated ones briefly hesitated and then quickly picked up speed on their path to avenge their brethren.

"I call it the Separator," Nort said proudly, reloading it with small cannon balls.

"Good name," Alex said, now feeling slightly better about the situation.

Nort and Jayda continued their barrage; round after round, arrow after arrow, but did little to slow the tenacious spiders.

The horde was closing in and less than a hundred feet away when Alex felt a strangeness wash over him. He suddenly felt warm and then a tightness all over his body, gripping him in place. He couldn't move or speak; it paralyzed him. He panicked and desperately wanted to yell out for help but no words came. All he could do was watch the terrifying spiders get closer and closer.

Then, seemingly out of nowhere, a deep voice growled, "Halt, minions."

◇ ◇ ◇

The spiders halted in place at the command coming from behind the horde. Jayda continued to fire her arrows — stuck in a frenzy of bloodlust — until Nort leaned his hand on top of her bow and gently lowered it. She resisted, but only for a moment on seeing a towering figure emerge from behind two dead spiders that she had just impaled through the head with her arrows. Nort had already set aside the Separator, though he was now wielding his dagger in its place.

"Enough," a booming voice bellowed loud enough for the entire forest to hear. Jayda slowly raised her bow in defense to strike.

Alex's sword still vibrated, so much so that party members glanced back at it in unison, temporarily ignoring the figure wielding the booming voice. None of them had noticed that Alex stood paralyzed and unable to speak.

"Not one step further, you vile demon beast," Karmac said and pushed his way in front of Jayda.

The hulking figure dwarfed Karmac and the rest of the party as it stepped closer with its huge hooves sinking into the forest floor. Though he was farther away than Nort or Jayda, sweat still dripped down Alex's forehead as he studied the beast: curved, thick crimson horns jutted out from the sides of its head; piercing, jaundiced, glowing eyes enhanced the menacing features of its protruding jaw line. A pair of dark, flame-colored wings bulged from behind it. The monstrous clawed hands gripped a massive scythe that was stained red and razor sharp. The beast stopped a few yards away, resting his weapon over his muscular right shoulder in a stance that said, I can destroy you all with one swipe of this enormous blade.

"So, you're the brave leader of this group," the demon said to Karmac. His voice was deep and intelligent and not at all what Alex was expecting.

"I am," Karmac commanded. His voice then turned to that of a diplomat. "Look, we're not here to disrupt whatever it is you and your pets are doing. We're passing through, that's all."

"No one just passes through this forest," the figure said, and then turned his attention from Karmac to the rest of the party. "A few soldiers of the king and a female bowman." Jayda huffed. "Another female cloaked . . . a sorcerer, perhaps?" He stopped and stared at Nort as if he knew him. A satisfying smirk spread across his face and he said, "Nortimer, I knew you would fall, eventually. I always liked you."

Nort stared at the demon as if trying to figure out how he knew the beast. He did not know any demons personally, but once they became demons in the underworld their forms changed.

"Nort, you know this demon?" Karmac suggested with disgust.

"Of course he does," the demon said in a dark voice, remaining fixed on Nort. "Shall I awaken your memory?"

Nort gave the demon a silent nod and allowed the demon to explain.

"Your human sister and I once held a bond." His forked demon tongue licked his lips.

Nort's face unraveled a menacing glare toward the demon. "Daal!"

The demon smiled, "Sinvexe, now. I've taken a new oath. A much . . . shall we say, clearer path."

"You went right where you belonged, you murderous waste of flesh!" Nort bellowed. "You deserve to be right beside the filth you always were!"

"I see you finally fell from your pedestal," Sinvexe said calmly. "I always knew we held a similar perspective."

"We share nothing! You killed my nephew, an innocent child. Your own son! You're a monster that needs putting down for good."

Alex noticed Nort's hands gripping tighter around his dagger with each word spoken.

The demon's hubris was obvious as he did not so much as flinch at Nort's words or his aggressive fighting stance.

"Before your little group perishes, I would like to extend an offer for your service in my ranks, Nortimer."

"You're wasting my time," Nort said.

The demon continued despite Nort's words. "Once you reach the underworld, things will change for you. You will see what I see and be glad for it. The master's vision is grand and we can be leaders in the coming of the new age: the old world. Search your feelings, Nortimer, you know this place will fall. The king is already dead and we have lords placed strategically on all fronts. Don't you want to be on the winning side of eternity?"

"What's he talking about, Nort? How do you know this . . . this foul thing?" Karmac demanded.

"You can stop the charade; I'm done with you, little knight," Sinvexe told Karmac. "I'll soon be leaving with my prize."

"What are you talking about, you filthy demon scum," Karmac retorted.

"I've heard enough from your insolent mouth!" Sinvexe roared and raised his right hand in a pushing motion toward Karmac.

An invisible force shoved Karmac to the ground, and he immediately revealed an open palm of surrender as he sat groveling and groaning in pain, shocked by the unseen power held by the demon. Karmac's sword lay a few yards away, but he didn't dare reach for it.

Nort turned his attention to Karmac and asked, "What charade is he speaking of? And what prize?"

Karmac struggled in pain as he made his way to a nearby tree and leaned his back against the trunk. Through exasperated breaths he told Nort, "I think we would all like to hear more about how you and this demon are acquainted."

The demon spoke before Nort retorted. "Yes, Nortimer, tell these mortals of our past profession."

"We were guards together, gatekeepers," Nort said, staring fervently at the demon. "The first line of defense to heaven, sworn to protect it no matter the sacrifice. No matter the persuasion."

Chills ran along Alex's entire body as the realization hit him. If he was hearing things correctly, Nort was a real angel of heaven.

"Trying to make your way back, I see," Sinvexe said and pointed to the small protrusions coming from Nort's head. "Futile, once you fall and see the truth; there is no going back. There is no redemption. It's a facade to keep you loyal."

Nort shook his head and sighed, "I'm aware we are pawns. but I'd rather be a pawn on the side of mercy rather than on the side of torment and agony."

Sinvexe laughed a deep, hearty laugh. "You and your weak friends will snap like the tenuous strands holding the levels of eternity in place. The lie we preserved will crumble along with the gates we guarded. You, all of you, will bleed and suffer under my command. Except for you." He stared at Alex. "My master has other plans for you."

"Alex, stay where you are," Nort commanded. Alex wanted to answer, but he remained paralyzed and unable to speak. He would have even stepped back a few paces if he were able. "Let's see what your so-called master has taught you," Nort said turning his attention back to Sinvexe.

Sinvexe snarled at the disrespect spoken of his master and then lunged toward Nort with a wide arc of his scythe. Nort ducked and then leaped toward the demon, translucent golden wings emerging from his back and then disappearing again as if they were never there. Nort struck Sinvexe across the chest, releasing a stream of black blood along his torn leather vest. Nort didn't hesitate but sliced again, this time removing a piece of the demon's right horn.

Watching helplessly, Alex wondered why the demon hadn't just used his power on Nort and knocked him to the ground as he did Karmac. He pondered whether the power worked only on certain species and not on angels or demons.

"Don't just sit there; assist your master!" Sinvexe yelled toward Karmac. "Grab the boy and bring him to me."

The party stopped what they were doing and looked over at Karmac. They were all waiting in suspense for his response to dismiss the demon's command. He did not.

Without saying a word, Karmac got to his feet and grabbed his sword from between two huge roots a few feet away from him. He moved toward Alex with his eyes fixed on him and his blade firmly in his grip. The group stared, shocked, not knowing what to make of the situation unfolding in front of them. Everyone, except for Nort.

"Karmac, declare your loyalty, now!" Nort warned as the knight maintained his silence and purposeful movement toward Alex.

Alex could feel his heart pounding in his chest as the knight marched toward him. The knight's eyes remained fixed in a trance with bloodlust pulsing through them.

"Karmac! Last chance!" Nort warned again, having now moved in front of Alex.

"Strike the little fallen angel down and retrieve the boy," Sinvexe bellowed. "Avenge your master!"

Karmac hefted his sword in the air and began to charge when two strikes came flying past Nort, one after the other, and into the knight's chest. Nort wiped his face from the splatter of blood as the knight fell lifeless to the ground at his feet.

The arrows did not come from Jayda this time. Karissa lowered her cloak and the bow in her hand, and said, "I knew he was a traitor the moment I laid eyes on him."

Alex was far beyond impressed this time. *Where did that come from?* he wondered. He was a little scared, but thankful that she was on his side, giving rise to a lump in the pit of his stomach.

"Bravo, Nort," Sinvexe said, while lightly clapping his clawed hands. "How touching that you have two ladies looking after you." He then turned his attention back to Karmac's body and rolled his eyes. "Pathetic. I'll just have to handle this myself."

"Jayda, Karissa," Nort said, "if those soldiers so much as blink, drop them where they stand."

The soldiers all lowered their swords, seemingly confused now that their traitorous leader lay dead.

"Let's finish this, shall we," Nort said, with his sword at the ready.

"Gladly," Sinvexe hissed. "I'll enjoy watching you snivel on the ground while I kill your friends one by one." He racked his scythe on his back and unhooked from his belt a whip with a metallic razor for a tip. Nort's strike to the demon's chest must not have hit anything vital. The demon did not even wince as he snapped the whip a few times in the air around Nort, tauntingly, Indiana Jones-style. "It's time you feel the pain of hell."

Nort smirked, angering the demon further.

Sinvexe began wildly snapping the whip in the air and then charged toward Nort. Once again Nort's agility was too much for the demon and he missed, striking a nearby tree and removing a large chunk of bark. Nort stood behind the demon with a wide grin stretched across his face. When the demon realized where he had gone, he darted furiously around. He reached back his massive arm, ready to strike, but

207

stopped midair when he saw Nort motioning to an object lying on the ground in front of the demon. Sinvexe quickly searched his own head and immediately let out a guttural yell when he noticed a piece had been sliced from his other horn.

"My master won't be pleased," Sinvexe said, backing away. He then yelled, "*Causam et festum.*"

Jayda looked over at Nort with a horrified expression and asked, "What does that mean?"

"Charge and feast," Nort answered.

CHAPTER 17

A Warlock's Residence

Sinvexe gave the command and disappeared behind his army of demon spiders. The party had mere seconds before the mob devoured everything in its wake.

"I don't have time to sort you all out," Nort scolded the soldiers. "Fight, and if you survive, I'll give each of you the opportunity to clear your name. Betray us and you will see the same fate as your traitor commander."

The men nodded in unison, and Nort quickly gave them orders on where to stand and fight — ensuring they remained within sight of Jayda and him.

Alex finally felt some movement returning to his muscles. The farther Sinvexe moved away, the better he felt.

"Are you all right?" Karissa asked Alex as he wobbled around with an unsteady gait.

"Yeah," he cleared his throat a few times. "Shaky," he managed.

"What happened? Were you bitten by a spider?" Karissa asked.

"Incapacitated," Nort interjected. "By Sinvexe."

"How?" Alex asked, his voice fully returning.

"I'm not entirely sure, but Krunk should be able to tell us. If we survive this, we'll ask him." He motioned toward the wave of spiders closing in on them.

Alex nodded and gripped his sword handle. Thankfully, he had almost regained all of his strength. Being controlled by a demon began percolating in his head. *What does it mean? Am I that vulnerable?* He placed the thought temporarily away as his mind quickly shuffled back to survival mode when the first spider leapt toward him and was quickly struck down by a soldier.

Jayda and Nort once again began rapidly expelling barrage after barrage of arrows into the spider herd. Karissa also had her bow out striking down spiders.

"We may have to make a run for it," Jayda exclaimed between arrows. "There's no end in sight to these disgusting creatures."

They seemed to multiply the more they killed. Alex tried steadying his hands from the deluge of adrenaline pumping wildly in his blood vessels, waiting his turn. Seconds later he made eye contact with a spider in the distance. He waited intently for it to reach him. He sighed in relief when one of Jayda's arrows sliced off its leg. But the relief was short-lived when the spider kept its pace toward him at an unbridled speed as if the leg had no bearing on its ability to move. He looked around for help, but everyone else had their hands full with their own advancing spiders. This was all him, and his grandfather's sword.

The spider let out a horrible hiss when it catapulted toward him, knocking him to the ground with its uninjured legs. Alex quickly grabbed his sword, which had thankfully fallen within arm's reach when he was knocked down. He sprang to his feet and began circling the spider. He did not quite know the purpose of circling, only that he had seen it in many movies and figured this was the procedure for dueling.

The spider made the first move, lifting its two front legs in the air as if to pounce; the stump of the left front leg oozed onto the forest floor. Alex swung his sword in a wide arc, hitting the front uninjured leg but not removing it. The spider hissed and stumbled backward. On seeing the spider vulnerable, Alex made his move. His instinct was to get as close as he could to the beast and lunge his sword into its body, but that's not what he did. Instead, he closed his eyes and swung his arm back, and then let go of his sword, hurling it forward.

He opened his eyes and saw that he had somehow impaled the beast to a nearby tree. He sighed and looked around, proud of his lucky strike, but again no one noticed his feat. He quickly realized how incredibly lucky he was and how stupid it had been to let go of his weapon without a second one at the ready.

"Get ready to run!" Nort shouted over the loud bang from his massive gun. "Alex, get your sword out of that tree and mount your horse, now!"

Alex did not argue nor hesitate. He raced toward the tree and retrieved his sword, ignoring the splatter of ichor now all over his arms.

"Everyone, get ready to mount your horses," Nort said. "I can give us only a few seconds with the few fireballs I have left."

Alex began untying the other horses as Nort loaded his weapon.

Boom! Boom! Boom! rang out into the forest, shaking the ground. The trees burst into flames in the area where the fireballs landed. Nort dismantled the Separator in seconds and began running for his horse. The others had mounted theirs and were moving away, but Alex waited for Nort, holding his horse in place for him.

"Alex, go, now!" Nort yelled. "Don't wait for me!"

Just as Alex was about to heed Nort's words, he noticed two spiders closing in on Nort from behind him.

"Nort, behind you!" Alex shouted. *He isn't going make it,* Alex thought. And then another spider joined the pursuit from above him. They were less than twenty yards behind him. Fifteen. Ten.

Suddenly, a blinding, bright light emerged from behind Alex, encapsulating the entire area in green illumination. Alex shielded his eyes, trying desperately to see whether his friend was okay. As badly as he didn't want to face another one of those spiders, there was no way Alex was leaving Nort behind.

When he could finally open his eyes, the light had disappeared and Nort was standing a few feet in front of him, all in one piece. Alex peered around anxiously in every direction, searching for spiders.

"What happened? Where'd they go?" Alex asked, confused and still on guard.

Nort leaned against his horse and took a much-needed gulp of air. "Krunk."

"Nortimer, I should have known you were the one stirring up the forest," a deep, stern voice said from behind them.

A tall, dark figure emerged from the trees behind them, wearing a tattered black cowboy hat and a black leather cloak. He was a little taller than an average man, Alex noticed, as he removed his hat. He had long, dark hair and a thin chinstrap beard doused with gray, enhancing his sharp chin. He wore dark pants that came down to a pair of rugged black boots.

"This place should have been destroyed long ago," Nort grumbled. "Environment aside, how have you been, Krunk?"

Alex stared curiously at the man. *This cowboy-looking warlock is the one they're seeking to train me?*

"And who is this young man wearing the king's robes?" Krunk said, walking up to Alex, who sat perched on his horse.

"That is the king's grandson, Alex Rayne," Nort said. "And the only reason I'm here in this dreadful part of the world."

"Come on, it's not all that bad," Krunk said, while studying Alex.

Krunk removed his dark, round spectacles, which looked like an overly thick pair of sunglasses. Alex noticed when the man got closer that his eyes seemed to change color from dark green to olive. He looked to be in his mid-forties, if Alex had to guess — somewhere around his dad's age. Only his face held many more lines, which Alex supposed was from living here in this forest. He carried an ornate staff, black and dark royal blue, and at its tip sat a miniature black-gray stone gargoyle. He also had a pair of gun holsters attached to his leather belt and a skull-shaped belt buckle. He did not see revolvers, but there was definitely something bulging from inside the holsters.

"So, Alex Rayne," Krunk said, "how is it that your grandfather has given up his robes? How did you convince him to go around the castle naked?"

On seeing Alex's forlorn expression, Krunk's smirk faded, and he turned immediately to Nort.

"Nortimer, why exactly are you here?" Krunk asked sternly, now with unease in his words.

"The king is dead; murdered," Nort said bluntly.

"Murdered?" Krunk stared at Nort as if he was waiting for another explanation for the real reason the king was dead. "You're serious, aren't you?"

Nort shook his head with a grave expression on his face.

"Let's not waste another moment out here then, where wondering ears are rampant. The rest of your party are at the forest's edge awaiting your arrival. I told them in passing that I would see you to them once you were safe."

Nort huffed. "I had it all under control, but thanks anyway."

Krunk nodded. "Good to see you, too, Nort."

Krunk whistled and a horse came from behind a nearby tree. The horse wore battle gear, matching the garb of his rider, all but the cowboy hat, replaced with a black leather face piece that dramatically enhanced the white glowing eyes emerging through.

Nort didn't waste any time and quickly began questioning each of the soldiers, though he had no intention of letting them continue on the journey. Maybe it was Nort's deadly tactics he displayed or his stern demeanor, but none of the soldiers contested his order to return to the realm and report directly to the council. They had specific instructions to avoid contact with Jarren at any cost and were any to disobey he promised he would see them face the gallows on his return.

The now much smaller party followed Krunk, to their dismay, back into the forest. Though it was only a few hundred yards, the dread on all of their faces could not be mistaken. They came to a specific tree; other than it being slightly larger there was no discernible difference between it and the surrounding ones. Krunk raised his staff in the air and made a half circle in front of the tree; the stone gargoyle on the tip unwrapped its wings and then furled them back again. Immediately, an invisible layer began to shed from the outside of the tree, as if its bark was sloughing off.

At the massive base of the tree, a wooden door appeared with a bronze half-circle handle. Surrounding the archway of the door, elaborately carved stone showcased a variety of symbols.

"Probably some spell protection," Karissa whispered to Alex as he watched in awe. Since arriving in Tristoria, he had been amazed every time he saw something extraordinary happen. He presumed that he would soon have time to learn more about some of this stuff, now that he was in the presence of his supposed teacher. He was excited to begin learning, but also leery about the idea.

The inside of the tree was much bigger than Alex thought it would be, considering the size of the trunk's exterior. There was a crescent of windows that faced a wide mountain range filled with green rolling hills. That was definitely not what was on the other side of the tree; another piece of aesthetics he had no explanation for, though on seeing Alex's confusion, Krunk explained that the view was of the Hills of Hal, an illusion so he does not go insane from the surrounding darkness. His choice of living in the forest was dangerous and required discipline and a crucial balance; the slightest teeter could end his sanity.

Exhausted from their latest battle, Karissa, Alex, and Jayda plopped down in the living room by the fireplace and began small talk. Well, at least Jayda and Karissa did; Alex just sat aside and did his best to not say anything embarrassing to the two beautiful women. Besides, he had some snooping to do, so he inched as close as he could to the kitchen entrance where Nort and Krunk took their private conversation. He listened near the threshold as Nort explained to Krunk what had transpired in the forest before Krunk arrived.

Krunk sat stewing over the information with his pipe in hand. After a few minutes of quiet puffing, he said, "So, I suppose you want me to train this boy in the warlock's way?" He exhaled a plume of smoke toward the open kitchen window.

"That's the idea, yes," Nort said and sighed loudly. "I wasn't expecting to take on such a huge task when I agreed to retrieve the boy for the late king."

"We're all in it now, aren't we?" Krunk said woefully.

"So, you'll train him then?"

Krunk sighed. "Need I remind you the age of ascension?"

"I'm not a warlock. So, yes."

"Seventeen, and he is fourteen, which means his powers, what few he has, cannot be tamed yet. This boy is going through a sort of puberty while actually going through puberty. It's hard to explain, but you can imagine the emotions he's dealing with. And now he's thrown into a world he never knew existed and is meant to rule it. How incredibly insane it must be to be him right now. And even if he were ready, there's no time to train him to defeat a powerful, determined demon."

"Yes, that is quite a lot," Nort lamented, changing his tone. "Why, then, did his grandfather bring him here if he wasn't ready?"

"What choice did he have? You didn't bring him here to defeat this demon horde. Obviously the king knew he was dying and Tristoria needed a king. The people need to know the kingdom is still being ruled by a Rayne as it has for a millennia. They don't care his age or abilities as long as he has that name. If Alex were not here, and the king fell without an

217

heir, mayhem would ensue around the kingdom. Throw in the invasion happening and you have a perfect storm for chaos. An optimum time to overthrow the kingdom and take over Tristoria."

"Then this Helenia didn't know about the next in line for the throne? She has to be the dumbest demon in a thousand years to leave an heir alive if her intentions are to destroy the bloodline and take over."

"Oh, I think she well knows of the bloodline, but reaching him, as in finding a portal to him, is another thing entirely."

"Am I missing something here?" Nort said. "Surely, they would have a plan to take out the rest of the family."

"She'll come for him now that that demon knows he's here. A tough choice his grandfather had to make to keep this place safe, placing the boy within reach of demons." He sighed. "What was the demon's name again? Sinvexe was it?"

Nort nodded. "Yes, he was once an angel long ago. We . . . have a history. What I'm trying to figure out is how he found us in this vast forest. We were here less than a day."

"Someone likely tipped him off when you all departed the realm and told him of your direction."

"Definitely Jarren, but how was he able to ambush us? No one knew the exact path we would take in the forest."

"Jarren, the king's hand?"

"Yes."

"Huh, I guess he fooled James and me. But I also never spent a considerable amount of time with him."

"Me, either, but I've never liked the guy."

"I suppose that has nothing to do with your, uh . . . surly demeanor toward the realm."

Nort huffed, not returning a comment.

"No matter the tip-off," Krunk said. "All that demon had to do was to be near Alex."

"What do you mean?"

"Warlocks put out a . . . let's just say a very strong scent that demons can detect."

So, Karmac wasn't lying about the scent. What about the Woodblood?

"That's a little scary and unnerving. Do you guys have a defense for that?"

"Yes, our sense of them is much stronger. But Alex has not yet developed his."

"Obviously, since Helenia knows he's here, she will go for him next," Nort continued. "And we have a bigger problem than that."

"And that is?"

"Trust."

"Yes, that is a problem," Krunk agreed thoughtfully. "What about the council?"

"I know very little of them and no one has spoken of their loyalty. The king seemed to trust them, though he made a point to me he did not want them training Alex."

"For good reason," Krunk said knowingly. "If James would not have a close eye on the training, then Alex could not be alone with the council. He would be vulnerable, and a warlock must not reveal his weaknesses to an outsider, meaning anyone outside the Rayne name."

"He must have trusted you immensely, then."

"We go back a long way, James and I. We held many debates over allowing a council to intervene and hold power in the kingdom. He knew of my stance and my distaste for the council."

"I don't particularly like the idea of a warlock monarchy. No offense, but your kind invites the evil to the front door, and you all have a craving for power."

"None taken," Krunk said, "and I completely understand the apprehension. I told James the people need a voice, a few of their peers, but . . . I emphasized voices not so powerful as to overrule him. I even iterated, just as you have pointed out, our thirst for power. But I could never convince him of the dangers of a coven of warlocks turning against him."

"Are you thinking the council is behind all of this? Teaming up with Helenia and ordering Jarren to take out Alex?"

"Honestly, I don't know, but I know warlocks, and they would sooner cast themselves into oblivion than let demons rule over them and the place they live. However, that doesn't rule out using them to get what they want. Or Jarren."

"And that is?"

"More power."

"Of course," Nort sighed, shaking his head.

"It's in our blood," Krunk said with a shrug. "Our curse."

Nort frowned. "How can we trust you, then?"

Krunk did not seem even the slightest offended by Nort's continual distaste for warlocks, or his personal distrust of Krunk.

"I can assure you I have no intention of ruling anything other than a few demons now and then. James was a good friend and I will not let the Rayne kingdom be supplanted by demons. I may not have wanted to be a permanent part of his kingdom, like yourself, but the Raynes have kept a balance in this world. This is my home, Nort, just as it is yours, and I like it the way it is."

"Temporary home," Nort pointed out. "And I too would like to finish my time in this place the way it is," Nort said. "Since we both agree to not let Tristoria fall, we need a plan."

"Yes, and allies," Krunk pointed out.

"Agreed. My village will fight with us, but that will not be enough. We need the king's soldiers on our side. Who knows how many demons have crossed over by now."

Krunk nodded. "Yes, but we don't know where the soldiers' loyalties lie."

"Which is why Alex is our best hope for the soldiers' allegiance," Nort said. "They follow the king. And if this deceit is true, then Jarren has probably told the kingdom of the king's death and claimed to be next in line because there is no heir. That sniveling traitor is probably sitting on the throne giving orders as we speak."

"I suggest we send a scout to see how far this has gone," Krunk said. "We need to see exactly where we stand. And then proceed accordingly."

"I agree, and if our scout returns with horrible news, what next? Who else do we have on our side?"

A girl's voice came from behind Nort and startled them. "I want to fight."

"Vitoria, what have I told you about evesdropping?" Krunk said.

"Only do it if I will not get caught," Vitoria said pointedly.

"Precisely," Krunk said.

"Sorry, just, I want to help," Vitoria said, pouting her lips.

"Nort, this is my daughter, Vitoria. Sorry for her rude interruption."

"Nice to meet you," Nort said with a nod of his head.

"You, too," she said cheerfully.

"Vitoria, you are in the same position as this boy, Alex," Krunk said. "Your powers have not matured."

"But you trained me since I could walk."

"You're no match for a demon witch, or a demon of any sorts for that matter. Now, since you are up and awake, go introduce yourself to the rest of our guests and let Nort and me finish our talk of urgent matters." He narrowed his eyes toward her and she did not argue back; she merely rolled her eyes and turned around and left the room the same way she had entered.

"She's testy," Nort said, taking a sip of his now cool tea.

"Just like her mother. Hopefully, she won't follow in her footsteps."

"Is her mother not around?"

"No," Krunk said forlornly. "I blame myself for moving here. She let her lust for the Woodblood absorb her and let her guard down one too many times. Suffice to say, a powerful demon took her from me." He stared longingly at the wall.

"Sorry for your loss," Nort said sincerely.

After an awkward few moments of silence, Krunk snapped back to the present and spoke as if he should have asked it earlier. "What about Henry? The boy's father?"

"As you know, he never finished the trials."

"Yes, but he's still a warlock. He passed the trials after ascension, and he closed all six of the seals, giving him the same powers as any other practicing warlock. In fact, if my memory serves me, James was impressed with how powerful his son Henry had become."

"That may be true, but from what I observed, I doubt he's still a practicing warlock. He seems more of a struggling husband and father attempting to maintain what has become a turbulent household. In fact, that's how I got Alex alone: he was running away from his home."

"James always said Henry had his head up too far in a hole to see what was right in front of him."

"Oh, and one more thing," Nort said, remembering an important bit of information. "The Book is missing."

"When you told me that Helenia had gained entrance into the castle, I figured she would steal the Book."

"You don't seem overly worried, how come?" Nort asked.

"James was not naïve. He knew the importance of that book. He confided in me long ago that there was an unbreakable spell on it."

"Any spell can be broken," Nort reminded him.

"Yes, but this one can be broken only by one that is not able to cast a spell. And there's one more protection for the Book. It has a lock and key."

"Okay . . ." Nort said, "however that works. Where's the key?"

"That I do not know, but James told me it was never in plain sight of the Book."

"Fine, if you say so," Nort said skeptically. "If you're not worried about the Book, then I guess I'm not. But there's something else bugging me: if we do somehow survive this war, what if the boy doesn't want to take the throne and rule?"

"He's here by his own free will, isn't he?"

"Yes, but I sort of bribed him."

"What do you owe him? I'm sure we can figure something out."

"He wants his dad back to the way he was before he met his new wife."

"He left Samantha? Huh, that is peculiar. According to James, they were inseparable."

Nort nodded, "I do not know of the details, but this new woman, Margie, is no treat. I didn't spend a lot of time observing, but this woman was difficult on the eyes and her personality was even more atrocious. I also believe Samantha is dead."

"Really?" Krunk said surprised. He then took a deep breath and let it out slowly. "You certainly have a challenge. Changing one's fate is not an easy task, but changing one's heart is an even tougher one."

"I said what I had to and got him here," Nort said unapologetically. "I was going to talk with the boy and come to a compromise, but I honestly don't know what to do now that this situation has evolved."

Krunk sat thinking for a moment. "There is definitely something strange with that situation with Henry, but in the meantime, we must hope Alex will see the bigger picture. Seeing that you once had a grand vision of the good place, you will be the best at convincing him of those things involving the heart."

"I fell, if you recall," Nort said matter-of-factly.

"I do, so what? We all have flaws. You're not allowed any?"

"Back to the situation at hand," Nort said, changing the subject. "What about more allies? I know I will regret this, but are there any other warlocks that you trust to help us?" Nort looked as if he were attempting to swallow a swig of spoiled milk.

Krunk seemed to ignore Nort's expression and said, "I've been in isolation for so long . . . no, sorry, I don't. But there is a coven in the Hills of Hal."

"You just said you knew no more warlocks."

"They're not warlocks; they're witches."

Nort shook his head and mumbled sarcastically, "Great."

CHAPTER 18
The Coven of Hal

Jayda decided she was best suited for spying on her brother, Jarren. She needed no hard evidence of his guilt for she knew her brother and his past comments about the king. There were many occasions when she came close to warning the king of Jarren's ranting, but she had held her tongue. Jarren's rants had been only words until this point. The king had trusted him with his life, which now seemed a little too ironic for her to digest. After hearing Jayda's insight, Nort and Krunk did not need any more convincing that Jarren should never have been trusted.

Jayda packed some provisions and left immediately for her mission of spying on her brother. Once the information was gathered, she was to report back to Nort's village with her findings. Nort and the others would be along soon once their own mission was complete.

It was just the five of them now traveling the short distance to the Hills of Hal, where somewhere deep in the mountains was a settlement of witches known as the coven of

Hal. There is not much known of them other than they mostly keep to themselves and they practice dark witchcraft, Krunk informed the group. Vitoria predictably made objections to her dad's comments about the coven, explaining their practices as breakthrough spells that, once mastered, could help everyone.

Krunk knew of his daughter's aspirations to join the coven one day, though he didn't quite approve. He wanted her to join the king's ranks, but he knew criticizing the witches' practices was contradictory and would only cause resentment in his daughter's eyes. After all, he was a practicing warlock and made his own rules, but he also didn't completely disregard the king. He was careful and remained on the king's side of the very tenuous line of rule.

Krunk just wanted his daughter to use her powers for the greater good and not waste away chasing power as he has done. She was born here, which meant she could never leave, but with a little discipline she could live her life away from dark magic. She could help the weak and serve the king and hopefully live a fulfilling life in a not-so-great place.

Vitoria insisted on being the one to lead the group to the coven, describing how she had all but been confirmed and all she had left was to become of age and gain her powers. On hearing Krunk's explanation of her embellishments, Karissa and Alex both rolled their eyes at her boasting and presumptuous comments.

Krunk and Nort moved ahead of the three of them and began a quiet discussion on how to approach the coven.

"I don't trust them, Krunk," Nort began. "What makes you think they will even help us?"

"Look, I don't trust them completely either. Honestly, I don't really know them, having met them on only one occasion when a demon got loose and I had to track it and . . . anyway, I ended up apologizing for entering the Hills of Hal and we went our separate ways without conflict. But not until they made it a point that I knew that it was their land and I was trespassing."

"What do they do here? I mean, do they just live in these hills and do spells all day?" Nort asked.

"Much like me, I presume," Krunk said. "Write new spells, try them out, gain new insight. Rinse and repeat."

Nort huffed. "What a waste of . . ." He lowered his gaze. "Sorry, I just don't see the point."

"It's difficult to understand, I get it. It's an addiction, that's all. Something I prefer not to pass down to my daughter."

"From her words it sounds like you may be too late already."

"That's what I'm afraid of, but how can I discipline her for aspirations when her old man does the same thing."

"That's a dilemma I'm glad I don't have to solve." Nort looked in the direction they were riding. "How are we going to convince these witches? What do we tell them?"

"The truth. That Tristoria is being invaded."

"And if they don't care?"

"We improvise," Krunk said, motioning his head back toward Alex.

Nort shook his head. "I don't like that approach, Krunk, not one bit." He sighed heavily. "But it may be our only recourse."

Despite Alex's newfound confidence in his riding skills, his nerves began creeping up again as he rode between two girls his own age. Karissa was attractive, but this Vitoria girl was also pretty, in a dark, gothic sort of way. She had midnight black hair, purple eyes, and a scar on her right cheek just like Karissa's. Any remaining confidence quickly began to wane as his hormones bounced back and forth. He didn't have a clue what to say to either of the girls, so he decided it best to remain quiet. He even briefly considered riding up to Nort and Krunk to avoid them altogether, but he didn't want to appear lame or cowardly by running away.

"So, Alex, how long have you known of your powers?" Vitoria said smugly, keeping her gaze forward.

So much for remaining quiet, he thought. "Not long at all. I only —"

Vitoria interrupted. "My dad taught me since I could barely walk. Why didn't your dad teach you? Oh, wait, that's right; he wasn't strong enough to pass the last and easiest of his tasks."

Other than an informal introduction, this was the first time she had spoken to Alex. *What is this girl's problem? What did I do to her to deserve this ridicule?* As much as he did not want to defend his dad due to his recent behavior, he was still his dad.

"My dad chose his path," Alex said defensively.

"I heard it differently. I heard he fainted during the last trial."

"That's a lie."

"Whatever you want to tell yourself," she said with a whip of her dark hair and turned toward Karissa. "And you, what's your deal?"

Karissa had been waiting patiently for the inevitable interaction. "How do you mean, my deal?" Karissa said mimicking Vitoria's snideness.

"You're quiet, you wear a cloak, and you travel with an old man and this wannabe warlock."

Karissa took in a deep breath, calming her words before speaking them aloud. "First of all, that's your king right now. Have some respect. Second, if it's any of your business, which it's not, I'm a seer."

Vitoria sneered, "My father and I have no king. We're only helping to help ourselves."

Alex kept his mouth shut and Karissa shook her head in disgust while mumbling, "What a surprise."

Vitoria continued. "And what has being a seer done for your little group here?"

"For one it gave me the insight to calm myself before I said something foul to you that would go against my principles."

Vitoria huffed. "Good for you." She clapped mockingly. "I see you have the same scar as me. Well, obviously, that's the only thing we share."

"Thankfully," Karissa mumbled.

"And what makes you so special?" Alex said, defending Karissa. He had had enough; there was no excuse for the arrogance Vitoria was spraying all over the place.

"I've been chosen by the coven of Hal to take their trials. And once I pass, I will be part of their elite group."

"Suits you," Karissa mumbled a little too loudly.

"Thank you," Vitoria said emphatically. "It must be a sad little life not to be part of anything. I honestly feel sorry for you."

"Don't. And I was being sarcastic, by the way. I'm perfectly happy not being a part of a cult."

"How dare you call them . . . I should —"

"Stop!" Alex demanded, and cooled quickly on seeing their stunned faces. "We don't have to like one another, but we need one another right now."

"He's right," Karissa admitted.

"Yes, you all do need me . . . to convince the coven to help us," Vitoria said.

Alex and Karissa gave each other a shake of their heads and decided it best to not further escalate the conversation.

◊ ◊ ◊

The party remained silent as each of them took in their surroundings. The air had turned cooler, and the trees weren't plush and full anymore, but barren sticks jutting out from the ground, surrounded by dead leaves. Loud crunches as they rode through the dry leaves rang out through the silence, bouncing between the tall mountains they were currently riding between, balancing back out what little tension they had released.

The group tightened in a single line behind Krunk as the path narrowed. They ducked and swerved, attempting to avoid the canopy of naked tree limbs that seemed to grab at them like disembodied hands.

"Well, at least they'll hear us coming," Nort said with a roll of his eyes.

"It doesn't much matter anyway," Krunk said. "They already know we're here." He narrowly escaped a limb to the head. "We crossed over a line a few paces back that I am pretty sure was some sort of perimeter spell."

"I'm regretting agreeing to this," Nort said as the wind whistled through the tree branches, leaving a sound resonating like bones creaking down a dark hallway.

Alex reached down and checked his sword to make sure it wasn't vibrating. He sighed in relief at its stillness, though he kept his hand close enough to grab it quickly if needed. He was riding in line behind Nort, and just as he was about to comment to him about his sword, the sight in front of him caught his words and shoved them back in and deep into the pit of his stomach.

Three hooded figures, all in black, stood four to five horse lengths in front of the party. Nort and Krunk were no longer in a line but beside one another. They sat quiet and motionless on their horses and shielded the group behind them.

Vitoria quickly trotted her horse in front of her dad and Nort, ignoring their warnings to get behind them.

"Fellow witches," she said as if she were one of them returning home. "My father and his acquaintances would like a word with the coven. They have a pleading request."

One of the hooded figures stepped in front of the other two and lowered her hood. A woman's stern but beautiful face emerged. She had long black hair with a tint of dark purple that traveled just past her shoulders. Her face was pale with high cheekbones and full lips painted black.

Her words came out smooth and severe. "Young girl, as I have instructed you in the recent past, this is not your coven. And may never be. Until you ascend, there is no discussion of joining our ranks or even speaking with us. Now, leave these grounds the way you came and take the rest of these outsiders with you."

Krunk moved his horse next to Vitoria. He bowed his head and spoke respectfully, "I am Krunk, Vitoria's father. I would like to first apologize for my daughter's rudeness and intrusion into your coven."

"We know who you are, warlock," she said sharply. "Speak your business and leave."

"Yes," Krunk nodded and cleared his throat. "Lucianna, I'm aware of our differences and I appreciate your covens' quest for isolation. I wouldn't be here if there wasn't a dire situation at our doorstep. I'll get straight to the point; we need your help."

Lucianna sighed. "Whatever force is attacking Tristoria once again, we aren't interested. We, our coven, pride ourselves in our seclusion from the rest of the world. We are happy in our quiet hills."

"All the more reason to help. Look, I understand and feel the same way about seclusion, as does my friend here, Nort," Krunk stretched out an arm toward Nort, "but this is far worse than a few demons harassing a village."

Nort nodded in agreement, but all three witches seemed to ignore him.

Lucianna held up her hand in protest. "We have defended our lands for millennia and will continue to do so on our own terms."

"Yes, but the king has always done his part and kept most of the demons where they belong. I know your coven is more than capable of defending its lands, but this will take all of Tristoria to defend against. Not only is there a massive horde of demons gathering, but there is corruption within the kingdom."

"King Rayne would never allow corruption in his kingdom," she said dismissively.

There was a lump in Krunk's throat as he spoke the next words. "I agree, and if he were alive, that would be true."

"The king is dead? But how?" There was a tinge of concern in the witch's voice, though her face held stern.

"We believe a demon witch by the name of Helenia has killed the king and stolen the Rayne spell book. She's amassing a great army of demons and moving closer to the kingdom as I speak. We think the commander of the king's army, Jarren, has been turned and is likely turning the soldiers in his favor. If she reaches the kingdom, and the commander has turned the soldiers to join the demon horde, the rest of Tristoria doesn't stand a chance."

"How can that be? Wasn't she defeated and burned?"

"Yes," Krunk said. "I was there surrounding her as she perished, but the king insisted it was she who stabbed him in his private bedchamber."

"If what you say is true, then we are already too late."

"Not if we reach the kingdom before Helenia. Not if we overthrow Jarren and his corruption and keep the soldiers on our side."

"Why wouldn't you just do that in the first place? Why come here?"

"We only just found out this information, and we don't know exactly how deep it goes. But here's what we know so far. Nort and his party faced a demon lord in the forest. This demon lord held power over the captain that Jarren handpicked to join Nort's party."

"Why were they coming here in the first place?" Lucianna asked suspiciously, reinforcing her initial question.

"They were searching for me on the late king's orders. So I could train the boy." Krunk motioned toward Alex, who was attempting to avoid the witches' notice.

The head witch, Lucianna, and her two hooded companions turned and stared at Alex, silently studying him.

"Who is the boy?" Lucianna asked curiously.

Alex wanted to shrink inside his cloak and hide in there forever, but he knew his role was important, so he held his head high and kept the fear hidden the best he could manage.

"The king's grandson and next in line for the throne, Alex Rayne," Krunk said.

Lucianna seemed to process the information; her perfect pale skin barely wrinkling as her eyebrows furrowed. She then spoke smartly. "The boy is too young to have ascended; that much is obvious. The king is dead and the realm is without a Rayne ruler. The soldiers are being corrupted by a traitorous commander. We need to assist you on getting the boy to the kingdom and convince the soldiers to follow their king, hoping the demon witch, Helenia, has not reached the kingdom first. And if we make it in time and can convince the soldiers that this boy is their king, we still must face Helenia and her demon army. Does that about sum it up?"

Krunk nodded. "Yes . . . I believe so."

"One more question," Lucianna said. "You speak as if the kingdom doesn't know their new king. Why is this? Don't the soldiers follow the king with the name Rayne? This boy now?"

Krunk sighed at the complexity of the situation. "They don't know the king is dead. It's . . . complicated. The king wanted to protect his heir, his grandson. Someone close to him who had access to his private quarters had betrayed him."

"What about the council; why not go to them?"

"The one place in the kingdom you don't take a vulnerable heir," Krunk said. "In front of a group of power-hungry warlocks."

"I see his point, though I'm not sure if it was a smart move or a dumb one to have the boy so far away from his army."

"The boy is well protected," Krunk said confidently.

Lucianna stared at Alex for a long moment as if attempting to penetrate his mind. Alex felt the air leave his lungs for the briefest of moments and had a sinking feeling wash over him. He felt his bowels tighten. Krunk had just given these witches a vital piece of information. They were all definitely in a vulnerable situation, freely stepping into a den of witches with the boy king of Tristoria, as they so pointed out, without his army.

Lucianna spoke, "Time will tell, sooner rather than later, if your words are true. We must convene for a moment," the witch said and walked back to her two fellow witches, who had remained creepily stoic and quiet behind her the entire time.

"That's not a no, yet," Nort whispered to Krunk. "But I still don't trust them. And why did you have to tell them about Alex?"

"They had to know how dire the situation is," Krunk said. "If they say no, we're likely doomed anyhow."

"Not without a fight," Nort said angrily.

"Don't worry, there'll still be one if they help us or not," Krunk whispered.

A few minutes later, the three witches returned. Lucianna said, "If we join this fight, what do we get out of this?"

Nort answered this time, his voice riddled with impatience. "For starters, you get to keep your little place in the hills here."

The witch stared at him and studied him for a long second before saying, "Ah, angel man, I was wondering how long you could keep your tongue still. You must cringe inside being so close to warlocks and witches."

She turned her attention back to Krunk. "Not good enough."

"What do you propose, then?" Krunk asked, as Nort brooded quietly.

She turned to Alex. "If we survive this and you take the throne, we, our coven, want our time back."

Alex looked to Krunk for explanation, his eyebrows furrowed with confusion.

"The king of Tristoria is not only the ruler but the timekeeper," Krunk whispered. "I'll explain later, but for now just agree."

"Sure, okay," Alex said with a nod.

"If you break this promise, we will burn down the kingdom," Lucianna warned, expressionless.

"Don't worry; there will be no broken promises," Krunk assured her.

Alex nodded with as much confidence as he could muster, reinforcing Krunk's words. He finally let out a breath and wiped the sweat beading on his brow once the witches turned around and disappeared a few steps in the opposite direction. He knew that she was not bluffing because there was a darkness in her severe eyes that told him she would die trying if he even hinted at breaking his promise.

CHAPTER 19

Timekeeper

They began their return trip back to Krunks' residence in the Faceless forest. The journey back seemed quite different to Alex, and not only because they pushed the horses to top speed, but because he still was processing his place in the inevitable coming conflict. He felt as if he was being pushed farther and farther to the front line, like a volunteer with a raised hand while everyone else slowly backed away from him in silence. He knew that was not the case and that at the very least Nort and Karissa would stay beside him; but still, there was a loneliness encompassing him he could not shake.

"That went well," Krunk told Nort and Alex as they entered the threshold of the forest.

Karissa and Vitoria traveled behind the three of them, but kept their distance from one another.

"How can you tell?" Alex asked, returning his thoughts back to the group.

"Yes," Nort said, "please tell us, Krunk, how can you tell?"

Krunk sighed at Nort's sarcasm and said, "For one, we're still alive."

Alex's eyes widened at those words.

"And second, we're still alive," Krunk emphasized. "And they will help us."

"How can we trust them?" Alex asked. "I mean, I'm grateful that they're willing to help us, but they seemed pretty selfish to me. And not to mention, you just said we were lucky to survive our interaction with them."

"See, Krunk, the boy's instincts are right on target: cautious and perceptive," Nort added.

"Yes, just like a good leader should be," Krunk agreed. "We came here for multiple reasons, Alex. A king must not only know his kingdom and what creatures inhabit it but the responsibilities that come with it. For example, though these witches prefer their seclusion, they, like every being here, owe time. And also like every being here, they make choices. The universe allows us time, but how we spend that time is up to the wielder. Our choices interlace with our time and destiny from the moment we come to be, and will continue to be so until otherwise. This place is an extension and is no different; only the timekeeper is different. Every step in our fate must have a timekeeper, one who maintains checks and balances. And that gives you the best bargaining chip there is."

Alex thought on the information for a moment and said, "So, you're saying, time is like a currency I can use?"

"Precisely," Krunk said, impressed with Alex's quick understanding.

"And that's the king's job to keep up with?" Alex asked. "So, if I'm following correctly, you're saying I will have to make those decisions about someone's time? But what if I make the wrong choice, or . . . I don't know. . . ." Alex's mind twirled with the array of possibilities of bad decisions and the many lives that it would impact.

"Yes, there are consequences for everyone, including the king," Krunk continued. "But that's why you must know the importance of your choices and must weigh each of them carefully. It's part of growing up and becoming a leader. Most have the luxury of one at a time, but it is your unfortunate task to face both at once."

"I didn't choose this," Alex said defensively, feeling the impact of responsibility beating on the back of his head like an annoying kid. "I never wanted to be a warlock or . . ."

"You did," Krunk reminded him. "You agreed to come with Nort. True, you haven't yet embraced your heritage, but that choice is still brewing and in the making."

Krunk's influx of information made Alex's brain hurt. Krunk's words were profound and intense and just plain crazy. All of this, Alex felt, was insane at the very least.

"You're just one of the many synapses in the massive brain known as existence," Krunk said.

Alex turned to Nort before his head actually exploded. "You're from the most enlightened place known to exist, right? What's he talking about?" Alex pleaded.

"I wasn't privy to the information you're seeking. I was a gatekeeper. Yes, I was slightly more enlightened than some, but obviously I was just as vulnerable as the less enlightened.

There is only one heaven, Earth, and underworld, but five levels in the middle, which means many timekeepers."

"Wait, what?" Alex asked. "Isn't there a clear answer to what exactly we all are? What about your boss? Aren't they, you know . . ."

"All powerful, all knowing," Nort said. "Yes, but I was far from that knowledge. And now even farther. Let's just say the space where we live is much larger than any of us can imagine. . . ." Nort stared off into the distance for a moment as if he hadn't pondered the information in a long, long time.

This was too much for Alex to process all at once. What Nort implied turned his belief system into a never-ending cycle of unknowns.

"I actually understand less than when I came here," Alex said exasperated. "So, where do I fit into all of this?" The ones he thought would have all the answers had many questions themselves, it seemed.

"The same place you are for the moment," Krunk said. "You're the timekeeper and king of Tristoria. And to your original question about how we can trust these witches. Well, we don't have to, because they gave you their word. And you gave them yours. If either of you is treasonous, the consequences will be much worse than not intervening in the first place."

"Wait, why would I be the one in trouble? I thought the king ruled and decided here."

"Head already swelling there, Alex?" Nort said.

"No, I didn't mean I would be like that; I just thought —"

"There were no consequences for the king?" Nort said. Krunk smirked at this.

Nort continued, "Every being is responsible for every choice they make. No matter their place amongst the stars. The chosen leaders' choices are actually more consequential."

"So, you're saying I can't just go around and give and take time free will."

"I'm not saying you cannot. I'm simply saying it would not be wise," Nort warned.

"Has there been a king who has done that?" Alex asked, curious about the consequences of doing such a thing.

"Yes, many," Nort said nodding his head.

"Here?" Alex asked, looking to them both.

Krunk nodded.

"You mean one of my ancestors?"

"King Rubus Rayne," Krunk spouted off as if it were on the tip of his tongue the entire time. "He held an untamable darkness. He took every bit of horror given within his soul and cast it on the kingdom."

"What did he do?" Alex asked with terrified interest.

"He used their vulnerabilities by adding time if they did not agree to his biddings. Most of them were for personal favors or frivolous requests intending to add as much time to their sentence as possible. He even gave time back occasionally and then ripped it back away at opportune moments. He wanted to tug on the strings of the marionette and watch the kingdom burn."

"Wait, so did they get their time back? And what happened to the king?"

"Yes, by his successor. The injustices have a way of righting themselves. By the end he had become so mad that he roamed in the Faceless Forest until the Woodblood eventually drove him to kill himself. I imagine he is somewhere deep within the levels."

Alex gulped and felt his insides twist at the thought of losing his mind to the point of self-harm.

"Now you know why I hold such a distaste for a single warlock ruler," Nort said. "We should allow no one person so much power."

"But I would never . . ."

"Who knows what darkness lies beneath once the outer layer is peeled back," Nort cautioned with a long and uncomfortable stare toward Alex.

Alex knew Nort had a point, but he refused to believe he was capable of such things, and that there was something inside that he could not control.

"The battle for rule is always a nasty business," Krunk said. "Deceit, murder, and dark whispers from every corner are only a few of the truths behind the history of any kingdom." He lifted his voice. "But, of course, there is greatness there, too. Honor and loyalty are a much more powerful potion, especially when a leader creates and drinks that concoction."

"Do you think there are grudges still ongoing today, you know, from back when King Rubus ruled?" Alex asked, wanting not to repeat the name for it felt bad in his mouth.

"Yes," Krunk said. "Why do you think the witches were so bitter toward us being on their land?"

"But how would they know it was me? A Rayne?"

"Your scent."

"What? Again?" Alex said annoyed and then instinctively smelled under his arms. "I thought just demons could sense warlocks?"

Krunk smirked. "Just kidding." He laughed out loud and Nort joined him as Alex smiled back nervously. "They don't like anyone on their land, and especially uninvited guests from the realm. Loosen up a little, will you, we got a long journey ahead."

Alex smirked and nodded. "Okay."

"I have a few things to discuss with Krunk," Nort said. "Why don't you keep Karissa company for a little while. And while you're back there I think Vitoria could use some words of encouragement."

They all looked back toward her in unison. She seemed to dwell in self-pity, and even her horse matched her doldrums, dragging its head low. The witches' treatment of her really got to her. She wasn't as big a deal as she thought she'd be.

◊ ◊ ◊

"Make your snide remarks, but it's not over," Vitoria told Alex and Karissa as they rode beside her and attempted to spark a conversation. "That, I can promise you. I will be part of that coven if it's the last thing I do."

"Why?" Alex asked. "After how they embarrassed you?"

"I don't expect you to understand; you have a lineage of kings and can just sit there and be part of it."

"Wait a minute. You think I'm enjoying this?" Alex roiled. "I know nothing about this place and yet I'm supposed to rule it and make life-altering decisions for others."

"You're accepted no matter what you do," Vitoria sneered.

"That doesn't make it better if it isn't your choice," Alex said.

"I don't understand you, Alex, honestly," Vitoria continued. "You're an instant celebrity and you think of it as a burden?"

"Maybe he isn't as shallow and self-absorbed as you are," Karissa interjected.

Vitoria held her sneer and turned to face Karissa. "Your supposed ability is a sham. You of all people should want to be part of something real."

"What sham?" Alex intervened. "Are you kidding me; she's already told me two things that have come true that she foresaw." He was hurriedly trying to think of two things to make up to tell Vitoria.

"You expect me to believe that? My father told me how these so-called seers came to be. How they used the vulnerabilities of the weak and sick to gain time. Nothing ever came to be other than the obvious."

"There are many liars and frauds out there, but that doesn't mean the power or ability doesn't exist," Karissa said calmly.

"Why don't we ask Nort, then?" Alex offered. "I'm sure he can give some insight into her powers."

Vitoria smirked and turned toward Karissa. "Okay, miss seer, how about you tell me my future? Will I survive this coming conflict?"

Karissa said nothing in response, but Alex could see the anger rising in her cheeks. Karissa had lamented to him she really couldn't see much with this girl. That most people had an aura about them, a faint color that surrounded them, but Vitoria had nothing but a vague blur now and then. From what Alex had gathered about Karissa, it didn't seem in her nature to make up a lie about a horrible death, as tempting as it may have been to say so to Vitoria.

"See," Vitoria said and then sighed heavily. "What does it matter, anyway; there's so much doubt in her eyes and in her words that she obviously doesn't believe it herself."

Karissa deflated and Alex saw the defeat on her face. She hadn't fully embraced her ability, but that didn't mean it wasn't there. Nort knew it was there and had agreed to help her. He promised her they would find someone who could break open her abilities and teach her the craft. He offered his belief in her and support, and that was more than she had had in her life so far, according to her.

"Leave her alone, will you," Alex said. "Can you cast an actual spell? I haven't seen you do anything but criticize others."

Vitoria smiled deviously and pulled a small sticklike object from the inside of her cloak.

"What is that?" Alex asked. "Is that a wand?"

"Yes, my dad felt it was more ladylike to carry a wand rather than a bulky scepter."

She pointed the wand toward a nearby tree and whispered something Alex could not hear. A moment later, a soft, dark purple light shot from the tip of the wand and pierced the tree, removing a considerable-sized limb.

Alex was both amazed and a little frightened at this ability. *How could she know so much and be so young?* he wondered. He had yet to even gain a wand, or scepter, or much of anything other than his grandfather's sword. He felt an overwhelming excitement inside at the possibility of gaining such a power. But she was the same age as he was. How did she have powers already?

"Vitoria!" Krunk yelled from the front of their group. "What have I told you about using your wand to show off? You are not of age yet! One more time and I will take your wand until you are seventeen, so help me!"

Vitoria quickly placed the wand securely inside her robe. "Sorry, father," she yelled ahead with a satisfied look on her face.

"Okay, that was cool," Alex admitted.

Karissa shook her head at this, but said nothing. She sped up her horse to where Krunk and Nort were, not wanting to be part of Vitoria's show any longer.

"Jealousy is something we have to deal with, unfortunately," Vitoria told Alex as she watched Karissa gallop away.

"So, what am I supposed to use?" Alex asked. "Will I get a wand or something?"

"Since your friend is no longer listening, we can talk. We, my father and I, just don't think seers are real and we don't really associate with their kind."

Alex ignored her comment about Karissa and her ability only because he wanted some insight that Vitoria could give him. He knew she was arrogant and crude, but she was his age and was way ahead of him in using magic in this place.

She continued. "You come from a powerful family, Alex. I won't lie; I'm a little jealous myself, but that doesn't mean I like you or anything."

Alex furrowed his eyebrows at this and shook his head, agreeing with her. He admitted that she was attractive on the surface, but that was as far as it went.

"You are a warlock and I'm a witch. You gain some of your power from demons, whereas I gain mine from nature, meaning the elements."

"I'm not really looking forward to dealing with demons, to be honest," Alex said. "I've had a run-in with a few since arriving here and it wasn't pleasant."

"I don't envy you there, but I will say there is much power to unearth if balanced correctly between a demon and his master. I've seen my dad defeat hordes of them by hardly lifting a finger. But, of course, he is a very advanced warlock."

"Yeah, he was impressive for sure when he saved us from those huge spiders. One minute they were there and then the next thing I see is a bright light and then, poof, they were gone." Alex beamed inside at the thought of performing such a powerful act.

"Your family's spell book will be your best friend. There are so many perfected spells in there I've heard about that there's hardly anything you can't accomplish with it. I'm pretty sure my dad has tried to get a peek at it before." Alex looked at her curiously. "Not maliciously," she assured him on seeing his concern.

Alex sighed. "Yeah, that's sort of a problem. It's . . . kind of missing. After that demon witch stabbed my grandfather, she stole the book."

"That's not good," Vitoria said with alarm on her face. "Do you know what someone could do with that spell book if they knew how to use it!?"

"Yeah, I can guess and it isn't good."

"Destroy or even conquer this world and then even the next one. There's no telling what that book actually holds inside."

"That's why we're here; why we sought out your father."

Vitoria stared off into the distance and said in a dark, quiet tone, "I'd love to see what's in that book myself."

Alex shook off the oddness of her tone and said, "Wait, doesn't your dad have his own spell book? You know, one passed down from your family?"

Victoria snapped out of her trance. "Yeah, of course he does. He's shown it to me a few times, removing it from its hidden, secure spot. And believe me, he's with me the entire time, not daring to allow it out of his sight. But, your family's book, well, it's legendary. No one has been privy to see that book unless they're part of the lineage. I doubt even your friend Nort has seen it."

"Why would he want to; he's not a warlock or witch."

"It's power, Alex. It controls Tristoria. Whoever controls the middle holds the key."

"The key to what?"

"Everything." She stopped her horse and motioned for Alex to do the same. She glanced ahead to make sure no one was watching them. She then whispered, "My dad told me once that if the Raynes ever figured out their true powers, they could end everything."

Alex almost retched, feeling a terrible emptiness deep inside on hearing this news.

"What does that mean?" Alex asked as if he had not been part of the conversation. "You're saying my grandfather didn't know his own power limits?"

Vitoria shook her head. "And they say I'm not ready. You have a lot to learn about yourself and your family, Alex."

"Yeah, I get it, I'm clueless, so teach me something. Anything. Come on, I need to be able to defend myself in battle, at the very least. Nort showed me a few moves with the sword, but not anything to do with magic."

Vitoria smirked and then smiled deviously again. "Okay. First you need an outlet."

"An outlet?"

"A scepter or wand. You know, something to expel the power; a conduit."

"All I have is my grandfather's sword at the moment. Will that work?"

"I doubt it. My father enchanted my wand. He calls it my trainer wand. As you know, we cannot control our powers until we become of age. But, who knows, maybe your grandfather placed some enchantment on it you can use to control the chaos of energy inside you." She shrugged. "Why not? Pull the sword out and try it."

He eagerly pulled his grandfather's sword from its sheath and held it in the air awkwardly.

She smirked and shook her head, giving him instructions. "Now hold it out in front of you like you mean it and point it toward that tree ahead of you."

He mimicked her instructions, holding the sword firmly with more confidence.

"Think of what you want to happen. For example, the bolt of energy projecting forward, as I did."

Alex concentrated and pictured a bolt of energy exiting the sword's point, but nothing happened. He attempted it again, this time straining his mind. He could feel the veins in his forehead ready to burst.

"Nothing's happening," Alex said through exasperated deep breaths.

"Keep going."

Alex's face was nearly purple from holding his breath.

"Breathe; exhale as you feel the bolt exit the tip."

He attempted once again, this time concentrating on his breathing first, then the bolt. He closed his eyes to help with the rhythm of his breathing and his thoughts. He whispered angrily to himself, *"Come on, come on!"* He held one eye opened. Nothing happened immediately, but just as he was lowering the sword he heard the tree he had been concentrating on begin to creek loudly. It then detached from its roots and began to topple over. They got out of the way just in time as it smashed to the ground next to them.

"Where was the bolt?" Alex asked as his breathing increased with stunned excitement.

"Good question," Vitoria said curiously. "Try it again."

Alex pointed his sword, but this time to a tree a little farther away.

"Enough!" Krunk said from behind them. "Hand me your wand, Vitoria. I warned you."

Alex wondered how the rest of the group ended up behind them. Had he and Vitoria been there for that long, oblivious to their surroundings?

"Father, that wasn't me," Vitoria said, motioning toward Alex.

Krunk frowned. "He doesn't possess an outlet yet. Hand it over, now."

"It was me," Alex admitted. "I mean, I think it was. I had my eyes closed and focused on the tree and the next thing I know it fell over."

Krunk looked at his daughter with great suspicion. "If he has no outlet, how can that be? Hmmm, Vitoria, how?"

"He used his grandfather's sword. I don't know. I guess it allowed him to use it."

"Not likely," Krunk said. "That sword's bound to his grandfather and no one else. A Rayne's sword must be inserted in the tree once another Rayne rises to power. We all know that."

"What may have happened," Nort offered, "is Alex could somehow harness some unbridled power left behind by his grandfather."

Krunk eyed his daughter and Alex suspiciously. Finally, he sighed. "I suppose. Just please, the both of you, refrain from any more outbursts. Understood? We need not bring any unnecessary attention to us at the moment."

Alex nodded vigorously, while Vitoria calmly told her father, "Okay."

Alex wondered why Nort stared at him for a few lingering seconds while wearing a disconcerting glare. It was the same look his dad gave him when he didn't quite believe Alex. There was definitely something that he was missing with this newfound power that he unknowingly possessed just moments ago. He wasn't supposed to have controllable powers until he ascended. Sure, Vitoria had used her power through an enchanted wand, but she only knocked down a tiny limb. He had uprooted an entire tree.

CHAPTER 20

The Courier

A lex pondered why he could suddenly produce magic with no formal training. Nort had suggested it had something to do with his grandfather's sword, but did that make sense? Possibly, considering Alex knew very little about magic. There was definitely something missing, but he could not place it. He was no closer to figuring out anything when Krunk halted the group with a raised hand just before reaching the tree where the illusion shrouded his home.

"What is it?" Nort whispered from behind Krunk.

Krunk pointed his scepter forward and a narrow bright yellow light beamed ahead and lit the area brilliantly. "Reveal your identity!" Krunk warned. "And quickly before I change my mind and turn this beam of light into a substance capable of disintegration."

"I'm a courier with a message from the king," a man's voice quickly called out from the direction of the light.

"You must be mistaken; the king is with us," Krunk said. "I'm sure he sent no messages ahead. Are you alone?" Krunk moved the light around and searched the area.

"Yes," the man said.

The group had all gathered in close behind Krunk to get a better look at this courier. The man was wearing the Rayne family crest on his armor, but there was a marking across it: a crudely hand-painted pentagram in blood red.

"Hands where I can see them," Krunk warned. "Are you armed?"

"Only my sword, and it's securely sheathed," the courier answered quickly.

"Fine, you may come closer with your business," Krunk said, keeping his beam of light on the man just low enough so as not to blind him.

The courier rode toward Alex.

"That's far enough," Krunk warned.

He heeded Krunk's warning and stopped well in front of Alex.

"You are Alex Rayne, yes?" the courier said sharply.

Alex nodded carefully, looking to Nort and then to Krunk, who both nodded back to him assuredly.

"The king of Tristoria has asked that I personally deliver this to you."

Alex blurted, "My grandfather's alive? But how —"

"Don't be absurd, boy," the courier said. "He's quite dead and —"

"That's your king you're speaking to!" Krunk berated. "Choose your next words carefully." Krunk raised his scepter and pressed the tip firmly against the courier's neck. The bright light on the tip of the scepter turned a shade darker.

Nort outstretched his arm toward Krunk and said, "Whoa, just a second, let's hear what he has to say."

"Thank you," the courier said with a smug nod.

Nort didn't nod back, but stared hard into the man's eyes: a piercing stare that would scare any mortal man to the hills.

The courier nervously cleared his throat. "Yes, uh, King Jarren is looking forward to your surrender and has offered you and your friends passage home without harm. You only have to renounce your lineage and leave."

Krunk let out a hearty laugh that rang through the quiet, dark forest, causing the courier to shuffle uncomfortably in his saddle and his horse to whinny.

"And if I don't?" Alex asked.

"I'm afraid the king will have no choice but to erase any remaining Raynes from existence."

"I told you —" Krunk started through clenched teeth.

"Please, Krunk," Nort pleaded, and then calmly said, "We need more information." He slowly pushed Krunk's scepter down from the man's throat.

"He's threatening the king!" Krunk reiterated.

"Jarren is threatening the king," Nort said, staring back into Krunk's eyes with another plead to wait until the moment was right.

Alex's heart sank swiftly when he thought of his dad and sister. Sure, take Margie but leave his dad and sister alone. Would that be a bargain Jarren would consider?

Definitely not, seeing how far he had already gone to establish power.

"What's stopping us from obliterating you and taking this up with Jarren directly?" Krunk said.

"If I do not return with an answer in one day's time, King Jarren will assume the answer is no and will kill the boy's sister first and then his father . . . once the boy arrives to witness it firsthand."

"No! Wait," Alex pleaded.

"Alex, they don't have your sister or your dad. He's bluffing to save his own skin," Krunk said.

"I assure you, the king does not bluff, sir," the courier said, his words not as confident as before.

"Is it so easy to betray your king for another?" Nort said. "What about the other soldiers? Have they switched loyalty," Nort snapped his fingers, "just like that?" The snapping was loud, like a small firecracker going off, causing the courier to flinch.

The courier only stared back at Nort with no answer.

"If I surrender," Alex started, the words tasting bitter as he said them, "what will happen to Tristoria?"

"Jarren will rule Tristoria and the demons will be slaves to all of man. Helenia has agreed to leave us be. She will continue her ultimate path of conquering heaven. You and your family will return home unharmed."

"You idiot," Nort said to the courier. "Do you really think the ruler of the underworld will allow his followers to be slaves to man? Jarren really has all of you deluded. We'll all be slaves if Jarren lets this Helenia have her way. Him included. See reason, man."

"You, angel man, are a testament to our path. You have fallen, meaning heaven can and will fall."

Nort shook his head and said, "Wait, what!? What do you mean *our path?*" Nort stared at the pentagram painted on the courier's armor and then back up at him. "Why would you want such a thing? Mankind should never want such a wish. I assure you, the place below is much, much worse than here. And that's saying something, in my opinion. Once they conquer heaven, they will return here. Demons will never let mankind rule Tristoria, trust me."

"What is your answer?" the courier pressed Alex, attempting to ignore Nort's last words as he shuffled around in the saddle. "King Jarren is eager to begin his reign."

"You mean his enslavement," Karissa turned to Alex, not able to hold her words back any longer. "Alex, you really can't be considering this, can you?! They may not kill you and your family right away, but eventually Helenia will reach earth. As long as a Rayne lives, she can never really rule anywhere."

"Well said," Krunk agreed. "If they knew where we were, why not defeat us here? Oh, wait, that's right, they've already attempted that once."

The courier sighed. "Yes, a bit of a mix-up of orders. Too many hands in the pot, which is why I have come alone with the offer. The soldiers must witness a Rayne renounce the throne."

"How honorable," Krunk said, disgusted. "By the way, how did you find us?"

"The soldiers you foolishly let go led me here. I figured a warlock would hold an illusion over his home, but I just couldn't pinpoint the location exactly. Looks like I guessed the vicinity correctly."

Nort sighed and silently cursed himself for letting them go.

The courier continued. "And we know about their mission to speak directly to the council and to avoid King Jarren. Had they reached the council first, they would have seen that they had been removed from their stations and detained. In King Jarren's kingdom there will be no place for warlocks or witches."

Krunk clenched his scepter tighter, causing the wood to splinter. "Good thing we prefer solitude," Krunk said through gritted teeth.

"Helenia would like to meet with you, Krunk. She apparently has some unfinished business with you."

"Looking forward to it," Krunk said, revealing a sinister smile.

"What's it going to be?" the courier said to Alex as sternly as he could manage.

Alex noticed that the initial patience in his voice was wearing thin. "I need a moment to discuss things with my council," Alex said, tossing the word *council* back in the courier's face.

The courier sighed with an annoyed look on his face, but motioned that it was okay after seeing Krunk's scepter change another shade darker.

They moved out of hearing distance and Alex briefed them with his initial plan. They nodded in unison, all in agreement.

"So how do we do this?" Alex asked the courier when they returned a few moments later.

"You have one day's time to return to the castle. You will meet with King Jarren; he will have instructions for you. The rest of your party will be escorted to the viewing section where you can watch others be judged and punished. Once you have renounced your lineage, you and your family will go back home and we will judge the rest of your party."

"You said we would not be harmed," Vitoria said.

"Oh, did I? I apologize. Your safety is not up to me. We will banish Alex and his family from this place and the new council appointed by King Jarren will judge you."

"Are you finished talking?" Alex asked. "If you would have given me a moment, I would have finished my question. I meant how would you prefer to be bound, until we can judge you for treason."

"Wha —"

Before the man could even think about reaching for his sword or motion for his horse to move, he was suddenly sitting backward on his horse with his hands tied snuggly behind his back and a gag in his mouth.

"How refreshing," Krunk said. The courier squealed as the ropes binding his hands tightened each time he struggled.

Alex couldn't believe he had risked the lives of his dad and sister if this courier was being honest about them being captured. *It was the right choice*, he reiterated to himself. *It's time for action, not for following a traitor and giving up.*

"Okay, how long did he say we had, one day?" Alex said.

Krunk and Nort both nodded.

"So, what's the plan now that the smug little errand boy is no longer in our way," Vitoria asked.

"Well, let's discuss what we know so far," Nort said. "Jarren has sided with Helenia and her forces. His army has no solidarity until Alex renounces his lineage."

"Which he will never do," Karissa interjected sternly while glaring over at Alex.

Alex agreed with a vigorous nod, not wanting to upset her further after her interaction with Vitoria.

"Right," Nort said, "and they supposedly have Alex's sister and dad hostage. They also may have the spell book, which according to Krunk will be next to impossible for them to use." He glanced at Krunk, unimpressed. "We don't have numbers of the demons here, but honestly I don't think they are expecting a battle from our little group. Helenia came here for a war, revenge most likely, but found a different approach by using Jarren."

"Mark my words," Krunk warned. "How she's alive I do not understand, but she will destroy everything once she gets what she came for. Her goal, as it will always be, is to overthrow the king and turn Tristoria and the rest of the levels into another arm of hell and rule it. She is a direct spawn of Satan and believes that this is her world to conquer and rule. Jarren is a temporary pawn, and no more."

"How did you defeat her last time?" Alex asked.

"A coven of very advanced warlocks. But we have yet another problem: we need the council if we are to defeat her."

"What about the coven of Hal?" Vitoria interjected. "Don't forget how powerful they are."

"I haven't forgotten," Krunk said. "They will be a great ally; that is, if they can put their differences aside for long enough."

"Okay, so we need intelligence on a few things before we proceed," Nort said. "We need to know about Alex's family, if they're safe or held hostage. Hopefully Jayda will be at my village when we arrive and can offer some insight as to the kingdom itself and how many of the soldiers are involved, but we can't wait on Alex's family. One day's time is all we have, according to the courier." He turned to Alex. "Alex, we must get you back home. Once you know answers, you will return to my village where we will convene on everything we have learned." He lowered his voice, "If things turn out as this courier has explained we have some difficult decisions ahead of us."

Alex nodded and then realized what Nort meant. "Wait, you're not going with me?"

Nort turned to Krunk.

"It appears I'll be heading home with you," Krunk said to Alex. "Nort has to prepare his village for war, and Karissa and Vitoria cannot leave. There's only one problem: getting us there."

"You can't portal us there?" Alex asked hopefully.

"Only a Rayne can portal from Tristoria to Earth, and you haven't ascended yet. And even if you had, the process to learn is lengthy; mapping and coordinates and a bunch of other stuff you will eventually study."

"Bessie," Nort offered.

"Huh?" Krunk asked confused.

"You can take my Bessie," Nort said.

"There has to be another way," Alex pleaded, remembering how long it took his stomach to return to normal the last time he rode Bessie.

"Is this one of your contraptions, Nort?" Krunk asked.

"A flying machine, yes."

"How crude," Krunk said disappointed. "But I suppose it will have to do as long as it can get us there quickly enough."

"We can't all have fancy portals to slip in and out of," Nort sneered, and then switched to a wide grin. "Anyway, speed will not be a problem."

Alex gulped at the words, knowing they were all too true.

CHAPTER 21

Home Again

Nort gave Krunk and Alex a crash course on the operations of Bessie, including the backup safety glider. Alex reminded Nort, pointedly, about having to use the lever on his descent here and Nort responded, "which is the reason it is there in the first place; unforeseen circumstances."

After relaying good lucks and goodbyes, Krunk stood on Bessie's platform with the overhead propellers spinning while Alex sat close by mentally preparing himself. Though he had never been through a portal, he figured it had to be smoother than this flying contraption.

Alex gave in and sighed, stepping onto the platform. There was no other choice at the moment. He reluctantly grabbed ahold of the handles and squeezed them tightly.

"Okay," Krunk said, "where's the emergency lever, again? And where is the Go button?"

"Really?" Alex shook his head. "This can't be happening."

"Relax, I was only kidding," Krunk said, patting Alex on the back with a heavy hand.

"Great timing," Alex said sarcastically.

"Precisely the right time, I agree."

Alex looked at Karissa with a pleading expression and then cupped his hands and mouthed, "Pray for me, please."

She smiled nervously and nodded. Alex then glanced over at Vitoria. She waved and nodded and he shyly waved back. Karissa shook her head and glared toward her, but said nothing. Before he could think any more on the matter, they were mere dots on the ground and he was once again holding on for his life with everything he had.

He was thankful when he heard the loud boom a few minutes later, revealing they were back on Earth. The rain clouds surrounding them appeared huge and the wind was still, and then he remembered that once they were in the atmosphere of Earth, they were the size of a raindrop; actually, smaller and inside of a protective raindrop. "It's automatic," he had overheard Nort telling Krunk, "the machine converts to raindrop mode on entering the atmosphere."

"This is all very odd," Krunk said. "I have never shrunk to the size of a pea, nor have I desired to. Nort is a strange fellow."

"Wait, so this isn't normal for you guys when you travel here?" Alex asked dubiously.

"Definitely not. We have an array of obscurities and disguises. Some may be a little unorthodox, but nothing like this. It's okay to be seen just as long as your true identity is not. Nort is an eccentric tinker and obviously likes to push the limits with his inventions. I have been witness to some great inventions of his in the past and also some not-so-great, but I'm not sure where I'd rank this one and this shrinking business."

"It's kinda cool, but, yeah, strange," Alex said, "that is, as long as you don't have to ride it for a long time." Now that he actually knew what would happen this time, he wasn't quite as nauseous. "I'm still confused on who can and can't travel to Earth or leave Tristoria."

"Only those on orders from the king can leave Tristoria. Except those born in Tristoria, such as your friend Karissa and my daughter; they can never leave. Traveling here is by portal only and a Rayne must be the one that opens it. The king approved Nort's invention of Bessie, likely because of Nort being his most trusted mercenary."

"But I heard someone say a portal may have been left open somewhere, and that's how the demons got here."

"Yes, portals can be open to lower levels, but not upper ones. They're supposed to be regulated, though it's difficult to monitor all of them. If one is left open, the lazy spell caster who failed to close it will be punished accordingly."

"Okay, that makes much more sense now, though I still don't understand why those born there can never leave."

"That's a difficult one to answer, Alex. My daughter is one reason I have remained in Trisoria. . . ." he took a deep breath. "Anyway, once we clear the clouds, you will have to guide me to your house. Nort put in the coordinates before we left, but that only gets us close. I asked him not to get too close until we figured out what was truly going on."

"Sure," Alex said. He did not understand completely yet how things worked and imagined he never truly would, but he saw the loyalty in Krunk's eyes toward his daughter and the pain that came along with it.

Krunk glanced down at a small screen on his handles and said, "We have a few minutes yet. Is there anything I should know about your stepmom?"

"Other than she's horrible to be around, not really."

"That's strange, I mean, considering how beautiful and enchanting your mother was."

"You knew my mom? How?"

"When a Rayne marries, the spouse has to understand the implications of the union they are forming and the responsibilities that come with it."

"Huh?"

"Being queen to Tristoria. Your dad was next in line, before he gave it up."

"My mom went to Tristoria?"

"Yes, and she met with the council."

"What about Margie? Did she have to go before the council?"

"No, your dad had already renounced his lineage and his right to the throne. He made that decision long ago, a few years after bringing your mom here."

"Why would he do that?"

"That, you must ask him."

Alex nodded and sincerely hoped that he would get the chance. "So, Margie never met the council."

"No."

"I guess that's a good thing. If they had met her, they would definitely have kicked her and my dad to the curb. Probably never allowing him there again."

"She must be something terrible to detest her that much," Krunk said in a manner that suggested Alex might have been exaggerating.

"She completely manipulated my dad," Alex nearly yelled and then lowered his voice on seeing Krunk's eyebrows rise. "He's nothing like he was when he was with my mom. You said it yourself that she was enchanting. He was so different and lively with her and now he's dull and unfair and . . ." Alex sighed angrily and deflated. "He used to joke around with me, but now there's nothing. Like he's an empty suit."

"That certainly doesn't sound like Henry. Your parents couldn't be apart for longer than a few minutes even if they had tried. When your mother faced the council, your father insisted that he be by her side. The council agreed reluctantly to allow them to marry, but even they could see the love between them. That's what they were looking for, you know."

"What?"

"Love. And solidarity. I mean, sure, strength and intelligence and understanding and accepting of things to come, but there is no greater loyalty than honest love."

Alex longed for that time and to be there beside his parents. The memory wasn't that long ago, but heartache and deceit clouded it.

"So, even though my dad didn't pass his last test my mom still had to go before the council?"

"Yes, because there was always a chance for redemption. He hadn't renounced the throne at that time. He was still unsure of himself."

"I still don't understand how my dad could do that without telling me anything. It doesn't make sense."

"I agree, but sometimes we lose our way and by the time we find the door back in, it is closed and sealed shut."

Alex didn't want to believe his dad was lost for good and the door sealed shut forever. As tenuous as it was, he still held hope for his dad.

"Where do you think my mom went?"

Krunk was surprised by the question, pausing before answering. "You knew her better than I. What do you think?"

Alex felt it in his heart that she was somewhere better than Tristoria, somewhere away from war and suffering and demons.

On seeing Alex struggle for an answer, Krunk said, "I definitely think she is in the heavens."

Alex beamed, hoping with everything he had that it was true. In his heart he knew so, but things were also way more complicated than he could have ever imagined.

"I still don't really understand the level thing," Alex said.

"I know," Krunk said, "but a Rayne must know the process. Once this battle is over, I will make sure you learn the path of things."

"Thank you," Alex said, and continued to beam inwardly at the thought of his mom in the heavens. The warm thought of her watching over him from above briefly entered his mind. "So, my mom knew about everything, right? Then why wouldn't she tell me before she died."

"She knew the rules, all too well, having gone through it herself when she was younger. The time had to be right."

"Wait, what, how? Now I'm really confused."

"You don't know?"

"Know what?"

"Your mom was a witch. A demon hunter to be more precise."

Alex couldn't believe what he was hearing. His sweet, caring, eighties-loving mom was a witch and demon hunter.

"How does that work with, you know, being married to a warlock?"

"That may have been one reason your dad never came back to retake the last test. She would have wanted to kill all demons, useful or not, and your dad needed certain demons for his power."

"I guess, then, why marry in the first place if their professions would clash?"

"Love is a powerful thing, Alex. I know you are young, but one day you'll see that love sometimes obscures the logical."

Alex thought on the information, unsure of what to make of everything. His parents were both magic users, and so was he supposedly.

"Okay, we should be close," Krunk said seeing the alert on the small screen.

They exited the blanket of heavy clouds and the tiny faint lights of his neighborhood were visible.

"Over there," Alex said, pointing. "The house with the gray truck in the driveway."

"Okay, now let's see if I can land this thing without crashing," Krunk said with a wink. But Alex wasn't paying attention, for he was too busy being nervous, instantly flashing back to his and Nort's rough landings.

"That looks good, that empty lot there," Krunk continued. "Now, all I have to do is point this arrow on the screen to that location."

Alex craned his neck over at the small screen above his handles. The screen was displaying the ground beneath them and Krunk was moving his finger along the screen, guiding an arrow to the lot. He then pressed the Accept button on the screen, and a moment later they were safely on the ground in Alex's yard and back to their normal size.

"You mean this thing had autopilot the entire time?" Alex asked.

"Of course," Krunk said, nodding his head.

Alex cursed Nort silently, but hardly hid his anger with his expressions.

"He manually flew this thing, didn't he?" Krunk asked knowingly.

"Yes, and I nearly vomited the entire trip."

Krunk smiled and shook his head. "Let's see what we're dealing with here."

Alex nodded, thankful that he would not have to deal with nausea on the return trip thanks to the autopilot feature.

"Okay, it's around nine o'clock in the evening," Krunk noted, looking at a small digital clock on the screen. "The place seems quiet. Is this normal? Anything look out of the ordinary?"

Alex glanced around. "No, this is pretty normal for this time on a weeknight." *Wait,* he thought to himself. *What day is it? How long have I been gone?*

"Do you have any animals we need to know of?" Krunk asked before opening the fence gate.

"My dad's small dog, Rounder. But he'll be inside. Once he sees me, he won't bark."

"If Jarren's henchmen didn't already kill him," Krunk said.

Alex cringed at the thought.

There was a light on in the kitchen that Alex could see from the backyard.

"Where would your dad normally be at this time of the evening?"

"Likely in his chair in the living room, falling asleep."

"Where's the living room window?"

"Around the corner."

As they passed the kitchen window, Alex sneaked a peek inside. The kitchen was empty, but he noticed some dirty dishes in the sink. They could have been there for a while, but they could also be recent. It was hard to tell from his vantage point.

"If he is here, what are we going to do?" Alex whispered, just realizing that they had not discussed that contingency.

"We get him to safety."

"Right," Alex said, shaking his head. "Ouch, what is that?"

"What?" Krunk asked.

Alex's eyes widened when he looked down by his side. "It's burning my —. Krunk, my grandfather's sword is vibrating!"

◇ ◇ ◇

"There are demons about the place. Stay close," Krunk warned. "Let's hope we're not too late."

Alex gulped and a deep sadness reached his gut at the thought of his dad and little sister imprisoned, or worse, killed by demons.

"Is there a secret entrance so we can get a closer look?" Krunk asked, and nudged Alex when he didn't get an immediate answer.

"Sorry, no, there's not," Alex said, snapping back from the thoughts of his family. "But I snuck out a few times when I felt like I was being punished unfairly. My bedroom window doesn't have a screen and the lock doesn't latch securely."

Krunk wore a fatherly expression of disapproval, but let it fade quickly. "Very good. Let's go then; lead the way."

"It's just around the corner here," Alex said, leading him around the dark corner of the house. "This is it."

"The lights are off, good. But we need to be sure no one's in there," Krunk whispered.

They listened for just a moment and heard no voices or sounds. Alex peeked through the tiny holes in the blinds just to be sure and then bent down to begin shimmying open the window. Suddenly it moved upward without him touching it, making Alex flinch. He was so surprised by what he was seeing that he nearly fell over, but he caught himself on Krunk's staff.

Alex shook his head and said through a deep sigh, "You could have warned me first." He leaned back toward the now open window. "I don't want to go first, but I will. You know, since it's dark and I know my way around."

"After you," Krunk said with an outstretched hand.

Krunk followed Alex through the window, and once inside swept his scepter around the room, casting a light just dim enough to see outlines of objects.

Alex nearly lost his balance when he tripped over one of his own shoes, but caught himself just before knocking his computer monitor to the floor. He took a deep breath and sighed while bracing the monitor on the desk. "Sorry," he whispered.

Krunk smirked and said, "It appears empty, but let's crack the door and listen for a moment before we proceed."

While Alex waited by the door, listening for sounds and watching for movement, Krunk seemed infatuated with his bookshelf. He amplified the light of his scepter as he perused the books. He grabbed one from the shelf and began flipping through it before Alex could object.

"Hey, what are you doing?" Alex whispered loudly from the door. "That's personal. And I thought we were in a hurry."

"We are. So, hush," Krunk said and finished the passage he was reading and then placed the book back on the shelf.

"I had one myself, a journal, when my fevers first began. It's normal, you know."

"Thanks," Alex said, slightly irritated. He knew it was just his nerves and not Krunk's intrusion into his journal. Besides, not that long ago he would have given anything for insight into his fevers and odd visions. He got up from his position by the door and grabbed his journal from the shelf.

"Yes, it's unfortunate your dad never guided you once the symptoms began," Krunk said.

Alex shoved the book under his grandfather's robe and into the back pocket of his jeans.

"Good idea, bring it with us," Krunk said. "We'll go over it together once all of this is over."

Alex nodded. "Sorry, I'm just on edge."

"Understood. How's the hallway, anything?" Krunk said returning them to their mission.

"I can hear the television in the living room," Alex said, now back in position by the door.

"How many rooms are to the left?"

"Two, and the last room, my dad's, is in the house's front past the living room."

"Okay, let's clear these back two rooms and make our way there last," Krunk said.

"My sister's room first; it's across the hall. If she's here, she should be asleep."

Krunk nodded, and they moved across the hall to his sister's room. The door creaked open, but Krunk silenced it quickly.

"She's here and looks okay," Alex said in whispered excitement. "She's sleeping."

Krunk nodded and motioned to move to the last rooms next to where they were.

"I don't want to leave her," Alex pleaded.

Krunk nodded again and whispered, "Okay." He then mouthed that he would be right back. He returned a few seconds later and cracked the door behind him and whispered, "There appears to be two overweight boys snoring loudly."

"Margie's two kids."

"There's something amiss about those two," Krunk said.

"Tell me about it. Try living with them."

"I'll be right back; I need to check on your father," Krunk said. "Keep guarding the door. My scepter light shining under the door will let you know it's me."

Alex watched the door once again without blinking. He edged open the door on seeing the blue glow a few seconds later. "Your father seems unharmed in his chair; his dog is in his lap asleep. Now, what about his wife?"

"Who cares, the courier was lying. Let's get back and tell Nort."

"Not so fast," Krunk said, turning his attention back toward the living room. "Something's not right in this house; I can feel it. And your sword, remember." Krunk motioned his head toward the sword against Alex's waist.

He was so relieved that his sister and dad were okay that he had forgotten about his sword vibrating softly in its sheath.

"What if it's wrong, or it's malfunctioning or something," Alex said, denying that there were demons present.

"Do you want to take that chance with your family?"

"No, you're right," Alex said, shaking his head. "So, what do we do?"

"Guard this door, and no matter what you hear, let nothing inside. Not even me. You'll know when it's safe."

"Wait —"

Krunk was already making his way toward the living room, shutting the door softly behind him. Alex sat with his back snugly against the door and pulled his grandfather's sword from its sheath and sat it in his lap. The warm vibration was oddly calming despite what it represented. Maybe that was part of the intention of the spell, a calming sensation in a time of strife and angst.

After several minutes of quiet and anxious anticipation, Alex finally heard something. It was Rounder, his dad's dog, growling; he must have spotted Krunk.

"Who's there?" he heard his dad's muffled voice say. Next, he heard Rounder barking viciously.

There was a loud thump, like something or someone, hitting the wall. And then came Margie's unmistakable shrill voice.

"Boys, it's time! Take the child!"

It took Alex a moment to register what she had said as he continued to maintain his stance behind the door. He heard multiple crashes and curses, and then words he couldn't make out, a language he had never heard before. His attention turned to his sister when he heard her stirring in her bed. Whatever was happening out there his sister was his top priority. They may have to run for it and she needed to be ready.

"Sylvia," he whispered as he crawled over to her on his knees. He shook her lightly on her shoulders. "Wake up; it's me, Alex."

She opened her eyes and smiled. "Alex, you're —" he covered her mouth with one hand and then placed one finger of his other hand over his own lips. "Shhh, just listen. I need you to come with me when I tell you it's time. We may have to run, okay? And don't be afraid if I cover your face."

She nodded and tightly hugged her very frayed brown teddy bear that she had been sleeping with. She then hugged Alex around the neck and he hugged her back just as tightly.

"I need you to grab your jacket and put it on," Alex said as she finally released her embrace.

"Where are we going? I can't leave without Dad," Sylvia pleaded as she slid her arms into the only jacket readily available, which was her rain jacket.

"Dad's going with us, I promise. But, shhh, I need you to be as quiet as you can for me now."

The door handle began to rattle, and Alex pushed Sylvia safely behind him. He held his grandfather's sword tightly in his right hand and could feel the vibrating getting more intense.

"Oh Sylvia, Oh Sylvia, come out and play," the voices sang from the other side of the door. "Oh Sylvia, there's no time to pray."

It was Margie's two sons, both singing creepily through the door. This was strange, even for them.

"We know you're in there," they continued to sing. "Oh Sylvia, Oh Sylvia, come out and play. Oh Sylvia, there's no time to pray." The door handle jiggled more and more violently with each word.

Alex raced to the window and tore down the curtains. With shaky hands he released the latch and raised the window halfway up. It was a good four feet off the ground, but he could still get Sylvia out fast if he had to.

He pointed his sword toward the door, just as he had at that tree in the Faceless Forest. Could he do it again? Could he do it to a person? If he had to, and if there were no other choice to protect his sister and himself, he thought he probably could. He really hoped that it did not come down to that, though.

"Krunk, where the hell are you," he mumbled to himself.

"Why are they talking like that?" Sylvia cried and whimpered softly. He could feel her shaking behind him as she tugged on his shirt.

"I don't know," Alex said and turned to face her. She had tears sliding along both cheeks. He wiped them away gently with his thumb. "I won't let anything happen to you; I promise. Just be as quiet as you can for me for one minute longer, okay?"

Through more whimpers, she shook her head in understanding.

The door was still rattling, but thankfully the boys had stopped singing. Alex was becoming just as freaked out as his sister, and even more so when he heard a strange scratching sound, like a rake being dragged along the door. The door began cracking and splintering, and then bulging, until it was mere moments from blowing apart. He shielded his face with one hand while the other held the sword shakily in front of him.

The creaking suddenly stopped and a few seconds later came two loud thumps as if something heavy had hit the floor close by the door.

"Alex, open the door, please," Krunk's voice said. "The glow, remember. Look under the door."

Alex saw the glow at the base of the door, but also noticed that his sword was still vibrating strongly. "How do I know it's you?" Alex said in a shaky voice.

"Nort wants Bessie back in one piece."

Alex sighed in relief and opened the door cautiously. Before him stood Krunk and his father.

"Dad!" Alex exclaimed.

His dad had his right arm slung across Krunk's shoulders to hold himself up. He was barely conscious and appeared weak and dazed.

"We need to get him back to Tristoria," Krunk said warily. "Poisoned."

"Who did it?" Alex asked.

"Daddy!" Sylvia cried. "Daddy!"

"Sylvia, he'll be all right. He just can't talk right now," Alex told her.

"One of the three demons that were here," Krunk continued.

"There were three? Wait, what happened to Margie and her two kids?"

"They were the demons. Look, I'll explain on the way. We need to get your dad back to a healer, now. He's fading quickly."

Alex nodded in understanding and grabbed his dad under his left shoulder and gave instructions for his sister to follow them, reassuring her their dad would be okay.

"How are we all going to fit in the machine?" Alex asked through heavy breaths.

"We're not," Krunk said, placing Nort's umbrella snuggly in his thick belt.

"Then how —?"

"Portal."

"But I thought only a Rayne could —"

"I can portal down levels, just not up."

CHAPTER 22

Tough Decisions

K runk held his scepter at arm's length and began making small circles in the air. A few feet away, a burst of emerald green light shot out from a tear in the world and formed an oval of spinning space as if a blender had been turned on from the other side. Alex could feel a vibrating power emanating from the tear; the world seemed to be fighting back and trying to close the wound. Thankfully the spinning stopped when the portal reached its desired size, leaving a pleasant green glow. Alex wondered if he would come out the same on the other side, all parts intact and in the same place.

He didn't know how long the portal would remain open so, after seeing Krunk enter through without agonizing screams, he grabbed his sister's hand, instructing her to close her eyes, and then stepped through the oval as if walking through an out-of-place door in a fun house. *Quick and uneventful,* he told himself, *similar to walking down a short hallway. Not so much.* Instantly, a rush of air encompassed him, and then a pressure all over his body — not an uncomfortable pressure, but pleasant like a weighted blanket. Immediately following was a moment of euphoria as time and space moved seemingly along each cell in his body as if he had just touched every tendril in the universe all at once. Unfortunately, it was short-lived, and he snapped back to the situation when he heard Krunk's raised voice.

"Where is your healer, Nort?" Krunk asked. "I don't know how long we have."

Alex peered around and realized they were in the center of Nort's village. Nort, Karissa, Jayda, Vitoria, and Lucianna had all backed away from the portal that had appeared a few feet from them.

Nort immediately ran to help on seeing Alex's dad limp and barely standing. Nort placed his shoulder under Henry's right arm, taking over for Krunk while Alex took his place under his dad's left arm. Krunk looked at Nort and then to Sylvia. Nort nodded back to him in understanding.

"Karissa, please take Sylvia with you back to my house," Nort said. He then turned to Krunk. "What happened to him?"

Karissa nodded and greeted Sylvia gingerly. She glanced at Alex for approval.

"Sylvia, she's a friend," Alex said. "Let us take care of Dad, and I'll join you real soon. I promise." He could see the fear and uncertainty in her eyes. "Look at me, Sylvia." He shook his head vigorously. "I promise."

Sylvia finally accepted Karissa's hand once Karissa offered her a bracelet that glowed bright pink. "The pink glow represents bravery to the wearer," Alex overheard Karissa say as they walked away toward Nort's house.

Vitoria huffed and stared after Karissa and Sylvia as they walked off. "If you need me," Vitoria told her dad, "I'll be browsing at clothes in the store since we never leave the forest."

She then turned and left in the store's direction. Alex thought it was odd, even for Vitoria, to be that dismissive, but he had more pressing matters at the moment to dwell on.

Krunk nodded to Vitoria but kept his attention on Karissa and Sylvia. Once Sylvia was out of earshot Krunk said, "From the appearance of his pupils and his skin, he's been poisoned."

Now that there was sufficient light, Alex noticed that his dad's skin was slightly paler than normal and was tough and thick like leather.

"This way," Nort said, motioning with his head. "Just next to the inn there."

Next to the inn was a small store Alex hadn't noticed when he was here the last time. The wooden sign above the door didn't have any words on it, but there was a picture of two small potion bottles with the necks of the bottles crossed.

"What is this place?" Alex asked, as he helped heft his dad onto a wooden bench just inside the store. The inside was dim and cool, with walls of inlaid dark wooden shelves full of small potion bottles filled with a variety of colorful liquids and solids. There were even some that held faint glows inside them.

"An apothecary shop, what else," Nort said as if it should have been obvious. "Horace!"

"Yeah, okay, makes sense," Alex said, attempting to cover up his ignorance. But he knew what an apothecary shop was; he just had not heard it called that other than in his fantasy novels. *Why couldn't Nort just say pharmacy?* Alex wondered. But then he remembered his surroundings. There were no bright lights and shelves of advertised medications, nor people behind the counter in white coats counting pills and filling bottles, like he had seen at a typical pharmacy. This place wasn't like a pharmacy at all. Apothecary shop was very fitting.

A man with long gray hair and a full beard entered through a pair of saloon doors. He wore clothes similar to Nort's, appearing as a nineteenth-century gentleman, and was at least a foot taller than Nort. Horace immediately saw Alex's dad and motioned for them to bring him toward the rear of the store.

"Dad, hang in there. Just a few more steps," Alex said, noticing his dad was getting weaker by the second.

Through the double doors and to the left was a decent-sized room with a large rectangle-shaped, heavy wooden table in its center. One side of the room's massive inlaid shelves were full of dusty old leather-bound books, while the other had more potion bottles similar to those in the main shop. There were also odd-shaped tools scattered about the countertops.

"Place him on the table, please," Horace instructed. "And remove his shirt. Now, would anyone like to explain to me what exactly happened to this gentleman?"

Alex and Nort helped remove Henry's shirt while Horace rolled up his sleeves and swiftly searched the shelves of books for a particular one.

"Poison. From a demon witch. Likely long term," Krunk said.

Horace glanced over his shoulder and eyed Krunk suspiciously. "And how do you know this?" He looked Krunk up and down. "Warlock, I presume?"

"Yes. The name is Krunk."

"Ah, the famous hermit warlock," Horace said nonchalantly as he turned his attention back to the books on his shelves; he was now on a rolling ladder. "Once part of the king's council, if I recall correctly."

"Yep, that's me," Krunk said, unsure what to make of the man's tone.

"You mentioned long term. How long?" Horace asked.

Krunk looked over at Alex, whose attention was on his dad fading away on the table beside him.

"Alex," Krunk prompted.

Alex continued to stare off into space.

"Alex!" Krunk said again.

Alex snapped out of his trance and looked up at Krunk. "Sorry, what?"

"How long has your dad been acting strange?"

"Ever since he met Margie. A year or two; I don't know exactly."

"That's a long time for poison to be in the body and still be alive," Horace said, retrieving a heavy leather-bound book and slamming it onto a desk next to the table. He began thumbing through the pages. "Looks like I have my work cut out for me."

Nort explained to Alex that Horace was the best healer in the kingdom before he self-exiled.

"Why did he leave?" Alex asked.

"He wanted to explore Tristoria and search for new potions and herbs. Seek the creatures of the many lands here and learn new techniques."

"What's wrong with that?" Alex asked.

"Nothing, but others, namely your grandfather, thought his practices were good enough, and he didn't want to risk his best healer possibly being killed in the wild."

"But he left anyhow and never returned, right?"

"Exactly, it's called free will. You may be king one day, but you cannot suppress free will. You can bargain with time, but in the end you have to appeal to the person's needs and desires."

Alex nodded, processing Nort's words.

"Okay, got it," Horace said, and turned around and slid the ladder along the railing, stopping it in the center of the bookcase. He stepped up to a shelf and pulled slightly on the top of a book's spine as if it were a lever.

The shelves suddenly slid into one another like pocket doors and revealed a spectacular sight: a labyrinth of copper pipes with cogs and wheels and knobs. Multiple gauges were poking out amongst the pipes, along with a few lightbulbs, but not ordinary lightbulbs — some were long and thin, while others were short and fat. But the coolest part, Alex thought, were the nine differently shaped and colored potion bottles positioned upside down, with each having their own umbilicus linked to another pipe above it. A long pipe set into the wall separated the bottles — five on the left and four on the right. Near the mouth of each bottle were individual knobs to release whatever substance the bottles were holding. *It appears to be a complicated dispensing mechanism,* Alex mused, as he stared at it in wonder.

Horace immediately got to work and began turning knobs. A few seconds later came a bubbling sound and then immediately following was the sound of pressure being released. One bottle on the left side, a yellowish copper-colored one, had fluid inside that began to shift. Horace held a small wooden bowl underneath the faucet of the bottle and twisted the knob. A viscous dark blue glowing liquid came pouring out.

He set the bowl down and went to the shelves again and grabbed a bottle with a dry white herb in it. He then grabbed a mortar and pestle and began smashing the two ingredients together. He then went to the sink and filled a wooden cup with water and poured it in with the mixture. With a wooden spoon, he began methodically slathering the mixture on Henry's upper body. The smell was acrid, causing Nort and Alex both to cover their noses in unison.

"What is that stuff?" Alex asked, still holding his nose.

"The white stuff is death root from the smell of it, and the blue glowing liquid is demon oil, if I had to guess," Nort said.

"That's correct, Nort," Horace said.

"How do you know so much about these? Were you a apothecary?" Alex queried Nort.

"Dabbled a bit in herbalism when I first got here. But it did not hold my attention, so I switched to tinkering. Who do you think built this dispenser?"

"You made that?" Alex asked, amazed.

"Don't act so shocked, my boy. Bessie was much more difficult to build than this contraption."

"Can you please help me turn him," Horace motioned. Alex's dad moaned, but did not struggle as they turned him slightly so Horace could place some of the mixture on his back.

"Who exactly is this man?" Horace asked noticing the markings on the rear of Henry's upper left and right shoulders. "These are the markings of a Rayne."

Alex craned his neck closer so he could see the marks Horace was talking about. There was a tattooed wing on each shoulder: one was a demon wing and the other was an angel wing. There was also writing in Latin under each of the wings, which Nort interpreted as man's eternal struggle with good and evil. Alex had never given the tattoos a second thought when his dad walked around without a shirt. Now that he got a good look at them, he noticed the wings were small, but detailed. A mistake made as a teenager, he recalled his dad telling him once, and Alex never gave them much thought after that.

Krunk and Nort both nodded to Horace.

"Perceptive, Horace," Nort said. "This is the late king's son, Henry Rayne."

Horace appeared horrified by Nort's words. "Wait, what? Late? So, the rumor of the king's death is true? And . . . this is his heir?" His expression turned even more grim. "Wait, so, if he doesn't make it through this . . ." He hunched over as if he would be sick, and sighed heavily. "What happens if he doesn't make it? If I'm not able to cure him?"

"You will do fine," Nort said calmly while placing a firm hand on Horace's shoulder.

"If it steadies your hand, Henry gave up his seat long ago," Krunk added. "And the new king is well and in this very room."

"Huh?" Horace asked, confused. He turned and focused on Nort. "Nort? You're —"

"Don't be absurd," Nort grumbled. "I would never take on such a task or be part of —". He stopped short, as if his next words would have disrespected the late king.

"Then, who?" Horace asked. "The boy?"

Krunk and Nort both stared at Horace with expressionless faces.

Horace quickly scanned Alex from head to feet, making sure not to linger disrespectfully. "Looks like I need to get my act together, then. I'm in the presence of two Raynes." He bowed his head to Alex.

Alex instinctually bowed his head in return.

"Okay," Horace said, taking a deep breath and returning upright. He grabbed the bowl with the mixture and continued slathering it on Henry's back, taking much more care now that he knew who Henry was. After Horace finished, he left the room and returned with a thin white shirt in his hands. "Here, please help me put this on him."

Krunk motioned for Alex's help.

"Why is the shirt wet," Alex asked, as he helped Krunk put the shirt on his dad.

"It's soaked in a stabilizing solution. It creates a barrier for the salve I placed on him and also works as a stabilizer because of the salve's unstable properties. The mixture is inherently temperamental."

"*Stabilizer* meaning it's unstable, as in, it might explode?" Alex asked being much more careful with his hands and the shirt.

"Yes, but with the stabilizer, it will be fine," Horace reassured him. "So, make sure it stays on him." Horace shook his head and then said, "He shouldn't even be alive with the dose administered and the time he endured the poison."

Alex nodded morosely and then thanked Horace with a grateful handshake. Alex remained silent for a few minutes and just stared at his injured dad lying helpless on the table.

"He won't be alone. I'll be here with him," Horace told Alex. "I'm sure there are discussions that need to take place."

"Yes, we have many things to discuss," Nort said. "We'll be next door if things change."

Horace nodded. "Don't forget to wash your hands in the sink before you leave."

Alex reluctantly nodded an okay, not wanting to leave his dad, and then made his way to the sink where he rubbed his hands vigorously.

"I don't have those markings on my back, Nort."

Nort handed him a towel, and before he could respond, Horace chimed in. "You're marked at birth, but you cannot see them until you ascend."

"Okay . . ." Alex said.

"Come," Nort said, "we have much to discuss."

Krunk, Nort, Alex, Jayda, and Lucianna gathered at a secluded round table in the far corner of the tavern. Lucianna made it a point to voice her reason for joining the meeting other than her obvious role in the coming war. She saw a potential kink in the pact she had made with Alex now that his dad was in the picture.

Krunk started the conversation with an inquiry about Lucianna and her coven. With them being a huge part of their defense, he thought it wise to voice his interest and concern for their needs. Lucianna explained that she and her coven were staying in the town hall with plenty of amenities; basically, whatever they desired. Nort nodded and commented on how the coven's beauty smote the men of the town, and even the women looked on enviously. Lucianna did not object to the observations and even seemed proud, as if those were the coven's intentions.

The witches were mysterious and gorgeous and surrounded by mystique. They walked with an aura of confidence and seduction, wearing intricate gothic robes and dark, heeled, laced boots. Some wore pointed witch's hats while others preferred their long black hair to flow freely behind them. But most of the non-witches agreed that it was their violet eyes and pale skin that made them the most intriguing and appealing.

Wiley, the owner of the tavern, set a few pitchers of mead on the table, along with some tankards. He hovered as usual when an interesting patron or group was there, and with all the rumors about the king he sure would not miss this group. Krunk, on seeing the bartender hover, shot him a stern glare to leave them alone. Wiley turned toward Nort with a pleading look, but to his disappointment Nort matched Krunk's glare. But Wiley was no amateur eavesdropper, Alex recalled Nort saying. And over the years of running the establishment Wiley had become a master.

Jayda continued the conversation by retelling her interaction with her brother. Jarren's soldiers had captured her just after arriving in the outer realms of the kingdom, as if they had been waiting for her. She was blindfolded and taken to her brother. After Jarren's spiel about how disgusted he was with her decision to be a traitor, he gave her just enough information to reinforce the surrender option his courier had given to Alex. As part of his strategy, he also allowed her to see the king's soldiers lined up side by side with demons, portraying a unified, massive army.

"It infuriated me to my core when I saw the unity," Jayda exclaimed. "So much so I have declared that Jarren is no longer my brother. He might as well be a demon in my eyes."

"Wise choice," Nort said, taking a large swig from his tankard of mead that he had just poured and then set it down abruptly on the table. "Now that we are all a little more disturbed thanks to Jayda's news, we can begin." He lifted his mug toward her with a smirk and a nod. She nodded back, emotionless. "Unless there are any objections, this is an informal discussion, so interject at any point." There were no initial objections, so he sat the half-full tankard on the table. "The way I see it, we have two paths to discuss: one where Jarren lives and one where he does not." He turned toward Alex. "Sorry for the directness, but we have to discuss both alternatives."

Alex lowered his eyes, but nodded in understanding. The hard truth was staring him in the face. It was harsh and bitter and he had tasted it before with his mother when she died. Only this time it was different. There would be no one left if his dad died, leaving him and his sister to become orphans.

"I know I'm too young, but can —" Alex started.

"Yes, but only a little," Nort said, as if he knew the request was coming. He slid a half tankard of mead to him from across the table. "It comes from the mountains to the south where the giants roam. They say they feed it to their young and that's why they grow so huge and mean."

"Maybe on second thought," Alex said, eyeing the gold liquid.

"Nort used to be the size of a mouse," Krunk said. "And smiled more often."

Nort let out a loud, hearty laugh loud enough for most of the tavern to turn toward their table. Alex unfolded a nervous smile, but he was in no mood to laugh.

"Sorry," Nort said as he calmed his laughter, "but I needed that. There is entirely too much tension right now."

"Agreed," Krunk drawled, letting his smile fade. He then winked and turned toward Alex. "Even in the most uncertain of times there is still room for mischief."

Alex assured them it was okay with a nod and a half smile. He then cautiously brought the tankard in front of him to his lips. On smelling the sweetness of the mead, he braved a decent-sized swig. He instantly regretted that decision as his face contorted and twisted in pain as the liquid burned its way down his gullet. He futilely hid his reaction, for the group was already smirking knowingly.

"That . . . was . . . good," Alex managed and then coughed and wiped his tear-filled eyes with the back of his hands. "But I think I'll take my time with the rest."

"Yeah, maybe not gulp it down," Krunk agreed.

"I can see how it would make someone mean," Alex said, stretching his eyes.

The table laughed lightly.

"Okay, let's start with the bad first," Krunk said, bringing the tone of the table to a more solemn one as the laughter settled. "If Henry does not survive."

"Then we'll be back where we started, right?" Jayda said, as if she had been holding the sentence in since arriving. "I mean, no matter if it's Alex or his dad as king, it still doesn't change the fact that we must convince the soldiers that my brother is a traitor. And to do that we must have a way of getting inside the castle, right? We don't have near the number of soldiers they have to face them head-on on the battlefield. And that's not including the demon horde that this Helenia has brought here. I saw them with my own eyes and, trust me, there were a lot of them."

Alex was surprised by Jayda's directness, but he guessed the reason. It was the coming battle with her brother, knowing that only one of them would likely survive.

"Yes, that's correct," Krunk said. "But, if Alex's dad survives, he is a Rayne who has already ascended. Meaning he is a practicing warlock, and with the Book in his hands he could lend us the edge we need to win this war."

"But we haven't found the book," Alex reminded him.

"Oh, I didn't tell you, sorry," Krunk said. "I slipped it in my satchel when I saw your dad."

"That's a pretty important piece of information, Krunk," Nort said with a raised eyebrow.

"I honestly forgot until a few moments ago."

"Where is the Book now?" Nort asked.

"It's safe right here in my satchel," Krunk said, patting his hip. "It never left my side."

"It definitely does not need to be in a warlock's hand other than a Rayne," Nort warned. "Alex should be its guardian."

"Easy, Nort," Krunk said with raised hands. "I wasn't going to keep it. Besides, even if I did, I can't open the darn thing."

"I would feel better if Nort held on to it," Alex said. "He can keep it safer than I can."

Nort nodded in understanding. "I will bear this burden for now. Once your father wakes, we can hopefully figure out what to do with it."

"If his father wakes," Krunk said, tossing him the satchel.

Nort caught the satchel and unbuckled it, taking a quick peek inside. "Yes," Nort nodded and sighed. "And if he does not survive?"

"We have to find a way inside the castle other than the front door," Krunk said, acknowledging their group's numbers were much fewer than their adversary's. "That's why we're here, right, for a discussion."

The table was quiet for a few awkward moments.

"So, is that all we have, then?" Jayda said unconvinced and still irritated.

After another stretch of uncomfortable silence, Lucianna interjected. "I have a question."

They all turned toward her and listened. She demanded their attention despite her calm, soft tone. Alex speculated that she may even be using some spell.

Krunk nodded, "Please."

"Why has no one asked the most obvious question? Why was the Rayne spell book with the three demons at Alex and Henry's home?"

"Yes, I have thought on this ever since finding it in Margie's possession," Krunk said.

"Wait, what?" Alex asked. "Margie had it and not my dad?"

"Yes, but before I could interrogate her, she escaped as if she had been waiting for us," Krunk admitted.

"Had the security of the Book been breached?" Nort asked.

"It was locked when I found it," Krunk said. "I'm sure she tried many times, but I don't think they could open it."

"That's a relief," Nort said. "Things may be far worse if she had."

Krunk nodded, and then turned his attention back to Lucianna when she asked him, "What is your conclusion to this?"

"That she has to be colluding with Helenia. Margie must be one of her lords."

The words shocked Alex, even more so than finding out that Margie was an actual demon. *She's in cahoots with this Helenia? And she's a demon lord?*

"And when were you going to share this revelation?" Nort asked.

"I hadn't figured out all the details, but I don't think it's overly complicated," Krunk said.

Nort sighed. "Just tell us what you have."

Krunk shrugged, "I suspect it was their plot to end the bloodline."

"You mean kill my entire family, my dad, sister, and me?" Alex said, horrified, as he considered what that meant. His family was being hunted for extermination by demons from hell. And not just regular demons. There were demon witches, lords, and spiders.

Krunk nodded. "Yes."

"Okay, they're colluding in a plot to kill the Rayne bloodline; that's not surprising," Nort said. "But that still doesn't explain how a portal was opened in the king's chamber."

"What about someone else in the bloodline?" Lucianna offered.

"It wasn't me," Alex blurted defensively.

"Relax," Nort said. "No one here thinks it was you." He turned his attention to Krunk. "Could the spell work like that? If so, it could explain things."

"Maybe," Krunk said, leaning back in his chair thoughtfully. "I've heard rumors of such things happening: a prohibiting spell placed and a close family member who could bypass it; something with the DNA and the spell. Very smart, Lucianna."

Lucianna nodded and said, "It had to have been Henry. The closer in line the relatives are, the better the chance they have to break it. When my sister and I were children, we did it all the time; broke each other's spells. Those were simple children's spells, of course, but the theory is sound."

"My dad would never have done that to my grandfather," Alex said.

"Demon witches can be very persuasive, Alex," Lucianna said. "I suspect he did not do it under his own free will."

Alex suddenly felt a wave of nausea wash over him and placed his head in his hands. *Why had my grandfather not thought of this? Why weren't contingency plans in place for such an occurrence?*

"Unless he had a sister or brother," Lucianna prompted Alex. He lifted his head and shook his head no. "No, then it all fits: the spell book was there; he is a direct descendant; and there was motivation by his captor."

Alex, still ignorant on the whole warlock and demon thing, queried. "Okay . . . but how did Margie get there in the first place?"

"It makes perfect sense, really, if you think about it," Krunk said. "Your dad was still practicing demonology. Margie or Helenia wait patiently on the other side for your father to summon a demon and then make a mistake by getting too greedy. Once summoned, they overpower him and then use him to open a portal inside the castle. Helenia stabs your grandfather and takes the Book. Margie slowly poisons your dad while Helenia gathers her army through portals your dad opens for them. They use him and then kill him when they don't need him anymore."

"Greedy?" Alex asked.

"Overconfident and making a mistake by summoning too powerful of a demon," Krunk clarified. "You'll learn this soon enough."

"So, they could have many portals open here and many thousands of demons waiting to strike?" Jayda pondered. "To what end? Kill everyone and move on?"

"Kill the bloodline, as I mentioned," Krunk continued. "I suspect Helenia bargained with your brother, Jarren, to allow him the rule of Tristoria. She will attempt to take over the world and enslave mankind, ultimately to take over the heavens. She wants revenge, I assume. What Jarren doesn't realize is that her goal is to rule everything, including Tristoria. He will eventually be enslaved or killed like the rest."

"There is a silver lining in this discussion," Lucianna said. "We possibly now know how to open a portal inside of the castle."

"Yes, if Henry survives," Nort said.

"If the worst comes to be," Krunk said, "then I shall do my best to break the spell that locks the Book and hopefully find a way to open a portal inside the castle."

"Don't you think Alex would have a better chance than you, seeing how he is the king's grandson," Lucianna offered as if he should have known.

"As you are well aware, Lucianna, he is not of age and cannot produce a portal," Krunk said.

"So, I suppose this means you'll be in possession of the Rayne spell book once again," Lucianna said warily.

"Yes," Krunk said. "I suppose I will."

Alex noticed a darkness in Krunk's eyes that he had not seen before that left a chill lingering inside of him way too long. He suspected it was the darkness inside all warlocks that Nort had mentioned disdainfully. He briefly considered when he would face his own darkness. *Will it happen after I ascend? I hoped so, because I have enough going on at the moment.*

"With Alex by my side, of course," Krunk added cheerily, attempting to shroud the darkness. "After all, I do not possess the same DNA to perform the spell alone."

"Nort will also accompany you and the boy," Lucianna said sternly and smoothly.

"Yes, someone not seduced by the dark magic of this place," Nort said with discontent. "But I don't think it will be a problem anyhow. Even if there is a spell inside, and Krunk does find a way to break the spell, we don't have the key."

Lucianna nodded and then stared at Krunk suspiciously for a long moment.

"Of course," Krunk said. "The more the merrier."

Neither trusted the another, and they both knew it.

"I know you all know of my past, but I assure you my intentions are pure in this matter," Krunk said. "I am much stronger now. Besides, we have to at least try."

All around the table each nodded in understanding. What choice did they have at this point if Henry did not pull through? Krunk was right; he was the most qualified and Alex's grandfather had trusted him immensely. He even trusted Krunk with his grandson's warlock training.

"Then it's settled," Nort said. "Any objections?"

The table was quiet. Even Wiley, who had been listening from afar, remained conspicuously motionless at the corner of the bar.

"The situation we arise to in the morning will determine the first steps Alex and I take," Krunk said.

Alex knew what Krunk's words meant, but he didn't want to think on it anymore. He just wanted to be alone with his thoughts, and that's exactly what he did once the group dispersed for the evening.

Alex donned the hood of his robes and lowered his head just far enough so as not to run into anything as he made his away across the small village. The temperature had dropped significantly the short time he had been in the tavern, leaving a heavy, cool mist in the air. When he first arrived in Nort's village, it seemed so magical and majestic. The soft glow of the lanterns hanging from the trees, the whimsical slants of the chimneys and buildings. Now, everything around him was drab, full of grays, leaving a dismal emptiness inside him. He knew it was likely because of how things were taking shape, but he couldn't shake the feeling.

He needed to arrange the widely dispersed thoughts that seemed to scatter the more he mulled over his current situation. What would he do if things took that horrible route for the worse? He was in too deep now, even if he had wanted to leave. He was part of this place, regardless if he liked it or not. The delicate balance of good and evil in the world was in jeopardy, and his family was the weapon to either keep it in check or destroy everything. He could feel his insides tearing at the thought of being responsible for the outcome. He had never had to face such madness or critical decisions. No one his age should have to take on so much.

One thing at a time, he remembered his mother telling him when he would become overwhelmed. The memory of her voice calmed him to realize he needed to focus; there were way too many unknowns he had no control over and they were muddling the ones he could change. He needed a distraction to bring him back to center. What better way to get your mind back on track than a trip home? The memory of home would have to do for now.

He doffed his hood and entered the store, Wear from Home.

"Sir," the clerk said. He appeared middle-aged with some gray showing on his full head of hair slicked back and parted to the left. He looked straight out of the *Mad Men* series. "I apologize for the intrusion, but are you a Rayne?"

By now, the small town had heard talk of the king's family being in town. No one knew the truth about his grandfather's passing, but that didn't stop the rumors.

Alex nodded hesitantly, unsure of the man's intention.

"If I may, can I place a request for the next king to honor the accord between the realm and the town?"

Alex didn't hesitate with his answer. "Sure, if people are happy, I will not interfere." This seemed to be most people's greatest fear so far, according to Nort: change.

The man seemed honestly relieved. "Thanks. And get what you need; it's on the house."

"Thank you," Alex said. He hadn't given much thought to how he would pay. Maybe Nort had a line of credit or something he could have used. He was grateful the man offered to take care of his bill.

The closer he got to the eighties section the louder Twisted Sister's "I Wanna Rock" amplified all around him. He smiled at how absurdly cool the place was as he once again perused the eighties paraphernalia. He pondered if his dad had been in this place when he was younger, but then he realized this was the decade he was probably in Tristoria. He couldn't wait for his dad to see the place now so they could explore it together. He caught himself tearing up, so he quickly wiped his eyes and focused, making a beeline to the clothes section before he lost all control of his emotions.

He snagged a pair of acid-washed jeans, a pair of black-and-white Converses, and a Journey rock T-shirt, featuring the cover of their 1983 album, *Frontiers*. It was the same outfit his mom told him his dad had been wearing in the arcade when they first met. He thought on it for a few seconds and then grabbed the Sony Walkman and a few tapes.

He averted his eyes so as not to reveal his watery emotions that had leaked. "Thanks again," he said as cheerfully as he could manage. "And I'll be sure and pay you back for everything."

"No need," he heard the clerk say as the door closed behind him.

He debated with himself on returning to Nort's house for the night. His sister would need a familiar face, but she was probably asleep by now. Besides, Karissa was good with her. He could tell right away when Sylvia latched on to Karissa's robes. He needed to be there for his dad in case he woke up, or be there if he passed away. Either way, he wanted to be next to him.

He entered the dark room in the apothecary shop and laid the clothes he had gotten for his dad on the bench. He inspected his dad's chest for rise and fall, and once he was sure he was still breathing, he felt the weight of the day saturate his senses, leaving a heaviness in his eyes. He lowered his head on the folded clothes and fell asleep not long after.

CHAPTER 23

The King Has Returned

Alex's dad sat up on the edge of the table with his legs dangled over the side. The shirt that he had been wearing now sloughed off in pieces like tree bark. The mixture Horace had placed on Henry's skin was now part of the shirt that lay in crumbles on the floor at his feet.

"Alex," his dad said hoarsely. He cleared his throat and tried again. "Alex."

Alex had been shifting around, trying to get comfortable on the hard wooden bench next to the table for the last half hour. On hearing his dad's voice, he sat up groggily and grabbed ahold of his neck, feeling an instant stiffness from the makeshift pillow he had been resting on.

"Alex, what happened to me? And where the heck are we?" his dad asked, peering around the dark, unfamiliar room.

"Dad, you're awake," Alex said with relieved excitement. "It's an apothecary shop, but never mind that. You almost died." Alex noticed his dad's dog, Rounder, curled up next to his dad. "What's Rounder doing here?"

"Whoa, that's an intense headache," his dad said, grabbing his head at the temples as the intermittent sharp pain hit him. "He's my demon; he's always close by," he said, as if Alex should have known. "Where did you say we were again?" he continued to peer around the room while clutching his head.

"An apothecary shop. In Tristoria. You know, the place you never told me about," Alex said and then stopped, realizing what his dad had just said. "Wait, you have a demon? Is it dangerous?!" *Why would I be surprised that my dad has a demon?* Alex thought. *After all, warlocks and demons are real and now part of my language.* Rounder's unusual loyalty to his dad made complete sense now. No wonder the dog was full of anger most of the time; he had been living in a house full of demons.

"What, how —" Henry grimaced from the pain in his head. "And no, he's not dangerous; he's under my control." Rounder seemed unfazed by the conversation, as he was snoring softly.

"Your wife, Margie, is an actual demon who was poisoning you. I told you she —"

"Wait, what!? Wife Margie? What are you talking about, Alex?"

"Are you kidding me, really? Do you have amnesia or something? Did you hit your head? I didn't see any marks —"

"Alex, my head's fine," his dad said sternly. "Just tell me what's going on."

Alex stared at him a moment and realized that either he was doing a darn good job at playing dumb or he really didn't remember. It was a dark spell that had poisoned him.

"You brought this woman Margie into our house and kicked out Mom. She was a demon along with her two so-called children that also lived with us." Henry began processing Alex's words and stretching his memory for the truth. "The others said she was a . . . a powerful demon witch, I believe is the term they used, that you summoned, and she persuaded you by using some spell. I don't know how it all works or —"

"Where's Sylvia!?" Henry asked, suddenly realizing the situation playing out.

"She's fine, Dad. She's safe here with Karissa."

Henry let out a sigh of relief. "Who's Karissa?"

"A friend of mine I trust. I'll get Sylvia once you're cleared by Horace."

Henry nodded and suddenly another memory popped into his head. He was still very groggy, with a dense fog clouding most of his thoughts. "And your mother? She must be unhinged over this. She always warned me that this would happen if I ever started back up again. I suppose I have a lot of explaining to do to her."

"Are you serious?" Alex said, feeling his insides roil with anger and sadness, along with many other things that he couldn't explain.

"What is it? I know she won't forgive me easily, but she'll understand after I speak to her."

"Dad, stop! Mom's dead!" Alex yelled, but calmed slightly on seeing his dad's distraught and confused face. "She died of cancer over six months ago." It seemed to him as if someone else was speaking the words.

"No," his dad breathed, as if the words were exiting his mouth like a heavy spoonful of rocks. He shook his head in disbelief. "No, it can't be. No spell could have kept me away from . . ."

Alex felt the rage overpower his bitter sorrow on mentioning his mom's death. "You didn't even cry when you heard about her death!" Alex's eyelids swelled almost instantly and immediately a deluge of tears tore down his cheeks.

"No!" his dad yelled. The room shook, rattling every bottle on every shelf. Some fell to the floor and broke, spilling different colored liquids. "It . . . cannot . . . be! Not Samantha!" Alex stared at his dad's hands, which were turning different shades of yellow and orange.

"Dad! Your hands! What's happening to you?"

Henry didn't acknowledge Alex, not immediately. There was smoke coming from the table where his fingers were gripping it.

Alex stood and backed away to the corner of the room close to the exit. "Dad!" Alex cried out one more time.

When his dad did finally look over at him, his eyes were the color of the sun, matching the burning fire of his hands. They then changed to blue, then to green, and then back to the burning orange, cycling as if building to release something angry and powerful. Alex noticed Rounder had his eyes open now and was searching the room methodically, as if seeking a threat. The dog lowered his head back down once he saw there was no one else in the room besides Alex.

After a long moment that seemed like many minutes to Alex, his dad's hands and eyes returned to their normal state. Alex could feel his heart pounding through his shirt and realized how simultaneously terrifying and spectacular his dad was at that moment.

"What was that?" Alex asked, remaining a safe distance away.

"That was me almost losing control," his dad said with exasperation. "A time not long ago I would have destroyed this entire building with that much rage inside. Over the years, I have learned to filter by cycling. It's a form of deflating my emotions."

"Oh, okay," Alex said. "That's what you were doing."

The room was quiet as they kept to their own thoughts. After some time had passed, Henry motioned for Alex to come over and sit beside him. His dad stretched his left arm around Alex's shoulder and gripped it tightly. Alex felt his dad lightly trembling. They sat in silence for a long while.

Alex went to get Horace after a considerable time had passed. He wanted to be notified the moment Alex's dad woke, but grieving was more important. Though there was more time needed, Henry agreed that Horace needed to be summoned as requested.

Horace timidly entered the room a few minutes later, followed by Alex. Horace lowered his head respectfully toward Henry, who returned the respect with a nod of his head.

"I'm Horace, sir. Pleased to meet you," he said, extending a wary hand to Henry.

Henry shook Horace's hand with a grateful half smile and said, "I suppose you did this to me. Thank you."

"It worked," Horace whispered, looking down at the pieces on the floor and then back up to him. "And you're most welcome."

"You sound surprised," Henry said.

"A little," Horace admitted. "I have to be honest. You were leaning a little toward the side of not returning. Looks like Alex and Krunk got you here just in time."

"Krunk? He's still around?"

"How do you know Krunk?" Alex asked.

"He was there during my trials. As an observer doing a favor for your grandfather. By the way, where's my old man? I suppose it was him who broke the spell."

Alex lowered his head, wanting to avoid the question for just a little while longer. Might as well rip the Band-Aid off all at once. "It was Krunk, actually."

Henry looked surprised. "Really? Well, okay . . ."

"Dad, I'm here because Grandpa summoned me here. He was dying, and I was to take his place since you . . . you gave it up."

Henry shook his head, not at all surprised by the news. He took a deep breath and said, "He thought I was a failure, but that wasn't it. Not entirely. I never wanted it in the first place. He forced me to take the trials. Your grandfather could be ruthless and very persuasive when he wanted to be."

"I never said I wanted this, either," Alex complained. "I didn't even know all of this existed before a few days ago. But what choice did I have once I was told what was happening?"

"What do you mean?" Henry said. "What exactly did he tell you?"

"Not too many details, but basically our ruling of this place keeps the heavens from crumbling."

"He told you that?"

"Well, not exactly those words, but something like that."

"Yeah, I heard a similar lecture. But did he also say you must protect this place unselfishly, which includes judging fairly and timekeeping."

"No, but Nort and Krunk mentioned timekeeping. Why?"

"It's a tremendous amount of responsibility. That's why."

"I know, but Grandpa made it a point to say there had to be a Rayne on the throne. What choice did I have since, you know . . ."

Henry shook his head and sighed. "Like I told your grandfather, there's a council. They can expand the council and grow and vote on things for the people. 'Why a king,' I asked. He told me, 'The people need a leader and a much greater power chose us to take on that role.' And I repeated once again that a council for the people would suffice. It infuriated him and he stormed away."

"Sir, if I may?" Horace interjected.

Henry nodded, only slightly irritated by the interruption.

"Warlocks are not the most graceful of magic users, but they have their place and have the potential to become very powerful. There's a reason they have chosen warlocks, particularly the Raynes, to protect Tristoria. Your family has perfected the balance of good and evil and used it for millennia to keep the demons from usurping the world. Like your father told you, this honor was chosen for your family long ago."

"Precisely, which is why I relinquished my duty. I understand we were chosen, but I didn't have the self-control to balance good and evil. Just look at my latest path of destruction."

"Of course you do, sir. It's in your blood," Horace reminded him. "We all make mistakes, sir. A leader is not chosen for their perfection. Leaders are chosen for their loyalty and principles."

"Dad, he's right," Alex said. "Grandpa told me before he died that you would take your rightful place one day. That you had great potential, but had to find your way in your own time." Those lies sparked something inside him. On seeing this in his dad's eyes, he pressed on enthusiastically. "I'm not of age yet, so what good would I be? Besides, you have more of a reason to defend this place than anyone. The evil threatening mankind nearly killed you. It killed Grandpa and stole the remaining time with mom. If you don't take your place, I have to. I've already made the commitment."

Alex could see his short speech turning into bloodlust in his dad's eyes.

When Henry spoke, his words were calm and direct. "This will take some reflection on my part." He looked over at Alex. "In the meantime, Alex, are you sure this is what you want? I know you're not of age yet, but you have shown initiative and strength and have accepted the calling."

Alex shook his head. "It's not my time yet. I was doing it only because I didn't have another choice." Alex felt a huge relief of pressure deflate inside him at his dad's words of potential return.

"We all have choices, Alex. And you stayed," Henry said.

"And, thankfully, you're here now," Alex said.

Henry sighed. "Yes, I am. If I take the throne, the council will have to hear your words of relinquishment. Temporarily, of course, until it is your time to succeed me."

"But I never went before the council," Alex said.

Henry furrowed his brows. "There was never a ceremony, then?"

"No, Grandpa instructed not until after I was trained by Krunk," Alex said. "Dad, the council is only the beginning of the problems. Wait until you hear the rest of what's going on."

Henry sat back down and listened while Alex explained what he knew, leaving out many details, feeling they were better explained by Nort and Krunk, who were way more versed in matters of Tristoria.

On the news of his dad's death at Helenia's hands, Henry's anger rose to the surface, but much less than the news of his wife, Samantha. He admitted that he and his dad had grown apart over the years since their disagreement. He vowed to Alex it would never happen to them and Alex was more than grateful to hear those words. Before leaving, Alex glanced over at Horace and noticed that he looked just as pleased, if not overjoyed, with Henry's decision to take his rightful place on the throne. Even though Alex was more than grateful for his dad's decision to relieve him of the burden of ruling Tristoria, he still felt slightly offended by Horace's overzealousness toward Henry.

Alex assisted his dad as discreetly as possible across the village to Nort's house. The early morning hour helped them to avoid most wandering eyes. Nort was already awake and saw them coming up the cobbled walkway. He had been sitting in his chair, with his pipe in hand, next to his cracked open window, as was his usual morning routine. Krunk was also there, sitting on the back porch overlooking the enormous tranquil waterfall that flowed down into the forest below.

The smell of meats and breads filled the small house, and Alex felt his stomach rumble the moment he stepped inside. Sylvia was still asleep, but Karissa had awakened as they were let in the front door. On seeing Alex and Henry, Karissa hurriedly shuffled her way back to her room to dress more appropriately.

After pleasantries and morning routines were complete, they all sat around the kitchen table for a breakfast feast, compliments of Nort. Despite the tastiness of the food, most of the plates around the table still had food on them. The stale stench of war was in the air and there was no avoiding it. Jayda and Lucianna showed up at the door not long after. Another one of Nort's gadgets had summoned them: a tiny drone the shape of a bird. It was small and carried a tiny parchment in its ravenlike claws.

Sylvia, not wanting to leave her dad's side, reluctantly went to the next room and played with one of Nort's gadgets, a small replica of Bessie that flew, but was controlled with a remote. On seeing the model, Alex wanted to join her in exploring the toy's capabilities, but he knew there were much more pressing matters to discuss.

"There will be plenty of time for games once this war is over," Nort told Alex on seeing him linger by the door to the room Sylvia went to.

Alex felt himself twinge at the comment; it was both disturbing and much too real. He pondered if this was the line parents had to use all over his world during the wars that had taken place. It was a sad truth everywhere, it seemed — no matter what level one was in — that war was a common word in the vocabulary.

Henry greeted everyone around the table and thanked them appropriately. Nort and Krunk regaled him with the tale of what had taken place from their perspective with more vigor and intrinsic details thanks to their unique personalities and time spent in Tristoria.

Henry sat in silence for a few minutes, absorbing the details before beginning his questions.

He shook his head in disbelief. "How can Helenia be alive? My dad and you, Krunk, saw her burn. How is this possible, even for a demon witch?"

"Disturbing indeed," Krunk admitted. "If your dad wouldn't have made the claim himself, I would not believe it to be true."

"Is there a plan in place to take back the kingdom?" Henry asked.

"Sort of," Krunk said. "But now that you seem to be well . . ." Krunk glanced over at Nort, who nodded back to him. "What we'd all like to know is what your plans are now that you are back here, sir?"

"Yes, that is a more than fair question," Henry said. "It does appear that I'm back here." He frowned. He peered around the room and noticed that they were all focused on him and anxiously expecting his answer. He caught Alex's eye, and Alex looked back at his dad pleadingly with reassurance about his decision. "After discussing things with my son, we . . . I . . . would like another chance to take my place on the throne."

Relief spread through the room like a pressure valve had opened and released a plume of steam. The only one around the circle who didn't seem relieved was Karissa. Again, Alex felt slightly offended by the sighs of relief, though he completely understood them.

Karissa raised her hand and Henry nodded for her to speak. She slid her chair back and stood. "Isn't there a law or something about removing a sitting king? I mean, I don't think it's fair to push Alex to the side like he was never even here.

He watched his grandfather die and agreed to take his place as king even though he had no idea that this place even existed. He knew there needed to be a Rayne ruling this place, and he took on the responsibility, unselfishly."

Alex glanced over at Vitoria when she huffed and he saw the roll of her eyes and her sneer at Karissa's desperate words. He didn't know what to think of Karissa's words. Yes, they were flattering, but even he was more than glad that his dad would take his rightful place as king. He wouldn't even ascend for a few more years and he could hardly defend this place with intermittent prepubescent powers.

"Karissa," Nort scolded.

"No, no, she's right," Henry said. "Alex had to renounce the throne willingly for me to take his stead. He will have to do it officially in front of the council when all of this is over, since I initially relinquished my claim. No one is more proud of Alex than his own father, I can assure you." He focused on Karissa. "He has obviously shown great leadership and loyalty to have already surrounded himself with such fierce friends defending his honor."

Karissa nodded and accepted the answer, but with reluctance for a reason Alex could not figure out.

Henry continued, "Alex has given me full power of the throne." They all looked to Alex, and he nodded a vigorous yes. "I know I've made many mistakes and I have paid dearly for them. I can assure all of you that I have learned from my mistakes and my heart is ready for the responsibility of being king." Henry looked to each of them for assurance and objections. There were no objections this time around. "Very well. Then I would like to form a solid plan since swift action is imperative. What do we have?"

Krunk cleared his throat. "Since you're back and we also have the Book, we should now be able to portal inside the castle, correct?"

"Thanks again, Krunk, for retrieving the book," Henry said, patting the satchel that hung on his chair. "Honestly, I've never tried . . . I mean . . . I've never tried willingly. Apparently, everyone has deduced that it was me who opened the portals, though I have no recollection of doing so. If I can open the Book, there may be coordinates inside."

"Wait, you're not sure if you can open the Book?" Krunk asked.

"I need to spend some time with it," Henry said.

Krunk frowned and let out a long, heavy sigh. "Okay, well, once Henry figures out the Book dilemma and is able to get us inside, Henry and I will locate Jarren and take him out. Yes, he's in control of the soldiers, but if we can show the soldiers a Rayne is on the throne, I believe they will turn back and follow the king's command."

"In theory, yes, but we don't know what lies he has spread," Nort interjected. "And in all of my time I can't recall soldiers fighting side by side with demons."

"Disturbing indeed," Henry said. "It may be more of a challenge to convince the soldiers, but I'll bet they turn back to their own side once they see a path. Let's hope so anyway." He motioned for Krunk to continue.

Krunk continued, "While we're tending to the leaders, Nort's group will take the guards out in the small forest near the entrance to the castle. Once we give our signal from the castle walls in your direction, which will either be Henry or me waving a lit torch from side to side, Nort's group will act as a distraction and lead as many demons as they can to the deadly ore, daemonium mortem. Meanwhile, Lucianna's coven will then flank the remaining demons. All of us, no matter where we are, must focus on killing any demon lords. Take out the demon leaders and the rest will crumble easily. Which brings us to Helenia. While inside Henry and me will also focus on locating the council; hopefully, before running into Helenia. She will be challenge enough even with the council's help."

"If they're still alive," Nort said grimly.

"Yes, if they're still alive," Krunk agreed. "That's about the gist of it."

Henry nodded. "Okay."

"Wait, who do I go with?" Alex asked.

"And me," Karissa echoed.

Krunk looked at Henry to answer the question.

"Alex, you and Karissa and Vitoria will be safe here," Henry said.

"That's not fair, we —" Karissa protested.

Henry interrupted, "I know you all are brave, but —"

"Dad, we can fight and help you," Alex pleaded. "Let us do our part."

"You, the three of you, are the face of the future," Henry said. "We cannot afford to risk losing the young until we have to. Do you understand?"

Alex looked over at Vitoria for help in pleading their case, but she remained quiet as she had the entire time.

"Alex, I need you to understand," Henry said. "This is an important lesson all leaders must learn."

Alex finally nodded on seeing his dad's pleading face, and then glanced over at Karissa. She was shaking her head defiantly but remained respectful because of Nort's overbearing glares toward her.

Nort turned his attention to Jayda, who had been quietly listening from the other side of the table. "Jayda, I know you renounced your brother, but would you be willing to kill him?" He sighed lightly. "I know it's not fair to ask, but it will not be fair to the group if we are not all in. I think we'll all understand either way and will not fault you for saying no and staying in the rear to fight."

The group agreed with silent nods.

"I know it will not be easy, but I stand by my decision. He is a demon and will be treated as one," Jayda said confidently.

Lucianna, who had also been quietly waiting her turn, made a quiet interruption by clearing her throat.

Henry addressed her. "Lucianna, yes, please," he nodded. "And once again, thank you and your coven for your help."

"Thank you, King Henry," she said and then bowed her head slightly. "I assume you know my sisters and I are here for more than our survival and the kingdom's future?"

"Yes . . . I suppose," Henry said, uncertain about her intentions.

"I would like to have your word that you will honor the agreement made between our coven and your son."

Henry looked over to Alex and then to Nort and Krunk. They all nodded, reassuring him that the agreement was valid.

"Yes, I will honor the agreement," Henry said, turning his attention back to Lucianna.

"And know that we owe the kingdom nothing after this fight is over," Lucianna continued. "We go back to our land and you to yours."

"As you wish," Henry said, then turned his attention to the rest of the group. "So, I guess this is our army, then. A coven of witches, a few outlaws, a hermit warlock, and a hope that our soldiers return their loyalty. Sounds like a decent fight is in our midst." He looked over at Alex. "I can use a little revenge in my life."

"For Mom," Alex said, feeling overwhelming pride in his dad. His dad would finally fight for what he believed in. Alex pushed his chair back and stood, then reached to his side under his robes and pulled the sword that his grandfather had given him from its sheath.

"Is this . . . ?" Henry began, also standing.

"Yes," Alex said with an assertive nod. "It was meant for you to hold it last, not me. Besides, I'm staying safe, remember."

"Thank you, son," Henry said, taking the sword gingerly from his hands. Alex noticed that he held it like it was a sacred artifact. Henry's eyes welled up, but he quickly snuffed out his emotions with a powerful sniff and a clearing of his throat. He removed his eyes from the sword and said, "This will be a challenging feat with much bloodshed, but this

327

is hardly the first battle here and will not be the last. Every one of us knows of the eternal struggle of good vs. evil and we here in Tristoria ride the tenuous line that separates the two. All of you have my word. I will avenge my father, your former king, and take the kingdom back from these demons and traitors. To my wife Samantha, you will also be avenged." He hefted the sword high in the air. "We will fight and we will kill demons, lots of them. We will return Tristoria to the people and send the demon horde and their leaders back to hell!"

The group all stood and nodded, one by one, even Karissa. Alex could sense the changing of mood from somber to a brief illusion of hope, if only for a moment. He felt an overwhelming emotion of pride rising inside as he peered around the table at the faces he was begging to call friends, including Vitoria. The momentum of a rally was finally building amongst them as a team.

CHAPTER 24

Motley the Demon

Krunk insisted that Henry get started with opening the spell book; too insistent, Alex thought. In fact, Krunk had been acting a little strange ever since recovering the spell book. His irritation was obvious when Henry told him he needed a private word with Alex before starting, adding validity to Alex's theory about Krunk's appetite for the book.

Alex and Henry strolled along the Path of the Dead near Nort's home. Despite it being daytime, the path still held an enveloping feeling as the vast canopy of tree limbs hovered above them. There was an inviting warmth about the place, like a gathering of families and friends every day at the same time enjoying a nice filling meal.

"Dad," Alex began. "Why didn't you tell me about you and Mom, the warlock and witch stuff?"

"Honestly, it was my intention to do just that before all of this mess happened. In fact, your mother and I had already discussed the matter. Long ago, before you and Sylvia were born, we both agreed to shelter you and your sister from that life for as long as we could. And as you now know, the dangers to our family are great."

"Yeah, unfortunately," Alex said heavily. "And all the more reason to know what we were capable of. How were we to defend ourselves if we did not understand what we were?"

Henry stopped and sat on one of the many benches along the path and motioned for Alex to sit next to him. Henry stared off in the distance and then said earnestly, "Life is full of strife once you cross the boundary of understanding where you place in the scheme of it all. Children need to be children for as long as they can."

"But Dad, I became part of it anyway, and I had no idea what the heck anything was. I mean, come on, you brought demons into our house."

Henry sighed. "Yes, that I did. And I shouldn't have —"

"Why couldn't you just stop using magic?" Alex could feel the irritation creeping back inside at the thought of his mother. "None of this would have happened."

Henry turned toward Alex and pleaded, "The power is so seductive, son. That's part of the reason for keeping it from you until your mind is fully ready, fully capable of resisting. It will tug on you relentlessly, wanting more and more, never letting up. You're never satiated, never full. I was young and never completed the lessons that included advanced discipline and resistance. But I thought perhaps with your mother's strength that I would be okay. We would use our powers together, sporadically, just to satisfy the craving. . . ." his voice trailed off.

"So, you did love her?" Alex said, not believing the words that just left his mouth.

"Yes, of course I did," Henry exclaimed through now red-stained eyes. "She was everything . . . is everything to me."

The anger that had been building in Alex lessened with his dad's words. His own eyes swelled with tears as he stared down at his feet with clenched teeth. "I miss her so much!"

Henry scooted closer to Alex and wrapped his arms firmly around his shoulders. "Me too, son. Me too."

"Where do you think she is?" Alex asked softly. "Krunk said she's probably in the heavens."

"Krunk is a wise man. I agree with him; she's way ahead of us. If I know her, she's probably waiting patiently for us to finish our foolishness and meet her."

Alex smiled through tears at the thought. "I hope so."

When the sniffing turned to clearing of throats, Alex said, "Can you tell me about her? The stuff I never knew, like her witch days or whatever you all called it."

Henry smiled and wiped his eyes. "Sure, well, to start with she was a brilliant witch. Much better than I was at incantations. And she not only performed them well but could write her own." His voice turned passionate. "I remember one spell in particular she wrote. It was one that could return lost things no matter if you had forgotten what you had lost. She said she wrote it for me because I was so forgetful, which I was. Not too proud to admit that."

"That's pretty cool. Was there a school you went to or something? That Mom went to?"

"Me, no. Mine was all private because of the sensitive nature of our family name, but your mom was traditionally trained. An all-girls coven, The Sisters of the Wind."

"I've never heard of it."

"You wouldn't have because the school's public name was Cape Willow School for Girls. There are very few selected for this private school each year, given that there are so many factors involved in the selection process."

"Is there one for warlocks, a boy's school?"

"There is. There are many of them."

This is good, Alex thought. *Maybe I can finally get out of that school where I don't fit in.* "Can I go?" Alex pleaded.

"Believe it or not, your mother and I talked about that. We even considered it at one time, but the risks were just too high. Even with our name being changed, which I'm sure by now you have figured out."

Alex nodded. "Grandpa told me."

"If anyone were to find out who you were, well, you can imagine the possibilities."

He'd probably get picked on less, seeing how his dad will be king of purgatory with great powers. "So, I'm supposed to go back to regular school like none of this happened?"

"Yes, at least until you reach age seventeen and ascend."

"What about you? Are you staying here? Who will take care of Sylvia and me?"

By the look on his dad's face, Alex could tell he hadn't considered this yet.

"Let's get through this first and I promise you we'll work this out together with you and your sister."

Alex nodded, but felt uneasy about the situation. If his dad stayed here in Tristoria, he and his sister would have to stay with some other relative. The only living relative he had was his grandmother, his mom's mom. She could hardly take care of herself and was living in an assisted living community.

"Back to this warlock stuff," Alex said, changing the subject. "I need another outlet since I gave you mine." Henry had a confused look on his face and Alex motioned toward his dad's belt. "The sword."

"Outlet?"

"Vitoria told me we need an outlet to use our powers. She has a wand that her dad gave her. . . . "

"Yes, a trainer wand. Krunk likely enchanted it for her, but she also likely had much instruction by him. And this sword was your grandfather's and is not a trainer anything. Advanced warlocks do not need outlets other than their hands and minds."

"But I used the sword and damaged a tree."

Henry smiled. "That must have been Vitoria tricking you."

"No, she had her wand by her side. I saw it."

"Okay. . . ." Henry said, furrowing his eyebrows and thinking on it for a moment. "Wait a second, did you . . . nah," he argued with himself and lightly laughed.

"What?"

"You're too young to —"

"To what?" Alex said impatiently.

Henry mused, "Were you in the Faceless Forest when you damaged the tree?"

Alex nodded slowly, unsure if he should reveal any more.

His dad stood and walked around the area as if searching for something. His face suddenly unveiled a serious expression along with his tone of voice. "Alex, come over here, please."

Alex did as his dad told him without question. "Dad, what are you looking for?" Henry circled him and began whispering words that he couldn't quite make out. "I can't hear what you're saying."

"Shhh, one second, please," Henry demanded. Alex noticed that both of his dad's hands began to glow green as he spread his fingers apart searching the air with his fingertips and continued his whispering as if reciting lines.

A few seconds later, there was a whimpering and a loud hiss close by. Alex followed his dad's eyes to the ground near his feet. When he noticed the creature, he leaped back away from it as if it were a poisonous snake.

"Just as I suspected," Henry said concentrating on the creature.

"What is that," Alex said, now a safe enough distance to mix curiosity with the fear.

"This small terror is a demon. To be more precise . . ." Henry knelt down and got a closer look at the little fellow. "It can't be . . . is it really?" he whispered in awe.

"Really what?" Alex asked inching closer, but still well behind his dad.

The demon looked like a small dragon with tiny wings, but with fine white fur in place of scales. Suddenly its eyes changed colors from a glowing deep green to light green and then . . . it disappeared and in its stead appeared a slightly larger doglike animal with the same fine white fur, a split tail, and four ears.

"What happened?"

"He's a shifter," Henry said amazed. "I've only read about them, never seen one in person. They're really rare."

"So, he can change? Like into different creatures?"

"Yes, but I presume maybe just one or two varieties at his age. He appears to be young. Even more amazing, he also can meld with his environment."

"You mean cloak?"

Henry nodded.

"Is Rounder's demon form a dog, then? Or can he change?"

"The dog form is a spell from me he has no control over. His true form would likely scare you a little."

"Wait, like what?"

"He's an imp, with small wings and legs and arms."

"Oh, okay. . . . maybe the dog form is better," Alex said, turning his attention back to the demon. "By the way, where is Rounder?"

Henry shrugged. "He's always close by."

The shifter changed back to his dragonlike form and hissed at Henry when he reached out a hand toward him. "Easy, little guy," he said, trying once more, his hands glowing brighter. The demon, now docile, laid his head on the ground with the guitar pick-shaped tip of its tail slowly sliding back and forth as if content.

A thought suddenly hit Alex as he stood back staring at the curious creature. "Is he attached to me, you know, like Rounder is to you?"

"No," his dad barked. "Nothing like Rounder. Rounder was a gift to me during one of my first trials. I impressed one of the council members so much with my focus that he offered me one of his very own young demons."

"So, they normally don't just attach to warlocks? They have to be given to you? Or is there a demon pet shop somewhere?"

Henry smirked. "No, there's no shop. Yes, they can be gifted by another warlock, or they can attach when summoned. Or as in this case, they can be found in a demon-rich environment such as the Faceless Forest."

Alex's eyes met with the demon's now dark green eyes and he felt a sudden closeness to the little guy, as if they had known one another for a while. Like old acquaintances that had been doing business together for many years.

"Can I keep him?" Alex asked eagerly.

"Absolutely not; they're much too dangerous. And besides, you're not trained enough or of age to handle such a creature. Though he is also young, he could likely overpower your mind and manipulate you."

"But he already allowed me his powers; that has to mean something."

"Yes, he's beginning to manipulate you. It's better we get this over with now." Henry pulled his late father's sword from its sheath.

"Wait!? You're going to —"

"Kill him, no. Incapacitate and return him to the forest, yes. He's a demon, Alex, and you're not ready yet."

Alex stood between the little creature and his dad. "Let him stay with me until the war is over. Come on, I may need him if something happens to you and the others. I don't want to be helpless and weaponless; I gave you the only weapon I had."

"You may have a point," Henry said grabbing his chin with his index finger and thumb. He took a moment to think it over. "There are strict conditions."

"Anything!"

"He must stay in a cage at all times, unless I'm here with you. Got it? And only attempt what I teach you. Don't go searching for spells on your own."

Alex nodded excitedly. "Promise."

"They're dangerous. I mean it."

"Dad, I get it."

"I don't think you do." He pulled a leather sheathed dagger from one of his back pockets and handed it to Alex. "Here, this might come in handy if that demon turns on you."

"I'll be fine, " Alex contested.

"Take the dagger or I'll change my mind."

"Okay, fine," Alex said and slid the dagger in the back of his jeans.

"And when this is all over, we'll bring him back to the forest. Got it?"

"Got it." Alex said. "I think I'll name him Motley."

His dad shrugged, "Your choice, but don't get too attached. Remember, we're bringing him back."

Before Henry left to meet Krunk, he gave Alex brief instructions on defending himself by using the demon's power; one easy defensive spell along with offensive one. Alex was beaming and more than grateful after his first official lesson. His dad warned him, however, against too many spells at one time and overwhelming the demon, reiterating that Alex had limited knowledge, and the dangers that come with a lack of discipline in a young relationship.

There are several types of demons, but their goals were the same: possess, kill, and wreak havoc. As a warlock it was paramount to control the demon before it controlled him. Demons had a way of sensing a warlock, and to a point could read their minds, revealing their desires and most importantly their weaknesses. The most difficult part of any relationship is balance, and this truth resonates within every warlock every single day of their lives. Henry's passion in his warning to Alex was borderline anger, and rightfully so, after realizing what Margie had done to him.

Alex knew Motley had already read his mind. When he pointed the sword at the tree, he had wanted to shoot a burst of energy toward it and that's exactly what had happened. Motley knew it and made it happen. Now, Alex just needed to tap into that and do it consistently, not allowing Motley too deep into his mind.

◊ ◊ ◊

Henry managed to open the Book; though he did it, begrudgingly to Krunk, in private. They worked well into the morning hours. Nort also joined them, insisting that he would be the balance of the darkness in the room, but his real reason was to keep an eye on Krunk. There was no room for error; therefore, the portal casting had to be precise. The practice was long and exhausting, but Henry was sure by the end he could get to the location needed, which was a secret entrance mentioned in the Book and privy only to Raynes. However, though slim, there was still a chance Margie could have opened the spell book and found the coordinates. It could be their end the moment they entered through the portal.

While the three of them rested after the long night of practice, it was an opportune moment for Alex to spend some time with his demon, Motley. Alex used the excuse of a headache to be alone. Karissa agreed to watch Sylvia, though she eyed him a little suspiciously as he quickly locked himself in one of Nort's rooms that didn't have a bed in it, not giving her enough time to question him.

Alex was teeming with curiosity about the demon and his own undiscovered abilities. He could barely suppress the excitement pulsing through him as the possibilities unraveled in his mind of his future powers. *It's like practicing with a sword,* he told himself. *Motley is my only weapon if things take a terrible turn. Only, a sword would not turn on its wielder or attempt to take over its mind,* he reminded himself.

"Okay, Motley, how shall we start?" Alex asked, kneeling and opening the cage as the demon uncloaked and revealed its form.

Now that Alex had a closer look at him, he noticed Motley's dark green eyes sparkled like gems. His sharp black claws were shiny and matched the pair of small black horns that protruded from his head, as if they were just now forming.

"You sort of look like a dragon," Alex whispered. "Can you breathe fire?" He concentrated on the words in his mind, attempting to explain them telepathically. He had no idea if he was doing it correctly or not, but Motley gave the impression he was trying to understand, slightly tilting his head curiously from side to side.

"Now, don't bite me, please," Alex said, inching his hand inside the cage. He was careful not to get too close to the demon's mouth, noticing the rows of partly exposed razor-sharp teeth, and began gingerly caressing the demon's neck.

The demon curled its tail and rubbed its head against Alex's hand, as if giving him permission to continue.

"Okay, so how do we do this?" Alex said, slowly pulling his arm along with the demon out of the cage.

Alex felt a tearing sensation in his mind, as if something were forcing its way inside. "Is that you doing this, Motley?" he asked wincing. "If it is, can you please stop?"

Motley leaped from his arm and onto the floor and stared up at Alex, keeping eye contact with him. The pain immediately lessened.

"Are you saying we need eye contact?" Alex asked. Motley wiggled his head. "Then what?"

"How about let's try what we have already done before," Alex continued. He stretched out his arm and opened his palm toward the bookshelf along the wall. He closed his eyes and focused on the bookshelf. When he opened his eyes a minute later, the top row of books on the shelf was on fire. He ran and quickly grabbed them from the shelf and began stomping the fire out.

"What was that?!" Alex loudly whispered. "I didn't think of fire." Motley seemed unfazed by his words, remaining in his observant position.

"Alex, are you okay in there?" Karissa called to him through the closed door.

"Yeah, I'm fine. . . . Just . . . um . . . stubbed my toe," he said quickly.

"Let's try this again," Alex said. "And a little quieter, please. Now, I just want to knock off one book, not the entire shelf. Got it? And no fires."

The demon bowed his head as if to say he understood, but Alex had his doubts.

He held an outstretched arm and open palm stance once more and clenched his eyes shut. The tearing sensation in his head returned. He decided that this was Motley attempting to break into his mind, so he tried relaxing slightly more and accepted the pain. He was only allowing the tearing sensation a little at a time, remembering his dad's words about demons and control. It seemed to be working; a moment later the pain lessened and a warmth filled his mind, then darted down his outstretched arm into his open palm. It was a sensation like he had never experienced before — powerful invigoration filling his insides as if he had no limitations. But, suddenly, and without warning, his mind deflated and exhaustion encompassed his entire body and he fell to the floor.

"Alex," Henry said as he rapped on the door. "Can you open the door, please? We're about to leave."

Alex sat up from the floor at the sound of his dad's voice. "What happened," he whispered to himself, shaking off the dazed feeling. He didn't remember falling asleep, but he looked over at a hanging clock on the wall and noticed that a few hours had passed. He then remembered Motley.

"One second," Alex told his dad, getting to his feet and searching the room for Motley. "Motley, where are you!?" he whispered frantically. "Ah, there you are," Alex sighed deeply as the demon suddenly appeared beside him. "I need you in the cage, please, and fast. I promise, once my dad leaves, I'll take you out."

"What are you doing in there?" Henry asked with suspicion when Alex yanked open the door. Alex had not realized it, but he was sweating profusely and out of breath.

"Nothing. I mean —"

"You were messing with that demon, weren't you," his dad whispered. He stepped inside the door and cracked it behind him. "Look, remember what I told about the seduction. It's real, and it's very dangerous. If circumstances weren't so dire, I would not allow you to keep that demon."

"I can keep him!?"

"You know what I mean. In the cage, I mean it. Unless it's absolutely necessary. Now, come on, we're leaving. Walk with us to the portal."

Alex nodded. "Okay."

His dad shook his head knowingly and left the room.

Nort, his small army of villagers, and the coven of Hal left by horseback earlier that morning. Their mission was to infiltrate the small forest and deal with any opposing guards so they would be ready when Krunk and Henry arrived later and gave them the signal to provoke as many demons as they could and steer them toward the deadly ore. The coven of Hal was to flank the demons and assist with funneling them to the ore as well as slaughter any stragglers.

Alex wondered why Nort didn't tell him he was leaving in person and left a note instead. The note was vague and merely said to remain safe and stay out of mischief. Alex didn't quite know how long the war would be, but he would have liked to say goodbye just in case things did not turn out well. He had grown fond of the small, grumpy angel.

It was late afternoon in the center of Nort's village. The portal Henry had just opened blanketed the surrounding courtyard with a soft green glow. Sylvia cried softly into her dad's robe as he told her goodbye. Henry nodded and Rounder appeared out of nowhere and leaped into Sylvia's arms. She hugged him tightly and then, suddenly, she seemed content for the moment.

Despite remaining calm, Alex felt what his baby sister was expressing. He had just gotten his dad back and now he was going off to war with demons. Alex's emotions were a tangled mess, but at least he now had a reason behind his dad's deceit and could let his dad go without a marred memory of him.

"This will all be over soon enough, and we'll talk more about warlock stuff," Henry told him earnestly.

Alex nodded with a nervous grin. "Are you sure I can't come with you?"

"I'm sure," he said with a genuine smile. Henry hugged Alex tightly and whispered, "I'll see you soon." Alex hugged him back with all the strength he could muster, causing his dad to wince. "I love you too, son," he grunted.

"Sorry," Alex said. "I just got you back, Dad. Be safe, okay."

"I will," Henry said.

Vitoria and Krunk said their goodbyes with little fuss. Krunk gave her the same instructions as Alex, Karissa, and Sylvia. They were to remain together in Nort's village until the war was over. Vitoria attempted to argue, but Krunk quickly snipped it away with a stern glare. Henry gave Karissa a hug and asked her to help keep his kids safe. She nodded to him through the embrace but held something curious in her eyes immediately on releasing her hands from his robes.

A few seconds later, Henry and Krunk stepped through the portal, leaving the four of them in the center of the nearly empty village. Only a handful of guards remained, along with a few villagers, to tend the buildings. Two guards were there to protect the portal's integrity, along with eliminating any demons that attempted to enter through it.

"I don't know about you, but I'm getting as far away from here as I can," Vitoria said.

"As much as this pains me to say," Karissa said, shaking her head, "they ordered us to stay together."

"Look around you," Vitoria said. "There's no one left. And no one is coming back. If I were you, I would run as far away from this portal as you can."

"Alex, is Dad coming back?" Sylvia whined.

"Yes, he is," Alex said, glaring at Vitoria. "She's just upset she can't go is all."

"I wish it were that simple, kid," Vitoria said, looking down at Sylvia.

Karissa sighed. "I know you won't believe me, but I had a vision when I touched Henry's robe."

"Wait, what?" Alex said confused.

"It took me a moment to process. . . ."

"Karissa, what is it?" Alex pressed.

Karissa bit her lip and said, "They're in trouble. It's a trap. Not an actual trap, but somehow your dad will turn. I see him conflicted and taking orders, but it's unclear."

"I don't understand," Alex said. "Are you saying he will betray us?"

"You'll never understand," Vitoria interjected. "It's all nonsense."

Karissa shook her head as tears slid down her cheeks. "He's in trouble; they all are."

"Why didn't you say something to them when you felt it? Before they left!?" Alex said irritated.

"I couldn't — They left so fast and I didn't understand. . . ."

Alex leaned against a nearby brick wall and then sighed heavily after quickly regaining control of his emotions. Sylvia was next to him, leaning her head on his shoulder.

"So, what do we do about it?" Alex asked.

Karissa shrugged. "There's no one else around. I guess we ask Horace. He's the one who cured him. Maybe there's some side effect or something he didn't tell us about."

"What other choice do we have at the moment?" Alex said, getting to his feet and holding Sylvia's hand. "Vitoria, are you coming? It involves your dad, too."

Vitoria seemed to think on it a moment. She huffed. "Fine, I'll stay and see what this Horace has to say. If there's any possibility that I can get into this fight, I'm game."

CHAPTER 25

A Seer, a Witch, and a Warlock Walk Through a Portal

Horace opened the door with a puzzled look from behind a pair of bloodshot eyes. "Alex, shouldn't you be —" he slurred his words.

"Are you okay?" Alex asked, noticing how unsteady he was as he held open the door.

"I'm fine, I'm fine, come in . . . all of you," Horace said, attempting to conceal something on a nearby shelf behind him.

Alex noticed the bottle before Horace could hide it, along with the smell of its contents. Horace had been drinking mead and a lot of it. The group shuffled into the entryway and shoved together on a small wooden bench. All but Alex, who stood with crossed arms.

"We'll be quick," Alex started. Horace nodded slowly. "Are there any side effects to the medicine you used to cure my dad of the poison?"

"Is the king okay? I saw him leave through the portal. I haven't drunk . . ." Horace said and hiccupped. "He appeared fine to me."

"Is it possible for him to still be poisoned?" Alex asked. "You know, like he was before, influenced?"

Horace seemed to think this over for a moment. He suddenly realized and looked over at Alex with a horrified expression. He whispered darkly, "How could I have been so clumsy?" His shoulders slumped and then he slid down the wall he had been leaning against into a crouching position. "It's all my fault. Our only chance now gone, and it's because of me."

"What are you talking about," Alex demanded, standing over him.

"I overheard enough and should have warned him," Horace continued in a monotone, distant voice.

"What!?" Karissa nearly shouted, taking the words from Alex's mouth.

Horace sobered after hearing Karissa's raised voice. "There's still enough poison in the system. It takes a few days to clear out, which means he is technically still vulnerable."

Alex shook his head and exhaled slowly. "You're saying the demon that poisoned him can still persuade him?"

Horace nodded. "I'm sorry. I doomed us all."

Alex ignored Horace and looked to Karissa and Vitoria and his sister. "We're wasting time; let's get out of here. I have an idea."

◇ ◇ ◇

Vitoria and Karissa both were impatient on the way back to Nort's house, pestering Alex about his big idea. He held strong, though, and they finally relented, agreeing to wait to hear more details for the rest of the short distance back to Krunk's home. Sylvia remained close by her brother's side, asking occasionally if their dad would be okay. Alex consistently told her yes, leaving out details, which seemed to appease her until the next time she asked.

They all gathered in the living room, and Alex began his spiel next to the fireplace and its continuous fire. "As you all know, a powerful demon overtook my dad. She poisoned him and could control him, torturing me and my sister."

"Yes, yes, we know this. Get on with the plan already," Vitoria said fussily.

"Just let him finish," Karissa roiled.

Vitoria sneered, but said nothing else.

Alex nodded to Karissa. "Yes, uh, well, anyway, he's still vulnerable to the demon that poisoned him. If he comes into contact with her, they could use him against our forces. We have to warn my dad and Krunk before it's too —"

"Is your plan just to tell the guard by the portal, .because we could have done that on the way over here," Vitoria said emphatically.

"No," Alex said deviously, spreading a smile across his face.

"No?" Vitoria said. "Then what?"

"Yes!" Karissa said, nearly leaping to her feet. "When are we going?"

"Yeah, I want to go, too," Vitoria said. "One problem, the two guards by the portal."

"I'll be right back," Alex said excitedly.

He returned a few seconds later, clumsily carrying Motley's cage, which was many sizes too big for the small demon.

"What are we going to do with that? Throw it at the guards?" Vitoria said laughing.

"No, just a second," Alex said, and placed the cage on the floor. He tried focusing his mind with the words, *Motley, these are my friends.* Vitoria, Karissa, and even Sylvia edged closer to the seemingly empty cage. Alex unlatched the door. "He may be a little scared at first, so give him some room for a second."

They barely moved back a few inches, not removing their eyes from the cage. Alex held out his arm with an open palm and instantly felt Motley's sharp claws dig lightly into his skin.

Karissa noticed him wince. "What's wrong?"

"His claws are razor sharp," Alex said.

Alex noticed the confused looks on their faces and demanded, "Motley, reveal." When Motley didn't respond, Alex said, "He must be a little shy, one second." He focused his mind to plead with the demon, attempting not to show his growing embarrassment. He was about to begin pleading with the demon when he noticed all three gasped at once. Motley revealed himself, perched on Alex's shoulder in dragon form. Sylvia scuttled behind Karissa's robes, clinching them tightly. On hearing Sylvia's gasp, Rounder lifted his head and perked up for just a moment. Alex forgot about Rounder being a demon and became slightly nervous about the two demons in the same room, but Rounder lowered his head back down and watched from a distance, as if they were only slightly annoying to him.

"What is that?" Karissa asked.

Motley blinked his sparkling green eyes and curled his tail. He then let out a long, open-mouthed yawn, revealing his plethora of sharp teeth and his forked tongue.

"This changes things a bit," Vitoria said.

"He's my demon," Alex said proudly, "and his name is Motley."

"But you haven't ascended. I mean you barely found out you're a warlock and —" Karissa said.

"I know, right? It's kind of amazing," Alex beamed. "My dad said he must have attached to me in the forest. He's how I could knock down that tree."

"Can you control him? Like, sic him on someone?" Vitoria asked with a crooked smile.

"No, not really. I mean, I'm not sure, but he seems protective of me. And I've been working on focusing my mind. My dad said we sort of have a connection. Supposedly all demons and their warlocks share a mental connection."

"Sounds dangerous," Karissa said cautiously.

"Sounds powerful," Vitoria said fervently.

"Probably a little of both," Alex agreed.

"What kind of demon is he?" Vitoria asked, mesmerized by the creature. "Can I touch him?" She inched her hands closer.

"I wouldn't. Haven't you noticed his teeth?" Karissa warned.

"No, Karissa's right," Alex said. "His teeth are super sharp and he barely listens to me yet."

"Fine," Vitoria lamented. "What kind is he?"

"I'm not sure the technical name, other than *shifter*," Alex said. "My dad says he's pretty rare, though, and it's even rarer that he attached to me."

"So, he can take different forms? Like what?" Vitoria asked.

"This one and some strange dog-looking creature. My dad seems to think that's about it for his young age."

"So, he's a baby?" Vitoria asked.

"By demon standards, yes. By our standards, he's probably much older than we are, according to my dad."

"That's pretty cool, I guess," Karissa said wearily. "I suppose this will help us?"

"If he listens to me, yes," Alex said.

"What other choice do we have?" Vitoria said. They all looked to one another and shrugged. "So, what's the plan?"

"I was thinking of distracting the guards with Motley. That is, if he'll shift for me and lead the guard far enough away. Then we should be able to slip by. Once inside," he shrugged, "we wing it, I guess. We know what we have to do. Karissa has her bow. Vitoria, you have more experience with this magic than I do. And I have Motley. We got this."

"Okay," Karissa said. "Count me in."

Vitoria nodded. "Me, too."

"So, we're all in," Alex said. "Great, let's go, then." He was caught off guard by their unbridled acceptance of his meager plan.

"What about me?" Sylvia asked, still partially hidden by Karissa's cloak. "I want to help dad, too."

"Sylvia," Alex said, nearly forgetting that she had been in the room. He knelt down beside her. "I need you to be brave for me, okay?" She nodded. Alex looked to Karissa. "Is there anyone in the village you trust to watch after her until we return?"

"Yes, Brandi; she looked after me when I was younger. She was my babysitter when my dad would leave me with Nort, trying to get him to take me to the realm. Anyway, yes, I trust her."

"Sylvia," Alex said. "Will you stay with her until we return?"

Sylvia emphatically shook her head no.

"Please," Alex pleaded. "It's way too dangerous where we're going. Dad needs you to be brave and stay here. I need to know you're safe or I can't leave. Rounder will be here with you."

Her eyes swelled with tears. "I don't want you to leave."

"I don't want to go either, but I have to. I'll be right back, I promise. With Dad. Karissa will get Brandi and she'll watch you and Rounder here at Nort's."

"No," Sylvia insisted.

"Okay, let's do this, then. How about we have a glass of chocolate milk and we talk with Brandi? If you don't like her, we'll take you with us. Deal?"

She nodded heavily, wiping her eyes.

Alex looked at Karissa and then to Vitoria. They were both looking at him like there was no way it would work, but Karissa left to get Brandi anyhow, on his insistence.

When Karissa and Brandi returned ten minutes later, Alex and Sylvia were halfway through the glass of milk. Alex grabbed a pillow from beside him and placed it in front of Sylvia on the table. He could see her eyes weighing her down as she sipped the beverage. Seconds later her head hit the pillow in front of her and she was sound asleep.

"What was in that chocolate milk?" Karissa asked.

"Just chocolate milk. My dad taught me a defensive spell with Motley, which just conveniently was a sleeping spell."

◇ ◇ ◇

Karissa and Vitoria both approached the glowing portal warily. Alex wanted desperately to tell the two of them his odd yet euphoric and spiritual experience when he went through the portal with Krunk on his way back to Nort's village, but decided it best to let them figure it out on their own. He was glad no one told him anything before he entered, but that was after the fact. He wanted to know everything to expect of the unknown, weighing the best choice in a given circumstance.

"Let's go. Once the guards see us, it'll be too late," Alex said nervously, looking back over his shoulders.

Just moments before, Motley had leaped onto one of the guards' shoulders and smacked him with his tail. The guard yelped as Motley jumped down and darted off. The two guards chased after him, shouting curses. Once Motley reached a gathering of trees, he suddenly went into stealth mode, leaving the guards peering up at the naked branches.

"No more thinking," Alex said, and shoved the two of them forward into the green glowing oval. Alex felt Motley on his shoulder and quietly thanked him before stepping through. Thankfully, the two guards had not turned in time to see them.

A few seconds later, they found themselves in a dimly lit corridor with a few sconces flickering low-level light along the wall somewhere inside the Rayne castle. Alex immediately felt the intense heat emanating from the other side of a metal plate that was a little too close for comfort.

"Don't touch the metal," Alex warned. "There's a fireplace on the other side and it's lit." He was glad to have overheard his dad explain to Krunk what to expect on the other side of the portal involving the secret room.

"I'm trying not to," Karissa cried, nudging Vitoria.

"Okay!" Vitoria snapped with both hands held up in protest. "I get it."

"Quiet, guys," Alex whispered. "We don't know who or what is on the other side."

They both nodded.

Alex noticed that the dust on the floor had been disturbed, along with the cobwebs that were dangling from the ceiling and walls. Hopefully, his dad and Krunk were the only ones who had disrupted the room.

"Okay, this way," Alex said and motioned, cautiously leading the group through the next turn to a small room.

Alex noticed that there was a lever next to the eye slits in the wall. He did not dare touch the lever just yet without knowing what lay on the other side. He assumed that it would open the wall in front of them into the room, only there were no noticeable crevices in the wall.

"What is this place?" Vitoria asked glancing around.

"Supposedly, we're behind the Halls of War — the weapons and armor room from past wars."

"A museum," Karissa said. "Cool."

"Any warlock stuff, perhaps spell books?" Vitoria whispered excitedly.

Alex shrugged and then whispered, "Probably," all the while holding his index finger to his lips. "Come on, guys, we don't know what's waiting for us."

Alex stood on his tiptoes and pressed his eyes against the two makeshift slits. He quickly realized that his view was from inside a helm, likely a knight's helm, he gathered, from seeing the variety of suits spread out along the opposite wall. The room was full of weapons and armor as its name implied: suits of armor, ornate staves and bows, and many long swords and shields.

"Looks empty," Alex said. "Ready?"

They both nodded.

Alex reached up beside him and cautiously pulled the rusty lever. The stone they were standing on immediately began to move and rotate clockwise, and then they were inside the massive room of war paraphernalia. When Alex stepped off the stone platform and into the room, it began moving again, cycling back to its original place. Karissa and Vitoria quickly dropped their gaze from the sights around the room and leaped from the platform and tumbled onto the floor.

"Sorry," Alex said, helping them off the floor. "I didn't know it would do that so fast."

They didn't say a word after gathering their things from the floor because of the sight in front of them. The trio stiffly gazed at the three resting demons snoring loudly at the foot of a gilded throne some thirty feet in front of them.

Alex had forgotten about Motley. He sat perched on Alex's shoulder, silent and camouflaged. He crawled from Alex's right shoulder to the left one to get a better look at what had his master so unnerved.

"I thought you said it was empty," Karissa whispered irritably.

"It was . . . I mean . . . I guess I couldn't see that part from the slit I was looking . . ."

"Should we fight them?" Vitoria interrupted, gripping her wand tightly in her right hand.

Alex shook his head with a resounding no.

"I think we can take them," Vitoria said. "What do you think, seer? You think you can hit one with that raggedy bow of yours."

"I think I can hit you," Karissa snapped with narrow eyes.

"Guys, voices," Alex warned.

"I like your vigor," Vitoria said. "Use it on these beasts."

Karissa shook it off and readied her bow.

"One each, shouldn't be that hard," Vitoria said.

"Wait, why are we doing this?" Alex said. "Because you two have to battle one another's ego? The doors are right there, unguarded, let's go."

"No witnesses," Vitoria said, and then raised her wand and pointed it toward the demon on her left.

"Wait —" Alex started.

Karissa already had her bow at the ready and released her arrow just as Vitoria's wand shot out a purple flash. The beast Vitoria hit instantly fell over with a low groan, waking the other two from their slumber. Karissa's arrow just barely missed its mark, causing the demon to roar in anger. It darted toward her in a fit of rage, baring its huge teeth, slinging saliva in its wake. Karissa knelt down calmly and steadied her bow, releasing her arrow precisely toward her opponent's head and dropping the demon instantly. Its limp body slid a few feet and rested next to a statue wielding a sword and shield, rattling it and nearly toppling it over.

The third beast, the one Alex was to take down, took off in a full sprint toward Karissa. She fumbled to notch another arrow as Vitoria yelled over at Alex. "Alex, your turn!"

He instinctively reached by his side for his sword, but remembered he had given it to his dad. Then he remembered the dagger his dad had given him to defend against Motley. He snatched it out from the back of his jeans and held it out in front of him. Motley hissed and uncloaked himself. He leaped from Alex's shoulder, causing Alex to flinch as he dug his claws in him and took off fearlessly toward the demon dog.

"Motley!" Alex yelled.

Motley cloaked and uncloaked as he raced forward, causing the beast to halt and glance around dumbfounded. Motley weaved in and out of his own shadow and struck before his opponent knew what had happened. The beast lay exsanguinate on the floor, while Motley returned to Alex's shoulder to stand guard.

They all three stared in horror and awe at what they had just witnessed from the small demon companion.

"That's a little scary, but pretty brilliant," Karissa said.

"Awesome!" Vitoria said. "Just awesome."

Alex stood quietly stunned, grateful that Motley was on his side.

"Let's get out of here before more come," Karissa advised, making her way toward the doors.

"Wait, where exactly are we going?" Vitoria asked.

Alex looked over to Karissa and Vitoria followed his gaze.

"In my vision, I only saw they were in trouble," Karissa said. "Not their exact location or what to do, okay? It's not always clear."

Vitoria rolled her eyes and sighed loudly.

"It's okay. We were winging it anyway, remember," Alex said.

"Fine, you first, then," Vitoria said, offering an open hand. "You're the one with the most lethal weapon here."

Alex smiled back nervously.

CHAPTER 26
The Council

Alex took the lead and guided them blindly, but confidently, to the right and down a long hallway full of huge oil paintings, flickering sconces, and tapestries along the walls. Alex suddenly halted in place, and then the rest followed suit nearly running into one another. The vibration was subtle at first, but soon became all that they heard. Alex rushed from the hallway out to a balcony and clumsily peered out over the castle wall. The source of the vibration was obvious as he gazed upon hundreds of soldiers and demons marching out from the castle and through the small forest to an open field.

Once the entire army had all exited the small forest and were in the open, the army halted in formation at the raised hand of one of the soldiers on the front line. The lead soldier then quickly swiped a fist toward the ground and war drums rang in the air along with swords and staves bashing against shields, one after another on a one-two count followed by two consecutive battle cries, an obvious intimidation ballad meant for their enemy.

Alex peered out past the army and to the far hill. Another army peaked over the hill, marching in a not-so-orderly fashion. He recognized the montage of warriors and merchants and witches. Leading them was Nort on his dark horse and Lucianna on a steed of her own, a snow-white horse that seemed to glow in its entirety, creepily similar to the eyes of Nort's horse. Now that he got a better look, all of the witches' horses matched their witch leader. The numbers didn't seem fair, with the Jarren's soldiers and the demons outnumbering Nort and Lucianna's army two to one.

"Those numbers don't look promising," Alex said, more worry in his voice than he meant to share. "No wonder Nort didn't follow Krunk's plan; the demons must have surprised him and pushed his army back."

"But those demons don't fight for anything, and the soldiers are obviously being brainwashed," Karissa said. "Our people fight for their freedom."

"And their time back," Vitoria added.

"I just hope those witches have something up their sleeves," Alex said, immediately thinking of his mom, longing to know more about her powers as a witch. He felt for the quarter around his neck and rubbed it.

"You have no idea," Vitoria beamed. "A scorned and threatened witch is not one to mess with."

He really hoped she was right for all of their sakes.

Alex had been so distracted by the imminent battle he nearly forgot why they were there in the first place. "Do either of you see my dad or Krunk?"

"No," they both said scanning the battlefield.

"Or Helenia?"

They both shook their heads.

A horrible realization hit him in the gut. "If the soldiers are on the battlefield, it means my dad and Krunk didn't take care of Jarren and couldn't convince . . . which means they're . . ." He could not finish the sentence.

"They're not dead," Karissa insisted. "They may not have located Jarren or Helenia yet and could just be waiting for an opportune moment."

"Now seems like a pretty good time. And you were the one who said they were in trouble in the first place," Alex said with frustration.

"I know I did, but there are many ways of reaching that result."

"She said it herself, she's still figuring out her so-called visions," Vitoria sneered. "What does it matter anyway at this point; we're here and have come this far. We're not stopping until we know something for sure."

"Let's just focus on finding them," Karissa said, ignoring Vitoria's continued contempt of her abilities.

Alex took in a deep breath and nodded to them both. Just as he was about to turn and head back down the hallway a trumpet echoed loudly in the distance. Hundreds of boots and hooves pounded the ground and began marching forward toward the smaller army.

"Why aren't Nort and Lucianna moving?" Vitoria said. "What are they waiting for?"

Alex shrugged, wondering the same thing.

"Nort's probably letting them make fools of themselves, waiting for a precise moment," Karissa said.

The sky suddenly darkened, followed by thunder rumbling slightly louder than the men's and demons' roars. A moment later, rain began to fall lightly on the open field, and Alex swore he saw a smile unravel across Nort's face, though it was nearly impossible to make that out as far away as they were.

Lucianna rode forward and placed her wand in the air. A radiant lavender barrier materialized around their entire army.

The head soldier raised and lowered his hand again, and immediately two huge boulders shot from a pair of catapults at the center of the army. The roars of intimidation changed to roars of anger from the demons as the crude boulders shattered to dust when they reached the barrier.

"How long will a barrier like that hold?" Alex asked.

"I'm not sure. I think it has to do with the one casting it and what offenses are being used against it," Vitoria said. "But there are definitely limitations to it."

"Such as?"

"Demon witches."

"Like Helenia?"

Vitoria nodded, "Demon witches are more powerful than the barriers, but thankfully they are rare to come across."

"None of us saw Helenia, so that's a good thing for Nort and Lucianna's army," Alex said, scanning the battlefield again.

"But not for Henry and Krunk," Karissa said.

Alex nodded, "Okay, we know what we have to do; let's go." Alex left the obvious unspoken. If his dad and Krunk had fallen, it was up to them to save Tristoria; not a very digestible outcome were it to come to fruition.

Alex, Karissa, and Vitoria came to a winding staircase at the end of the hallway that led only one direction: down. Alex stood at the top of the stairway, chewing over the decision to proceed down the dark stairwell or go another direction. With the imminent battle, time was not on their side.

"Aren't we on the first floor?" Karissa asked, glancing down the stairwell.

Alex nodded. "I believe so, yes."

"So, that's the dungeon area, which means prisoners, right?" Vitoria said excitedly.

"You think his dad and yours are being held down there?" Karissa asked.

"Why not?" Vitoria shrugged. "It's possible. Besides, if they're not, there may be some soldiers to help us."

"We just saw the battlefield; the soldiers are not on our side," Alex said.

"If we tell them who you are, they might help us," Vitoria said.

"Or kill us," Karissa said.

"We have to at least look," Vitoria said.

Karissa frowned, but nodded her approval.

They needed all the help they could get. "Okay, but whatever's down there —" Karissa started.

"Just go, already," Vitoria said impatiently.

"Alex?" Karissa said, searching for his endorsement.

Alex nodded. "Motley and I will take the lead."

Motley sniffed the air approvingly. Alex slowly began his descent down the stairs and snuffed out the torches as he came to them, leaving the one at the bottom of the stairs lit so as not to draw attention to their presence. They stood in the shadows and listened, hearing a variety of low voices and moans. None of them recognized any of the voices.

"Use your seer powers and see who the guard is," Vitoria whispered, holding back a snicker.

"For the fifth time . . .", Karissa sighed. "You know it doesn't work like that."

"Come on guys, seriously," Alex whispered, shaking his head. "I'm getting a better look to see if I can recognize anyone." He took a few steps down and stood at the threshold of the bottom stair and the first cell. A whiff of dank, cool air filled his nostrils, and he held back a cough. He quickly switched his breathing through his mouth only, focusing on shallow inhales and exhales.

He edged his head around the corner and sighed inwardly when he saw multiple guards gathered around a small table playing cards. They wore the pentagram on their chest armor, which meant they were under Jarren's command. He still couldn't make out who, or what, were in the cells: the light was too dim, and the prisoners were being uncannily quiet.

Alex attempted to focus his mind and connect with Motley's, wanting to keep his words to a minimum so as not to draw attention. He wasn't sure yet if Motley even understood his thoughts, but they had been doing well so far. Motley came out of stealth mode and walked along Alex's right shoulder to his left one. Alex stared into Motley's green eyes in the torchlight, and after a moment they seemed to understand one another; or at least it seemed like it to Alex.

Motley cloaked and Alex felt the small demon leave him. He motioned with a wave of his hand up the stairs from behind him for Karissa and Vitoria to join him.

Alex whispered, "I told him only to wound; no killing the soldiers, if we can help it."

"Fine, but if one attacks me, then it's fair game," Vitoria warned, her wand at the ready.

"Just be ready, okay," Alex said.

Karissa nodded and then notched an arrow.

"What the hell is that thing?" one guard yelled as the screeching of chairs along the floor filled the small space. There was a loud clunk, and then a rattle of the cells as if someone had slammed against the bars. Another clunk came a few seconds later.

Alex glanced back around the corner and saw that the two guards were lying supine on the floor, and to his pleasant surprise not in a pool of their own blood.

Alex grabbed the torch from the wall closest to him and rounded the corner cautiously. He flinched as Motley made his way back onto his shoulder.

"Tell us your name, boy," a deep voice came from the shadows of one cell.

"How about you tell us yours first," Vitoria snapped.

"Vitoria, daughter of Krunk, your mouth precedes you."

"How do you know my name?" Vitoria asked, inching closer to the dark cell, her wand held out in defense.

"Put that thing down before you put your eye out," the voice commanded.

Alex lifted the torch to light another sconce next to the cell. He squinted his eyes and saw that in the cell were six robed figures, all cloaked but one, whom Alex presumed had been speaking. As the flickering light hit the man's face, Alex saw a head full of long, gray hair and a face with a maze of well-defined wrinkles. His eyes were gray and intelligent, matching his deep, deliberate voice.

"You're the council," Alex said with unexpected excitement.

The man nodded. "I am Crolin, and these are my colleagues." The group of cloaked figures nodded. "And who might you be?" the gray-haired man said, stepping closer. The man studied Alex a moment and then said, "Alex Rayne, you are the spitting image of your grandfather when he was a younger man."

Alex nodded. "Yes, and we're here because my dad and Krunk are in danger. Karissa has seen it. She's a seer —"

"Karissa Spurnlock?"

"Karissa Shade," Karissa said emphatically, stepping closer and into the light. "Please. If you don't mind me asking, sir, how do you know me?"

He nodded knowingly. "We all know of your father's many attempts to earn favor with the king. Your mother had the same sight as you —"

"Can we get a move on," Vitoria interrupted.

"A young Krunk in the making I see; disregard for others and a quick mouth." He shook his head. "Karissa, we'll speak at a more appropriate time."

Karissa nodded her head, but held an eagerness in her eyes that Alex recognized. His own eyes held that same intensity when he heard his mom had been a witch.

Crolin continued. "This is quite the group you have assembled, Alex Rayne. But even more curious is the unseen member of your group; the demon perched there on your shoulders."

"You can see him?" Alex said curiously.

"No, but his aura is bright to one who knows where to look," Crolin said.

Alex scrunched his brows, not sure what aura he was talking about. He suspected it had something to do with a warlock's sense of demons, or something along those lines.

"That's some rare demon for a boy your age to have of his own. You have not ascended, yet have gained a rather powerful and rare demon. How intriguing."

Alex shrugged. "He attached to me in the Faceless Forest. No idea how or why."

Karissa had removed the keys to the cell from the guard's belt and was ready to place the key into the slot when Alex stopped her with a light brush of his hand.

"Please understand my caution. I need to know where the council's loyalty lies," Alex said.

"Come on, Alex, they're prisoners. Why else would they be in here?" Vitoria said.

"No, he's right to be suspicious," a woman's voice came from the shadows. She stepped into the light and lowered her hood. "His life has been shrouded in deceit and hidden from him. It's in his nature not to trust, as it is in all of us warlocks."

She appeared older, but not as old as the other man. She had gray-streaked brunette hair and eyes the color of deep arctic blue. She was still beautiful and must have been stunningly gorgeous in her day.

"My name is Inora," she said, nodding to them. "We are the king's loyal council and are here in this cell because of that loyalty."

"Nice to meet you, all of you, but we don't have much time. My dad and Krunk are in trouble. My grandfather is dead, and my dad has decided to take his rightful place next in line. Will you help us?"

Crolin and Inora turned to face their colleagues. There were loud mumbles with a few words of contestation that Alex couldn't quite put together. A moment later, Crolin stepped forward and cleared his throat and said, "You have confirmed what we feared. The king is truly dead. Sorry for your loss and the kingdom's. The matter of your father. He gave up his right to the throne years ago, which would explain you being here. We, the council, have always strived for a balance in the kingdom. We all took our vows and pledged our allegiance to the Rayne Kingdom. We are loyal council to any Rayne on the throne who has passed the tests and become king. Lineage is but a word used to describe the next ones able to take the test."

"So, you're saying you will not follow my dad?" Alex asked, unsure.

"Although he didn't pass every test, in a time of war, such as this, we make exceptions. Normally when a Rayne passes on, we continue with the next in line until the tests have been taken and completed. Which, in this case, would be you, Alex."

Alex began his protest, but Crolin lifted a hand. "Until this crisis is over, we will honor your wishes to a point we, this council, deem appropriate."

"Alex, that means they can change their minds if they want to," Vitoria warned. "They could basically do what they want if they 'deem' it appropriate."

"The girl isn't wrong," Inora said, taking in a heavy breath through her nose "But, we pride ourselves on what is best for the kingdom. And demons in our lands and ruling our soldiers is not appropriate."

Alex nodded in understanding. They had been loyal to his grandfather, but his grandfather had also warned of them. If Alex left them there in the prison, it would cause resentment if they lived. Not a good thing for a new king to contend with.

"Let them out, Karissa," Alex said.

Karissa placed the key inside the cell door and unlocked it without question. Vitoria sighed with a shrug as the door flung open and the council members filed out.

"You made the right choice," Crolin told Alex. "Inora, our weapons, please."

Inora went to a tall wooden cabinet against the wall and retrieved the council's staves and wands.

Alex hurriedly told them what he knew about his dad and Krunk, as well as Margie and Sinvexe. Helenia they knew all too well, though they still didn't completely believe she had returned from her demise. He also told them of Nort and Lucianna and the battle that was temporarily stifled by a magic barrier. The council cringed a little at the thought of allying with the coven of witches, but understood the sheer number of demons and their own soldiers they would have to fight if they could not be turned back.

CHAPTER 27

Battle Warlock

Crolin advised Alex that the throne room was the best option to begin their search for his dad and Krunk. It represented power and dominance, so it was the perfect place to intimidate and torture Helenia's opponents.

The few guards along the halls and in front of the huge doors were easily dealt with by the council members, although Alex noticed that the council seemed a little too indecisive when killing the two demons accompanying the soldier guards. Though he had been told that the idea of being ruled by demons disgusted warlocks to their core, the warlocks also needed the demons for their powers. He himself had Motley. *But that's different,* he argued with himself; *we share a bond.* Still, he wondered if in time he would become sympathetic toward all demons, as the elder council seemed to have become. *Maybe the council see destroying demons as destruction of a wasted resource. Could they be that shallow? Will I become that shallow?* he wondered.

There was only one way into the Throne Room. Alex and the council knew how to get there, but he also realized his family presumptively held many more secrets yet to be revealed and there was likely a hidden door somewhere. They hardly had time to push on every seemingly out of place stone, or pull on every sconce, to find a hidden passageway.

"On your count, Alex," Crolin whispered.

Alex glanced back at Karissa and then to Vitoria. They both nodded with their weapons at the ready.

"Slowly and methodically," Crolin added with an outstretched arm. "There's a slight chance we may go unnoticed and can plan our attack accordingly. Or we go in swinging." He shrugged as if either was fine with him.

Alex nodded nervously and felt for Motley on his shoulder, patting him lightly on his rigid back, all the while attempting to meld with Motley's mind and prepare him for what may lie on the other side of the doors. Though they seemed to be getting through to one another, he had yet to receive any thoughts from Motley: none that he had recognized as not his own.

Thankfully, the huge doors to the Throne Room had been left cracked open, meaning no noisy knobs to turn. There were also no guards on the other side of the doors. Though Alex could hear a few voices speaking, they were distant, far off into the room.

With his staff, Crolin nudged open the door a little farther, just enough for them to slip into the room. He entered first and hurriedly scanned the room. On seeing a clear path, he motioned for the rest to follow and he led the group to the right and behind a pair of huge statues of armored soldiers wielding banners. The statues mimicked another set across from them as a joining force leading to battle. Alex, Crolin, and the others all knelt and quickly situated themselves. They looked to one another with surprise that they seemed to have entered the room unnoticed.

Alex snuck his head out from behind the large statue just far enough for a view of the massive room. Huge ornate stone columns lined the room like fingers jutting up from the floor and holding the massive space in place. Upright demons wearing the Rayne soldier armor and wielding crude weapons were lined in a single file along one side of the long, crimson-and-black carpet leading to the throne; their lesser subjects, the demon dogs, at each of their feet on all fours occasionally snarling and then quickly snuffed when their masters yanked on the collars.

Directly opposite the demons was a single row of soldiers in full battle armor, standing at attention as if awaiting orders. The dark iron throne sat perched at the top of a six-tier set of steps. Two intricately carved statues on either side of the throne knelt with their heads pressed firmly against it: to the right was a winged demon staring out menacingly; to the left was an angel with its eyes shut and the head angled slightly downward, giving the impression of disappointment. A massive, gothic, arched stained glass window depicting a battle between a demon and a man sat behind the dark throne, enhancing the throne's already ominous appearance.

Alex strained his eyes to make out the figure sitting on the throne. It was a man, but it wasn't Jarren, as he had suspected. It was his dad! Alex strained his eyes and looked again to make sure his eyes weren't deceiving him, but sure enough it was him. He had replaced his robe with full gunmetal battle armor. And standing next to him was Krunk, in a dark red robe, staring out into the room. They both appeared oddly still and expressionless.

"I have seen nothing like this in my time," Crolin whispered, poking out his head next to Alex's.

"My dad and Krunk on the throne, or demons in the throne room?" Alex said. "What the heck is going on?"

"Demon and man in the same room as one fighting force," Crolin said, and then looked over at Alex. "This should come as no surprise. Karissa warned your dad would be in trouble, did she not?"

"Yes, but . . ." Alex considered his words and remembered how his dad had acted since meeting Margie. In a trancelike state, repeating words that she had placed in his head. "Okay, but where is Jarren, or Margie, or this Helenia?"

"I suspect very close," Crolin said hauntingly.

"I don't like this, Alex," Karissa whispered, inching up to them.

"Me, either," Alex said, and then turned to Crolin, "Any ideas?"

"We must find the source of the trance."

"You mean Margie or Helenia."

"Yes, and then subdue her long enough to free your dad and Krunk. I suspect it was her plan all along, to bring your dad here so the soldiers would see a Rayne on the throne and follow his commands."

"I thought that was Jarren's role," Alex said.

Crolin stifled a laugh. "If I had to guess, Jarren was merely a temporary pawn, used as a tool to gather the soldiers. Expendable at best."

Just then, they heard a loud rattling from above, and then were pelted with small pieces of debris that came raining down on top of them. A large, winged creature came hurtling from the rafters above and cornered the group. The creature towered above them over fifteen feet high with a wingspan twice as wide. It resembled the demon Sinvexe they had faced in the forest, only much bigger and female. The massive horns on its head jutted back and curved slightly downward, giving the impression they were aerodynamic.

Crolin whispered something under his breath and a second later, a powerful beam of light shot out from his staff toward the demon's head; an unseen force immediately deflected it. The rest of the council also released volleys of fire and light from their staves, but none could penetrate the demon's unseen defense. Their weapons suddenly flew from their hands and into the air and were slung to the middle of the room, landing in a neat pile.

The voice was deep and female. "How adorable is this? Alex has a team." The demon laughed darkly as its massive wings curled in close to its body.

Alex remembered the huge painting in the Great Hall of the demon surrounded by the warlocks. *This is Helenia; it has to be.*

"Helenia," Crolin said. "We killed you. I saw your head on the stake. How is this possible?"

377

The demon laughed again. Her voice was loud, her words vengeful. "Yes, you saw my sister's head on the stake and soon all of your heads will be on display."

"Sister?" Crolin said confused.

"Twin sister," she hissed.

"If I'd had known Helenia had a twin sister, I would have ventured to the underworld myself and killed you," Crolin said angrily.

"Here I am little warlock, do your best," she said tauntingly and then smirked. "Oh wait, you just tried and failed miserably."

As the demon spoke, Alex noticed something familiar about her voice.

"Margie?" Alex said under his breath, though the demon still heard him.

"I prefer Margonna, but yes, it is your lovely stepmother."

"That's your stepmother!?" Karissa asked with disgust. "Your dad married that!?"

Alex glanced over at Karissa and shrugged. He peered back up at the demon. "But how —"

"How was I able to change forms? Easy," she huffed. "A simple spell with the right ingredients and participants. Dense little warlocks couldn't see through the thin veil." She turned her attention to the throne. "Pathetic, really, just look at him. Your poor, emasculated little father is still obeying me as if we had never left your house. The only one who saw the true me was your mother. It's a shame, really; she had such potential to be a great dark witch like myself. Pity I had to kill her."

"Liar! Cancer killed her," Alex yelled, feeling his heart pounding in his ears as the fury began building.

"She fought until the end; she really did. She tried to resist my influence, but I was just too strong for her. That's why she never could tell you who you really were. What those strange fevers and visions meant. It was my idea to send you to the head shrink. Brilliant on my part, I'd say. Your entire family thought you were crazy."

The tears welled up in Alex's eyes at the thought of his mom being killed by this demon, her last memories of him not her own. He felt his voice shake as he spoke. "For your information, my mom was the only one who didn't think I was crazy. She told me the fevers were a sign of my strength and power. Now I know it was her true self finding its way through your lies."

"Enough!" Margonna yelled, and then suddenly calmed her voice to a soft, sinister one. "It doesn't matter anyway, now, boy. You will soon join her in death. All of you will, and Tristoria will be no more. No more Raynes will exist. No more middle world. We'll destroy all of them in time and there will be only one place after death." She turned her attention to the throne. "Henry, stand and obey your master." Without hesitation Henry immediately stood. "Boys," she motioned to the two short, fat demons next to the steps. She then turned to Alex. "You've already met my two imps."

Alex squinted and took a moment to study them. They looked like shorter, fatter versions of Margonna, only their wings were tiny, nearly nonexistent, and out of place as if they were malignant growths. They were the two stepbrothers he had shared a house with. This was their true form. "How fitting," he mumbled.

The imps wobbled over toward Alex as other demons moved in to guard each member of the group. The imps formerly known as Alex's stepbrothers grabbed him by his arms and led him to the bottom step leading to the throne. They breathed loudly through their noses as they walked, like a pair of pugs. Alex would have laughed if the situation were not so grim. Karissa, on seeing him taken away, struggled from the grasp of the demon who was guarding her, though it was no use.

"Before I sic your father on you, I want you to see true, raw power," Margonna said. "Bring me the girl," she commanded. A moment later, a demon emerged from the shadows nudging his little sister, Sylvia. She had a cloth around her mouth and her eyes were wide and full of terror. She struggled and moaned from behind the cloth when she saw Alex. The demon pushed Sylvia to the bottom of the steps leading to the throne.

"She's a child!" Alex pleaded. "Leave her out of this!"

"I cannot," Margonna said darkly. "After all, she is a Rayne. And we must exterminate all of you."

"I don't know what you're planning but —"

"But what? Huh? You're defeated. Your family will be no more. You will feel the loss of family as I have."

"I already have!" Alex yelled.

"Not enough!" she spouted and then smiled widely. "Soon this will be over and I can move on, but in the meantime I shall enjoy your suffering. Henry, kill the girl. Now!"

"No!" Alex pleaded. "Take me!"

"Don't worry, I will. You're next."

Alex stared up at his dad from the bottom step. Henry had his sword unsheathed and held down in his right hand. Alex noticed Jarren for the first time, standing on the other side of the throne." Jarren, she will kill you next, once we're all dead. Don't let her kill my little sister!"

Jarren stared at him just as emotionless and stoic as his dad and Krunk.

Alex wiggled his way loose from the two fat demons and made his way in front of Sylvia.

"How cute," Margonna said. "Henry, proceed; ignore the boy."

Henry robotically made his way down the steps and in front of Alex and Sylvia.

Alex stood his ground in front of his sister and instantly felt the vibration coming from his grandfather's sword, now wielded by his dad. Thankfully, the sword still relaxed down by his dad's side, but Alex shuddered at the thought of his dad raising it and using it on him and his sister. Alex could almost taste the steel, he was so close. He felt Motley edging closer, preparing to strike on his command or the sword coming toward him, whichever came first. He did his best to calm the demon with his thoughts, reminding him that this was his dad and not to hurt him. *Stop him if necessary, but don't kill him.*

"Dad, I know you're in there, so listen. This isn't you. You're a good man, a good father, and a good husband. You and Mom's first date, the game *Dragon's Lair.* The quarter mom put on the game's marquee saving the next game for her. The sounds of joysticks and the smell of pizza." His hands shook as he pulled the quarter from around his neck and tossed it to his dad. It hit Henry's chest and fell to the floor. "Look at the date, 1976."

Henry's eyes followed the coin to the ground and stared at it.

"Stop wasting our time, boy, with this nonsense," Margonna commanded. "Now, Henry, get on with it and kill the girl!"

"I forgive you," Alex said, sniffing through tears. "For everything. I want my dad back." Alex wiped his face and stared hard into his dad's eyes and could see the struggle taking place inside him. And at that moment he swore he saw his dad wink just before he raised the sword high above his head with his right hand, and with his glowing left hand, he pulled a dagger from his belt. He slung himself around and hurled the dagger toward Margonna's chest.

Alex watched the event as if in slow motion as Jarren leaped in front of Margonna and allowed the dagger to impale him in place of his leader.

"Noooo," Alex yelled.

"That's a good pet," Margonna applauded with a wry grin as Jarren lay bleeding on the floor at her feet.

Henry, without hesitation, charged toward her with his sword ready to strike. Margonna, on seeing his sudden rage, jolted into the air, her wings knocking over a pair of demons close by. Henry grabbed Sylvia and tossed her to Alex, and he quickly unbound her with his own dagger, which he had stuck in his back pocket.

Henry turned to the soldiers. "Soldiers, I release you! Avenge your king and rid these demons from his castle and your lands! Tristoria will never fall! Defend her!"

The soldiers drew their swords in one giant sweep. The sound of fifty swords being unsheathed at the same time was brilliant, and gave rise to chills down Alex's spine and arms. In unison they all let out a guttural yell and charged the demons across from them.

The council snatched up their weapons from the floor, while Karissa and Vitoria did the same. Karissa shielded Sylvia behind her, and Alex joined them, forming a makeshift wall. His dad finished a demon near him and joined them. Vitoria made her way to Krunk, where they fought beside one another, father and daughter. Vitoria beamed as bolts shot out from her wand, matching her dad's staff toward the same demon target.

"What do you say, Dad?" Alex said nodding toward Krunk and Vitoria. He then looked over at Karissa. "Karissa? Want to get some?"

Henry nodded, along with Karissa, and they both smiled.

"Soldier," Henry yelled to a nearby soldier. The man halted in place. "My son needs a sword."

Without hesitation the soldier yanked a short sword from its sheath around his waist and tossed it to Alex. Alex snatched it from the air and gripped the handle tightly, lightly swinging it in the air.

"Thank you," Alex told the soldier.

"Hey, watch it," Karissa said as the blade came a little too close to her hair.

"Sorry," Alex told Karissa tensely. "How about those two imps that harassed me at home?"

"Agreed," Henry said.

The two fat imps huffed away as fast as they could manage as Alex, Henry, and Karissa charged forward. They quickly put the imps out of their misery.

"You'll pay for that," a voice came from above them.

They had nearly forgotten about Margonna, but thankfully the council had not. The council had already formed a circle in the center of the room. One of them used chalk and hurriedly drew a round, intricate symbol on the floor. The symbol instantly glowed a dark crimson, and when the council began a soft chant, it pulsed with their words.

Margonna laughed loudly above them, only this time Alex heard apprehension in it. "Defend your queen," Margonna yelled to the remaining demons. "Kill the council!"

On hearing this, Krunk and Vitoria turned their attention to the center of the room. Alex, Henry, and Karissa were already taking their places to defend the council.

"Crolin!" Henry yelled. "No matter what you do, don't break the seal. We'll hold them off!"

Crolin nodded, but kept his focus and concentration on the chant.

A loud burst rang out against the doors to the Throne Room. "What now?!" Henry said annoyed.

"Sounds like there are more demons out there," Alex suggested as the doors shook violently and bulged.

Luckily, when Alex, Crolin, and the group had entered the Throne Room, one of the council members had the foresight to place a rod through the large handles of the door to brace it closed.

"On that door! Get some men on that door, now!" Henry yelled.

Three soldiers who were close by headed for the door and braced against it, while two others finished off the demons they had been fighting.

"Henry," Krunk said from the other side of the council circle. When Henry didn't respond Krunk yelled, "Henry!" This got Henry's attention, and he turned toward Krunk. "Distraction," Krunk urged him.

Henry furrowed his eyebrows, but when Krunk motioned toward Margonna above them, he realized what Krunk meant.

"Karissa," Henry said turning toward her.

"Sir," she said in a way that suggested he was her commander and she was his soldier.

"I need your archery skills. We need to break Margonna's concentration. Her hide is thick and not easily penetrable, which means we need to find a weakness. There is always a weakness. I need you to find it."

"Yes, sir," she said with a firm nod, and pulled a few arrows from her quiver and set them on the floor next to her.

"Alex, protect her," Henry said.

Alex nodded and he and Motley stood close behind her.

Karissa looked over her shoulder at him from her kneeling position and smiled. "Thank you, my protector."

Alex turned many shades of red at that moment and then smiled. "You're . . . you're welcome," he clumsily replied.

Karissa began her pursuit of Margonna's weakness and combed through the demon's hide with arrows, but none seemed to faze her much more than an annoying gnat would.

Demon after demon came hurdling toward the council, but the council fought them off like mosquitoes on an electric bug zapper.

The council kept their concentration, mostly; they were interrupted twice, but held together. Margonna seemed to get more and more annoyed. She was using all of her concentration to resist the council's power to send her through the portal that had appeared in the center of the floor and was slowly cracking open. Her army was falling. The tension was palpable as the council's chant grew more intense and the portal opened wider. The room felt like it would burst at any moment.

Karissa was still attempting to find Margonna's weakness, though she was now running low on arrows.

"Dad, what happens if we can't get Margonna in the portal?" Alex asked.

"We fight until the end. I fight until the end. You find Nort and get Sylvia someplace safe. That's an order."

"I won't leave you."

"You will if I say you will."

Suddenly two of the council members burst into a ball of flames. Alex leaped backward so as not to get burned and cringed at the sight in front of him.

"Should we put them out?" Karissa asked while frantically scanning around her for something to smother the flames.

"Do nothing!" Henry yelled. "The council members must not break their spell. This is their duty, leave them be. I need that distraction, Karissa. Now, please."

Karissa knelt back down and grabbed her last two arrows, trying to maintain her concentration.

Alex watched in horror as the two burning council members continued their spell, chanting through the flames, holding the circle intact for a few more seconds. He shielded his eyes as the portal at the center of the room grew bigger and brighter.

Margonna let out a loud, horrible shriek from above them.

Karissa shot her final arrow. "Got it!" she yelled as the arrow landed in Margonna. Alex looked up and saw Karissa's arrow was jutting out from the demon's left wing, near a protruding claw. Blood spilled down her wing and dripped onto the floor below, letting off puffs of smoke as each drop landed.

Alex reached his hand down to help Karissa up from the floor when she suddenly flew into the air and was flung across the room, thudding hard against the far wall. He watched helplessly as she lay motionless.

"*No!*" Alex felt himself say, but no words exited.

Margonna flailed and gnashed her teeth, spouting out unrecognizable words in a language that Alex assumed was demon tongue. The council continued their spell with boundless focus, despite two of their members reduced to charred husks on the floor beside them. The rest of the room stopped their fighting for the briefest of moments when the portal darkened to near black and began emanating a soft orange glow.

"What's happening?" Alex asked himself as he climbed over a few dead demons on his way over to Karissa. He could feel the panic rise in his throat at the thought of the portal failing. Or worse, what if they opened the wrong portal and more demons poured out?

When he finally made it to Karissa, he knelt down beside her. "Karissa, can you hear me?" She didn't budge, so he tried again in a much louder voice. "Karissa!" He pulled her hood down and turned her toward him. Blood streaked across her forehead where she had hit the wall. "Come on, Karissa, please."

The doors to the Throne Room burst open, knocking the men who had been bracing them closed to the floor. Alex glanced over his shoulder and toward the doors. He wiped the tears from his eyes and saw Nort and Jayda marching through, followed by a regiment of Rayne soldiers. They all got a front row view of Margonna's terror-stricken face and her last horrible screech before the portal sucked her through to the other side. Seconds later, the portal disappeared, leaving the floor unscathed, as if it had never appeared.

On seeing their leader banished, the remaining demons lost all semblance of structured control and became erratic and scattered, which made them easy to kill.

Nort, Alex, and Henry hovered over Karissa while Krunk rubbed some concoction into her limp mouth and onto her gums.

"Is she still alive?" Alex asked in a panic. "What's that stuff you're putting in her mouth?"

"It's a remedy, to nourish and cleanse the body," Krunk said calmly. "Made from herbs from the Hills of Hal." He winked and whispered, "Don't tell them, but I snuck over to the witches' lands a few times."

"Don't worry, Lucianna and her coven are guarding the entrance to the castle, disposing of any remaining demons," Nort said.

"Is she going to live?" Alex demanded angrily, wondering how Nort and Krunk could carry on a conversation so calmly while Karissa lay dying.

"Yes, yes, see, she's starting to come around," Krunk said reassuringly.

Alex felt his stomach slightly lift out of its slump when he saw her move her head and softly moan.

Nort knelt down beside her and gingerly touched her shoulder. "Karissa," he whispered. She lolled her head from side to side. "Karissa," he said again, this time slightly louder. She groggily opened her eyes and peered up at the array of concerned faces staring down at her. "You did good, kid."

"Alex and Sylvia and Vitoria?" she managed.

"We're here," Alex said, poking his head closer so she could see him and his sister. She smiled, and he smiled back.

"Is that a tear I see," Karissa teased.

Alex wiped his face hurriedly as his cheeks burned red. "No."

She smiled through a wince. "Gotcha."

"I'm here too," Vitoria said, craning her neck beside Alex's. "I guess you didn't see this one coming."

Karissa smirked through a grimace as she moved herself to a sitting position. "Good one. And Margonna?"

"Banished by the council," Nort said. "With your help . . . with all of our help."

"Banished? Did she die?" Alex asked curiously.

"She will suffer a much worse fate than death," Krunk offered.

"Huh?" Alex said.

"They sent her to a very dark place where the most sinister and evil warlocks rule and torture demons: Vanoraz."

Alex suddenly felt anguish and fear wash over him, along with a horrible feeling of dread in the pit of his stomach. Motley rummaged around on his shoulder, digging his claws into his skin.

"Where?" Alex asked wincing through the odd feeling overwhelming his senses.

Krunk continued. "Named after the demon, Vanor, who began his ascent from hell and only made it to the first level. Little did he know the first level was teeming with the darkest and most powerful warlocks, forever stuck in power and bloodlust. His name quickly became known around the realm of demons as the 'foolish one'. Though he was thoroughly warned, he was determined to ascend every level. His foolish tenacity was his demise, and they adopted his name for the place as a future warning to others wanting to achieve such a feat."

Nort shook his head and said, "I'll never understand the amount of stupidity allowed in the universe." He turned to Alex and focused on the cloaked demon on his shoulder. "Even the youngest of their kind can sense danger when a name is mentioned."

Motley blinked in and out of sight for Nort, and Nort winked back. *How did he know?* Alex wondered, as the feelings slowly subsided and he regained control of his emotions. "Finally," Alex mumbled to himself and to Motley, "we make a solid connection and now I have to leave you here."

Their attention turned to muffled crying coming from near the throne. Jayda was holding her limp brother in her arms, and Alex could see her green eyes flooded with tears as she rocked him slowly.

"It's not your fault," she said just loud enough that the silent room echoed in sadness.

"I was foolish and selfish," Jarren managed through a wince. "Forgive me. . . .", he said with his last bit of energy and then slumped in her arms and took his last breath.

"No more than I," she whimpered. "No more than I. We'll meet again, brother." She closed his eyes gingerly with her fingertips and then gripped him in a tight embrace.

Karissa, on seeing Jayda's anguish, hobbled over to her and knelt beside her, offering a comforting hand. Jayda seemed to accept it as she leaned into Karissa's shoulder while still clutching her brother.

Nort stood beside Alex and placed a hand on the shoulder opposite of Motley and whispered, "Though Jarren betrayed his fellow soldiers and the king, here in Tristoria one knows the meaning of remorse and its value."

Alex held on to these words for a long while and considered their meaning. He knew that one day the words would make more sense when it was his turn to take the throne, though he hoped it would be a long while.

CHAPTER 28
A King's Duties

The four remaining council members stood in front of the Tree of Kings in their tidy black with gold trim dress robes, facing the small crowd that had gathered for the Transition of the King ceremony. Henry and Alex stood side by side between the council and the crowd, both wearing a neatly pressed pine green robe with the crest of Rayne embroidered over the left breast. Sylvia stood next to Nort and Karissa on the front row, along with Krunk and Vitoria. Rounder, with his front left paw bandaged, sat proudly on his two hind legs next to Sylvia, and watched as his master took the oath to become king. Rounder had protected Sylvia brilliantly when the demons kidnapped her from Nort's house, but could not contend with higher level demons, especially a group of them. Brandi had also been injured in the effort to protect Sylvia from being taken, but Horace advised she would survive her injuries.

Alex was more than elated to have his dad back with an unfettered mind. It had been a strange and arduous journey with much effort and sacrifice from everyone involved. Destiny had spun the web that connected them all, and the universe parted its hands and allowed another piece on the board in the vast expanse of existence. *Now that Dad has found his rightful place, what does destiny have waiting next for him? What's next for us both?*, Alex mused.

Crolin lifted his hands and addressed the crowd, interrupting Alex's thoughts. "The twin demon witches will not enter Tristoria ever again." The crowd cheered softly and clapped approvingly. "Let's hope there wasn't another sibling," he continued and laughed lightly. Mumbles resonated through the crowd with a few uneasy laughs. Noticing the uncertainty traveling around the crowd, Crolin quickly said, "Yes, well, let's get to it shall we." He outstretched a hand for Henry to step forward.

Henry softly patted his son's hand and took a step forward.

"The sword," Crolin nodded to Henry.

Henry unsheathed it from his right side and held it out in front of him, admiring his father's blade for the last time.

Crolin continued, "Please retire the sword to its rightful slot. The sword and its master have served the kingdom well. May they serve their next guard as justly and loyally."

Henry stood at the base of the massive trunk of ornate sword handles jutting out toward the gray sky. A short and stocky bearded man who had been sitting behind the council began playing ceremonious music with a bagpipe. He had an impressive auburn beard that twirled down to his waist.

Alex watched proudly as his dad slowly inserted his father's sword into the waiting slot next to the hilt Alex assumed was his great-grandfather's. Alex noticed that his dad was holding back emotions that were obviously bubbling inside. Alex was attempting to hold back his own emotions for he knew this was not just a ceremony to say goodbye to the previous king and greet the new one; this was also a goodbye to a father from his son. Tears slid down Alex's face as the music and emotions overwhelmed him. Motley curled his tail softly around Alex's neck, and the loneliness he had been feeling shifted as if Motley had taken some of the burden. He thanked him silently.

Henry stepped back from the tree trunk and sighed, quickly shoving aside a rogue tear before facing Crolin.

Crolin addressed the crowd once more. "Henry James Rayne has accepted his son's temporary relinquishment of the title as king. Henry has shown himself to be true and worthy. He has portrayed great leadership and loyalty to Tristoria and its people. The council will accept his reinstatement as next in line for the throne once he has passed the final test."

Crolin and Henry nodded to one another.

"Henry Rayne, will you accept the responsibility of placing Tristoria's safety and solidarity in front of your own, up to and including your own life? And will you rule honorably and justly and uphold the old laws and the new?"

"I do and I will," Henry said confidently with dutiful honor.

Crolin loudly exclaimed, "I give you your new king of Tristoria! King Henry Rayne!" Henry knelt, and the rest of the crowd quickly followed. Though Nort and Krunk didn't follow the king's rule, they, too, knelt out of respect for Henry.

A moment later, after King Henry stood, the crowd followed and began cheering loudly. Alex clapped vigorously and let out a deafening whistle, all the while smiling at his dad, brimming with pride and respect for him. Alex saw the quarter he had tossed to him in the Throne Room around his father's neck and broadened his smile, feeling a rush of overwhelming emotions for his mother. He wanted her to be there and see her husband take his rightful place, but somehow he knew she was watching from a higher level.

Once the crowd calmed, Crolin addressed them once more. "A king needs a sword." He turned toward another small, stocky man, also sporting an impressive beard. "Rhenli," he said, nodding to the man.

The short and stocky man held out his arms in front of him and presented the draped item to Henry. Rhenli removed the drape and presented the sword. Henry bowed his head respectfully.

Rhenli nodded back and spoke in a thick, gruff voice, "Don't go making a fuss out of it, will ya. Take the thing and use it wisely. It'll cut through anything, especially demon bone. That's a dwarf's promise." He gave a quick bow and marched back to his position next to the bagpiper.

Crolin said to Henry, "He's a little rough around the edges, but no race makes a better blade than the dwarves from the Darken Highlands."

Henry smiled and then drew the sword from its sheath. He wrapped his right hand around the leather-bound grip and stared in awe at the amazing craftsmanship and the featherlike weight of the blade.

"It's fully customizable," Crolin said with a wink.

After a moment of staring at the magnificent blade, Henry turned to the crowd and said, "Let's retire to the Great Hall for the feast."

As the crowd began to file out of the area, Alex glanced over at the trunk of blades and noticed an open slit slowly reveal itself below his grandfather's sword handle. He felt an uncertainty of emotions wash over him as one gate closed and another opened, knowing one day he would have to face this same ceremony.

When Alex entered the Great Hall, his uncertainty was pushed aside as the carnival atmosphere and roaring fires warmed his insides. His stomach rumbled when he saw the colossal spread of meats, breads, and fruits lined along the massive rectangular tables. The constant seesaw of emotions and battles with demons had left him famished. He took his seat next to his dad and Sylvia at the center of the massive U-shaped table facing the stretch of six rows of tables in front of them. Also on the center row sat, Nort and Karissa next to Alex, and then Krunk and Vitoria and Jayda sat on the other side next to Henry. The council members took their seats on the far side, giving the impression they were important to the kingdom, but not rulers.

Lucianna and a few of her high-ranking witches were already seated and waiting patiently for the ceremony to be over. Their coven and the kingdom had always held a mutual understanding of the importance of one another's existence, especially since recent events. They could disagree and still respect one another's wishes.

As predicted, the soldiers gushed over the beautiful witches, with some scuffles over the seats closest to them. Lucianna warned both sides of inappropriate behavior and then sat silently back in her seat, remaining in her reserved manner. The dwarves were also there and already on their third round of ale.

Once everyone was seated, King Henry stood and hefted his large mug of ale in the air. "Please, eat and drink, and honor the dead. Let the burdens wash away if only for a day."

The room nodded and lifted their mugs in unison. Immediately, the sounds of plates and silverware and cheerful voices rang throughout the hall.

After some time had passed and the mead and ale had lifted voices above average ranges, Crolin asked the king for the floor for one more announcement. Henry proudly gave his permission.

"Sorry for the interruption, but this will only take a moment," Crolin said. The room's volume lowered slightly. "Thank you. I'd like to acknowledge three young soldiers who showed bravery and disregard for their own safety to help another. Alex Rayne, Karissa Shade, and Vitoria Locklin, please stand and take a bow. Alex and Karissa looked to one another with dubious expressions and all three stood. "The people of Tristoria will never forget your deeds. Thank you." The crowd cheered, and Alex and Karissa humbly bowed through red-tinged cheeks. Vitoria also bowed, though she reveled in the spotlight with a huge smile draped across her face.

King Henry nodded to Crolin and then stood and addressed the crowd. "Thank you, Councilman Crolin. Yes, the three of you have reminded us bravery can arise from any place and at any age." He nodded to them with a raised mug. "And while we're discussing acknowledgments, I would also like to thank two more heroes of the battle, Nort and Krunk. Thank you for saving my life and keeping my son and daughter and the kingdom safe." They both bowed their heads respectfully. "To Jayda, your loyalty to the kingdom will not be forgotten. The loss of family leaves a bruise on our hearts unlike anything else." His voice shook, but he never lost his composure. Jayda nodded her head with heavy eyes.

Henry cleared his throat and continued, "Lucianna, you and your coven's sacrifice were vital to our victory and you and your coven will always be welcome in our kingdom. Our agreement remains intact." She nodded back with a wink, and Henry felt a weird tingling all over, likely what the soldiers all felt when they looked at her, he mused, and then smiled softly back at her. "And to the soldiers, without you there would be no kingdom. Thank you!" Henry nodded to them around the room and they, too, raised their mugs. "And finally, to all those who perished. We will never forget." Henry bowed his head in respect, and the crowd followed. After a moment of silence, he continued. "Whatever the deepest and darkest pits in existence send our way, we will defeat it. We will protect

Tristoria and preserve the worlds above us and below. No evil will destroy a united Tristoria."

The room burst into loud rumbles and cheers. The soldiers stomped their boots in unison and began chanting, "Rayne! Rayne! Rayne! Rayne! Rayne! Rayne!"

Henry lifted his hand, and the chanting slowly halted. "May we all remember this moment when the flames of hope are snuffed out."

The room erupted once more in jovial cheers and more "Rayne" chants.

By the end of the meal and as the evening wore on, the size of the crowd had thinned out dramatically. A few soldiers had passed out on the table, having foolishly attempted to outdrink the small group of dwarves.

"You didn't tell me there were dwarves in Tristoria," Alex whispered to his dad. "Those are dwarves, aren't they?"

"Yes," Henry nodded. "And they're just as you likely think they are: grumpy, like to drink, and can build just about anything."

"That's definitely cool," Alex said.

"Yes, it is, and there's much more in Tristoria," Henry said. "Wait until you see the giants."

Alex's eyes grew wide as he mouthed the word *giants*. His mind began filtering through the many creatures in his fantasy novels and wondering how many were real.

Council members Crolin and Inora approached the table and said their good evenings to everyone, but briefly stopped in front of Krunk and his daughter.

"There's room on the council for you, Krunk," Crolin said.

Krunk wasted no time chewing over his answer. "I appreciate the offer, but I cannot accept. I take pride in my seclusion. Besides, the Woodblood would be lonely without me."

"Perhaps your daughter, then, one day," Inora offered.

Krunk turned toward Vitoria beside him for her answer. She shook her head confidently no and said, "The forest is my home until the witches accept me." She then turned toward Lucianna.

Lucianna overheard her and nodded her head in approval, but did not offer any words. And that was good enough for Vitoria for she grinned and turned back around.

"Very well," Crolin submitted and then faced Henry. "We will retire for the night, King." Both Crolin and Inora nodded to him and left the room.

To the dwarves' and soldiers' dismay, Lucianna and her witches left soon after. Alex and Karissa and Vitoria moved a few chairs on the other side of the table to face Henry, Krunk, and Nort.

"Dad, I have a question for you," Alex began. "I mean, we have a question for you," he motioned to Karissa and Vitoria. They both nodded in agreement.

"Okay," Henry said with furrowed eyebrows. "Is this an interrogation?"

"No," Alex said laughing. "We were just curious about something."

"Okay, shoot."

"Karissa saw you in her visions being subdued. How did you . . .?"

Henry smiled knowingly. "Ah, I took the proper precautions," Henry said. "Your old man still has a few tricks up his sleeves." He looked over at Krunk. "Clever friends are just as important as being clever yourself."

"What do you mean?" Alex asked curiously.

Krunk smiled and said, "I dabbled in alchemy. After all, I am a warlock. Antidotes and reversals are as crucial as the poison or potion being made. And it isn't difficult getting ingredients you need from a town alchemist who enjoys the comfort of mead a little too much."

"So, you were faking the entire time in the Throne Room?" Karissa asked amazed.

"Yeah, not bad, huh," Henry said with a smirk.

"Not bad at all," Alex said impressed.

"We honestly didn't know what we would do if Margonna didn't buy our act," Henry admitted.

"You winged it," Karissa said, smiling toward Alex.

"I suppose we did," Henry said with a wide grin and nodding back toward Krunk.

With a full stomach and an open mind, Alex followed his dad up the winding stairs of Tower Number Three. Alex had no idea where the tower led, and his dad had yet to elaborate. All he knew was there was a ton of security and many guard points leading to the tower.

"Where are we going?" Alex asked for the third time, attempting to keep up with his dad's two-steps-at-a-time pace.

"Almost there. Last one. Come on, don't let your old man outdo you," Henry said. "Trust me, it'll be worth it."

"I hope so," Alex grunted, pushing himself up a few steps behind his dad.

When they reached the top step, Alex glanced over his dad's shoulder through the small window while catching his breath. He noticed the thickness in the air and wondered if it was fog he was seeing or clouds.

"Are we —?"

"At the peak of the tallest tower, yes," Henry said. They were standing in front of a stone wall, no different from the walls surrounding the stairs they had traversed. "Now, let me show you what we do as Raynes, and what Tristoria is really all about. My dad took me here when I was a few years younger than you."

"Dad, there's just a wall here," Alex said.

His dad faced the wall and, with his right hand, pressed against a specific stone in a specific area. Seconds later, each individual stone separated from one another and built a short passageway in front of them. Wide-eyed he followed his dad around the short curve and into a massive room. He was immediately awestruck and speechless at the sight before him.

The ceiling background was black as night and filled with countless stars and galaxies illuminating the room. Mammoth-sized gears and hands fluidly moved inside of the enormous, gilded timepieces spread throughout the area. Monstrous hourglasses filled with a rainbow of colored sand seemed to float in the heavens above, while smaller versions of the giant gilded clocks flew around, flapping small mechanical wings on their sides and intermittently soaring around like birds.

"I told you," Henry said. "Amazing, isn't it?"

"I didn't know . . . I mean . . . I had no idea."

"Yeah, I felt the same way when my dad first took me here."

"What is this place?"

"We call it The Toll. This is the intricate detail behind our real purpose. These hands and gears and the seconds they pump out, along with the hourglasses of sand, represent each of the lives in Tristoria. We are responsible for every moment of that time, and dismissal of even just one second can have devastating consequences to not only their lives, but the world as well. There's a constant influx of good and evil that floods through the gears and glass like a poisonous viscous fluid, and it's our job to filter through it and deal with the consequences."

"Consequences, meaning more or less time here?"

"Yes, and to send souls back a level if necessary. Or two. Or progress forward."

"Wait, we can send them down more than one level? Even all the way to . . ."

"Yes, but that is very rare, and if that is to happen it would have to be justified. For if it is done selfishly or for personal reasons, they will judge us."

"Who would judge us?"

"There is a council that exists that oversees the rulers of the worlds. We are not above the rules of existence."

Alex thought on this for a moment and felt humbled by his future responsibility. He certainly wasn't ready for it yet and wondered if he ever would be.

"I know this place is beautiful and enticing, but it requires discipline and caution. It demands an unwavering loyalty just to be in its presence. We must account for each grain of sand and tick of a clock," Henry reiterated, as Alex inched closer to a glowing purple hourglass floating near him.

Alex couldn't help being mesmerized, but heeded his dad's warning, taking a few steps back, not wanting to disrupt anything.

"I'm glad you're taking your rightful place," Alex said, shaking his head at the sheer enormity of what he was seeing along with the immense responsibility of being king.

"One step at a time" his dad said, gripping his shoulder gingerly.

Alex noticed a floating book and made his way toward it. When he got closer, he noticed it was approximately five feet from the floor as if sitting on an invisible pedestal. "You brought our family spell book here?"

"Yes," Henry nodded. "Its new home until I can have my new quarters built. Besides, I will not be practicing any spells for a while. Not until the kingdom is completely repaired and I have some time to practice ruling."

"So, you can open it? Break grandfather's spell?"

"It ended when he died."

"So, it was vulnerable?"

"Not without the key."

"Oh, yeah, the key." Alex looked down at the book and noticed a tarnished golden clasp. When he looked closer, he saw the Rayne crest etched in the center. "Where's the keyhole?"

"It's not a traditional lock, son. Remember where you are." He pulled his sword from its sheath and showed Alex the bottom of the hilt. "Do you see the crest?"

"Yes, so how does it work?"

Henry turned the book on its spine and lightly pressed the hilt of the sword to the etched crest on the book. A soft glow emanated when the two crests touched and then an audible click, releasing the clasp.

"Can I?"

"Go ahead," Henry nodded.

Alex tried to open the book, but it remained sealed shut. "Why won't it open? Grandfather's spell is gone right."

"Yes, but I placed my own. One similar to your grandfather's, with a few added tweaks."

"I know I won't understand what's in it, but I just wanted a glimpse," Alex said deflated. He remembered Vitoria talking about it and how excited she had been.

"Don't worry, your time will come soon enough," Henry said placing a hand on Alex's shoulder. "Come on, let's get some rest. We have some important logistical questions to answer tomorrow."

Alex felt his insides churn as he shook his head in understanding. The next morning would not be an easy one.

CHAPTER 29
Not that Machine Again!

The next morning came fast, though not without many restless hours before Alex's eyes finally shut. He knew this moment was inevitable, ever since his dad recovered in Horace's shop.

Alex and Sylvia stood before their dad, the king of Tristoria, in the Great Hall after breakfast. Alex had his arm around his little sister's shoulder, and she returned the gesture with a strong hug of his leg. He was wearing his jeans and T-shirt, just as he had when he first arrived in Tristoria. The servants of the king had thoroughly cleaned his clothes and returned them to him. The servants had also cleaned and folded the green robe his dad had given him and placed it neatly in a leather-bound backpack that Karissa had given him as a goodbye gift.

Nort and Karissa stood close by, along with Krunk and Vitoria and Jayda. Alex had already said his thanks and goodbyes to the coven of Hal and their leader, Lucianna.

Henry began. "This is difficult, children, but unfortunately it is necessary. Many things have been set in motion that have to be continued for the sake of our existence." He sighed. "You have been through more than any children should have to go through. No children should be ripped from the arms of their parents, whether it be illness or war or manipulation. But, no matter our distance, your mother and I love you both eternally. I wish there was another way, but for now this is what has to be done. In time understanding will shine through the opaque clouds of this moment." He wiped a tear from his right eye and glanced over toward Nort.

"Ouch!" Sylvia said.

"Sorry," Alex replied after a moment. He had been gripping her shoulder tighter and tighter while his dad spoke, attempting to hold back the deluge of tears eagerly waiting to burst out.

His dad continued, "There are few beings out there who hold others above them at the most opportune moments for themselves. Nort has proven himself repeatedly, deed after deed, and I have granted him the passage back home. On my telling him the news, he graciously rejected my offer by stating that he had one more mission to complete. He wants to be the guardian of my children until they are of age, and then he will return to his post as a gate guardian to the heavens."

Alex looked over at Nort and smiled through the flood of free-flowing tears running down his cheeks.

"As long as the two of you are accepting of my offer," Nort said humbly.

Alex nodded. "Yes."

Sylvia liked Nort, but she was six and wanted her dad. Henry knew they would have to alter her memory so she would be okay with the arrangement.

Alex would miss his dad immensely, but he understood what had to be done. He knew he could visit Tristoria occasionally, and at least this time he was not being manipulated by a demon witch, and he could be happy about that.

"Wait," Alex said as a thought suddenly hit him. "What about Karissa? Can she come with us? If Nort leaves with us, she won't have anyone."

Karissa blushed.

Nort lowered his head. Henry also shook his head, disappointed in his own limitations, and said, "I'm sorry, Alex. I wish I could; I really do, but I don't have the power to allow that."

"So, who will take care of her? She can't go back to her dad. He'll try to give her up again."

"That's why I have decided that she can stay here in the castle. I have already arranged for her seer training. She will become a great asset to the kingdom. I will be her guardian until she comes of age."

Alex turned toward Karissa and said, "That's good, right?"

She nodded and wiped the tears from her eyes.

"Wait, that means you'll be my sister," Alex said, unsure how he felt about that realization. He had some feelings for her that were definitely not sisterlike.

"Odd, but I guess in a weird way I will be," Karissa said.

"As much as I like you, I mean . . . you know what I mean . . . Let's just call you a close friend of the family," Alex said.

"I like that," she said, and gave him a long hug goodbye.

Krunk stepped forward to Alex, and Vitoria followed behind him.

"I look forward to training with you soon," Krunk said and shook his hand firmly. "You definitely have potential like your old man and grand old man. I'll show you a few tricks along the way." He winked and stepped aside.

Alex nodded back gratefully.

"Let's not make this all mushy," Vitoria said. "You got some skills in you, but I'm better. Remember that. I'll miss all of your lame clumsiness." She extended her hand to him.

Alex smiled and shook her hand. "I'll miss you, too."

Alex turned toward his dad and whispered, "I'm glad you're back, Dad. I love you."

"Love you, too, son," Henry said and grabbed him in a tight embrace.

Alex hugged him back, but made sure not to linger or make a big fuss in front of Karissa and Vitoria. He was a teenager after all and had a reputation to maintain, though he had yet to understand what that reputation was quite yet.

Sylvia hugged her dad as tightly as she could muster and cried softly into his robe. He hugged her back and told her he would see her, both of them, soon.

Nort made his way to Sylvia after seeing her not letting go of her dad. He leaned over and whispered in her ear and she immediately took his hand and followed him to where Alex was waiting.

Nort lifted his trusty umbrella in the air and twirled it above his head.

"Come, on, Nort. Not in the machine!" Alex pleaded.

Nort smiled. "Just kidding. Come, we'll cheat and go through a portal."

Krunk nodded and opened the green, glowing, oval-shaped doorway. Alex took one last look around the odd place, and to the group of friends and family he was leaving behind. He waved a heavy hand and followed Sylvia and Nort into the portal.

Alex got ready for school as usual, though things were definitely not usual. He now had an angel for a guardian, and he was the future heir to Tristoria, the pinnacle of the middle world. He still had not made plans to return and wondered when he would see his dad next.

He had to go back to his normal school until he was seventeen and he ascended. His powers were still developing, which meant he was vulnerable to demons and others wanting to destroy Tristoria. Once he ascended — he had already begun counting down the days until that happens — he would be accepted into the College of Warlocks and he could finally be around his kind.

For now he at least had his best friend Nick. Nick was still at a different school, but they could see one another after school and on weekends, with no one interfering this time. His mom was apparently in the process of dumping the deadbeat guy she had been dating; at least, that is what she told Nick. Nick felt that since his dad was now gone, he had to give his mom another chance. For now, it was a better option than the orphanage.

Sylvia had her mind wiped clean of the events that had occurred and was told Nort was her dad's brother and would take care of them until he returned. The story was flawed, but thankfully, she was only six years old and many details were not necessary.

This was Alex's first day back to school. Though he had been gone for weeks, to everyone else only a weekend had passed.

At least he could control the fevers and visions now, thanks to a few quick lessons from his dad and Krunk. Mrs. Tindal only sneered at him once and it was because he was daydreaming and ignored her attempt to embarrass him with a question about her lesson. He answered her question, but this time correctly.

After school he decided he would walk home, telling Nort before he left that morning. Nort was not ready to drive a car just yet, but he was working on it. In the meantime, unless it was raining, Alex would walk. Before he even made it off school grounds, Robby and Ted, his two favorite bullies, saw him walking alone and made a beeline toward him.

"Wait up, teeny Sweeny," Robby said.

Alex exhaled and tried not to acknowledge them, but it was inevitable. It was a long walk to his house, and they were tenacious morons, pestering him until they got the response they wanted.

"Well, well, look who's walking home alone," Ted said. "Didn't your mommy tell you it isn't safe to walk home alone?"

"Oh, that's right," Robby said. "She's dead."

"Poor, poor, Alex. No one to guide him home," Ted mocked.

Alex appeared calm on the outside, though his blood violently boiled inside. "Is that all you got? Between the two of you, not one neuron linked. Such a shame. No one at home to teach you to use your brains." He shook his head in mock disappointment.

"You'll get it for that one, Sweeny," Robby said, pulling back his right fist. He stopped mid-swing and dropped his arm down by his side and lurched backward, nearly toppling over his own two feet.

"What's wrong with you?" Ted asked on seeing his friend slowly back away. When he saw what had his friend so rattled, he too backed away.

When they felt they were a safe distance, they both took off running and shouting over their shoulders. "You're a freak, Sweeny!"

"It's Rayne, you morons," Alex mumbled and resumed his walk home.

His eyes returned to hazel green from the glowing crimson they had become for the few seconds he and Motley had their minds melded. Motley shuffled around on Alex's shoulder and then settled in his favorite spot with his tail snuggly against his master's neck.

ACKNOWLEDGMENTS

I would like to thank John Bosch and Joshua Cragun for taking the time and reading an early draft of the novel. I'd also like to thank my sister for her beautiful artwork and my copyeditor for her invaluable advice. And as always a very special thanks to my wife, daughter, and mom. Thanks for allowing me the extraordinary amount of time it took to finish the book.

Made in the USA
Coppell, TX
21 July 2021